THE ERLKING'S DAUGHTERS

THE ERLKING'S DAUGHTERS

A SLOW BURN ROMANTIC FANTASY

THE KARNEESIA CHRONICLES
BOOK ONE

CLAIRE TRELLA HILL

The Erlking's Daughters

Cover Art by Kay Fine

Cover Typography by MIBLArt

Paperback ISBN: 979-8-9883463-1-9

I hope you like this book.
But this book is for me.
Specifically, for the me I used to be.
Look at us go, girl.

PROLOGUE

INGRIDON

The war band hid at the edge of the tree line, swathed in black cloth against the light of the crescent moon rising above the trees. Ingridon cautiously poked his head over a fallen log for a better look. His Second, Hadrian, crouched beside him.

"Look at that," Hadrian murmured, staring down at the empty fields and the wooden palisade. "There is a settlement."

"Of course there is." Ingridon shot him a look. "My father traveled here in his youth. He was right when he told our people there would be food."

In addition to the palisade, the settlement had some simple earthworks, but no one on guard at the gates, and only one tower to survey the land for dangers. The only threats these people routinely faced were timber wolves and mountain winters. If they had more weapons than a few hunting bows, he'd be surprised. Hardly much of a challenge for their war band.

But an orange-red light still burned in one cottage's high window. Not all the humans were abed for the night, then.

Ingridon squinted against the glare and ducked back down. "Once the light is out, we move," he murmured to the war band. They nodded their acknowledgement and stilled their movements, the warriors waiting with hands on swords, the thaumaturges flexing their fingers, readying their Arts.

"So, Ingridon, will you take a prize all for yourself tonight?" Hadrian asked him with a raised eyebrow.

Ingridon's white teeth gleamed as he chuckled. "You know me," he murmured. He was the Heir. He could do what he liked, and no one questioned it. "What about you?"

Hadrian shrugged and looked away, uncharacteristic for him.

"Don't tell me you're still pining over my sister from afar," Ingridon said, incredulous. "I thought you scratched that itch ages ago."

Toren, the head thaumaturge assigned to the Heir's war band, lifted his head and stared at Hadrian, a dangerous light in his dual-colored silver and black eyes.

"I tried," Hadrian bit out, wrapping his hand around the hilt of one of his daggers. "Six cycles ago. She made her feelings clear."

"Well, obviously you didn't do it right, because that's when she got even worse," Ingridon hissed. Morwë, younger than him by three years, was the bane of his life.

"I don't understand her." Hadrian stared off into the middle distance, disgruntled. "One minute, things were grand, the next...." He shrugged.

Ingridon rolled his eyes. "So force the issue."

"Force the issue?" Hadrian said, turning to stare at him, his eyes wide. "With your thaumaturge sister?"

"Scared, Hadrian?" Ingridon sneered. "Need me to hold her down for you?"

"He is prudent," Toren interjected. The dark circles around his eyes, a result of excessive magic use, gave extra weight to his hard look. "Thaumaturges are volatile when crossed."

Ingridon scoffed. "But she isn't a fully-fledged thaumaturge, is she, Toren? She never finished her training." He stared hard at the man. They weren't anything close to friends, and Toren didn't have the status to win a stare down with the Heir, no matter how much power he held. Slowly, Toren dragged his unsettling eyes down in obeisance, and Ingridon smirked. He lifted his head above the embankment to check the status.

The light was gone.

"Tell you what, Hadrian," Ingridon said, pulling his black hood forward over his silver hair. "We'll get Morwë a present, too. See if that'll do the job. Then you can try your charms again; you don't want to lose your chance before she's leg-shackled to some courtier or other." He shot Toren a slant-eyed look that the other man did not see.

"The charm works," Hadrian mumbled, pulling his sword from its sheath. "It works on serving girls, chamber maids, even Enzella. But not Morwë."

"Don't take it so hard," Ingridon said, clapping him on his black-clad shoulder. "You can always wait for Zel to grow up." Ignoring Hadrian's grumbles, he turned to the war band and made the signal to move.

As the black-clad men swarmed over the ground without a sign, Ingridon bared his teeth in a grin.

ONE

ENZELLA

Enzella tripped going down the cold stone stair as the newly formed cavern gates groaned inward, like the maw of a gigantic dark beast. She caught herself against the rough wall. The stone scraped her palms, so different from the dark forests and loam tunnels that made up the taiga of her childhood. Recovering, she picked up her trailing skirts, ready to descend further.

The war band entered the large cavern, bearing a crowd of captives. Checking herself, Enzella hovered, squinting in the shadows, until the gates shut out the cruel moonlight.

The members of the war band pulled off their helmets and unwound the black scarves around their faces. The pale witch lights, crystals infused with magic that hung from the cavern ceiling and studded the walls, illuminated her brother's silver hair as he shook it out. Enzella's heart jumped as he spied her hiding place.

Ingridon grinned at her, a wild look in his eyes. "Is that you, Enzella? Get down here, imp."

Dry mouthed, she padded down the last few steps. Enzella yelped as he snatched her up and swung her around. He threw his head back and howled like a mad wolf. Not angry with her, then. Clutching his arms, she waited anxiously until his euphoria waned. He had let go and sent her flying before when his mood turned.

He dumped her on the ground without warning and laughed. "We'll have a feast tonight, imp—we got a good catch."

Enzella picked herself up and dusted off her hands, peering at the throng of wights behind him, still and quiet. The thaumaturges assigned to Ingridon's war band held them in thrall. She had never been allowed to see other wights so close before. But here she didn't have minders every second of the day—the Unseelie were too busy trying to form the caverns into some kind of livable space before everyone went mad.

"Disband," Ingridon barked to his men. "Take the wights to the thaumaturges' distillation chambers." The band dispersed silently, prodding the mass of captives ahead of them. Only two remained—a man and a woman, guarded by Hadrian, Ingridon's Second.

"Those are mine," Ingridon said, following Enzella's eyes. "You like them?" He smiled, flashing his sharp teeth, as he looked at the woman. He stepped up to her and ran a hand down her round cheek.

She gasped and jerked back as his touch woke her from her stupor. Her unseeing eyes flew past Enzella's face, and she started to cry. The witch lights that lit the caverns were bright and plentiful, but they were not made for wight eyes. To them, the cave was all murk and shadow.

"Don't worry." Ingridon ran his fingers through the wight's hair. "You won't be around long enough to get used to the dark."

"Ingridon." Their mother's coarse, angry voice cut through his honeyed tone.

Enzella turned guiltily.

Mother leaned against the wall at the top of the stair. Her dark, gray-streaked hair straggled down around her shoulders, unbound and uncombed. Her mother's sunken eyes glared over Enzella's head to hit her brother full force.

"Mother," he responded provokingly, lip twisting.

"Let that girl go." She coughed. It rattled deep in her chest. Her thin hands dragged over her mouth, the witch light bracelet around her wrist glowing faintly.

"Why?" he asked innocently.

"You took her from a village? She's a mountain girl, she belongs out there—"

"And?"

"All those years I kept silent, but now—you won't steal from them! They are my people," Mother snarled, venomous life flashing through her eyes for a moment. "If you had any decent feeling for me at all, you wouldn't do this."

Ingridon laughed. "Why should I care about you, hag? You're just like us now! This is who we are! And who cares where they're from? All you wights are the same to us."

"Ingridon—"

"And anyway," he continued, smiling, "I'm hungry." Too quick to see, he grabbed hold of the woman and pressed his mouth to hers. She struggled for a moment, but blue light swirled around their lips. Ingridon swallowed. He broke the brutal kiss, and she slumped in his hold.

"Enzella!" Mother's voice cracked. "Come here!" She coughed again, and Enzella could smell the blood coming up. She froze in indecision.

"Enzella, Mummy's favorite monster-child," Ingridon taunted. His eyes grew dark. He brought his hand back, and Enzella squeezed her eyes shut, braced for the coming blow. He checked his hand so close to her face the air stirred her pale hair.

He chuckled. "Well, someone's got to run after her, and it's not going to be me." He tugged her hair, and then pinched the tip of her pointed ear, making her flinch. "Get on with you."

Enzella skittered up the steps as he turned away. Everyone knew Ingridon would be Erlking after their father, and no one dared cross him except Morwë.

"Enzella, my handkerchief," Mother mumbled, lowering herself onto the steps as Enzella reached her. Her hands shook.

Digging in her mother's pockets for it, Enzella heard Hadrian ask, "And the other wight?"

"I told you, a little something for Morwë," Ingridon said offhandedly. "To raise her magic levels and cheer her up. Then you can take another crack at her."

Enzella found the cloth and wiped the blood and phlegm from her mother's face and hands. How Mother had gotten this far from their family suite, she didn't know.

"The one thing I've done right," Mother rasped, cupping a shaky hand over her daughter's head. "You're the only one who doesn't resent me." Enzella gathered her mother's waist-length hair and began to braid it to quiet the twisty feeling of guilt in her stomach.

Ingridon laughed. "What's this?"

Enzella glanced down. The male prisoner, coming out of thrall, was putting up a struggle, trying to reach the girl Ingridon held. Hadrian punched him, and he fell. Ingridon's sword met his throat an instant later, and the prisoner froze.

"Feeling chivalrous, boy? She's mine. Fight all you want; it won't get you anywhere."

The tip of Ingridon's sword pulled a pendant from the neck of the prisoner's tunic. Hooking his sword under it, Ingridon pulled up, slicing through the leather. The sword left a shallow cut on the prisoner's jaw.

Enzella swallowed, her pulse beating hard in her throat.

The leather thong and pendant dropped into the dirt, and Ingridon kicked it out of the way, even as the prisoner tried to reach for it. "Whatever you might have been out there, you're in the deep dark now. And you're just food." Ingridon slapped him with the flat of his blade, knocking the prisoner over. Blood dripped into the dirt as Enzella tied Mother's plait.

"Mother? Mother, how did you get up here?"

Enzella looked up at her sister Morwë, her face silhouetted by the witch lights against the stairway arch. Morwë's hair, black as pitch like Mother's used to be, curled and flowed down her shoulders to her waist, mixing into the dark glossy feathers that made up her gown. Enzella used to wish that her hair were like her sister's. Morwë was one of the most beautiful girls in Unseelie court—men wanted her hand, but she would have none of them, and drove the stubborn ones away with her sharp tongue and her Arts.

"Zel, did you bring her up here?" Morwë said, voice clipped. She came forward and helped their mother stand on trembling legs, supporting what remained of her scant weight.

Enzella shook her head rapidly.

Morwë's sharp eyes took in the tableau below in one sweeping glance. "Moonlight, I leave either of you alone for ten minutes...." Morwë muttered.

"Take me back to bed," Mother mumbled, turning her face away.

WALKING from their suite all the way to the gate cavern had taken too much out of her, even with both her daughters supporting her on either side. Mother barely made it back to her bed. She would be too tired to attend the feast.

Enzella shivered. Father would be angry, but there was nothing they could do.

Enzella held Mother's hand while she fell into a doze, feeling the odd warmth of her mother's fingers compared to her own. It felt a little like when Enzella had tried to grasp the witch lights as a baby.

Her mother's chamber held a large bed piled with blankets and furs, plus a chest, washstand, and wardrobe. Water trickled in the garderobe to the side, and the walls were covered with hangings. In the center of the room stood a brazier full of witch lights. As she held her mother's hand, Enzella kept one eye on the door that led to her father's chambers. It remained closed, but she never knew when it would open.

Morwë opened the main door to their mother's chamber and swept in, her gown trailing along the floor. She laid an icy hand on Enzella's shoulder, the tips of her fingers permanently stained black from using magic. Enzella's skin crawled.

"Time to go, Zel. I've brought your court dress." Morwë held up the heavy, ornate gown of black velvet and lace.

She tilted her head back to see Morwë's face. "Do I have to?"

"Yes." Her sister straightened and helped Enzella out of her dress. "Don't whine. You know the rules as well as I. Besides," Morwë said, a bit gentler, "Ingridon should not have things all his own way." The corner of her mouth turned up as she tossed the court dress over Enzella's head.

"He's got a captive to give you," Enzella confided as she wrangled her arms through the sleeves. "The one from the gate cavern. He said you needed cheering up."

"He did, hmm?" Morwë did up the last of her buttons and smoothed the fabric straight. "I'll show him who needs *cheering up*."

Enzella shivered in anticipation. When she was out of the line of fire, Morwë and Ingridon's fights were a delightful sight to behold.

They walked down rough tunnels only recently hollowed out by their thaumaturges. Enzella missed their old home in the cold northern taiga forests, where they had had a veritable honeycomb of tunnels and mounds to live in, and walked in the night under the dark firs grown together to keep out the light. But the barbarians had realized what was stealing their people, and had forced them out with burning oil and flame.

The forest might be completely gone, Enzella thought sadly. Burned to the ground. But Father had said this would be a good place to start over, with a new food source and a mountain range between them and their former neighbors. But no one was allowed outside the mountain yet, except for the war bands.

The old familiar shiver of curiosity ran through her. She wanted to explore every inch of this new place, underground and above. Enzella fisted her hands in her gown to curb the wanderlust that got her palms lashed when she disappeared for too long.

They entered the great hall, the largest cavern the thaumaturges had hollowed out so far, at the height of the Unseelie Court's festivities. Witch lights glowed in every corner, and the imps and sprites gibbered at the lower tables, eyeing the first and second daughters of the Erlking, their graying faces sharp and envious. Because she was Second Daughter, Enzella was required to attend the feasts when none of the other younglings could. She wished she didn't have to go. Tonight was one of the more riotous feasts, a result of pent up tensions from the long journey and unfinished living quarters.

Enzella followed her sister to an out-of-the-way table near the wall, close enough to the high table to avoid comment, far enough away to breathe easier. She felt her father's dark gaze on them. She chanced a quick glance up. The Erlking was not watching *her* —he had his pitch-black eyes trained on Morwë. He stared in silence before turning to speak to the man with two different colored eyes who stood beside him. Enzella ducked her head before she was noticed.

As she and Morwë found seats, most of the Unseelie courtiers around them scooted away at Morwë's icy glare, leaving a space around the two daughters of the Erlking. All except Hadrian.

"Good feasting, Morwë, Enzella," he said, coming up to them with a smile on his face.

Enzella smiled back at him as she slipped into her seat. She liked Hadrian. His hair was not dark or pale, but some shade in between, and Hadrian didn't smack her like Ingridon. Most of the time he spoke to her, too.

Morwë glanced at him out of the corner of her eye as she placed some of the hot, oily meat from the table's platters on Enzella's plate. It had been cycles since they had had meat like this—the journey from the taiga to the mountains had been a lean time for the Unseelie. "Good hunting, Hadrian."

Enzella tugged on her sleeve in plea, and Morwë placed another helping onto her platter.

"The hunting was due mostly to Ingridon."

"Well Ingridon isn't here, is he?" Morwë said tartly. "If you must sit, don't speak of him." She sat down on Enzella's right and reached for a cup of wine and an empty goblet.

"I'll sit by Zel," he said, sitting on Enzellas's other side. "She doesn't snap at me like a hungry wolf."

Enzella giggled as she chewed the meat, but saw Morwë roll her eyes. "She's mad because I told her about the prisoner," Enzella admitted.

"Whenever you open your mouth, knowledge bubbles forth," Hadrian laughed, taking a tankard for himself.

Morwë bent towards Enzella's ear. "You should keep it shut more often. Until you know what's to be said and what's not."

"I do," Enzella whispered. "I just tell what I think you should know. Like a moment ago, Father was watching you."

Morwë stilled, but said in a low voice, "He watches everyone and everything, Zel. He is the Erlking. Knowledge is power. Don't give it away lightly."

They ate in silence for a time, letting the conversation swell and ebb around them until the meat course was taken away. Then Morwë stiffened beside her, and Enzella knew that at the high table, Father had stood. Enzella kept her eyes on her plate as the hall's voices hushed in a great susurrus.

"This night is momentous for the Unseelie," her father said, his powerful voice rolling forth and filling the entirety of the great hall. "We have come to a good, prosperous land, full of magic for us to use and grow strong. I made a vow to return the Unseelie to their former glory. Tonight marks the beginning of our rise. Bring out the kneph, and let us drink… deep."

Then the doors at the far end of the hall creaked open, and the part that Enzella hated about the feast began.

As the thaumaturges brought out the ice-cold cauldrons of blue kneph, the great hall went wild.

Much of the kneph was reserved for the powerful thaumaturges, to rejuvenate their magic stores and enable them to keep hollowing out the mountain. But the rest of the kneph stores were distributed to the imps and sprites, all who could only do a little magic, if any, to keep the kneph-sickness at bay. Without kneph, the Unseelie developed white flaking patches of skin and a terrible hunger. This would be their first real taste since they left the taiga.

The scene went from spirited to downright riotous and frantic as the cauldrons were distributed to the tables.

The crowd dived for the wide-mouthed cauldrons, dipping in their cups and goblets to bring them out brimming with the freezing liquid. They slaked their thirst, gulping the liquid as it ran in rivulets around their cups and down their faces. Visible flaking patches on faces or hands of the lower Unseelie imps shimmered and smoothed back into normal pale or gray skin as the kneph rejuvenated them from the inside out.

Enzella shrank into Morwë's side. High-pitched screams and laughter filled the air as the imps and sprites moved with abandon, some dancing, others kissing, while a few fistfights broke out here and there if someone didn't get their kneph quick enough.

Hadrian scooped a cup for himself and then set a full goblet in front of Morwë. Morwë wrapped her fingers around the goblet's stem and lifted it to her lips but did not gulp as Hadrian did.

Enzella looked away. She was not allowed to drink—you couldn't partake in the kneph until you came of age. And from what she saw at each feast, she hoped she never did.

"Sister," Ingridon called, "look what I got you!"

Ingridon approached their table with his arm slung around his wight woman. Her cheeks were shiny and wet, and his arm was probably the only thing keeping her upright. The male captive trailed behind them, tripping every time Ingridon yanked on the rope tied to his hands.

Ingridon pulled on the rope again. The captive stumbled forward, keeping his gaze on the rushes of the floor—if he could see them. Maybe he could. There were more witch lights in the great hall than almost anywhere.

Morwë stared across the table at Ingridon. "What is that?"

"Food," Ingridon said. "Like so." He kissed the woman briefly, their fused lips glowing blue. Her knees went out from under her, and she nearly collapsed.

"You're disgusting. Learn some restraint," Morwë sneered. "That wight's half gone already."

Ingridon gave a satisfied sigh. "But I feel better than I have in weeks, sister dear. Straight from the source is always best. Try a sip."

"Why, so you can congratulate yourself for curing my attitude?" she drawled, taking a sip from her cup of normal wine.

"I don't remember mentioning your disposition, Morwë." Ingridon glanced at Enzella and Hadrian.

Enzella shrank down in her seat. She knew what Morwë meant about her mouth.

"Not in the last hour, maybe, but it's a constant conversation topic with you, brother." Morwë sneered. "Have you realized that my attitude might be due to *you*?" She picked up her wine cup and stood. "Let me know when you finally grow half a brain, Ingridon." She turned and started to walk away.

Growling, Ingridon dropped his prize and vaulted over the table one-handed to grab her by the hip. He slammed her into the wall and pinned her there.

"Get off me!" she hissed, locking her hand around his throat. "I'm warning you—"

"Your Arts don't work on your own blood, Morwë; did you forget that?"

She snarled. "More's the pity, you weasel."

"That's no way to speak to me, sister of mine—"

"I'm sorry I misspoke, you *brat*."

Ingridon's face twisted with hate. "*Morwë....*"

The loud prattle of conversations cut off like someone had slit every throat in the great hall. All could hear Yemelyan Onyxeyes, Erlking of the Unseelie, say, *"Children."*

Enzella slipped off her bench and dropped under the table. She wrapped her hands over her head as a shudder twisted its way through her body.

Father's low voice slithered powerfully through the Hall. "First Daughter. Ingridon. What is the meaning of this… disruption?"

Enzella inhaled sharply. She was only a foot away from the captives. The young man was clumsily trying to help Ingridon's woman, who had fallen to the ground.

He looked up, his eyes searching for the sound.

Enzella swallowed hard, staring into his eyes as he squinted at her. Could he make her out in the shadows?

After a long, pregnant silence, Ingridon said, "Father, Morwë refused to accept my gift to her."

"Why is that, First Daughter?"

Morwë's voice was subdued. "Father, I did not refuse. But I don't need to replenish my magic stores. This one can go to someone else."

"Morwë, your brother was thoughtful enough to give you this gift. You will accept it. Do not squabble over trifles, children. Apologize to each other. Tonight is for feasting, not fighting."

Enzella did not hear her siblings' half-hearted apologies. She watched the young man's eyes until someone jerked him to his feet and he disappeared from her sight.

TWO

MORWË

Morwë heard the coughing as she put Zel to bed, but it kept on for a long time, a rough, deep cough from the chest, full of phlegm and blood.

Morwë let out a long, slow breath. What little kneph she had sipped at the feast had finally drained out of her body, taking its cravings with it. Releasing the tension from her shoulders, she eased open the door to her mother's chamber. The witch lights, the Unseelie's only source of light underground, barely glowed; no servant had replenished their magical stores. But then, whose duty was it to attend to the Erlking's wight wife?

Mine, Morwë thought, sending her Arts into the lights. They flared up, sending sheets of green and blue light across the carved stone ceiling.

In between coughs, her mother gazed wide-eyed at the ceiling, only half awake. She managed to whisper, "Northern lights… I never thought I'd see northern lights again…."

"Drink this, Mother. It will ease your cough." Morwë poured from the jug beside the bed and held the cup to her mother's lips.

Mother could only get half the cup down before she had to lay back and wheeze, though the awful sounds from her chest had stopped. Morwë silently mopped up the spilling liquid and the flecks of blood on her mother's lips.

"The feast?" her mother whispered. "Was he angry?"

She meant Father. "I don't know," Morwë said. "He said nothing about your absence, which only made the rabble curious." She had ushered Enzella away as soon as it was deemed proper. The feast was undoubtedly still raging in the new great hall. She gazed around the room. "Has no one come to give you food?"

"No," Mother sighed, leaning back into her pillows. "But I'm not hungry."

Morwë turned to replace the cup and the jug. "You need to eat; you won't get well on potions alone. I'll fetch you something—"

"You did not drink, at the feast."

The cup rattled as Morwë set it down. "What?"

"Don't give me that, girl. I know the look of an Unseelie who has tasted kneph, the mad light in their eyes as they drain their goblet dry." Mother cast the door that led to the Erlking's chambers a black look. "Among other things. I know it well. You did not drink."

Morwë picked at the sleeves of her gown. "Zel was with me. I only sipped."

Her mother gave her a long look, her gaze indecipherable in the way she had learned to be from all her years in the dark. The silence hung between them for a long time before her mother broke it. "You know I'm dying, don't you, Morwë."

Morwë clenched her hands in the feathers of her skirt.

"Yes, I am." Her mother looked up at her, eyes baleful but dull. "I have been dying by inches your whole life."

Her tongue was lead in her mouth, and she was cold—so cold. She managed a single nod.

"At least now I can rest," her mother whispered, the lines of her face deep in the witch lights' glow. "At least now… I'm home." She drew her hand from under the coverlet, examining what she held for a long moment. "I'm home," she said again. "Here. Put this—" She coughed, covering her mouth as her frame shook from the force. "Put this in my trunk," she whispered when she had her breath back.

Morwë took the object—a simple hunk of stone, with a small glimmer of silver running through it. A faint tingle ran through her finger as she traced it over the silver vein. Frowning, she opened her mother's heavy wooden trunk and placed it inside, on top of a few of her gowns. When it left her hand, she felt—odd. The back of her throat felt tight.

"Lock it," Mother rasped. "And keep the key." She coughed again. "It will be yours and Enzella's."

"Mother, you are not dying as quick as that," Morwë said, though she turned the key and pulled it from the lock.

She turned back, and the frank look in her mother's eyes made her pause. "What is it?"

Mother opened her mouth—and then paused as coughing overtook her again. Morwë raised her up so she could cough up the phlegm in her lungs. Mother spat a wad of mucus and blood into her handkerchief. When Morwë eased her back onto the pillows, the inscrutable mask had returned, tiredness leeching into her mother's body.

"When I'm gone, he'll marry you off."

Morwë's hand twitched, the bloody handkerchief falling to the stone floor with a wet splat.

"He's got to think of his power base. It's gotten shaky since the move, with so much turmoil. He's not one to squander a powerful piece on the gameboard," her mother rasped, closing her sunken eyes. "He could buy a lot of loyalty with whoever he chooses for you. I know you hate me, but I've tried to spare you that."

Do I? Morwë wondered. In the Underground, knowledge was power. If someone knew you cared for something or someone, they could use that against you. What few deep feelings an Unseelie possessed were kept locked away. Only the superficial and petty emotions were safe to show.

Rarely did Morwë take her feelings out and examine them. It

was too dangerous, and she wanted to survive. She kept herself wrapped in ice so that nothing could break free.

But she didn't think she hated her mother.

"Someone has to look after Enzella," Morwë said in a flat, distant voice as she picked up the handkerchief and wrung it out in the basin.

"Someone. Not the Erlking's First Daughter. They'll foist her on someone, and you—" Her mother coughed again, a long, drawn out rattle, and Morwë's chest clenched in response.

"Hush." Morwë swallowed. "All this talk will make your cough worse." She hung the cloth up to dry.

Her mother passed a shaking hand over her face. "If I had a little broth, maybe I could drink that before I slept again," she whispered.

"Yes, Mother." Morwë rang for attendance and settled in to wait. The lazy imps that made up the kitchen drudges would not arrive punctually, distracted as they were by the revels of the feast, though they *would* arrive. She had put a little power behind the call so they knew who had demanded their presence.

When at last a page arrived, ducking his head to hide the sly look in his eye, Morwë was in fine form. "A large bowl of broth for the Erlking's wife." Icicles dripped from the words. "*Immediately.*"

His gray face blanched whiter and he bowed wordlessly from the room, pointed ears twitching in fear. In a few minutes, a tray of soup and bread arrived, steaming with heat in the cold room. The imp laid it down with shaking hands that belied his blank face. "Will there be anything else, milady?" he whispered in a voice like dry leaves.

"No," Morwë said, dismissing him with a wave of her hand.

The imp backed out of the room, eyes still on stone.

Morwë turned back to her mother and handed her the spoon, helping her sip at the broth. Her mother did not meet her eyes as she slowly ate. Morwë tore chunks of bread from the soft loaf and handed them to her. She dipped them in the soup and chewed slowly.

"Why do you think I hate you?"

Her mother paused with the bread halfway to her mouth. "You told me you did."

"When?"

"Enzella was a baby. You were helping me with her care." She paused to catch her breath and chew the bread. When she regained her voice, she said, "You threw a basin on the floor because you couldn't attend the youngling classes anymore."

"Did I?" All Unseelie children were taken from their families at age three or four and placed together in dormitories, the better, more efficient way to raise and educate children in a society whose population was plummeting. They'd return to their family units when they reached sixteen annuals or so. Morwë had been pulled from the program at ten annuals to help attend to her mother and baby sister after the birth. She had never gone back, and Enzella had never attended at all. She had assumed special provision had been made for the children of the Erlking.

Her mother sipped at the spoon and didn't respond.

"I don't."

The spoon paused.

"Hate you," Morwë clarified.

The spoon shook for an infinitesimal second, and then continued its progress. After three more bites, her mother asked, "Will you send your Arts into the witch lights again?"

Wordlessly, Morwë pushed power into the crystals. Green and blue waves flowed like water over the stone ceiling. Her mother sighed, her gaze locked on the faint colors.

She remembered the word her mother used. "What are northern lights?"

"Relics from a past life," her mother said brusquely, but her eyes didn't waver from the sight. "Lights in the night sky. Maybe I could've seen them from the taiga…if he had ever let me out. I can barely remember what they look like. But the witch lights jog my memory."

Morwë handed her another piece of bread. When the magic ebbed, Morwë set the lights glowing again.

The bowl was half empty, an accomplishment for her mother in recent days, when the handle between her parents' rooms turned.

Morwë froze with her eyes on the tray as her father stepped through the doorway in silence. The confrontation of the feast swept over her again—she didn't know what mood he'd be in after her public spat with Ingridon. But one had to push back with Ingridon, or he would think he could bully you forever. It was all power to Ingridon, and he thought he deserved to make everyone else crawl, since he was Heir.

Morwë steeled her spine. If Father was angry at her, she would not flinch.

Mother continued tearing away pieces of bread and eating them.

It astounded Morwë, as it always did, that her mother, the *wight*, was the one person who did not react with fright to the Erlking's presence, as if she did not know what he did to stay in power underground. But she did, clearly—he had stolen her himself.

"First Daughter." Her father's quiet words snaked through the air. "You do your mother honor by attending her."

Head still bowed, Morwë forced numb lips to move. "Thank you, Father."

"Your absence was marked at the Feast, Wife."

Mother rasped, "Please give them my apologies."

Morwë dared a glance at her mother and caught the flash that passed between her parents' eyes. Then a cough overtook her mother, and Morwë held the cloth for her again.

Morwë didn't move as her father's long-fingered hand, stained black all the way to the knuckles, stroked her mother's hair from the crown of her head to her shoulders. When his hand reached her chest, he pushed the faintest bit of power into the still-coughing woman. Her breathing eased, lungs clearing and relaxing as she breathed fuller, deeper breaths.

"Go to your room and take your rest, First Daughter. I will attend your mother."

Morwë's gaze flickered to her mother's face. With nearly the same gesture Morwë had used to send the imp away, her mother shooed her on. The faint gesture swept her fingers across the back of Morwë's hand, faint warmth blooming on her skin before it faded. Almost like a benediction.

Morwë set the spoon carefully on the tray before she curtseyed and retreated from the room. She caught a glimpse of the Erlking taking her vacated place as she closed the door with a soft click.

CHAPTER

THREE

ARKEN

Solid old Bess shied as Arken reached the well-trodden path to Peridun, tossing up her head and mouthing at the bit. Arken reined her in, pulling the cart to a stop as she stamped, copper ears laid back against her head.

"Whoa, girl, we're nearly home," he said, speaking softly to her. He gazed around at the sparse forest on this side of the Lady's Mirror; the trees didn't clump in such thick stands on this side of the lake as they did to the east towards the larger town of Cairenoch. There wasn't enough cover for timber wolves to come up so close without him noticing. Bess might have smelled a fox, or perhaps caught the scent of bear—but then there wasn't enough tree cover to hide a bear, either, unless the wind had blown the scent down from the mountains that rimmed the Cirondel valley.

Arken continued to speak to her in a low voice, and slowly her ears flicked back to listen to him. He clucked her on, and the cart rolled forward along the path, but there was some hesitation in her step that didn't leave.

That gave Arken pause. He would have thought Bess would be eager to get home, to her own stall and grain after their four-day trip to Cairenoch. He had taken his mother to help assist with his older sister's first baby. Selma was a week or so away from her lying-in, but Luned informed both her sons in no uncertain terms that babies could come when they pleased, and fie on any carefully laid plans—so he had taken her early to Selma and Leofric's farm, and Micah had stayed in Peridun to mind the house and keep up with his apothecary apprenticeship.

Arken was eager to get home, too—the trees on the mountain had been burning their fall colors for nigh on two weeks, and the nights were already frigid as frost crept along the ground. Soon the snows would come and cut off Taliesin's Gap, the pass between the mountains and the lowlands, and they would be in for another long winter. He wanted to have enough projects to last him through the snowy months.

But Bess's step slowed even further as they passed the stone marker that pointed the way towards Peridun. The overcast sky loomed with gray clouds, obscuring the sun. On the breeze came the sound of wailing. A child's cry—one of hopeless despair.

Arken set his teeth as his heart sank. What had happened? Was it the pox? They had heard tell of it sweeping through Trellester and the other lowland countries from the summer merchants, but they hadn't heard of a case yet in Altesia. And wouldn't it have struck a larger town closer to the border like the capital, Cruever, or Cairenoch? Why Peridun?

Urging the horse and cart on, he came out of the trees and entered the wide section of cleared land around the village—wider still now. The village's palisade walls lay broken on the ground.

Arken leaped down from the cart. Bandits? This far north? Raiders? He ran through what used to be the gates and stopped at the sight in front of him.

Around the well in the center of the village, flanked by two large horses, children gathered in a cluster. He recognized the Hennessy child, both of Joana and Lar's children, and all of the Johansen brood, except for the oldest girl—twenty children or more. They all looked up and stared at him in shock, and those that weren't already crying burst into tears.

"Arken!" Sara, one of Elara Johansen's girls, about six, ran to him and flung herself on him, crying. Her older brother Derwin followed her, his face bleak.

"Sara? What's wrong? What's happened?" He gazed around at the silent cottages, dread building in his stomach. "Where is everyone?"

Out of the nearest cottage came Father James, his priest's robe torn and dirt-streaked, followed by Ora, a girl Micah's age. They both carried sacks of grain. Father James dropped the sack at the sight of him. "Arken! God be praised!"

Arken, towing the little girl who refused to let go, moved to the old priest's side, taking his shaking hands. "Father, what's happened?" he demanded.

"We were attacked. They came in the night—they took everyone —"

"Who?"

"We couldn't see," Father James said, passing a brown hand over his weary face. His gray locs fell over his shoulders in disarray, not neatly pulled back like usual. "It was—so dark. But the way they appeared—moved, a great swarm of creatures, stealing our people away...."

"Where is Micah?" Arken scanned his eyes over the group of children, but Micah was not there. The children in the group ranged from infancy to about twelve. Micah had turned sixteen last month. "Where is my brother, do you know?"

"They took him."

The words hit Arken like a physical blow.

Father James's eyes filled with tears. "We've searched. I sent Derwin to find out if anyone had been spared—"

"I rode the flume." Derwin flushed and ducked his head for interrupting.

The flume was a waterway on trestles that was used to transport logs to the Lady's Mirror, where they would then float across the lake to Cruever. Flume boats were small, flimsy things used in emergencies, uncontrolled in the flume's fast moving water.

"That's where he found me," Ora said. "I was posted on lookout that night. We think that's why I—I'm still here. They missed me." Her voice cracked.

Arken blinked, uncomprehending.

Father James shook his head. "Everyone is gone, except the children and those too elderly to travel. And me. I'm so sorry, Arken."

Arken stared at Peridun's priest, a great roaring in his ears as his world shrank to a single focus. Swallowing back the stark fear that threatened to engulf him, he asked, "Bandits took my brother?"

"*Faefolk,*" Sara hiccupped from her grip on his side. She wiped a trail of snot from her face. "They were faefolk. They took Mama and Papa and Alia."

At Arken's blank look, Ora shook her head. "I wasn't here. I didn't see."

Arken picked the girl up. "Sara, I know you were very scared, but the men who attacked Peridun—"

"No, Arken." Father James shook his head and closed his eyes with exhaustion and sorrow. "She's right."

"*Father—*" Arken said, astonished. He stared at the man he had known his whole life, and suddenly realized how old the priest was—nearing eighty, and it showed in the deep lines on his face and the sudden haggard cast to his eyes.

"You weren't there, Arken. You didn't see them. I don't know what else they could be." Father James tugged on his locs, twisting them in his veined, arthritic hands. "I've never seen faefolk before, but the world is home to many mysterious creatures, and these attackers were not men." His tone brooked no argument.

"Faefolk," Arken repeated, echoes of his mother's stories surfacing. "But they lived hundreds of years ago, before the Sundering. I thought they had all gone away. Died, perhaps."

Father James shook his head ominously. "Not all of them." He glanced up towards north. "They came from the direction of Ceridfel's peak, under cover of full dark. They attacked us in our beds, and fought those who resisted, but subdued rather than killed. They *laughed*, Arken, laughed at their task. It *must* have been magic. Once they had rousted us from our houses, all became still and stupid, like cattle. They bound up their captives and drove them away. They said...." he faltered, eyes darting towards Sara.

Arken put Sara down and gave her a gentle push. "Sara, go with your brother and help him with the supplies. Everything's going to be all right." Derwin took her hand.

When she was moving, Arken set a hand on the priest's arm. "What did they say, Father?"

Father James had to swallow twice before his voice would work. "They separated out all the young children and left them. To let them grow up, they said. That the stock needed to replenish itself." Father James shook. "The same way hunters cull a herd. As for the Widow Elim and Grandmother Foley and I, they ignored us. We were no threat to them, and they didn't seem to want us." He wiped his eyes with a handkerchief. "Too old."

"They stole much of the livestock, too," Ora said. "I brought Sam and Jack with me from the station." The two horses were used to wrangle recalcitrant logs when the need arose. "We've been gathering what supplies we can, to make the journey to Cairenoch."

"I need to *find Micah*. Which way did they go?" Arken lifted his eyes towards Ceridfel's peak. "You said they came from the direction of the mountain?"

"Arken, listen to me. We need your help." Father James seized Arken's hands. "We are more than twenty children, one teenage girl, and three infirm adults to make a two-day journey—likely longer, with only two horses. We need your help, my son."

Arken had a deeply selfish desire to tear his arm out of the priest's grasp. His brother needed him; he had always looked out for Micah growing up. To be out there, scared, captured—Micah was *counting* on him.

But Father James had said "my son."

Arken's late father had raised him to do the right thing. Arken could not leave such a procession unprotected, even if it tore at his very soul.

Arken swallowed. "I... I will take you part of the way, Father, past the Mirror's eastern edge, but once Cairenoch is in your sights, I must come back. I *have* to find my brother."

"What will I tell your mother?"

"Tell her I'm going to bring Micah home."

The priest finally nodded. "I understand. Thank you, my son. And while we travel, I will give you what little help I can," Father James promised through tears.

"We'd best get started," Arken said, feeling the weight of responsibility drag through him like a stone. Well, he'd make sure to get them moving as fast as possible, even as the need to go hunting nipped at his heels. "Who had the biggest wagon? I'll go unhitch Bess."

He turned towards the horse and cart as his mouth twisted. As he went, he caught sight of Grandmother Foley amongst the children at the fountain. Her face looked calm, except for the tears that streamed down her wrinkled cheeks. With a pair of shears, she walked down the line of children and carefully cut the braid of each child.

Arken's throat closed.

Altesians, as a rule, kept their hair long. Working men and women might keep it trimmed to shoulder length for practicality, but no one cut their hair any shorter. Hair was a badge of honor, a symbol—Altesians only cut their hair in times of great mourning or bitter war.

Child after child walked away with hair around their ears.

Abruptly changing his course, Arken stopped and sank to his knees before the older woman. "Grandmother." He could say nothing else.

She wiped her cheek, even as the tears continued to silently fall, and reached out with the shears.

A brown ponytail dropped from his head and fell into the dust. His head felt strangely light. *Micah, hold on. Hold on until I can come for you.* His brother was not dead. He *wasn't*.

With his belt knife, Arken evened the strands until his hair wouldn't fall into his face. He set his eyes towards Ceridfel. His heart burned.

I promise I won't leave you.

CHAPTER

FOUR

ENZELLA

The witch light in Enzella's chamber had flickered out, and she had no Arts to replenish it. Of all the Erlking's children, only Morwë had inherited the magical gift.

Enzella didn't usually wake before the first bells rang, signaling the dimming light up above, but she hadn't slept well. Her nerves still jangled from the uproar at the feast two nights ago. Ingridon and Morwë's fights were never so public—and Father never called them out before. The long months of travel had worn them all down to a frazzle. But after the riotous feast night, the rest of the Unseelie had been quiet, sated.

Apart from her mother and Morwë, Enzella had spoken to no one the whole day after. She had spied Ingridon once, but she had hidden before he saw her, and he had left their family suite after exchanging verbal jabs with Morwë in passing.

Mother hadn't risen from her bed again. She had taken the potion that the thaumaturges had given her, but she still coughed up blood.

Enzella rolled over in bed and shivered. She didn't want to think about that. She turned her thoughts to the young man with light eyes.

Had he really looked at her? What had happened to him?

From under her covers, Enzella pulled out the cut leather thong and the flat wooden disc a little smaller than her palm with carvings on it. She had crept out the night before and snuck down to the gate cavern to see if it was still there. After a long time searching around in the dirt, she had found it—with her foot. Her arch still smarted.

The carvings were faint, worn down by age and daily wear, but their lines had been repeatedly darkened by ink. On one side it looked like little mountains, but the other...she didn't know what it was.

She'd have to ask Morwë. She pushed back the covers and reached for a dress that wasn't too wrinkled.

AFTER IMPS BROUGHT up trays to break their fast, Enzella crept into Morwë's room.

"What is it, Enzella?" Morwë asked.

"What happened to your gift?" Enzella asked, biting her lip.

Morwë looked over her shoulder as she brushed out her hair. "What? Oh, the wight. He's in the cells, I expect."

"The cells?" Enzella exclaimed, plopping onto the bed. "Morwë, you can't just leave him there."

"Well, if he's my gift, I can do whatever I like with him," her sister muttered. "What do you want, Zel?"

She drew her knees up to her chest. "I saw that man when Ingridon brought him in, and—"

"Boy, Zel."

Enzella pushed her hair out of her face and frowned. "Really?"

"He can't be more than sixteen annuals." Morwë tackled a particularly tough snarl. "A boy, at least to me."

"But that's only four more than me!"

"Exactly." Her sister raised an eyebrow. "Was that all you wanted?"

"*No.* Ingridon cut a necklace off him, and I went back to find it." Enzella dug in her pocket and held out the rough wooden pendant. In the light she could see the lines twining around and around in a circle. "What does it mean?"

Morwë peered at the rough woodcut and shrugged, setting the brush down to work on the tangle with her fingers. "It's a badly carved pendant. It doesn't mean anything."

"So you don't know?"

"No, sprite. But if you're so curious about why Ingridon cut it off the boy, go pick his twisted mind, not mine."

"Ingridon only does things out of spite; that's no secret. I want to know about the *pendant.*"

"Can't help you," Morwë said, frowning at the knot in her hair.

Enzella slumped, and then jolted like someone had stuck her with a pin as inspiration struck. She'd ask *Mother*.

Leaving Morwë's chamber, Enzella crept into Mother's room, casting glances for any sign of Father.

In the great bed, Mother lay alone, coughing. Enzella grabbed a handkerchief from the nightstand and hurried to her side, holding the cloth as Mother coughed up wet, sticky blood. Lungs clear for the moment, her mother whispered, "Water."

Grimacing, Enzella discarded the stained cloth and picked up the glass, half full of the water from the underground springs. She held it for her mother to sip and laid her back against the pillows as her breathing eased.

"Thank you, Enzella… the only thing I've done right," Mother whispered.

Leaning against the bedspread, Enzella fished the pendant she had rescued the night before out of her pocket. "Mother," she whispered, "do you know what this is?"

Her mother blinked and tried to focus. "Where did you get that?" Her fatigued voice held a hint of wonder.

"I found it on the ground. A prisoner dropped it. What is it?"

"It's a knot carving," her mother said. She reached out a trembling finger to touch it. It swung gently on the leather at her light tap.

"So you've seen it before?" Enzella asked, leaning forward. Why hadn't she ever asked Mother about wight things before? But she knew why—she had never seen any wight things before they came to the mountains. No one really cared about wights—only what they could give the Unseelie. Even Father.

Enzella pored over the marks cut into the wood. "A knot carving. What does it mean?"

Her mother rasped, "There are many kinds, but this one means… family ties."

Enzella frowned. "Family ties of what?"

"Love."

Enzella stopped pouring over the curving and swirling lines of the pendant. "What's that?"

Her mother's hands wandered restlessly over the bedspread. "I've forgotten, down here."

"Don't we have it?" Enzella asked curiously. "Father says everything worth having up there, we have underground."

"He might say it is—but they've ruined it." Her mother coughed again.

She never referred to herself as one of them. She was always the outcast, the Erlking's wight wife.

Resigning herself to playing nurse until she got answers, Enzella held the handkerchief again. "Well, what do we have?" she pressed. "And what is it really? Can't you remember?"

But her mother wasn't listening. She turned the pendant over with shaking hands to look at the other side of the disc. "The mountains," she whispered, touching the inked wood. "White Mountain, Watchtower, Queen's Crest. Fulla's Sorrow, Lady's Mirror Lake."

Enzella peered at the tiny carved map on the disc.

"So that means...." Mother coughed, but no phlegm or blood came up, only a rattle. She gave herself a minute to catch her breath, and then continued. "We're here." She pointed to the last peak. "Under Ceridfel." She lay back against the pillows, spent. "Ceridfel. So close," she whispered again, and covered her face.

"Mother," Enzella said again, touching her arm. "Mother?"

But she turned away, burying her face in the pillow.

Something in Enzella's chest twisted.

Leaving her mother with the cloth and water within easy reach, Enzella slunk out of the room in disappointment. Maybe Mother didn't remember correctly. She *had* been underground for... Enzella wasn't sure. At least twenty-five annuals, because that was how old Ingridon was.

But there was one last person she could ask. She grinned gleefully and headed up to the prison levels.

FIVE

MICAH

Micah shivered in the darkness, clutching his arm against his chest. He had heard the bone snap as the white-haired man jerked him away from Alia. He couldn't see a thing in this cell, but there had been enough light in the huge cavern to fight off the dark gloom. He had done his best to hold on to Alia, but she had been dragged away weeping into the throng of faefolk.

I wonder if she's dead. Micah swallowed hard. *Like the others.*

Before the banquet, he had been in this cell, too—or a cell just like it. He couldn't see well enough to tell. But if it was the same, it was completely bare, made of three walls of rough stone and a door of iron bars. He had run his hands over all of it and found nothing to help him. And then Micah had heard the cries.

Not screams, really—desperate, animalistic moans, the sort a cow makes as its throat is cut. After what seemed like an eternity, the sounds had stopped. But then came the banquet. Losing hold of Alia. And then he had been thrown back in here. Alone in the dark.

Micah passed his unhurt hand over his face to swipe away tears. This would kill his mother and brother. To not know what happened—to not have been there when Peridun was attacked—

though he was desperately glad they were not in this hellhole with him. He knew most of the village folk, but in his gut he felt like he would recognize his family's screams. He didn't want to listen to them die like the others.

Why am I still alive?

Micah drew his knees up to his chest and pressed his face against them. He didn't know how long he had been left alone, but it felt like an eternity in the dark. No one had come to feed him. His stomach stuck to his backbone. Were they going to starve him to death?

In some other cell, a lone drop of water fell into a pool, the only sound in this tomb. But then… a whisper of noise. Micah sat up straight, heart pounding.

Quiet, as light as mice steps, someone advanced.

He pressed into the stone at his back and waited, eyes straining in the dark.

The sound grew closer, and with it, the barest glimmer of light. The figure stopped outside the bars, saying nothing.

Micah had to swallow twice before his mouth was moist enough to speak. He was glad his voice didn't waver as he demanded, "What do you want?"

The figure jumped.

"What do you *want*?" Micah peered hard into the shadows, trying to make the figure out.

The figure leaned into the bars. "Hello. I want to know something."

He squinted, swallowing hard. The voice was feminine—and young, very young. She didn't sound dangerous… but it could be some kind of trick. "Good luck getting me to talk."

The girl leaned back from the bars with a huff, bringing up the hand that held the shard of light.

"Saints above and below," Micah whispered, finally seeing her face. "You—you're the little girl from the banquet. The daughter of the lord."

"I've twelve annuals," she said defensively, frowning at him, "and Father's called the Erlking. I want to know something, and if you tell me, I'll give you your pendant back." She pulled something from her pocket and let it thump against the cold bars.

Micah sucked in a deep breath, his eyes lighting on the pendant that Arken had carved from a scrap of wood after their father had died in the accident. *"So you'll always find your way home,"* Arken had teased him, putting the map on the back.

Micah's good hand traced the cut on his jaw, the dried blood on his skin. He thought he'd never see it again. And to have it back... to have something to cling to down here in the dark....

"What do you want to know?" he asked in a rush, taking the gamble.

SIX

MORWË

"Well," Jezra said, opening the door to Morwë's chamber and stepping inside. "*This* is more like it, Morwë." The other girl's cat-like eyes shone as she took in the interior—the large bed set on a stony outcrop, the wide chest of drawers and the witch lights crusted atop it, the vanity with its great clawed feet, a vast wardrobe and the natural spring that fed running water to the washbasin and garderobe.

Morwë's tomes were safely hidden in the bottom of the wardrobe, away from prying eyes. She had squirreled them away one by one from the royal archives, and a good thing, too—who knew when the labor would be spared from the work crews to unpack and set up a new archive room.

Jezra sat on the edge of the bed and ran her hand over the black furs piled on it. "A room for the First Daughter, indeed. A far cry from what *we've* got down there in those caverns. It's practically a refugee camp, but this…."

Morwë bit her tongue to keep from pointing out that for all intents and purposes that's exactly what was in the lower caverns. The Unseelie had left their torched forests and come here for refuge.

She closed her door behind them—she didn't want anyone like

Zel wandering in—and the door swung shut on silent hinges, perfectly hung by the team of thaumaturges that had designed and hollowed out the royal family's suite of rooms.

"You have good taste, Morwë," Jezra said as she nodded her approval. "Everything's so sumptuous and delicious."

"I had nothing to do with it," Morwë said as she sat on the vanity's stool. "The thaumaturges made it all, and I suppose Demyen charged drudges to furnish it. I was just told, 'this one's yours.'"

Jezra threw back her head and laughed, her hair cascading around her like rivers of ink. "Oh, that *would* be Demyen's way, the old, gnarled stump. He probably shook one of his lists at you, too, didn't he?"

Morwë let a small smile grace her lips. "He may have waved parchment at the door, yes." Demyen was her father's councilor and advisor; he handled much of the administration of the Unseelie Court, and his lists had been instrumental in the great undertaking to move their people south from the frozen taiga forests to the mountains.

Jezra's chuckles died away. "Still, it gives me hope that they'll do an equally fine job, once his lists get to us. Whenever that will be," she mused darkly.

Morwë's hand twitched, but she clenched it to her side, out of Jezra's line of sight. "I'm sure the thaumaturges are working very hard. It's a difficult working to shape stone."

"Why aren't you on a team? Your Arts are strong; I remember that."

"I haven't finished my studies… and I've had to take care of family matters. Mother isn't well, you know." Morwë privately thought that defined her whole life—unfinished at the expense of her family.

She and Jezra had first met in youngling classes. Out of their whole age group, Jezra was one of the only ones who neither avoided her because of her heritage nor fawned because she was the First Daughter. Jezra merely laughed and teased and criticized freely without bias, and Morwë had stuck by her mainly from relief.

When Morwë had been pulled from the youngling classes to help her mother, she had finished her general studies piecemeal with an amalgam of tutors and instructors, and then studied on her own, soaking up knowledge from her tomes. It had been a boon in disguise—if no one knew just how powerful or skilled she was, they would be more wary of crossing her. No one was truly safe among the Unseelie, not even the Erlking's First Daughter.

Morwë half wondered if she and Jezra would have grown closer if they had finished out their classes together. As Jezra got up and began to prowl around her room, Morwë wasn't sure if she wanted that.

Jezra's dress rippled like water as she investigated the nooks and crannies of the room. "Yes… your mother. Have you not heard the rumors, Morwë?"

"What rumors? You know those imps generate gossip as easy as breathing. I can't listen to all of it like you can."

"Well, it's probably nothing—just living almost on top of one another has everyone on edge. And the thaumaturge teams don't seem to be doing a moon-cursed thing to change the living situation. It's *terrible*, Morwë."

"Spit it out, Jezra," Morwë said, voice flat.

Jezra looked over her shoulder furtively at the shut door. "Well," she murmured, "Your mother wasn't at the feast two nights ago."

"She wasn't feeling well."

"She hasn't been feeling well for moon cycles, Morwë. Annuals, even. And—well, there has been talk. About the Erlking, and how he put all the sprites that opposed the move or couldn't stand the journey to death, but he keeps a sick wight as his wife… it's bad luck, they're saying. A bad omen for our start here."

"They've always hated her; I don't see why that should change." Morwë clenched her fist, hard.

"No. They thought it odd—a strange foible in a ruler, to keep a wight around for so long. But now it's something more. They're saying he's losing his grip on the court." Jezra sighed and turned away to open Morwë's jewelry box. "Do you know anything? Anything of his plans, his vision for our future here that I can pass on...." Her hook dangled in the air, but Morwë was uninterested in the bait.

"I have been too busy with my own tasks, Jezra. My father has always kept his own council," Morwë said, somewhat testy. Her nails dug into her palm.

Jezra stirred the contents; the clink of metal and precious stone mixed with the burble of water from the washbasin. "Oh, well. It was just a thought."

Father never confides in anyone, least of all me, Morwë thought. *He makes all his decisions on his own. He decided to move us to these mountains when our forest burned, and those who objected were left in the taiga on spikes.*

She did not find it at all profitable to question her father anywhere where someone could overhear her. Only in the privacy of her own mind did she say what she thought—and even that was dangerous, if it showed on her face.

She hoped Jezra didn't speak like this to others. General unrest and unhappiness after such an upheaval was one thing—unrest with a root was another. The Erlking was quick to rip any unwanted shoots from the Unseelie Court.

"What's happened with that sprite you were seeing, what's-his-name," Morwë said, trying to redirect Jezra's attention to her favorite subject, her romantic life.

"Abraxis? I dropped him some days ago; he bored me." Jezra smiled and sprawled across the bed again. "I like Vadim now—he's a member of the war band, so big and strong. In fact, just the other day...." Jezra launched into a long story about the prank she had pulled on her paramour.

Morwë nodded along at the right parts of the story, her mind still whirling. It was an open secret that most of the Unseelie Court found her father's choice to keep a wight wife and bear children with her inexplicable. One theory had to do with the Court's steadily declining birth rate and experimenting to see if wight women were a viable solution to the problem. It was second only to the belief that the Erlking just had a predilection for wights. But Morwë hadn't known that the opinions had turned from puzzling and odd to ominous.

Jezra laughed and covered her mouth with her hand, but her delight still shone from her eyes as she reached the story's punch line. She rolled over on the bed. "Oh, you should have seen his face, Morwë! It was hilarious!"

Morwë brushed absently at the black feathers on her gown, "I'm sure," she murmured, her mind still going around and around.

"You know, we need to get you someone," Jezra said, leaning forward conspiratorially. "You'd be more fun then."

"No," Morwë muttered, shooting Jezra a glare. They might be friends of a sort, but she wouldn't tolerate being pushed towards anyone.

She scoffed. "Why not? That wight Ingridon brought back for you was a little young, but—"

"*No*, Jezra. Didn't you hear our row at the feast?"

"You said you didn't want the wight to bolster your Arts' levels," Jezra said, her smile wickedly sharp. "You can still tumble him."

"No," Morwë said emphatically, crossing her arms.

Jezra groaned and sat up. "Fine, how about Gavril? I've had him. He's good enough, if you don't mind him falling asleep after. Or Hadrian, with those strong shoulders—you know he always watches you, Morwë. He'd be good."

"No, he wouldn't," Morwë said softly, remembering hands on her body—grasping, possessive. Right before she had tossed him into a briar bush.

"Well, how do you know until you try? You need to live a little, before your father pairs you off with who-knows-what to strengthen some connection for his throne. Because you know who else watches you? Toren, with those creepy eyes." She shuddered theatrically. "What does he see with that one silver eye?"

"The thaumaturge?" Morwë shook her head. "His eyes are just an odd coloring quirk. Why would he watch me? We've never spoken."

"What better match for a powerful thaumaturge than another powerful thaumaturge, sure to make thaumaturge babies? And you know he'd never let you dissolve the marriage alliance and go your separate ways if your children showed signs of being powerful. He'd want to get as much out of you as possible."

He'll marry you off. Morwë's stomach sank.

Jezra continued, "So that's why you've got to live a little *now.* Great depths, girl, haven't you tumbled *anyone*?" Jezra's lip curled like she might have some sort of disease.

"*Yes*," Morwë bit out. The lie sat cloying on her tongue.

Jezra planted her hands on her hips. "Well, who?"

Morwë pulled a loose black feather from her gown and stared at it. Maybe if she had finished out youngling school, she would have been used to the casual intimacy that Jezra reveled in, would have been willing to be pulled into dark corners for trysts. But she hadn't, and so she didn't, keeping herself apart, rejecting all such advances. They were all the same, anyway. They all wanted something from her. It lurked in every corner, panted after her in the shadows. And Jezra, with a new swain every moon cycle, would never understand.

She didn't want Hadrian. Didn't want Gavril. Didn't want anyone who made her feel like a thing—like she was just another wight that they wanted to eat, consume her and be done. Like her mother.

She let the feather fall, watched it spiral to the floor in the greenish cast of the witch lights.

"Morwë, tell me!" Jezra insisted. "That tall one from Ingridon's war band? What's his name, Sephtis?"

"No."

"Well, don't tell me it was—" She broke off, staring at Morwë oddly.

Morwë raised an eyebrow. "What?"

Jezra leaned in and cast a glance around the chamber, though they were the only occupants. "Ingridon?" she whispered.

Morwë jerked back. "*Jezra!*"

"Sorry," Jezra said, a bit disappointed. "Only, I know you both fight like cats and dogs, and sometimes...."

"He's my *brother*," Morwë snapped, stiffening as a cold finger of terror ran down her boney spine. "That's disgusting."

"That doesn't stop some. It's only rumor, but I heard that—"

"Stop!" Morwë held up an emphatic hand. "No more rumors. I don't want to know."

Jezra raised an eyebrow. "I haven't even said anything juicy yet, Morwë."

"I don't care, Jezra." Morwë took a large gulp of water from the pitcher by the bed to wash out the sudden horrible taste in her mouth. It was unnatural—though that word didn't have much weight down in the dark. She felt gooseflesh break out on her skin. Her and Ingridon... no. Never. She'd hate him more than she already did.

She'd step into daylight first.

A fist knocked on the heavy chamber door, and a male voice called, "Morwë?"

Jezra answered for her immediately. "She's in here, come in!" She arranged her skirts' folds so her legs dangled into view. "Why, Hadrian," she said in honeyed tones as the guard opened the door and stepped into the room. "We were just talking about you."

Morwë shot her a poisonous look.

"Really?" Hadrian said with a smile, leaning in the doorway. "What about?"

"Nothing important; you know what she's like," Morwë put in before Jezra could admit to anything more damaging. "What do you want?"

"Ingridon sent me off to find you and Enzella. You're wanted," he explained. "A family matter. But I haven't found Zel yet; she's not in her room."

A family matter? Cold dread pooled in her stomach. That was never good.

Morwë stood and brushed off her skirt. "I'll find Enzella, Hadrian. Goodbye, Jezra."

The other girl sent a big wink her way, which Morwë chose to ignore. Jezra left the royal family's suite one way, and Morwë quickly turned the other direction, aware that Hadrian was close behind her.

Enzella often disappeared, but she had been acting odd lately. Morwë would check her usual haunts, but if she wasn't there, she'd probably have to go up to the prison levels. Zel had been asking about the wight boy—

A hand closed around her wrist and jerked her to a stop. "Wait a minute, Morwë."

"Do you want me to find Enzella or don't you?" Morwë snapped, eyes hard.

"I want you to tell me why you've been avoiding me."

"Have I?" she asked cagily.

"Yes, for cycles, Morwë. Why?"

"Could it be because I don't wish to see you?" Morwë hissed. "No, that would be too sensible. Go bother someone else, Hadrian. Jezra, maybe. She likes you."

"You liked me once," Hadrian said, pressing forward to stare into her eyes.

She wouldn't give ground, wouldn't press into the wall—she was strong. She *was*, moonlight take his sight! "No, I didn't." She clenched her fists. "Let me go, or I'll do worse than toss you into a few thorns." If he wouldn't move, she'd *make* him move.

"Is this about before?" he asked, eyes widening. "Because Ingridon said—"

"What?" she said in shock.

"Ah…." Hadrian realized his slip. "I—"

"No," Morwë growled, shoving out with her Arts. The force

from her hands pushed Hadrian across the corridor to the other wall, and the inky cobwebs of her magic stuck him there like a fly in a trap. "What. Did Ingridon. Say," Morwë whispered as power crackled in her veins.

"He said… it would loosen you up," Hadrian whispered, staring at her.

He was right to stare. She didn't use her Arts in showy displays—not often. She didn't want others knowing her measure, and as the Erlking's daughter, she didn't often need to. But when she did….

She laughed without humor. "Loosen me up."

"But I like you, Morwë," Hadrian added. "I like you, loose or wound. I don't care that you're—"

"That I'm what?" Her voice was no louder than a whisper, but grew in strength. "Rigid? Unyielding? *Cold*? Good. I'm not going to change any time soon." Her hands opened; with a great push, she threw him back down the hallway with her Arts. Morwë stalked away, ignoring the thump as he landed against stone.

Yes, she was cold. Cold as ice. As cold as these tunnels. She had to be. It was her armor.

Unbidden, memories rose of a mouth on hers, plundering, stealing her breath…. She gagged but kept walking. *That must be what it's like,* she thought, *to be a wight in thrall.*

To be stolen from.

SEVEN

ENZELLA

Enzella beamed at the wight boy in pleasure, her curiosity bubbling forth. "I want to know *everything*. But what does this mean?" She pointed to the side of the disc with curved lines.

The boy peered at it. "It's a knot design. My brother carved it for me when he first started learning to shape wood. He wasn't very good." He swallowed.

"Yes, my mother told me that," Enzella said impatiently. "But she said it means family ties. What does *that* mean?"

He stared at her blankly. "…The bonds you have with your family that keep you connected, knit together."

She frowned down at the pendant. "So it's a *bad* thing."

"What? No!"

"Then what? Being bound isn't *good*."

"It's the bond of shared blood, but it's a connection you choose as well, built on care, respect, love…."

"What's that?" Enzella pressed against the bars, eyes widening.

"Love?" He hesitated. "Don't you know?"

"I asked Mother, but she said we don't have it down here."

He blinked at her, uncomprehending.

She tilted her head to the side. "So what is it?"

"How about," he said slowly, "a question for a question."

Enzella narrowed her eyes. "Deal. But my question first."

He watched her from the corner of his eye. "There are different kinds of love. Sometimes you feel romantic. Like kissing."

"Oh, I know about that," she broke in. "I've seen imps in the shadows canoodling."

His jaw sagged a moment before he snapped it shut. "Yes. But mainly, love is caring about someone."

"How much?"

"More than anything." His eyes shone with moisture in the light of the witch light she held.

Caring about someone more than *anything*. Enzella pondered this. No wonder they didn't have it down here. "How do you do that?"

The boy licked his lips. "It's my turn, remember?"

She hesitated, and then sat down outside the bars. He was right. And she had already asked a few questions. "Fine. Fair's fair."

He swallowed hard, chin jutting out. "Are you going to kill me?"

She shook her head quickly, eyes wide. "No."

"Who, then?"

"Nobody. Remember the big scene at the feast? Ingridon gave you to Morwë for a present. Ingridon's my brother—the leader of the war band that brought you here—and Morwë's my sister. It would be Morwë, if it was anyone, but she doesn't want you. She'd rather moonlight take her eyes than for Ingridon to get what he wants." Enzella smiled cheerfully. "So you're all right. My turn!"

The boy shivered, passing a hand over his eyes.

Enzella cleared her throat, a strange feeling twisting in her stomach as she watched him shake. "What do you do with love? Or how do you do it?"

"I... I don't know. You just feel a certain way about a person, here." He put his good hand on his chest. "You decide to care." He licked his lips, staring at her oddly. "You put someone else's needs before your own. You'd do anything to make them happy or keep them safe."

Enzella mulled this over. Had anyone ever done that for her? Had *she?*

The boy scooted closer to the bars. "Why was my village stolen?"

Enzella lifted her eyes to meet his. "We need kneph for our thaumaturges, our magic users. Most of us have some Arts, but for small things. Only a few have real power. Kneph refills your magic stores. Not me, though," she mumbled. "I'm not old enough, and I haven't got any Arts." She made a face. "Ingridon doesn't either, but he likes the rush the kneph gives him."

"But what *is* kneph?" the boy broke in. "Why take us to get it?"

"Kneph is what we get from you wights. It's life force. Spirit. Breath."

EIGHT

MICAH

For what seemed like an age, Micah couldn't speak from the horror that gripped him.

"The thaumaturges take it and do something to it," the pale girl continued blithely, "and they put it into the cauldrons —could you see them?—at the feast. But Ingridon is messy enough to drink from the source. That's why his wight fell down. I saw you helping her—"

"Stop!" Micah shouted, his voice echoing loud in his cell. "Just —stop!" He squeezed his eyes shut and pushed himself away, even though the movement jarred his broken arm. He hissed through his teeth and bit down on his tongue. The pain helped. It cut through the despair that tried to overtake him. Dead, then—all dead for sure, even Alia by now.

"What's the matter?" she asked. "Is your arm—"

"Shut up! Just shut up!" he cried, glaring at her as tears spilled down his face. "What's the *matter*? All of my friends, neighbors— people I've known my whole life—they're all dead, and because of you! Because you stole us for, for, for food! You're all monsters!"

Micah watched her face crumple. Her shoulders hunched, and

she looked down and away, the light from her glowing crystal illuminating a trail of liquid down her face.

He swiped at his own cheeks. This place... evil leaked from the walls, almost palpable to him. It leeched through solid stone to try to wrap its grip around his throat. He had a right to be afraid. He had a right to hate the wisp of a girl outside the bars for being one of *them*.

But he remembered when he had first seen her at the feast. She had been cowering under the table with him. She, too, had been afraid.

"I'm sorry," he whispered in a thick voice. "I didn't mean to make you cry."

She sniffed and turned back to him, eyes round and luminous in the greenish light. "You're crying, too."

"Yes." His voice cracked. Micah tried to snuffle quietly into the arm of his tunic, but the movement jarred his broken arm again. He winced.

He heard a scraping noise, and the girl dragged a bucket of water up to the bars. "Here," she said, holding out a dipper, "it won't fit through the bars."

He took the dipper in his good hand and swallowed gratefully. The water was cold and stale, but it was wet, and that was the important thing. And it was more than he had had in days.

"What's the matter with your arm?"

"It's broken." He drained the dipper and handed it back.

"Oh." She scooted close to the bars and whispered, "You're sad because... you loved them?"

The pain rose again, and he wanted to lash out once more with barbed words, make her recoil and feel at least some of the misery he was trapped in. But when her face, so open and guileless, stared up at him, he found that he couldn't. "Yes."

"Who loves, where you come from?"

"Parents love children," he said when he could get the words out. "Families love each other. Friends. Husbands and wives love each other." What kind of world had she known, full of darkness? A world without love?

"Does…." she faltered to a stop, her face going blank.

"What?"

"If we don't have love here… does Mother love me?"

NINE

ENZELLA

"Does my mother love me?" Enzella pressed. "She came from up above once. She's like you, a wight. Doesn't that mean she does?" *But she said she's forgotten down here,* Enzella thought, growing still.

The boy looked away and forked his good hand through his dirty hair. "I... I don't know. Do you love her?"

"I hold the handkerchief when she coughs." Enzella looked away, dubious. "And I do what she asks. Mostly. But she likes me best, out of all of us. She says so. She says I'm the one thing she's done right." Though Enzella was never sure what she meant by that.

"Then maybe she does," he whispered, eyes flicking back to hers. He reached out and touched the bars, right above where her hands gripped them. "What's your name?"

"Enzella. What's yours?"

"Micah." He closed his eyes and wiped his face on his tunic again. "What are you?"

"Hmm?" Her nose crinkled in puzzlement.

"You said your mother was like me—wight, human, whatever you call it. So what are you? Why do you live down here in the dark?"

"The light is awful. Father says it burns and it'll eat right through our skin to our bones. And we're Unseelie."

"Tall tales and monsters," Micah murmured, almost too quietly for her to hear. "I've fallen into a story." He passed his good hand over his eyes for a moment and took a shuddering breath. "So… what *are* they going to do with me?"

Enzella stopped to think about this. "I—I'm not sure. I can find out, though," she said quickly. "I can find out lots of things. Oh." With all the questions and answers and crying, she had forgotten. But a bargain was a bargain. She held out his pendant, tying the break in the thong. "Here."

Micah took it from her with a shaky hand, and his finger grazed hers. She jumped. His skin felt warm, even here in this cell. He flinched as well and hissed. It must've hurt his arm. The leather slipped over his head to rest over his breastbone, the rough whorls barely visible in the glow of the witch light.

"Enzella!"

They both jumped again, violently. As Micah gasped in pain, Enzella turned to see Morwë standing in the stairway, hands on her hips. "We've been looking for you everywhere," Morwë hissed. "Father wants us. A family matter."

"Father?" Her heart skipped. "Why?" She hated that it came out as a whine.

"I don't know. It's orders." Morwë held out an impatient hand. "If you hurry up, I won't tell about you visiting the prisoner." Her eyes caught the disc on his chest. "And giving his necklace back."

Enzella hurriedly rose to her feet and dusted off her skirt. "Who are you going to tell? I won't get in trouble; he's your wight. His name is Micah. Isn't she pretty?" she asked Micah over her shoulder. "I told him you were pretty, Morwë—"

"Zella!" Morwë caught her by the shoulders and shook her, hard. "What have I told you about talking? Knowledge is *power.* Keep it to yourself," she hissed. "Come on." Morwë's grip tightened and pulled her down the stair.

Enzella clung to Morwë's hand and tried to keep up without

falling down the steep stair. As they hurried to the bottom and down the hallway, she realized: Morwë was afraid.

Morwë's never afraid! She thought. *She's the bravest person I know! She can look at Father when he rages!*

But if Morwë was afraid… what did that mean?

She began to be afraid, too.

TEN

ENZELLA

"Here we are, Father," Morwë said in a clear voice as they stepped into their parents' sitting room. "I'm sorry for our tardiness. It took me some time to find her."

Enzella trained her eyes on her slippers scuffed with dirt from the prisons.

"No matter, First Daughter. Go and help your mother," Father's smooth voice said, slicing in between Enzella and Morwë. Morwë dropped her hand and left for their mother's bedroom.

"Come here, Second Daughter."

Enzella swallowed, feeling her stomach turn to lead. But she had to obey. She scooted forward, eyes still on the floor.

"Look at me, child." His voice was still smooth and refined, but it was clearly an order.

Enzella forced her head up to meet her father's eyes. The Erlking of the Unseelie gazed steadily back. His straight hair flowed down his chest, white against the black of his robes, but it in no way indicated his age. He steepled his thin fingers together, stained black as all thaumaturges were, as he stared at her. His eyes glowed like dark coals in the recesses of his face. "Were you hiding?"

The weight of the words pushed down on Enzella relentlessly. "N-no, Father," she whispered. "I was… playing. I didn't know I would be wanted." Her voice trailed into silence, shoulders tightening. Would he lash her palms, the way her tutors did when she didn't arrive for lessons on time, or something worse?

He blinked, obscuring the onyx orbs for just a second. Even that was a relief from the penetrating gaze. "Next time, tell someone where you are, Second Daughter. We cannot have you wandering over this new territory unsupervised."

"Y-yes, Father." Enzella bobbed her head, clasping her hands behind her back.

"Good." He reached out and ran his fingers over the crown of her head.

Enzella locked her knees and stood perfectly still as the icy touch washed over her. She forced herself not to look up, and almost forgot to breathe.

Her father stood in one fluid movement, his black robes rippling like water. The black feathers on his wide sleeves, the sigil of his rule, rustled together like grim whispers.

Morwë reentered the room supporting Mother, who could barely stand without help. Enzella saw Mother grab her sister's hand and hiss something in her ear before Father walked over to them and obscured her view.

Ingridon sidled up to her from the corner where he had been lurking. "It's your fault, you know," he said, lip curling into a smile.

"What?" Enzella blurted out.

"All this. It's your fault. Mother had Morwë and me when she was in her prime—full of rage and hate, and with plenty of her spirit left. But you weren't planned. You came when she was weak—and she's just gotten weaker since." He shrugged. "No point in keeping her around."

"What?" she said again, now scared but still not understanding.

Father took Mother from Morwë's grasp. Morwë left to join Enzella and Ingridon, putting her hands on Zel's shoulders. The weight was not comforting.

"And yet, you're still Mummy's favorite monster child," Ingridon murmured. "Even though you're the one who's killed her."

"Morwë?" Enzella breathed, eyes darting around the room.

Morwë's grip on her shoulders tightened.

"For twenty-six annuals you have been by my side, Wife," Father said, staring down at the woman in his arms. "Far longer than many other women would have lasted. You have born me three children. For this you will have honor, and no more of this wasting away."

Mother merely stared at him, dead-eyed.

Enzella whispered, "Mother?"

Mother did not look at her.

Father took her face in his hands, tilting it up. "Goodbye," he said simply, and then kissed her. Blue light pooled around their mouths, and Father swallowed. And kept swallowing. And Mother didn't struggle; she just hung there in his grasp, limp.

"Mother," Enzella cried. "Mother, Mother!" She could hear it; it was a sucking noise. She tried to run to her, but Morwë held her fast, wrapping her arms around her.

"No!" Enzella fought back against the hold, screeching. "Let me go! Mother!"

She was starting to convulse now. He was killing her.

Morwë flipped Enzella around, but she could still hear. Enzella screamed into Morwë's abdomen and thrashed, but still couldn't get free. Morwë clutched her with the strength of her Arts.

The sucking noise finally stopped.

Enzella's frantic cries subsided into hiccupping sobs. She sagged against Morwë for a moment, and then shoved with all her might to be free. She had just enough time to turn and see

Father standing over a limp form sprawled on the floor before Morwë blocked her view again.

"Come on, Zel," Morwë muttered in a thick voice, trying to pull her out of the room. Enzella began to wail softly.

Ingridon grabbed Enzella by the hair and slapped her. "Shut your mouth," he said over her yelp. "She's gone; crying over an empty husk is a waste of time."

"*Leave her alone*, Ingridon," Morwë growled, prying his hand away, digging her nails into his flesh. "She's *twelve*." Morwë hauled Enzella out of the chamber and into the hallway. "Come on, let's go to my room," she whispered, "come on."

"Why—*why*?" Enzella forced out through hiccupping sobs. "Why did he—she's—our *mother*—" she shuddered against Morwë's side as her sister tugged her down the dark hallway.

Morwë tried to speak twice before forcing out, "He's the Erlking."

"That's no reason!" Enzella yelled as Morwë pushed open the door to her chamber.

"I know," her sister whispered.

Enzella ran to the bed and threw herself on it, shaking but unable to cry anymore. She hunched away from Morwë's hesitant touch on her hair, clasped a pillow to her chest, and wailed.

ELEVEN

ARKEN

"Don't go, Arken," Sara wailed, coiling around him like a snake, nearly knocking over his full pack and the quiver of arrows beside it. "Please don't go."

"I have to." Arken brushed the dark hair from the little girl's face and wiped her eyes. They had traveled for two full days, slowly making their way along the trail to Cairenoch with their party of children and infants, and the whole time Arken had felt the connection between him and Ceridfel's peak pull at him, growing tauter with every step.

But now they were halfway to Cairenoch. The party would be able to make it back without him. If he left the trail now and made straight for the mountain, he could be there in a day and a half.

He needed to find Micah.

"But you'll die! We'll never see you again," Sara sobbed.

"That's not going to happen," Arken insisted.

Father James came over and placed his hands on Sara's shoulders. "He must go, Sara. We will pray for him. Do you remember what the Psalms say? 'I lift my eyes to the mountains—where does my help come from? My help comes from the LORD, who made heaven, and earth, and the mountains.' And again the Psalms say, 'In His hands are the depths of the earth, and the mountain peaks belong to him.' The Caleahanachs have always been our refuge—God made it so. Arken will come back."

Father James made eye contact with Arken. "I have something for you, my son. Let me get it."

Arken nodded, tamping down his frustration and need to leave right away. He looked back down at the girl, who rubbed her running nose on her sleeve. "You're going to be strong, aren't you, Sara? You're going to listen to Father James and Grandmother Foley, and Ora and Derwin too?" he asked, speaking of the oldest children in the group. He had done his best to give them a crash course in wilderness survival and how to look for threats to the party.

Sara nodded tearfully.

"Will you take care of Bess for me? I don't want her to be lonely. She likes her grain and the occasional carrot, does Bess. Can you do that for me?"

She nodded again.

"Good. That's your job now. I'm glad I can count on you." Arken hugged her and then gave her a gentle push towards her older brother. She went reluctantly, wiping her nose along her sleeve once more.

Father James came back from his rummage in the wagon with a vial in his hands. "My son, the only thing I can give you is a blessing. If we are to believe these creatures were faefolk, dark elves, what have you—and I see no reason not to—they could be fey creatures that thrive on trickery, bargains, and the like. Or they could be like nothing we have heard before. I don't know what to tell you."

"Don't trust anything," Arken said darkly. "Right."

Father James corrected him, "Trust *God*, trust yourself, and trust the land to reject evil. Search for places where the light does not reach, and follow your feet." He took a deep breath. "Here is the blessing." He dipped his fingers into the vial and made a cross in oil on Arken's forehead. Then, quick as a wink, he smeared the oil in both of Arken's eyes.

"Agh!" Arken winced at the burning sensation.

"I added fernseed to the oil," Father James explained as Arken blinked his vision clear. "In older days, when magic was more vibrant and alive in the world, fernseed was thought to have a certain virtue to grant invisibility and to see things that are hidden. I pray it gives you clear sight, my son."

"Thank you, Father."

Father James blessed him and hugged him. "I will bring word to your mother," he said in a choked voice. "God be with you."

"Tell her I love her and will see her soon." Arken hoisted the pack and quiver over his shoulder, set his face and heart towards the mountain, and did not look back.

TWELVE

MORWË

Enzella had finally cried herself to sleep after what felt like hours of weeping.

Morwë moved like an old woman as she got up and walked to the garderobe. Her eyes felt dry and scratchy. Splashing water on her face, she stared into the mirror, her eyes fixed on her reflection.

She could see her mother in her face.

Morwë grabbed a comb and forced it through the snarls in her hair as the scene replayed over and over again. A phantom hand gripped her wrist with the last vestiges of strength and squeezed. *"If you truly don't hate me, promise me you'll take care of your sister,"* Mother had whispered urgently. *"Keep her safe. Promise me, Morwë!"* Her eyes showed only wretched desperation. Those eyes had pulled the words from Morwë's paralyzed lips: "I promise, Mother."

Once Morwë had spoken the vow, her mother's will had drained away. She had walked to the Erlking without resistance, even though she *knew*—

Morwë braced her hands against the stone counter and took several shaky breaths.

Ingridon had known she would be killed. He acted bored with the whole proceedings. He hadn't even cared.

Morwë hadn't wanted to believe it possible, even though she knew the reality. No wight had ever lasted as long underground, though that was partly due to Father's extreme restraint... and eccentricity. Most Unseelie didn't keep wights around at all, let alone long enough to bear three younglings. Wouldn't that have earned her...?

Earned, Morwë thought scornfully, grinding the heels of her hands into her eyes. As if the right to live was something to be wheedled or bought. *Yet here it is.*

Why had she had a wight mother and not an Unseelie mother? Surely birth rate would not be the only reason to sully a bloodline with a wight taint. Why Mother, specifically? Morwë only half-remembered conversations from when she was very young—full of curiosity, like Enzella—before she learned to keep her mouth shut or Ingridon would use her words against her.

No one had ever publicly questioned Father's choice.

And I never asked, because asking reveals too much. Fool, she berated herself. She opened the door to her wardrobe and pulled the stack of moldering tomes from their secret compartment. Turning over the pages, making sure the brittle ones didn't crumble, she searched for any mention of her mother in the histories, looked for any clue that might speak to her father's reasoning in the older volumes.

But the books remained frustratingly oblique. Why would a wight get a mention in an Unseelie tome, after all?

But Zel might have asked. She still spoke what was on her mind, though she was learning to keep important matters close.

She might even know more than she realizes....

Morwë stood and tiptoed to the door to look in on her sleeping sister.

The bed was empty. Her sister was gone.

CHAPTER

THIRTEEN

MICAH

Micah curled up in the weak glow of the crystal Enzella had left and tried to think as tiredness tugged at his frame. He wiped tear tracks from his face and closed his eyes, trying to slip off into dreams of better times. What would his mother be doing now? Any other day, Luned Sawyer would probably be baking or doting on his older sister Selma, whose baby was due soon. She might not even know he was gone yet.

But Arken would. He was supposed to return after dropping their mother off at Selma's house in Cairenoch.

This was the—third? fourth?—day of his captivity. By the best of his recollection, the war band carried them northeast from Peridun, towards Ceridfel. They were underground, possibly even under the mountain. When Micah thought about so much earth and stone surrounding him, his mouth dried and his heart raced. He forced the thought from his mind as much as he could, staring at the bluish-green crystal.

Was it possible he would die here? Alone? He had dropped every piece of lint and string in his pockets, precious little though there was, trying to give pursuers something to track. But the winter would soon set in, and a snowfall would cover any tracks or trail he had tried to leave. And who was left to come for him?

Even if Arken was back in Peridun, he wouldn't know where to start looking.

Face it, Micah told himself, shutting his eyes tight. *It's hopeless.*

Something stumbled in the darkness. He could hear panting, a whimper.

His heart jumped, and he pushed himself up, cradling his broken arm. "Hello?" he called, straining to see. "Who's there?"

A hiccup, and then the girl stumbled into view—Enzella. Tears streamed down her face, and she swayed where she stood. "Micah, she's dead," she cried. "She's dead and I didn't... I didn't ask her...." she broke off with a sob.

"Who?" He tried to scoot forward once again.

"M-Mother. Father killed her," she forced out, and then pressed against the bars. He watched, astonished, as she managed to force her skinny self through the bars. She threw herself at him, and he gasped and bit back a cry of pain as her headlong lunge jarred his broken arm.

"Enzella," he whispered, "Right side. Please. My arm...."

She scooted to his right side and tried to burrow into him, snuffling against his tunic. On instinct, he wrapped his good arm around her pointy shoulders. She sobbed, a low, gut-wrenching sound.

Her mother was dead by her father's hand. Unseelie or not... it was a terrible thing.

"I'm sorry." As he gingerly rubbed her slight and boney back, he found that he really was.

"I didn't ask her if she loved me." Enzella sniffled. "Now I'll never know."

Micah brushed the light strands of hair out of her face. His gut wrenched. "You may not be able to know that, but I think *you* loved *her*."

She looked up at him. "How do you know?"

"If you didn't love her, you wouldn't be so sad." He swallowed. "If you hurt when you feel loss, it means you cared very much."

"Ingridon doesn't love her," she said with finality. "He didn't care." She sniffed and scrubbed at the tears on her face. "He slapped me and told me to stop crying." Before Micah finished reeling from this revelation, she asked, "Do you have a mother, Micah?"

"Yes." His throat closed, thinking of Luned. He hated to think of her crying over him.

"Do you love her?"

"Yes."

"How many annuals are you?"

"You mean years? Sixteen. Why?"

"I wondered if it's something you grow out of," Enzella whispered, pressing a hand to her chest. "It *hurts*."

"I know. My father died six years ago. I loved him very much." He raised a hand to his head, the hair that straggled out of his dirty ponytail. "Everyone in my family cut our hair. That's what we do in a time of mourning."

Her eyes, round and sad, looked up at him. "Did that make it stop hurting?"

"No, that's just a way to—to demonstrate a loss." Micah smiled a little. "My priest calls it 'structured agony.'"

"Does it *ever* stop?"

He thought about it for a minute, and the old familiar ache awakened in his chest again. Darren Sawyer had died in a logging accident when Micah was only ten, and his memories of him were turning fuzzy. But he remembered his dark beard creased in a smile, his deep belly laugh, the way his father had swung his mother around their small home in a dance, and the way he had listened, rapt, as Luned told stories. The way Darren hugged Micah to him and called him his boy, making Micah feel safe and loved. "No, it doesn't. But it eases. Gets easier to bear."

Enzella looked away, her face drawn and pensive. "I don't want it to," she whispered.

"Enzella?" A woman's frantic voice filtered up the stairs. "Zel, where are you?"

"Who's that?" Micah whispered, tensing up.

"Morwë," Enzella murmured in a low voice, making no move to call back the beautiful sister that she had lauded the day before.

"Zella!" The voice was growing nearer.

"Hadn't you better tell her where you are?" Micah asked.

Enzella merely buried her head back into his side.

He swallowed and called, "She's here. She's safe."

Morwë emerged from the darkness and walked right up to the bars, gripping the metal tight. "Enzella! Get out of there!" she demanded. "Don't run off like that!"

"No," Enzella said mulishly, refusing to budge from Micah's side.

"How did you even get in there?"

"She squeezed through the bars," Micah said.

The dark haired woman stared at him like she was affronted at the very idea of him addressing her. Micah flushed and looked away.

FOURTEEN

MORWË

"Enzella, come here this moment or I will drag you out. I promised Mother I would look after you, and I can't do that if you're disappearing." Morwë set her hands on her hips, trying to tamp down the wild feeling in her chest. She had never panicked at missing Enzella before. But she had promised to look out for her. How could she have failed already?

"I loved Mother," Enzella declared, finally sitting up to look at her. Her pale hair stood out from her face like a lightning storm, framing the determined set of her jaw. "And now she's gone. Did you love her? Are you sorry?"

Morwë flinched. Love? No one loved among the Unseelie. "What are you talking about?"

"Micah says he loves his mother. And he's sixteen, Morwë. Is it something you stop doing? If we get old, do we stop loving?"

"What stupid things has he been filling your head with?" Morwë demanded, shooting the boy a look that could flay skin to cover her fear.

The boy protested, "I only answered her questions."

"Well, if I were you, I'd keep my thoughts about love to myself," she said, smiling without any humor. "Considering my brother thought you'd be ideal to cheer me up."

He gulped.

"It's not just kissing," Enzella said impatiently. "It's wanting someone to be happy and safe, trying to make them happy and safe." Her voice faded.

Morwë pressed her lips together. "Zel, what have I told you about knowledge?"

"Knowledge is power," Enzella whispered, hanging her head.

"And what do we do with power?"

"Keep it. Don't give it away for nothing."

"If anyone else heard you say you loved Mother, they'd think you were just like her, a weak wight. And they'd use it against you. Never hand your enemy a weapon freely."

Enzella glanced at Micah, a considering look on her face. "What about a trade?"

Morwë shook her head. "What?"

Enzella stared at Morwë, a canny look in her eye. "A trade. I let you know where I am, what I'm doing."

"Visiting your new friend?" Morwë suggested silkily.

"Maybe," Enzella said, frowning hard. "And you *let* me, because knowledge is power, remember?"

Morwë sighed, her shoulders slumping. "You're finally growing up," Morwë said quietly.

"Wasn't that what you wanted?" Zel demanded.

Morwë opened her mouth, and then shut it. No. She wanted to keep Zel wrapped up, safe, her promise fulfilled. She didn't want to ruin the happy demeanor that Enzella had somehow kept for twelve annuals. That was the only thing about her mother's children that remained unsullied. But nothing lasted forever, and at least up here she'd be away from most dangers. "Fine. What do you want in return for this trade?" Morwë crossed her arms over her chest.

"I want...." Enzella turned back and looked at Micah. "I want you to fix his arm."

"What's wrong with it?"

Enzella gave him an encouraging look, and the boy said, a little bewildered, "Broken, I think."

"This is really what you want, Zel? For me to fix your wight's arm?"

"Yes. *Is* he mine?" Enzella asked, interested.

"Why not? No one else wants him," Morwë muttered. "All right, you; stand up." She reached a hand through the bars.

Enzella helped him to his feet. "Morwë's the best thaumaturge in the underground," she told him in proud, confidential tones.

"Not *the* best," Morwë conceded, "but good. All right, you—"

"His name," Zel said pointedly, "is Micah. I told you."

"Mmm." Morwë narrowed her eyes. "Let me see it."

Micah gingerly held out his injured left arm, and she took it. He recoiled at her touch, but she held his arm steady as she felt the bone. "Yes, it's broken. It's not out of place, but it's a bad break. It'll need a couple healings. I think," Morwë added doubtfully.

"Don't you know?" Enzella poked her nose in between them to watch.

"He's a wight. I've never done a working on a wight before." She took a firmer hold on his arm and met his gaze. "This might hurt."

The boy stared in frightened amazement as her Arts, black like ink, flowed from her hands over his forearm. Her Arts coiled around his arm and sank down through the skin and muscle to the bone.

Micah hissed. "Ahhhh, it's cold!"

Enzella grabbed his good hand—she knew better than to grab Morwë when she was doing a working. "Morwë!"

Morwë let her Arts recede a bit, and tried to sooth the hurt. "I did tell you I've never done this on a wight before."

"I was just—surprised," he squeaked.

She felt him shaking under her hands, and knew he still felt pain. She did her best to convince the bone not to move, and then let go.

Micah flexed his fingers clumsily.

"All right?" she asked shortly.

"My arm's numb. Feels like I slept on it wrong," he said, opening and closing his hand.

"It will fade in a bit. But it's just the start. I'll have to come back to make the bone knit itself whole." Morwë gestured towards her sister. "And to check on this imp."

"Don't call me an imp," Enzella muttered. "That's what Ingridon calls me."

Fair, Morwë thought. "All right, Zel. But you do need to go to bed. We don't know what will happen tomorrow."

Enzella sighed but squeezed her thin form back through the bars. "Okay. I'll be back tomorrow," she told Micah.

"I'll be here," Micah replied, looking pathetically glad.

Morwë turned to follow Enzella down the stairs.

"My lady," the boy whispered before Morwë disappeared into the darkness. "Thank you."

She watched him inscrutably, nodded once, and then vanished into the black.

FIFTEEN

ARKEN

Arken panted at the pace he had set for himself over the rougher terrain along the lip of the valley, but he refused to slow down. The clouds overhead hung low and gray, threatening a snowfall before nightfall. He needed to find a trail before then.

He had hunted in this area of the Caleahanach Mountains many times, but he had never come from the east before. It was hard to recognize familiar landmarks, but he kept his eyes set on Ceridfel looming above him, the familiar sight menacing in a way he had never considered.

Not many people liked to hunt or travel outside the Cirondel valley, even though a few explorers had named the mountain peaks and traveled to valleys further east. Partly because there was no good pass to enter them, and any journey over the mountains was no small undertaking. But also… who knew what lived in the Caleahanachs?

The mountain peaks protected their valley from human raiders and bandits, but timber wolves roamed the mountain slopes and sometimes attacked lone travelers on the road. Yet the old stories and legends held that forest cats would protect, sharing beneficence with the good and meting out justice to the wicked. He wasn't sure how cats accomplished that, but it made for a good story.

But what other creatures might lurk in the hidden hollows and dells?

Many stories spoke of ghosts, spooks, or magical beings that haunted different countries in Karneesia. Before now, Arken had written them off as tall tales, myths that lived on after most of the magic in the land had died away. After all, the last griffin in these parts had been seen when he was a tiny child, flying west towards the sea, and no one had seen a dragon in the flesh since his great-grandfather's time. Elves, hidden ones, and faefolk had been relegated to story.

Now they blazed alive in his mind, full of horror and foreboding.

Arken's mother liked to tell the old stories that most scoffed at as superstition—stories where faefolk, full of tricks and wiles, doled out magic at a price. Hidden ones whisked away maidens in the dark of night, stole human babies and left something else in the cradle. Men wandered away and showed up a hundred years later, fuddled by spirits.

But Micah was neither a maiden nor a baby, and faefolk weren't spirits. No, whatever faefolk were, they had solid flesh, and they could be tracked, and found, and fought. Arken just had to make it in time.

Arken swiped his dark hair out of his eyes and took a drink from his water skin. Ceridfel grew closer with every step.

Trust the land, Father James had said. Every Altesian knew the story—the first settlers had stumbled through the mountain pass, refugees of the constant warring on the plains and the terrible wizard magic used in the battles. The refugees had pushed through the lowlands, some putting down roots, but most drawn by some indecipherable force to stumble at last through the pass, led by a man named Taliesin, for whom the gap was named, into a place of refuge. Not to say that the valley was peaceful or idyllic, far from it—but the mountains protected their people. The fells knew who belonged to them.

Arken's father had always told him that when they were up in the mountains with the other woodsmen, felling and rough dressing trees to be turned into boards and sold. Up in the mountains, surrounded by the familiar, it had always seemed true. Even when his father had died in a tree felling accident, Arken had never blamed the land or the mountains. It had been exactly that —an accident, the product of a dangerous life. But now....

Do they really protect? Arken wondered bitterly. The mountains hadn't protected Peridun, or Micah.

Arken set his face like a flint. He wouldn't lose another family member. He crossed himself and continued into the sea of pines. *Micah, I'm coming.*

SIXTEEN

ENZELLA

Enzella winced as Morwë dragged a comb through her straggling pale hair.

"You need to brush this more," Morwë chided. "It's a rat's nest."

"I don't care," Enzella mumbled, staring into the wavering mirror over Morwë's vanity. It stretched her out, made her look thinner than she already was. Nearly a ghost.

"You should." Morwë pulled out a dark ribbon from her box of hair things and braided Enzella's hair back.

"I want to cut it all off. That's what Micah did when his father died. He cut his hair to show he was grieving."

Morwë tugged her hair a little harder than necessary when she pulled the ribbon taut to tie off the braid. "You can't. Everyone will be watching. You can't give them an opportunity to exploit weakness. Don't show them that this affects you."

"But it hurts," Enzella said, looking up at her, eyes swollen from crying. Enzella saw something twist behind Morwë's eyes.

Morwë swallowed and set her face in an impassive mask. "They don't care." She lifted Enzella's black dress off her bed. "Arms up."

"Then why do we have to *do* this?" Enzella exclaimed, shoving

Morwë's hands away. The great wave of emotion swelled up within her, threatening to crash down and pummel her again. "Why do we have to pretend and have this stupid show to bury Mother when none of them *care?*"

"It's to show we're strong." Morwë wrung out a cold cloth and handed it to her, and then continued. "To show that Father is strong. That he can do what is best for the Unseelie people, and that includes—"

"Killing Mother." Enzella drooped. She had cried more in the past few days than in her whole life. She wasn't used to it. If Morwë created a strong enough gust of wind, it could knock her over without a problem.

"They will see it as eliminating a weak wight," Morwë said, voice tight. "That Father has been odd about for more than twenty annuals."

"Killing Mother," Enzella repeated dully.

"Yes," her sister whispered.

Enzella stood and let Morwë slide the black-feathered dress over her head.

"You have to be strong now," Morwë said as she did up the clasps at the back of the dress. "Strong, and guarded enough that nothing can touch you." She straightened Enzella's braid so that it hung straight. "Not what they say, or the faces they make, or the looks they send your way. You're a pool of water. No ripples. They can't see under the surface."

Enzella tried to quell the tremble in her lips. "But it hurts *so much*. How can I pretend it doesn't?"

"I didn't say pretend it doesn't," Morwë said, examining her own feather dress and coiffed hair in the mirror. "I said don't let them see. You hold it, here." She made a fist and pressed to her abdomen. "Hold it down. Keep it away from your face. Once you're away from them, then you let it float to the surface again." She raised the fist and opened her fingers. "Try it while I finish dressing. Keep that cloth on your face."

Enzella obediently tried to envision wrapping the tangled web of her emotions into a ball while Morwë fixed onyx eardrops in her ears and beads around the high collar of her dress. "Now, are you ready? We've got to join the funeral party."

Her emotions were in a ball, but instead of staying in her stomach, it leapt into her throat. "Don't leave me with Father," Enzella begged, clutching her sister. "I don't want him to kill me, too."

Her sister's cold hand closed around hers. "I won't leave you."

In the ante chamber to the royal family's suite of rooms, Ingridon waited, still wearing his black war band uniform, but with a crest of black raven's feathers added around his neck and the onyx medallion that showed he was Heir. He did not carry a sword, but he played with a wicked looking dagger.

"Time to get this over with," he grumbled. "I still don't know why we have to have a funeral for the hag. It's not like she was one of us."

"We will have this funeral because she was your mother, and you *will* be respectful." Yemelyan's cold voice shivered down Enzella's spine as he exited his private study with Demyen behind him. The shorter man bowed respectfully to the Erlking's children, smoothing his gray goatee.

Their father's robe whispered along the stone floor as he approached them. "She gave her life for yours when she bore you," he said, flicking his eyes over them to rest on Ingridon. "Is that understood?"

"Yes, Father," Ingridon said, standing up and sheathing his dagger.

His black gaze shifted to rest on Morwë and Enzella. Enzella desperately wished to hide her face in Morwë's skirts, but knew that Morwë would pinch her viciously if she tried. She couldn't let them know she was afraid.

"Yes, Father," Morwë said evenly, her voice a still pool of water undisturbed by ripples, just like she said.

"Yes, Father," Enzella echoed. She hid her trembling hand in her skirts.

He blinked slowly. "Good. Come; it is time." He swept out of the antechamber, merging with the shadows cast by the witch lights imbedded in the walls.

Ingridon followed behind him with a swagger. Demyen bowed slightly, waiting for the daughters of the Erlking to complete the procession.

"Come along," Morwë whispered, squeezing Enzella's hand as they fell into step in the procession. "Remember."

Don't let them see. Don't let them see. Enzella tried to stand as straight as Morwë, as straight as the great fir trees that had been the pillars of her world for twelve annuals until the fire and their exodus. Gripping her sister's hand with all her strength, Enzella stared ahead of them as the great crowd of the Unseelie court stretched out ahead of them, nearly three thousand strong.

Her heart quailed. *How do I not let them see the truth when it's reflected in their eyes?* Enzella wondered. *My mother is dead, and no one cares.*

CHAPTER

SEVENTEEN

MORWË

T he casket lay in state, an ornate carved stone monolith that sat alone in the newly dug deep catacombs. Atop it, a vague likeness of her mother's face had been formed.

Morwë did not think it looked anything like her—not a beautiful, idealized version of her mother in her prime, nor a death mask of her body aged and worn. Just the visage of a stranger that stared out with blank eyes into the darkness.

That, at least, was right.

Enzella could not look at it, and Morwë could not blame her. None of the imps and rabble were allowed near the casket, but the royal family had been stationed right by it for the duration of the ceremony, which mostly entailed a recount of her mother's life, or the parts that Father was most concerned about, namely giving birth to his heirs and continuing the bloodline.

It did not escape Morwë's notice that all Unseelie ladies wore their best finery and draped themselves with jewels. The Erlking was finally free of the wight queen—such a blow to their hauteur and pride that he had chosen such a one over them. But who was to say who might be the next consort, now that the business and mess of children was dispensed with?

The powerful thaumaturges also had a special place of

honor among the crowd, all looking very sour and put upon that they must cease their important duties to attend a wight funeral. In the throng, Morwë spotted Toren. His bi-colored eyes were trained not on the coffin or on the Erlking, but on her.

Jezra's words rang in her ears.

Morwë kept her face impassive and bit down on the inside of her cheek. It was coincidence only. She continued to squeeze Enzella's hand to remind her sister she could not show any reaction to the dry recitation.

Enzella had been in no state for a formal interrogation of what she knew of their mother's history after meeting with the wight again. What little Morwë had gleaned by probing only reinforced what she already knew. This enumeration certainly didn't add anything.

Who had her mother been, besides *Mother*? A captive wight, a woman married to the Erlking for twenty-six annuals. Where had she come from, and why, why oh why, had she clutched Morwë's hands like a lifeline? *Promise me, Morwë. Promise me.*

On the stone above the tomb, words were inscribed in Unseelie script over the archway, but only one sank into Morwë's mind.

Igrainne.

I didn't know her name, Morwë thought as she pressed numb lips together. *I didn't know my own mother's name.*

Father never used it. He always addressed her as 'Wife' or 'your mother.' He had taken even her name. Morwë could not fault her mother's bitterness and anger.

Maybe she had inherited more than looks from her after all.

Igrainne. Morwë wondered what it meant.

As the Erlking finished his recitation, a hush fell over the crowd, and the funeral toll began. The first bell, the Toll of Passing, rang out with a loud and heavy clang. Morwë felt Enzella jump and shake beside her. She squeezed her sister's hand and set her shoulders. The second bell, the Death Knell, rang at a lower pitch, its clapper muffled by leather. Then the third and last bell, the Lych Bell, rang quietest of all.

All was silent. Morwë found it hard to even breathe.

The Erlking raised his hands. The ceremony was over.

The Unseelie audience dispersed slowly, leaving the royal family alone in the new catacombs.

Their father swept away without a word to his children, Demyen at his heels.

"Finally," Ingridon sighed, cracking his neck. He cast a deriding look at the stone casket and spat before sauntering off into the darkness.

Enzella leaned against her side, and Morwë let her. "You did well," she ventured, feeling the weakness of the words.

"I hate him," Enzella whispered.

"Me, too," Morwë sighed, her mouth twisting.

Enzella looked up at her. "I meant Father."

Morwë pursed her lips. "…I hate him, too."

Enzella walked towards the casket, tracing the intricate carvings in the stone. "I loved Mother."

If Morwë didn't hate Igrainne, did that mean she had loved her? How could she have loved her if she didn't know her? Morwë looked away.

After a long moment, Enzella slipped her hand into Morwë's. "Can we go now?"

Morwë nodded, relieved. "Yes. Let's have dinner."

"By ourselves?"

"Yes, just us. No one else."

The sisters slowly walked out of the catacombs up the long and twisting stair, leaving the casket alone in the dark.

EIGHTEEN

MORWË

Insistent clangs shook Morwë from sleep, the violent ringing hurting her ears and driving her out of bed.

"Oww," Enzella whispered, curled up on the other side of the bed. She curled her arms over her head. "What is that?"

"The alarm bells," Morwë said, grabbing her dark robe off of the chair. It could be nothing else. The magical warning system had never rung in Morwë's living memory except a few months ago, alerting them that their taiga forest, carefully crafted and grown to keep out any hint of sunlight, was on fire.

Her heart raced, thinking of the terror from that time, the flames that had licked away their protection. What was happening now? Were they in danger again?

And then, suddenly, the bells stopped.

Morwë stood stock-still for a moment, and then thrust her arms into the robe and cinched it tight, obscuring the pale white of her nightgown. Now where were her slippers? She scoured the floor.

"Where are you going?" Enzella demanded, scrambling out of bed and rubbing her eyes.

"I'm going to see what's happening," Morwë said, sliding her feet into the shoes. "Stay here."

Enzella protested, "But what if it's dangerous? What if something happens?" Her pale hair straggled out of its braid. "The alarm bells aren't supposed to just *stop*. They're supposed to ring for all-clear."

"All the more reason for you to stay here," Morwë insisted, reaching for the door.

"But then you won't be looking after me," Enzella pointed out. "You promised. And I'll only sneak out later."

"I don't have time for this." Morwë cursed and grabbed her little sister's hand. "I'm going to rue the day I ever taught you anything, aren't I," she said, pulling Zel out of her chamber, down the hall, and through the suite's antechamber doorway.

"Probably," Zel said smugly.

"Well, you'd better do exactly what I tell you," Morwë commanded as they merged into the sea of bodies streaming towards the gate cavern.

"Nothing to see here," a burly guard, big for an Unseelie, boomed at the entrance to the stair. His impressive girth helped his squad keep the sea of fearful and curious sprites at bay. "Go back to the lower levels. Only a false alarm, no need for worrying. Look here," he said as Morwë elbowed her way to the front of the crowd, "No one past this point."

Morwë sneered and drew herself up straight as a rod. "Do you know who I am?"

The crowd drew back from her and Enzella, whispering.

The guard blanched as his second in command elbowed him hard. "Ah… my apologies, my lady, but I—I have my orders…." Confusion crossed his brutish face.

"Orders for the rabble," Morwë said. "Not for the daughters of the Erlking. Move aside or I'll report you to your watch commander." The anger washed through her like an icy wave. If he refused, she'd stick him to the wall.

"Milady," he murmured, stepping aside with a bow and knuckle to his forehead. The other guards made a gap in their perimeter for them to pass through.

"Better," Morwë muttered, tugging Zel along.

Past the guards, the corridor was deserted, silent except for their footfalls and far-off sounds in the gate cavern. As they emerged from the hallway at the start of the long stair that led down to the gate cavern, Enzella slipped on a damp patch of stone and almost went down. Morwë hauled her to her feet.

"Be careful," Morwë hissed.

The chamber only contained Ingridon, Hadrian, and one other man. Ingridon circled the stranger menacingly, his sword drawn. A pack, bow, and quiver had been tossed to the side, and Hadrian stood over them.

Shackled at the wrists and neck, the stranger did not seem like a threat— but at the sound of her whisper, he swung his head up.

Blue eyes burned holes into her.

Morwë clutched the neck of her robe, feeling horribly exposed. He shouldn't be able to see her. The witch lights in the cavern were weak and low, not yet replenished.

He does not see you truly, her head insisted. *He merely turned his head toward sound.*

But she could *feel* his gaze.

"Zel," she whispered, "stay *here,* do you understand? If you follow me, I'll make you so sorry—"

"Promise," Zel whispered, eyes locked on the confrontation below.

Morwë hesitated, but decided that was all she would get. Dropping her sister's hand, Morwë gathered her robe in one hand so she wouldn't trip and slowly descended. She did not miss the fact that the stranger's gaze followed her down.

Hadrian noticed her presence and came to meet her at the bottom of the stair. Morwë crossed her arms over her chest. "Who is he? What's going on?"

"He found the entrance to the mountain," Hadrian said. "Set off the wards and alarm bells."

She gasped. "But it's hidden!"

"He can see through the dark," Hadrian crossed his arms and stared grimly at the intruder.

"How?"

"We don't know."

Morwë felt cold, remembering flames and swords charmed to scorch and burn. "If he can find us...."

"Others could, too," Hadrian finished.

Ingridon's mocking voice cut off Morwë's next question. "Your people must have some rude form of magic, to give you this sight. So which eye is it? Right?" He set his sword point at the base of the prisoner's beautiful eye. "Or left?"

Beautiful? Morwë blinked.

The prisoner did not answer, just glared at Ingridon.

"Well, if you won't tell me, I'll just put them both out and save flipping a coin." Ingridon smiled, a baring of teeth.

"Stop," Morwë snapped. All heads turned to her, even the prisoner's. "Don't be a fool, Ingridon. He found us and set off the wards. Father will want to question him. With *both* his eyes."

"I didn't do anything," the man said in a low voice, startling her. "I was on a long hunting trip in the mountains, and got lost —" He broke off when Ingridon laid his sword at his throat.

Ingridon drew his sword along the prisoner's neck, a line of blood welling up. "Got *lost*," Ingridon scoffed. "And yet you can see through the dark, when no other wights can. Forgive me if I don't believe you."

A line of red dripped down the stranger's neck as muscles in his jaw flexed.

"As much as it pains me to say this, you're right," Morwë muttered. "Put him in the cell block and send someone for Father. Don't damage him any further."

"Already done," Hadrian assured her. As his gaze lingered on her, she scowled and turned on her heel. Enzella was waiting for her.

Ingridon's voice followed her up the stairs. "Abandon any hope you have left, wight. You've left the land of light and kindness and entered into the dark, never to return. And the only women you'll see are cold-hearted, like my sister." He laughed and Morwë heard the flat of his sword strike flesh, but she did not turn.

She fixed her eyes on the crouched form of Enzella at the top of the stairs and kept walking.

"Who was he?" Enzella whispered, getting to her feet as Morwë reached her.

She took hold of Enzella's wrist and towed her back down the hallway. Enzella winced and tried to pull out of her grasp. "Oww, Morwë."

"Shh." Morwë lessened her grip slightly. "Not until we get back to my chamber." They hurried in silence back past the guard barricade—they had succeeded in turning away the majority of the crowd—and wound their way through the general caverns to the royal family suite as finally, the bells pealed the all clear.

Enzella tugged at her skirts as soon as they passed through the antechamber. "Morwë, tell, tell!"

"A wight," she said, dropping Enzella's hand. Morwë pushed open the door and used her Arts to light the witch lights.

"Why is he here? What does he want?" Enzella crawled to the middle of the bed and watched her as she opened up her wardrobe, pulling out a plain dark gown.

"We don't know," Morwë said. But she needed to find out. She ducked into the garderobe to shed her robe and nightgown, and pulled the simple dress over her head.

"You're going to question him, aren't you? Can I—"

"No, Zel, you can't come. Father is going to be there, and you need to keep out of his way."

"For how long?"

"A while." Morwë opened the door and ran a comb through her hair. She'd need to give Enzella a task to keep her busy, or she'd just follow. Drat. "I want you to go to your room, get dressed, and break your fast in the great hall. If anyone asks, you know nothing. By now the news will be all over the mountain. So *listen,* but do not speak, and I'll meet you back at your room when I can."

"Are we a team now?" Enzella asked, bouncing on the furs atop the bed.

"If you do as I say," Morwë said, shooting her a look as she braided her hair over her shoulder.

"Promise," Enzella agreed readily.

"Scamper then." Morwë opened the door and gave her a push.

Enzella cast a glance over her shoulder. Morwë made sure to shoot her a gimlet look, and Enzella put on speed in the direction of her room.

That's taken care of, Morwë thought, tying off her braid. *Now for the intruder wight.*

That would not be as easy.

NINETEEN

ENZELLA

Enzella slunk into the great hall, looking for Jezra. No one had a bigger mouth; if anyone knew anything, it would be her. And Jezra wouldn't shove her away because she knew Morwë would get her for it. Jezra might even like her a little.

Enzella spotted her surrounded by her swains and paramours, ensconced in a deep discussion. Enzella let herself hover in Jezra's eyeline until she was noticed.

"Princess," Jezra cooed. "Where is your sister?"

"She was gone when the bells woke me," Enzella lied. "What happened?"

"Come and sit," Jezra said, pushing aside the sloe-eyed Unseelie with his arm around her. "Move, Armir." Jezra patted the patch of bench he grudgingly relinquished.

Enzella slipped in to his place and Jezra gestured at a serving imp to bring Enzella a plate. "I've never heard the alarm bells go off except for when the fire came," Enzella said cannily, watching the group from under her eyelashes. She didn't have to feign her shudder. "But no evacuation sounded."

"*I* heard that it was the wild beasts in these mountains slavering at the gates," one swain said, smiling at Jezra.

Jezra laughed. "What sorts of slavering beasts?"

"Oh, wolves, griffins—maybe even a dragon!"

"Persis, it's too cold for dragons." Jezra's smile cut like a knife, making the swain recoil. "Why would you say something so idiotic?"

Enzella artfully paused, reaching for the pot of gruel. "Do you think it was something that… scary?"

Armir snorted. "A drill, that's all it was. The war bands wanted to test our readiness. We'll never be caught unawares again."

"Are we sure it was an outside threat?" another swain asked. "There have been too many mutterings. Maybe some fool stopped muttering and started doing something."

"Like what? Open rebellion?" Armir shot a sidelong look at Enzella. "Of course not. No one would dare move against the Erlking," he added in a hearty, carrying voice.

"I'm not saying the justice wouldn't have been swift, but it's still possible," the swain objected.

"Treason is never possible down here," someone hissed. "*Shut up.*"

Jezra slipped an arm around Enzella and cooed, "Perhaps it was one of the stragglers? One of our missing people that's found their way here."

"Don't be stupid; they're all on pikes or burned," Armir retorted. "How would they survive in the daylight anyway? They would've had no shield against the sun."

Slowly, Jezra pivoted on the bench. Then, quick as a striking snake, she reached through his open shirt and pinched his nipple, hard. Underneath his yelp, Enzella just barely heard Jezra whisper, "Don't ever call me stupid in front of the princess again" as she twisted the flesh in her grip.

Enzella trained her gaze on her plate and kept her smile to herself.

TWENTY

ARKEN

"Inside." The man called Hadrian opened a cell door.

Arken took a step forward but stumbled when Ingridon tripped him. Biting back a growl, Arken recovered his footing and forced himself to stay focused. Micah had to be here somewhere. Arken just hoped he'd have enough sense to keep quiet until they were alone.

The door clanged shut behind him.

Arken turned and shook his hands, making the chains rattle. "Aren't you going to take these off?"

"I rather like seeing you shackled like a dog," Ingridon sneered.

Arken studied him. They were about the same height, but Arken had a sturdier build compared to the other man's whip-thin frame. Ingridon's small eyes, set close together, glinted in the dark like a rat's.

"Stick your hands through the bars," Hadrian said, shooting Ingridon a look.

Arken did. "I wasn't aware you knew what a dog was," he said conversationally as the shackles opened.

Something struck him on the side of the head. Arken recoiled with a yell. Reaching up, he felt blood well up by his hairline.

Ingridon smirked. He had cracked him with his sword hilt. "I know you beat untrained curs into submission."

"Ingridon."

Arken's eyes darted towards the darkness as both men turned. Fear slid down his spine as a trickle of blood ran down his temple. He had not seen or heard this new man enter. He was simply there, in the shadows.

Arken swallowed hard.

Of all the creatures he had seen thus far, this one was the most inhuman. Tall and thin, with long white hair, he swept soundlessly towards the cell. Dark, deep-set eyes seemed to peer through every shadow—and reflect no light at all.

With them side by side, Arken could see the resemblance between Ingridon and this man—father and son, perhaps? The father had an odd, dark cast to the skin around his mouth that made Arken's skin crawl.

Hadrian backed away and bowed low.

"That will be all, Hadrian," the man said quietly. His voice had a low but lilting quality, like the rattling of chains, promising danger. Arken clenched his fists and forced himself not to back away from the bars of the cell.

Hadrian silently bowed again. He moved to leave, but had to dodge to avoid the figure on the stairway.

"First Daughter," the father murmured without turning, his eyes still on Arken.

"Father."

The man blinked slowly, and Arken sucked in a harsh breath. Even that much of a respite from those eyes was welcome.

The odd, discolored mouth opened again. "Come closer, daughter."

Arken tore his gaze away, and his breath caught in his throat.

The woman took a guarded step further into the prison. Before, this woman's black hair had flowed free about her shoulders; now it was braided, with strands still straining for escape.

The style allowed him to see the shape of her pointed ears. She watched Arken like a wild hawk eyeing its prey.

"Ingridon, report," the father commanded.

"The wards sounded the alarm, so Hadrian and I went outside to investigate." Ingridon jerked his head to indicate his prisoner. "He was standing right outside the cave entrance, Father, not doing anything. Like he was waiting for us to find him."

"Hmm." The father tilted his head to the side. "Tell me, young sir, what your name and purpose is."

Arken swallowed and kept his mouth shut.

The man's shadowed mouth twitched up in what might have been a smile. "You must have a name, surely, unless Ingridon has driven all wit from you."

Ingridon laughed, his teeth shining like knives.

"Not likely," Arken hissed.

"Ah, so he has a tongue after all." The black eyes kindled with a strange light. "Speak, then."

"I went hunting; I got lost," Arken said, shaking his head. "That's all there is to it."

"No, I don't think so," the father mused. "If you had, you would have run like a scared rabbit when the entrance first began to open. Unless you were simple, and we have already established this is not the case."

No help for it now. "Maybe I was frozen by fear," Arken said brashly.

The faint amusement in the man's demeanor shriveled and died. "Young man, you are in the Unseelie Underground now, and I am its Erlking, Yemelyan Onyxeyes. You will tell me what I want to know, and then you will die."

Arken would not show how far his heart dropped. "Not much incentive for me, is there?" His lip curled.

"Incentive," Yemelyan repeated slowly, tasting the word. "Your incentive is that I will allow your death to be quick and painless. I do not afford that mercy to many."

The Erlking blinked again, for only the second time. Arken dug his thumbnail into his fist hard enough to break the skin.

The black eyes opened again. "Maybe I will allow you pleasure with a woman before you die. A kindness, for your last moments."

Arken's skin crawled. His eyes unconsciously flickered to the girl standing silent in the dark. Were all their women so wild and haunted?

"Do you like my daughter?" Yemelyan raised an eyebrow. "If your tale is true enough, sweet enough, I would permit you to have… even her."

"Father!" the girl exclaimed, stricken with anger. Her already pale face went white.

Her father turned and met her glare. "Silence," he whispered.

All sound in the cellblock died.

The daughter choked and dropped her eyes, shaking.

Arken took an instinctual step forward and ran into the cell door. What kind of man would do that to his own flesh and blood? "Don't trouble yourself," he said harshly, gripping the bars.

Yemelyan turned back around, watching him as a snake watches prey. "If I wanted to, I could crack your skull open and pry your secrets free. Your whole life would unspool before me. But I'm a patient man. I can wait for your tongue to loosen."

His eyes dropped to Arken's hands, clutching the bars. "Such bravery, born of foolish ignorance. I could end your existence with a thought." The corner of his mouth twitched upward.

The skin on Arken's right hand writhed, suddenly as cold as death. Arken cried out as the bones and muscles wasted away, leaving the hand shrunken and withered. He clutched his wrist with his good hand, afraid to touch the now paper-thin skin.

"Humans are so fragile," Yemelyan sighed. "Yet so inclined to think they are unshakable unless shown otherwise." He licked his lips with a dark tongue. "Do you know why we placed the prison levels so near the surface, Ingridon?"

Ingridon clearly did, judging by his smile, but he said, "Why, Father?'

"Because nothing kills the will as much as hope that never bears fruit. Only a few feet of earth separates you from your sun; do you know that? But you will never see it again. You will soon wither and die—not from my Arts or the dark, but from that little bit of hope." The Erlking smiled slowly. "It will slay you more thoroughly than I ever could. Think on my words."

And then he was simply not there. He had disappeared without so much as a puff of smoke.

Arken let his breath out slowly, trying to calm the hammering of his heart. His knuckles ached and creaked; it hurt to straighten them.

"You should take him up on it," Ingridon said, his voice startlingly loud after his father's quiet but deadly tones. He smiled a crooked, mocking smile as Arken refocused on him.

Ingridon reached through the bars to grasp the collar around Arken's neck. He yanked Arken flush against the bars to unlock and remove it. "Take Morwë in hand," he advised as he pulled the collar free. "She needs it, and life would be much easier for everyone." He smirked. Then he turned—right into the full force of his sister's malevolent glare.

"Stop trying to pander me off, Ingridon." Every word dripped with hoarfrost.

That glare could curdle milk and whither loins, Arken was sure of it. He rubbed his neck with his good hand and prepared to duck if need be.

"Just speaking the truth, sister dear," Ingridon sneered. He dropped the manacles in a tangled heap before he stalked off.

Morwë stared down at the mess of metal and shook her head slowly.

"Not much family feeling, I take it," Arken said.

Her eyes flicked up, and he was once more reminded of the scrutinizing gaze of a bird of prey. She moved as if to go.

The word escaped his mouth before he could pull it back. "Wait."

She stopped, tilted her head to the side. "What?" Her voice was low and dry.

Arken licked his lips. "I still have two eyes, and I think you're mostly responsible for that."

She laughed, but her eyes did not. "But a crippled hand," she said, glancing at his shriveled limb. "I did you no favors. For a wight among the Unseelie, it's better to be blind. There are some things your kind was never meant to see."

"I don't believe that."

"Oh?" She stepped closer. "Didn't your blood freeze in your veins when you faced my father? I don't think you've had the *experience* of watching a soul sucked from a body until all that's left is a husk." Her eyes froze over.

His skin crawled, but he could not look away. "So that's my fate, is it?"

"No." The word was soft. "Father will want a more painful death for you, no matter what he says. But," she added, "They might make you watch. That's worse." She turned away.

He breathed a prayer and took a gamble. His words rang out after her. "And you'd know, I suppose?"

She froze, still as death.

"I think you do know," Arken said. "I've seen death, too. They brought my father home to die when a tree fell on him. It was the worst day of my life." Second was learning Micah had been taken. "Who did you see die, Morwë?"

An odd tremor ran through her, but she pivoted and laughed, her face a cold mask of hauteur. "What makes you think you know me, wight?" she hissed. "Do not try to gain my sympathy. I am the First Daughter of the Erlking."

She lifted her right hand as lines of darkness ran up her fingers like ink, coating her skin. "I could end your life in an instant. I am no one's savior." Morwë closed her hand in a fist and stalked away.

TWENTY-ONE

MORWË

The wight's eyes followed her. Morwë could feel them: heavy, accusatory, angry. When she disappeared from his line of sight, she breathed a shaky sigh of relief and leaned against the icy tunnel wall for support. What was the matter with her?

The wight's eyes had blazed like blue fire through the brown hair that fell into his face, hot enough to—

No. Her ice was too thick. Nothing could touch her.

Not even that wight.

Morwë rubbed her arms to dispel the goose bumps and staggered on until she reached her room.

"Morwë!" Enzella jumped off the bed and hurtled towards her. "What happened? I went to breakfast like you said. Tell me everything!"

Rolling her shoulders, Morwë groaned and collapsed onto her bed. "You first," she said, pulling a blanket over herself.

Enzella clambered up beside her and sat with her skirt gathered up around her knees, rattling off her information. "Well, I sat by Jezra, and of course she wanted to know what was going on but I said I didn't know, and then they all said what rumors they had heard, that maybe it was a beast, or just a drill, or maybe just stragglers that finally found us. Later on, Ranat came up and said a company of wights had forced the door. She was scared we'd have to move again, but everyone else shot her down. No one would come out and say it, but I think they were afraid to question our security, for fear of Father. And then everyone started leaving, so I came back here. The food wasn't very good, just gruel. I was only here a minute before you. So who was he?"

Morwë rolled onto her stomach and closed her eyes. No good. The blue still burned through her eyelids. "I don't know," she whispered into the pillow.

"*Morwë*," Zel whined, poking her in the side. "You promised."

"They took him to the prisoner level," she sighed. "Father questioned him. He wouldn't talk. Well," she amended, "he didn't give away any information."

"Father should have offered him a trade," Zel said.

He did, Morwë thought darkly, shivering. *Me.*

Would that be better or worse than married off to a courtier for the chance to beget a powerful thaumaturge?

He's a wight, he wouldn't have the power to hurt me.

But Father could.

But the wight hadn't taken the trade.

If the torture was bad enough, he might yet.

She closed her eyes. She wouldn't think about that.

"But what else?" Enzella asked. "Was he tortured?"

"Not really. Father crippled his hand and decided to let him stew for a few days."

"But there *must* have been more, Morwë! *Tell* me!" Enzella shook Morwë's shoulder in frustration.

Morwë groaned. "If you're so keen to know, go see for yourself," she grumbled.

Enzella sat up straight. "Really?"

"Go on before I change my mind. Just remember—" Morwë broke off. Enzella was already gone. She groaned again and curled up into a ball. *I'm not very good at this. I'm sorry, Mother.*

"*Who did you see die, Morwë?*"

She squeezed her eyes shut, but no matter how hard she tried, the image of her mother's empty body falling to the ground would not go away.

A few minutes after Enzella left, someone knocked on her chamber door. Morwë pushed her head into her pillow and did nothing. Her wards would keep them out.

The knock came again, loud and insistent staccato raps against the thick wood that did not cease.

"I don't care who you are; go away!" Morwë yelled.

Hadrian's voice came through the door. "Morwë, talk to me."

She gritted her teeth in a snarl. "I *especially* don't want to talk to you, Hadrian."

She heard another voice a little further away, muffled. "Oooh, are you and Morwë having a spat?" it cooed. Jezra, most likely.

"I'd love to have a spat," Hadrian told her, "but I don't even get that."

"Morwë, open the door and let the poor man in," Jezra coaxed. Her mouth must have been right up against the door, or she was using her small amount of power to project it.

Morwë growled and pulled her pillow over her head. "Go away or go aboveground, Jezra!"

Jezra laughed. "Well, if she wants to be a recluse, let her. Let's show her what she's missing."

Hadrian murmured his assent before Morwë heard the thump of bodies against her door, followed by heavy breathing and the sound of mouths on skin.

This was absolutely the last straw. Morwë sat up, reached with her Arts towards the defenses of her wards, and screeched, "Do that somewhere else! Moonlight take *both* your eyes!" She clenched her fists. With a shout, she threw up her hands and set off the wards around her chamber. She heard Jezra shriek. The spell had worked.

Morwë got up and threw open the door. She came face to face with a hissing Jezra and a cursing Hadrian. They were peppered with magical burns in large splotches.

"Never cross me again," Morwë warned them in a low voice.

Jezra looked up at her with outrage and unconcealed venom in her eyes. "Moonlight —moonlight *take*—" she gabbled.

Any vestige of camaraderie Morwë had with Jezra died. "My curse took first," she sneered. "I am the First Daughter of the Erlking, and you'll not forget it." To Hadrian she said, "Never speak to me again, or you'll *wish* for pain like this."

She sealed her room and stalked off to find somewhere else to sit and stew. She wanted to be *alone*.

Bodies on the floor—a dead husk—

Morwë was cold, so cold, and tired.

TWENTY-TWO

ENZELLA

Enzella hurried down the hallways that led to the prisons, excited to see the new wight for herself—only to recoil at the sight of Ingridon in her way. "Well, look who it is, the monster child," Ingridon said, smiling mirthlessly.

Mummy's favorite monster child. The words whizzed through her head.

Monster or not, she loved me. She loved me. Enzella tensed and turned away, waiting for him to pass.

He didn't. "What, no smart mouth today, Zel?"

She eased past him and slipped out from under his grasping fingers.

"Where are you off to?" he demanded.

"I want to see the new wight," she whispered.

"He's nothing to look at," Ingridon sneered. "The dog didn't even put up a fight." He rolled his eyes. "Oh, go on and gawk at each other, what do I care." He walked down the stairs.

Enzella breathed a sigh of relief. Today must have been one of his melancholic days instead of manic. She started up the steps to the prison block.

"Hello," she said when she reached Micah.

"Enzella! Who is it that they've caught?" he whispered. He

pressed against the bars, trying to peer into the sheer dark and failing. "They brought him up, but I couldn't see...."

"An intruder," Enzella said. "He was right up by the gates and set off the alarms. Ingridon and Hadrian brought him in."

"Who is it? What's he called?" Micah insisted.

"I'll ask," Enzella said, and set off purposefully down to the far end of the cellblock.

The strange wight peered through his bars as she approached. "Hello," she said boldly, staring at his eyes. They were a pretty color, shining in the dark. He was tall, too, with shaggy dark hair that he had to brush away from his face. "What are you called?"

He stared at her and said nothing.

"I'm Enzella," she said. "Did you see Morwë? I think you must've. Morwë is my sister. She's grand." She waited a moment, but he still didn't speak. "What are you called?"

"Why do you want to know?" he asked finally, eyeing her suspiciously.

"I like knowing things," she said, rocking back and forth. "And my wight wants to know, too."

"What?"

"One of you people," she explained. "Morwë said I could have him because no one else wanted him. His name's Micah."

"Micah?" the stranger whispered. He gripped the bars, and she stared with fascination at one strong hand and one thin and withered hand. The stranger looked over her head down the hallway. "Micah? Girl, tell him that it's Arken. Tell him—wait, *wait*—"

She turned and skipped back down the row of cells.

"His name is Arken," she told Micah.

Micah paled enough that she could see his bruises in sharp relief. "That's my brother! He found me—" His voice caught and broke.

She stared curiously. "Is this a love thing?"

He nodded, eyes full. "Enzella, can I see him? Please."

"Father would skin me if I moved him." She glowered, thinking of her father. She usually had the urge to hide under a table when the Erlking was mentioned, like she had at the feast. Now a hot rage bubbled in her chest, like a kettle on boil. "But you're my wight, so I can do whatever I want with you," she decided. "I'll move you."

"But I'm locked in—"

She glanced at the lock quizzically. "The keys are just by the wall there." She pointed.

"I can't see in the dark, Zella," Micah reminded her. "I can barely see you at all."

"That's all right," she said, heading for the keys. Stretching, she could reach the nail on her tiptoes. After a minute of searching, she found the right key. Micah helped her turn the key in the lock, and the door groaned open.

"Here, hold my hand so you don't fall," Enzella said. She led him through the dark as he clung to her, almost blind. "Watch your step," she said. "The floor is pitted in places. The thaumaturges didn't finish out this level well."

"How do you stand it?" Micah whispered. "This crushing dark."

"It's not dark to me," she pointed out.

"How do you live without the sun?"

"The sun burns us, Father says."

"Is your father always right?" He stumbled, and she steadied him.

Enzella made a sour face. "You know about that."

"Micah!" the new wight exclaimed, reaching through the bars with his good hand as they neared.

"Arken? Arken!"

Enzella helped him reach his brother.

She thought, *it must feel good to have someone love you like that.*

TWENTY-THREE

ARKEN

rken pulled Micah as close as he could and clutched him tightly.

Alive. *Alive*! Arken finally let go of worries he'd refused to name on the frantic journey here. "I've found you; I'm here," he said, clutching the back of Micah's neck with his good hand. His brother looked bruised and shaken up, but not nearly as hurt as he'd feared.

"How is Mother?" Micah asked, blinking owlishly, straining to see.

Arken cursed himself for not asking Father James for some of the fernseed oil to take with him. "She doesn't know; I left her with Selma. Father James is bringing her word."

"Father James is alive?" Micah gasped.

"Yes, he and all the children are alive," Arken assured him. "They're headed to Cairenoch. I went with them part of the way."

"So they're not all dead." Micah drew in a shaky breath, tears running from his eyes. "I was sure I was the only one left."

"I'm here now," Arken said, running his hand over his brother's head. "I'm going to bring you back. I'll get us out of here, I promise." He tried to wrap his good arm over as much of Micah as he could.

His brother suddenly hissed in pain.

"What?" Arken asked, instantly alert, looking for a wound.

"My arm's broken," Micah said through gritted teeth. "But I'm all right."

"Morwë's mending it."

Arken looked down at the pale little girl. He had forgotten about her entirely. *Never let your guard down,* he chastised himself. *Always be aware of your surroundings.* She stood there staring at the both of them, holding a ring of… keys. Keys he could use to get them out of here. Then her words registered. "The tall girl with the dark hair? She was down here earlier?"

"Yes," the girl said, sighing like it was a chore to repeat this news again.

"She's doing what to him?"

"She's healing my arm," Micah explained, wiping his eyes. "I think. Apparently it will take a while."

Enzella's head whipped around and she froze, listening to sounds Arken couldn't hear. "You need to get in a cell," she told Micah, sorting through the key ring with tiny skeletal fingers. "In case someone comes."

Arken looked hard at Micah. "You trust her?" he muttered, nodding at the girl. Father James's warning rang through his head: *they could thrive on trickery, bargains, and the like.*

Micah shrugged with one shoulder. "We've got no choice. Enzella, you can't tell anyone that Arken and I are brothers. Do you understand?"

"Yes," Enzella said, as the cell alongside Arken's creaked open. "I won't tell anyone except Morwë."

"Not even her," Arken insisted. By her own words, Morwë had no compassion to rely on.

The girl looked up at him and frowned. Arken was much struck by the look in her eyes. "Don't tell me what to do," she said in a flat voice.

Micah looked shocked. Arken raised an eyebrow. This was apparently new territory with this girl.

"I know what I'm doing. Morwë won't tell anyone." Enzella shut the door and locked it after Micah stepped in. "If they knew you had come to rescue Micah, they'd kill you both, and we'd have to watch. I don't want to do that again."

Arken watched, wide-eyed, as she walked back down the hallway and hung up the keys. Again?

I was right.

TWENTY-FOUR

MORWË

Morwë spent the better part of the day in the unfinished top level of the caverns. She was guaranteed not to run into any other Unseelie—it was too close to the crust, too close to the outside of the mountain, far too near the *light*—but that was what she craved, distance from everyone who wanted to drag her down.

Besides the prison cell blocks and the gate cavern, the only other areas on this level were the open cavern they used as a pen for the horses, and the rookery right beside it. The rookery was small, surviving from generations ago when they had had contact with other colonies of faefolk and had sent messages via birds. The only reason they still had a few ravens and crows was symbolic; black-feathered birds were the symbol of her father's reign.

In the rookery, Morwë called a stack of her tomes to her, pulling them through the wards of her room. They appeared in front of her with a puff of air, and she set to reading, searching for some alternative to the fate of a First Daughter—a commodity to be traded and consumed. Just like her mother.

The books detailed an increasingly bloody series of reigns, ending in her father's coup to take the throne from *his* father and an older brother after Yemelyan returned from his long journey south with a wight woman in tow. But they were entirely concerned with the Erlkings and their Heirs. No mention was made of any girl children.

They weren't even worth a line.

After scouring the volumes until her eyes nearly crossed, Morwë sent the books back and stood as they disappeared, stretching achy joints. Morwë left the rookery and opened the gate to the round pen, soothed by the sounds of horses feeding and the rustle of wings. Even so, she could not completely forget the presence of the cellblock on the same level.

They had many more horses than usual—they had needed more to transport their colony south, and Ingridon's band had stolen many from the settlement they attacked. These new horses turned to look at her with round, interested eyes. With the witch lights studded all around the gate cavern, they had some vestiges of light and were not yet blinded by the darkness.

A dark mare came over and sniffed her palms. "No food," Morwë whispered, feeling the velvet-soft muzzle brush her hands. "I'm sorry." The horse sighed, a warm gust of air.

In fact, it was quite warm in here, from so many bodies so close together. Morwë leaned against the mare's neck, listening to a steady thump. The horse's heart?

Her own?

If only I could ride out of here! she thought. *Go far enough to find one of the lost colonies the tomes made mention of. Surely there are other faefolk somewhere in the world.*

Her fingers twisted in the black mane. But she couldn't leave Enzella. And taking her sister along would be imminently riskier. It would be harder to hide with two, slower to travel, more difficult to carry enough food and provisions. And they would be vulnerable in the daylight.

And no matter what, we are still the Erlking's daughters. He would send someone after us.

Outright rebellion could not be tolerated. Punishment would be swift, as she well knew.

She shuddered. Her father's anger would be terrible to behold, for no other reason than he had not allowed the decision. And it would be downright terrifying if he suspected that she had run to get away from his machinations. He was too strong a power to defy. She would be dead inside a moon cycle.

She couldn't put Enzella at risk like that. And she couldn't leave her behind, either. She had *promised*.

Morwë bit her lip hard enough to draw blood. She could not get out. Eventually Father would decide to do something with her, and he'd pick someone to pair her off with—for political reasons. He'd already offered her up to that prisoner, as if she was nothing more than a bargaining chip. And then she'd be trapped and… and she couldn't face that.

She was weak, too weak. She could pretend not to feel if that happened, but when the Unseelie looked at her the same way they looked at wights, like they wanted to eat her, suck out her soul and leave her empty—she couldn't. Couldn't.

But Enzella would still end up alone; even then Morwë would break her promise. She would be expected to tend to her husband's needs and leave Enzella behind. Who would look out for her sister then? No one, that's who. Oh, some would volunteer, eager to curry favor with the Erlking, but would they look after her? Would they talk to her? Would they sing her to sleep?

Not that I've ever done that, Morwë guilty heart whispered. Where had that come from?

The horse shifted beside her, and Morwë buried her face in its neck, smelling the undeniable scent of horse—a musk that was warm, and alive, and a comfort.

In her mind, a half-buried fragment of memory surfaced. She was so small, clutching a cloth toy to her chest—a doll—and someone held her. They were moving back and forth to ease her into sleep, and she could hear singing.

"Hush a-bye, don't you cry," Morwë whispered into the

horse's neck. "Go to sleep, ye little baby. When you wake, you shall have all the pretty little horses." She sat up straight and patted the horse's shoulder, as the memory grew stronger.

Blacks and bays, dapples and grays. Go to sleep, ye little baby.

It was her mother's voice.

She stared into the dark, astonished. Mother had sung her to sleep. Something turned under her breastbone, and she hesitantly touched her cheeks. They were wet.

All of Zella's talk of love—had Mother loved her once? Why else would she hold a baby she was forced to have? Why would she—

Morwë stumbled to the curving cavern wall to collapse on the floor. She pressed back into the stone, as if she could sink into it as panic clawed at her chest. Too late, it was too late—Mother was rotting in the ground, she—

A shiver ran down her back, the solidness of the mountain steadying her, lending her strength. *She loved you once.*

Morwë covered her face. Is this why she and Zella were so different from the rest of the Unseelie? Why she felt like she was wasting away?

I'm the one rotting in the ground.

The knowledge pierced her like a sword-thrust. "I'm half-wight," Morwë said aloud, a truth she had carried since birth, but never admitted to its weight. The horse's ears twitched. "I'm half food."

And I have half a soul.

TWENTY-FIVE

ARKEN

The little girl could talk; Arken would give her that. She'd talked at Micah until she ran out of steam, and then she'd badgered him into telling stories about "up there," as she called it. Micah recited anecdotes from their growing-up years, the fish they caught in the summer, their sister's failure at canning, and his and Arken's adventures at the lake's edge, pretending it was the ocean. Micah was a good storyteller—genuine—and he'd need to be. It would be useful for winning her loyalties.

But Arken wanted to talk to Micah, to ask him all the things he'd learned about these creatures, to tell him all that had happened since their people had disappeared. *Wait,* he told himself.

She can't stay up here forever.

Abruptly, Enzella cut Micah off in the middle of a sentence and wriggled back through the bars. "Morwë!"

Arken leaned forward to peer through the darkness.

Morwë moved like smoke, slow and fluid, skirts rippling as she walked. "Zel, time for bed."

"Morwë, this is Arken! Micah is his brother!"

Her sharp eyes met Arken's in a flash of electric understanding. For a second, he wondered if this was what wild animals did when they met—eyed each other warily, trying to gauge the other's intentions before ripping each other's throats out.

"Oh?" she said, cool enough to freeze blood. "What an interesting kernel of knowledge."

Arken's jaw tightened.

Her sister tugged her skirts. "He came to rescue Micah—"

"Yes, I deduced that," Morwë murmured. She raised an eyebrow. "How is that going for you?"

"Just dandy so far," Arken snapped.

"—because he loves him!" Enzella continued, oblivious. "Micah says it's what families do. Why don't we have that?"

Morwë's expression changed; Arken could have sworn an expression of pain crossed her face. "Zella—"

"Why not?" Enzella said, voice turning beseeching. "I want that."

A tremor passed through her body, and the raven-haired woman pulled her small sister into an embrace—a hard, painful-looking one, but an embrace nonetheless. "We'll talk about this later," she whispered harshly. "All right? Let me look at the wight, and then bed."

"All right," Enzella mumbled.

Morwë gestured to Micah.

"What are you doing?" Arken demanded, reaching to pull her away.

Her eyes flashed with warning. "I'm fixing his arm for Enzella."

"Not for *him*?"

"Enzella is the one who asked me to."

"It's all right, Arken," Micah said, extending his arm through the bars.

Black stains pooled on Morwë's arms, flooding to her hands. She gripped Micah's arm. Micah hissed through his teeth.

"Stop," Arken said. She ignored him.

"Stop!" he said, reaching through the bars.

Quick as a striking snake, Morwë grabbed his wrist and glared at him. Her hand was so cold it burned—like she had plunged it into a frozen lake and pulled it out again.

Her eyes pooled black. "Don't interrupt a thaumaturge when she's working," she hissed.

TWENTY-SIX

MORWË

Morwë finished her working on the boy's arm and shook with anger and something like fear. If the power in her hands had been misdirected, there was no way to know what might have happened. Jezra and Hadrian's piebald burns flashed through her mind.

"It's really all right, Arken," Micah gasped.

Morwë kept her glare trained on Arken, who gave as good as he got. The black ichor in her veins subsided, and she dropped Micah's arm like it was made of fire.

"You were hurting my brother," Arken ground out. His blue eyes held her, no matter how she tried to look away.

"I haven't ever tried fixing a wight before," she said. "And I'm only doing this because Zel asked."

"Arken, honest, it just feels cold," Micah said. "I'm fine. Thank you, Morwë."

Morwë looked through the bars at the boy's anxious face, eyes that pleaded with her just like Zella's did. Slicing through her like a knife to her chest.

She nodded through the phantom pain and grasped Enzella's hand. "Come on."

"Bye, Micah, bye, Arken," Enzella said, waggling her fingers at them before she let Morwë drag her down the stairs. "Arken's been looking for Micah since he disappeared," Enzella said. "He—"

"Hush," Morwë said strongly. "No more until we're back in our rooms."

Enzella subsided as they slipped through corridors and down several floors. "Can I stay with you again?" she asked in a small voice as they passed through a cavern filled with sprites.

Part of Morwë wanted Enzella far away from her rotting self, because Mother had been correct—Zel was the one thing she had done right. But there was no one else—

Morwë stiffened as she caught sight of Ingridon making his way through the crowd. "Yes," she said quickly. "Now watch it. Trouble."

The crowd parted for the Erlking's heir, and Ingridon swaggered over to them, smirk firmly in place. A dark malice lingered in his eyes. "You missed dinner," he said.

"And?" Morwë countered, raising an eyebrow. Their presence was only required at formal dinners and banquets. "I wasn't aware you were my minder."

"Where were you, sister?"

"Not that it's any of your business," Morwë said, icicles coating every word, "but we were up in the stable loft."

"And before that?" Ingridon asked, voice deceptively light.

Oh, moon glow, what's he on about? "All that business with the intruder, *if* you'll remember," she said tartly. She tugged Enzella around him and headed for the far passageway. There was no avoiding the oncoming explosion, but she'd be torched if she'd let it happen in front of the rabble.

"Enzella, you usually can't shut your mouth, but today, not a peep," Ingridon said. He was following them, just as she suspected. "What's clogged up your throat?"

Morwë squeezed her sister's hand hard to keep her quiet. "Go and bother someone else, Ingridon; we're tired." Morwë tried to keep her steps purposeful but not hurried. Ingridon could smell fear.

They made the first curve of the passageway before he cracked.

"Don't walk away from me," he hissed, shoving Morwë against the wall hard enough that her head cracked against the stone. Sparks pin-wheeled behind her eyes.

Enzella yelled, "Stop it, Ingridon!"

Morwë heard a slap. "Keep out of this," Ingridon warned.

Morwë's vision finally cleared enough to see her brother looming over her, mouth twisted in a snarl. "You magicked a member of my guard, Morwë."

"So that's what this is about?" Morwë drew a ragged breath. "He irritated me. And I'll do it again if his behavior continues. Get away from me."

"That's hurtful, Morwë," Ingridon said, fingers gripping her upper arms hard enough to bruise.

The pain in her head made nausea roll through her. She couldn't think.

Moonlight, I wish *I could use my Arts on blood kin!* Even if she could, she had already done two large, powerful workings today —she didn't have the strength. "What do I care," Morwë snapped, doing her best to pry his hands off. "I'm the First Daughter, and he'll remember it, or I'll burn him again."

"And I'm the *Heir*," Ingridon hissed. He leaned close enough to her face that she could feel his breath. "You remember *that*, sister dear." With a last twist to her arm, he stalked off down the hall.

"Morwë?" Enzella said, voice quavering and panicked.

"I'm all right." Morwë put a hand to the back of her head. She felt the stickiness of blood.

TWENTY-SEVEN

MICAH

Micah squinted up at the tiny crack in his new cell where a tiny flicker of weak sunlight trickled through the stone. "Could we get out by digging, I wonder?" he asked Arken.

"From the looks of things," Arken grunted from his cell, "We would have to dig through several feet of solid rock. Without tools, I doubt it."

"How did you get here?" Micah whispered in case anyone was close enough to hear.

"I returned to Peridun and found it gutted—it must have been right after you were taken. Father James and all the young children were still there. I agreed to take them part of the way to Cairenoch." Arken paused.

"You did the right thing," Micah told him, sensing the reason for his pause. "They needed your help. Without you…."

"It still tore at me," Arken said, "to leave you like that. But I got them halfway there, and from what Father James was able to tell me about the attack, I headed towards Ceridfel, trying to pick up your tracks. It was a combination of lucky chance and divine providence, I'm certain. I didn't know I had found anything at all until I set off some kind of magical alarm. Then I was captured, thrown in here...."

"What?" Micah said, his breath catching at what Arken left unsaid.

"Oh, their ruler—Erlking, they call it—he magicked me, trying to scare me, but I'm all right."

"What happened?"

"My hand."

Micah reached out blindly into the gloom and nearly recoiled. The hand that clasped his felt like an old man's—boney and wrinkled, with arthritic knuckles and veins, no strength to the grip.

"Arken—!"

"It doesn't hurt. Don't worry about it. It could be worse."

Micah closed his eyes against the possibility of *how much worse* it could be. "You can see—how?"

"Fernseed oil—thank Father James," Arken said. "He gave it to me on a hunch and a prayer."

"Fernseed. I've heard stories...." Micah mused. "I thought it made you invisible.

"Well, I don't know about that. But I can certainly see through this murk." Arken took a deep breath. "So what about these— these girls. You trust them? Because the cat's out of the bag about why I'm here now. That might've been what was keeping me alive," Arken said darkly.

Micah sighed and passed his good arm over his eyes. "Enzella seems innocent enough. She wants to know anything and everything."

Arken tapped his finger against the bars, the sound tinny in the deep silence. "Do you think she would help us escape?"

"Don't know. You saw how she reacted when we asked her to keep quiet."

"Yes, what was that about?"

"Her mother died just the other day. Murdered by her father's hand, she said."

"Mountain's bones. I believe it," Arken murmured. "I've seen him."

Micah shivered as Arken described the Erlking.

"Enzella's terrified of him," Micah said. "And she has no idea what love is, Arken. She had to ask me if her mother loved her. It was heartbreaking."

"Don't forget she's one of them," Arken warned. "What about Morwë?"

Micah tried not to bristle. Arken hadn't been here to see Enzella's tears; he had the right to be wary. "She has some kind of magic; you saw it," Micah said shortly. He tried to recall the few times he had seen the woman. "Cold. Withdrawn. But she seems determined to take care of Enzella." He pictured the energy surrounding Morwë, the tightly held emotion that only showed through her eyes. "Do you remember last winter when we set traps for rabbits, and we caught a fox instead?"

"Yes," Arken replied.

"It was pained and weak, but not quite dead. And it had a wildness in its eyes... Morwë makes me think of that," Micah admitted.

"I thought of a hawk or falcon tied to jesses," Arken said. "So Enzella is sympathetic, and will keep secrets she thinks are important. We might be able to gain her help. But the sister might intervene if she sees us as a threat to Enzella."

"She wouldn't get Enzella in trouble, though," Micah corrected him. "She cares, as much as they *can* care, about her sister. Their mother is—was—human," he whispered.

"That explains a few things. How have they treated you?" Arken asked.

"Well, the war band broke my arm, but since I've been in here, nothing."

"And the others? Where are they?"

Micah swallowed hard. "They're dead, Arken."

"*What?*"

Micah closed his eyes. He didn't want to speak the truth into being, but he had to. There was no one else. "They were... killed. To provide fuel for these people's magics. The only reason I'm alive is that Morwë's brother gave me to her as a sort of gift. He's a real piece of work."

Micah flinched as his brother slammed his fists into the bars. "Damn them," Arken muttered. "Micah, we only have a small window of time before their *Erlking*," Arken spat the word, "comes back to pry my reasons out of me. And that's only if the girls don't tell."

Micah dug his nails into his palms as panic clawed through his chest. "What do you think they'll do?"

"I want to be well away from here by then," Arken said grimly. "And to do that, we need those girls on our side."

CHAPTER

TWENTY-EIGHT

INGRIDON

Ingridon crossed his arms over his chest and laughed at Hadrian's muffled curses.

His Second shifted in his bunk in the war band's barracks, trying to find a position that didn't irritate the splotchy burns. "It's not funny," Hadrian said, spitting the words through his clenched teeth.

"It's a little funny," Ingridon said, grinning at his discomfort. "Why don't you get a thaumaturge to look at those burns?"

"And have them know another thaumaturge gave them to me? No thanks," Hadrian said bitterly. He rolled onto his stomach. He had caught the worst of it on his back.

"Well, swallow that pride," Ingridon commanded. "I need you back in top condition. For a little… revenge." He rang for a serving imp and rested his hip against the table in the middle of the room to wait.

Hadrian huffed. "On Morwë?"

"She's gotten too uppity," Ingridon said, face twisting into a scowl. "We're not younglings in a scrap anymore. She needs to remember her place."

"I don't think I'll be any help," Hadrian said, resting his head on his forearms. "Going after Morwë is only going to make her angrier. I could end up with worse than *this*." He flinched. "Though I don't really see how that's possible."

"We're not going after Morwë directly," Ingridon said quietly, fiddling with the hilt of his sword.

"How, then?"

Ingridon made him wait as the serving imp arrived, an unnatural smile carved into its face. From a brawl in the lower caverns, most likely. "Bring Thaumaturge Toren to me here," Ingridon commanded. "I've a few tasks for him. Let him know the Heir insists on him personally." He smiled as the imp bowed out of the room to fulfill his request.

"Damn, Ingridon, I told you I didn't want a healer," Hadrian groused.

The smile dropped off his face. "I don't care what you want. I need you for leverage. If that slut you've been keeping time with sees you healed, she'll do whatever you ask to get the same thing."

"Jezra?"

"I don't care what her name is."

A spot of blackness grew in the center of the barracks, solidifying into Toren, who bowed. Ingridon bit back a snarl. Only the most powerful thaumaturges could appear and disappear at will like the Erlking. Toren was flaunting his status as the likely candidate to take control of the thaumaturges' cabal.

"Finally," Ingridon snapped. "I want you to fix this." He gestured to Hadrian's burns.

"My prince," Toren said, bowing slightly, "the Erlking has decreed that all thaumaturge power be allocated to the cavern excavation—"

"And yet you decided to appear here instead of walking." Ingridon set his hand on his sword hilt. "Fix him. Now."

Toren hesitated just a shade short of being insulting, and then nodded and set his hands on Hadrian, black curling on his hands like snake tendrils. Hadrian snarled as the burns on his skin began to peel and shed. But eventually the shiny burns disappeared, leaving him swearing at the thaumaturge.

"If that is all, my prince…." Toren said, an edge to his voice.

"No." Ingridon crossed his arms. "There's something else. My revenge plot requires a little magic."

Toren's eyes went flat.

Hadrian pulled on his shirt and cracked his neck. "How are you going to put Morwë in her place? I don't want to face off with her again."

"We're not going to face off directly." Ingridon smiled. "We're going after her weakness."

"Morwë hasn't got any weaknesses. She's a pillar of ice."

"Every block of ice has a fissure, and if you tap it just right, it shatters."

Hadrian's confusion slowly bled away. He stared at Ingridon. "But she's—"

"The only thing Morwë cares about," Ingridon said, cutting him off smoothly. "It's nothing you haven't done before."

"And my presence is required because…?" Toren asked.

Ingridon considered parting Toren's head from his shoulders, but he needed him, much as he'd like to rid himself of those awful bi-colored eyes.

"Because Morwë knows she's got a weakness, and she protects it fiercely. You're going to get us past those protections," Ingridon sneered.

"I have no stake in feuds," Toren said calmly.

"Oh, don't worry—you'll get something out of it. I know what you want." Ingridon sunk a lake's worth of meaning into the words, his eyes fixed on Toren. The thaumaturge did not outwardly react, but that was how Ingridon knew he had him.

Ingridon smiled. "Now, here's what I want you both to do…."

CHAPTER

TWENTY-NINE

MORWË

The rap on her chamber door was soft and subdued. "Morwë," Jezra's low, husky voice called.

Morwë looked up from Enzella's sleeping face. Willing away her pensive frown, she got up and opened the door, settling for impassive hostility. "What."

Jezra's face still showed signs of fading burns. "Could we talk?" she whispered.

"What is there to talk about?"

"Morwë—please." Jezra twisted her hands, actually seeming hesitant, a foreign expression on her.

Morwë pursed her lips. "Not here." Black skirts swirling around her legs, she swept past Jezra down the hall to the antechamber. When Jezra entered after her, she closed the door that led to the royal family's rooms and crossed her arms. "Well?"

Jezra bit her lip, and Morwë sighed inwardly. Even from a former friend—if she could be deemed so—this false remorse seemed a bit much. "I shouldn't have needled you so," Jezra finally said. "Especially not about Hadrian."

"You are right," Morwë said. "You shouldn't have."

Jezra eyed her uneasily.

"Is that it?" Morwë said, raising an eyebrow.

Jezra swallowed. "No… we—we were wrong to provoke you."

Morwë blinked and waited.

"And I'm asking you to… fix this." Her hand moved, a tight, controlled gesture, to take in her waxy burns.

"There it is," Morwë muttered. "Jezra—"

The wards around her room broke. The force behind it made Morwë reel backwards.

A high scream of pain echoed down the hallway.

"Zella," Morwë gasped. She shoved Jezra out of the way as she ran towards her room.

Another scream came as Morwë dashed down the hallway. She barely registered Hadrian standing in the hallway, holding an object covered in glyphs—an object filled with enough power to break her wards. She threw him aside without thought and ran into her room.

Ingridon lifted his bloody knife from their sister's body. "Hello, Morwë," he said, flashing wicked teeth.

Shaking with rage, Morwë called up her Arts, staining her hands and arms black as she reached out—

"Ah, ah, ah," he snarled. He grabbed and twisted her outstretched arms with nearly breaking force. "That's not how it *works*, Morwë," he hissed in her ear as she cursed and struggled. "You can't use Arts on your own blood, remember?"

"Zel!" Morwë cried, twisting around to see her little sister's body. "If you've killed her—you—I'll *burn you*, I'll—"

"*You* did this," Ingridon yelled, shaking her. "You tested me once too often, sister dear." He laid his bloody dagger against her cheek. "And now what you care about is compromised."

Morwë flinched away from the blood, but it coated her skin in a cold, tacky glaze.

"If you keep on this track, I might hurt her worse. I am the Heir to the Erlking. *Not* you." He threw her on the bed.

Morwë clutched Enzella and tried to staunch the blood flow as her sister whimpered. He had stabbed her twice and sliced her face.

"You're the one who controls what happens to Enzella. Make the right choice," he hissed.

"I'll tell Father!" Morwë shrieked in a voice she hardly recognized, balling up the sheets to stop the bleeding. "I'll tell him what you did!"

Ingridon laughed. "You think he'll care?" He licked his lips. "Enzella's a girl, and a second girl, at that."

Morwë bared her teeth, fury and grief battling for dominance. "She is your *sister*!"

Ingridon shrugged. "What does that matter to an Unseelie? Remember what I said, Morwë. Make the right choice."

As soon as he left the room, Morwë used all the power she had to summon her father's best thaumaturges immediately. "Hold on, Zel," she whispered in a broken voice. *I can't lose you now. Not you.* "Hold on."

Morwë watched like a hawk as Toren and Zyra, the highest court thaumaturges, stopped Enzella's bleeding and healed some of her internal injuries. Their hands moved quickly as their Arts flowed to Enzella in inky streams.

As Zyra began to bind Enzella's wounds, Toren turned to Morwë and bowed, his long plait of dark hair falling over his shoulder. "She is out of danger, my lady, but the Erlking has commanded all thaumaturges to devote the majority of their power to the excavation and tunneling process. Healing requires much of our Arts; we cannot heal her fully."

"And such rules apply to even the Erlking's daughter?" Morwë demanded.

He nodded, and his two-colored eyes flashed in the witch light glow, one black and the other silver. "Yes, my lady. A ban has been put on healing anything but the most drastic wounds, to both conserve our Arts and to cow the rabble in the lower caverns from brawling. But we will prepare healing draughts for her, to aid her in the process."

Zyra looked up from bandaging, her gray hair straggling down her back. "The Erlking did not—"

A sharp glance from Toren's two-toned eyes made the older woman's teeth click together. His silver eye almost seemed to glow.

"Healing draughts take little magic," Toren said in a light, deceptive voice. "They will aid the little princess in her healing. It is an honor to serve the Erlking's daughter." He turned back to Morwë and he bowed low, a formal obeisance usually reserved for high court.

Morwë ignored this toadying. She had no patience for it now. "But she will recover fully?"

"There may be some minimal scarring, but yes, my lady, she will."

She remembered Toren; he had been one of Ingridon's year-mates. He hadn't liked Ingridon much, and Morwë had always thought it sensible of him. But Toren had a talent for misdirection. He could fool you into thinking one eye did not know what the other looked at. And according to Jezra, his eye had been on her.

But did she trust Jezra's word now?

"You were about to say, the Erlking did not make special provision for healing draughts," Morwë said to Zyra, who had just placed the last bandage on Enzella's face. "You spoke with him after I summoned you?"

Zyra exchanged a wary look with Toren. "The thaumaturges were reporting on the cavern process when your summons came, my lady. The Erlking informed us that our strengths should be concentrated on the mountain before he dispatched Toren and I to attend you."

"I see." Morwë's lips tightened with anger. Father could not even stir himself to concern over his daughter's injury at the hand of his son.

"It is in the nature of expediency, my lady," Toren said quietly.

"The rabble grows restless. If we do not dig more, dig deeper into the stone to expand our caverns and give them space, there will be trouble."

"I did not ask for an explanation." She couldn't care less about uprisings right now. And she had not forgotten that someone had given Ingridon an object spelled with enough magic to break her wards. Few could have done that. Maybe even one of these thaumaturges. An honor to serve the Erlking's daughter, indeed.

Her throat tightened. "You are done here?"

"Aye," Zyra croaked. "She may wake soon, but she will sleep again. Rest will bring healing."

"You will make healing draughts as soon as you are able." It was not a request. Morwë's mouth twisted, and both Unseelie flinched. She wondered what they saw in her eyes. "You are dismissed."

After a hasty curtsey, Zyra slunk backwards from the room without a word, but Toren bowed again and said, "Your wish is my command, my lady," before he left.

As soon as they were gone, Morwë redoubled the wards on her room to allow no one access except herself and Enzella. She sat down by her sister's still form and closed her eyes. "Oh, Zel," she whispered. "What are we going to do?"

THIRTY

ENZELLA

Enzella blinked slowly, fingers fumbling at the heavy weight around her middle.

"No, no," her sister's voice commanded. Hands pushed her arms to her sides. "Leave the bandages alone, Enzella."

Gradually, her sister's image resolved before Enzella's eyes. Morwë sat on the edge of the bed, struggling to smile. Enzella had never seen that look on Morwë's face before. Her skin was so pale, it was almost translucent. "How do you feel?" Morwë whispered.

Enzella hesitantly touched her stomach, which felt very tightly wrapped, and frowned—or tried to. At the pain in her cheeks, she gasped, lifting her hands to pat at the gauze on her face.

"Leave it alone, Zel." Morwë pulled her hands away again.

"Wha...." Enzella mumbled. "Ingri—"

"I know," Morwë whispered. She glanced over her shoulder. "I know. Zel, I'm... this was my fault. Ingridon wanted to punish me. I didn't mean—I—"

Enzella reached for her hand. "I know," she whispered. She remembered Ingridon looming over her, smiling. A flash of a knife. "He said."

Morwë's hands clasped hers, and her face settled into her icy mask. "He will regret this. On my blood and bones, I will make him regret it, moonlight take his sight."

Enzella relaxed. Everything would be all right. She sank back into the pillows, feeling the ache in her middle returning.

"Drink this before you fall asleep." Morwë held a cup for her to drink.

"Don't want a draught...." Enzella mumbled, flinching away from the phantom bitter taste.

"Draughts come later. The thaumaturges have to make them. This is just water."

Reassured, she sipped at the cup. The water slid down easily, washing away the awful taste in her mouth of coppery blood.

"I'm going to make this right," Morwë promised, setting the cup on the table.

Enzella, yawning, didn't respond. She was so tired. But she forced her eyes open. She couldn't sleep. What if Ingridon....

"Don't worry, Zel. Go to sleep. The wards will keep you safe."

Her eyelids closed gratefully as the comforting abyss of sleep dragged her down. As she drifted off, Enzella felt Morwë hesitate by the bed.

A light touch on her hair, as soft as a breath, made her eyelids flutter. But it could have been a dream.

THIRTY-ONE

MORWË

In the freezing passageway to her father's council chamber, Morwë steeled her spine and locked her weaknesses away. The only emotion she let herself feel was anger. Exhaling, Morwë watched her breath cloud and then disperse. Only then did she step through the doorway.

In the antechamber, her father's counselor looked up from his seat at the desk. "My lady, what brings you here?" Demyen's brow wrinkled; and there was quite a bit to wrinkle, thanks to his receding hairline. He stood respectfully and bowed.

"I want to see my father." Morwë narrowed her eyes when Demyen did not move. "Well?"

"He's having a conversation, my lady," Demyen replied, unruffled. "If you'll wait until he is finished—"

"He'll see me now." Morwë stalked to the inner door of the chamber and pushed it open.

Seated by the remains of a dying witch fire, Yemelyan kept his eyes trained on the brazier in front of him. "First Daughter."

From the chair opposite her father's, Ingridon lounged and smiled.

"Father." Morwë gathered her wits and let ice encase her heart. She'd need to use all the resources at her disposal for this encounter. "I thought you should know that Enzella will recover from Ingridon's stab wounds." With a bit more venom than necessary, she added, "Only a coward strikes a little girl."

Ingridon's smile fell. "Coward?" he snarled, coming up out of his chair. His hand reached for the knife at his belt.

Yemelyan sighed and drummed his blackened fingers on the arm of his chair, carved in a semblance of a beast's claws. "I dislike it when my children squabble. Sit down, Ingridon."

Ingridon's knees folded under the weight of the command.

"Demyen," Yemelyan continued, "Bring a chair for Morwë."

Morwë hid her flinch. She hadn't realized Demyen had followed her in. She sniffed, but deigned to sit when the chair was brought.

"Children," Yemelyan said when the councilor had vacated the chamber. "On occasion, your antics have been amusing, possibly even diverting to observe at a distance. But you are both of an age to put away childish things. This bickering should be put aside. Our people do not need division from the Erlking's family, and this story will spread."

"You deem Enzella's attack *antics*?" Morwë clenched her hands in her lap.

"Nothing irreparable happened." Ingridon toyed with his knife and murmured, "This time."

Morwë hissed, wordless.

"Enough," Yemelyan said, voice flat. "Ingridon took action because you continue to challenge his status as the Heir, First Daughter."

"How, pray? By not bowing and scraping in his presence? This 'action' he took was to stab Enzella; if he felt so threatened, he should have come after *me*."

"Ingridon struck at your weakness in a clever way, as befits the Heir." Yemelyan's eyebrows drew together in a frown.

Morwë's heart constricted. Enzella. Her weakness. "She is innocent in all of this! She is his sister—your *daughter*—"

Yemelyan cocked his head, eyeing her curiously. "Why, Morwë. Where did you acquire such a… human concept?"

Morwë went very still.

Ingridon's eyes glittered with feral laughter.

"What else did you wish to say, Father?" she forced through numb lips.

"There will be no more fights between the two of you. Not until the situation in the tunnels is resolved. Is that clear?"

Ingridon stretched, thinking he had gotten the last parting shot in their battle of wills. "Of course, Father." He smiled magnanimously. "You are the Erlking and to be obeyed."

"And Enzella?" It was galling to admit to the weakness, to *care*, but she had promised. She must take care of Enzella. No one else would.

"What of her?" Yemelyan raised a brow.

"You want fights between your children to cease. Does that include fights involving Enzella?"

Ingridon's lip curled. "You want the imp safe, keep away from my Second."

Morwë rounded on him. "Then control your men and keep him out of my way. I know Hadrian helped you. I'd better never lay eyes on him again or I won't be responsible for what happens to him."

Ingridon laughed. "Will my promise make you happy, Morwë?" He stood and grabbed her chin, forcing her face up to his. "Of course, I'll expect you to be appropriately grateful," he whispered.

She smacked his hand away. "Why would I be grateful for something worthless?"

Ingridon laughed and stood, the sound crawling through her. "Have a care, Morwë. Have a care." He took his leave.

Morwë sat very still, her skin remembering the sensation of his hands. She could feel her father's eyes on her, regarding her with a keenness she did not like.

"Your devotion to your sister is to be commended, Morwë."

She stared at the witch lights in the brazier without seeing them. He almost never called her Morwë.

In the same silken tone, her father asked, "Do you require a promise of me?"

She swallowed. Say yes, and she suspected he *would* give his word and abide by it—but she would pay a steep, unknown price, and it would imply distrust in her father, in his motives and judgment and rule, an entirely dangerous thing. But if she said no, he was left unbound. Or, worse yet, that she thought his word as empty as Ingridon's. And she must speak, and quickly, or prove her indecision.

Before she could marshal her thoughts, Yemelyan continued. "Enzella is your mother's daughter. I would not hurt something of hers."

But you did kill *Mother,* thought Morwë. *And you aren't inclined to protect Enzella. So what weight do your words carry?*

And what about me? *Am I not also my mother's daughter?*

She murmured, "Yes, Father."

Yemelyan sighed. "I will need to do something about you soon. I should have remedied it years ago, but your mother asked for your presence after Enzella's birth, and I refused none of her requests. She made so few of me."

Morwë stopped breathing.

Yemelyan's look was entirely too knowing. "Yes, something will have to be done about you, Morwë. I shall put my mind to it very soon." He drummed his fingers on the arm of his chair, and then stopped. "But not at this moment. Go and attend your sister, First Daughter."

She was dismissed.

Morwë took herself out of the study, shaking as the door swung shut behind her.

In the antechamber, Demyen called after her as she made to exit. "My lady, Toren informed me of your sister's injuries. However, he is very skilled; I have no doubt she will make a full recovery."

Morwë cast a glance at him over her shoulder. Toren had never struck her as wont to gossip. Why was Demyen volunteering this information? He was firmly Yemelyen's eyes and ears in the colony. He viewed it as a step down to impart information to anyone other than his master.

Demyen bowed to her. "Let me know if there is anything you or your sister require during her convalescence and it will be done, my lady."

Demyen had never given her so much as a conciliatory word before today. And Toren had bowed. Multiple times, with extreme deference. He had never done that either.

She nodded in acknowledgement before stepping into the dark hallway.

Yemelyan's words echoed in her mind: *"Something will have to be done…. I shall put my mind to it very soon."*

She shivered, foreboding spreading through her bones. Her time had just run out.

REACHING OUT, Morwë mentally tested the protection she had placed on her room. It still stood firm, and from what little she could tell at this distance, Zel's condition had not changed.

She stalked up the long flights of stairs guided by instinct and need.

Nothing mattered except keeping Zel safe. And she could no longer do that here. That was clear enough. To protect her sister, Morwë would be forced to step into her father's plans. But she wouldn't be able to care for Enzella. They would always be leveraged against each other. And Ingridon's word was worthless.

I cannot. I cannot.

Is there another way? Fear gibbered in the back of her mind.

Not one less dangerous. But hope is always dangerous.

Reaching the prison levels, Morwë stopped short. They had placed a guard.

She lifted her chin, fueled by a bitter rage. "You there," she called, stalking up to him. "Why do you stand here? What is the purpose of your post?"

The gray-skinned Unseelie with a hooked and broken nose recognized her instantly and bowed. Morwë sniffed, slightly gratified.

"My lady, as the unrest in the lower caverns is growing, security has been tightened. Two Unseelie attempted to leave the mountain earlier and were detained. I'm to guard the top levels against any who would seek to leave the mountain."

"I see," Morwë said, nose wrinkling in annoyance. "These two imps. What happened to them?"

"They await the Erlking's judgment, my lady."

Morwë took a long, slow breath and exhaled it through her nose. "Very good. Carry on."

Then she sent him to sleep.

As the guard slumped against the wall and slid down to the ground, she touched his forehead and addled the memory of the last few minutes, so he would not remember she had been there. Then she paced up to the cellblock, making the two imprisoned imps unconscious as well as she headed for the two cells that housed the wights.

Arken looked up, eyes sharpening when he saw her approach.

"What was your plan once you found your brother?" Morwë demanded without preamble. "You must have had one."

"What makes you think I'll tell you?" His eyes flickered over her shoulder warily.

"I put the guard to sleep," Morwë said impatiently. "You don't have to whisper."

Arken stood, voice deepening. "And why would you do a thing like that?"

Morwë straightened her spine, refusing to shrink back or glance around like a frightened rat or wight. "I can help you."

His eyes narrowed. "What has brought about this sudden apostasy?" His voice dripped with suspicion.

"I need to get Zel out of here." Morwë's voice sounded shrilled and strained, surprising herself. It was almost sure suicide. She knew that. But if there was the slightest chance—the barest possibility—then she had to take it, for Zel's sake.

They could not remain pawns in their father's game.

"Why? What's happened to Enzella?"

Both of them jumped at the sound of Micah's voice.

Morwë turned to him. Her nails cut into her palms, she clenched them so hard. "She was attacked."

"Attacked?" Micah repeated, eyes wide behind his cell bars.

"By my brother." Morwë swallowed, a tremor running through her. "It isn't safe for her anymore, not that it ever was, but I've no other choice now. I must get her away. If I help you, you must take—" she tripped over the words. "Take us with you."

Both brothers stared at her, eyes wide.

She pursed her lips and lifted her chin, waiting.

"Mountain's bones, sit down." Arken reached through the bars to touch her arm.

She stared at his hand, baffled.

"No offence meant, my lady," Micah said quickly.

Arken shrugged. "Or not. Do what you want. But there will be nothing we can do if you faint."

Morwë stared at Arken's hand—the uncursed one, strong and capable, with her sleeve in its grasp. She could not recall such a touch from… from anyone, save Enzella and her mother. But now she could feel the muscles in her legs twitching from fatigue.

She moved to sit. Halfway to the ground, she overbalanced and pitched sideways, but Arken was ready. He seized her arm and steadied her, easing her to the stone.

Once Morwë was seated, he slid his hand down her arm. His warm callouses rubbed against her fingers and made her jerk in surprise. He held on for another moment before his fingers let hers go.

When the warmth left her, she felt bereft.

"Tell us what happened, Morwë," Micah urged, sitting down as well.

Her eyes darted between the brothers as she slowly recounted the tale, doing her best to explain how and why Ingridon had stabbed his own sister. The whole time, Arken's dark blue eyes bored into her. "I still don't trust you," he said after speech had exhausted her.

"You don't have to," she rasped. "Look, once Enzella's better I can let you out. We can take horses—I can open the gates. But you have to get us out of here."

"*I* have to? Why not go on your merry way?" Arken asked, suspicious. "Why do you need *us* for your plan to work?"

"*Arken,*" Micah hissed. "Are you arguing *against* escaping?"

Morwë ground her teeth together. "I don't know where to *go.* Only the raiding party is authorized to leave the mountain right now. And we're new to this place."

Micah said, "What, you've only recently come to this mountain? Where did you come from?"

"North of these mountains. We lived under the deep northern taiga forests," Morwë said, a deep sadness etching its way into her bones, mourning the only home she had ever known.

"I still don't understand *what* you are," Arken put in.

To convince them, she'd have to impart everything she knew of Unseelie past, their history. Well, that was fine. In for a drop, in for an ocean.

Morwë closed her eyes. "When younglings are taught our history, they say that when the world was younger, we did live above the ground, and magic that fueled our Arts was plentiful, bubbling up like a spring from the earth, infusing every living thing and even the very air with life." Her voice sank into a cadence. "But without warning, the wellspring of magic ceased. We knew of no cause for such a thing. We could still feel the magic, locked away in the earth, but we could not extract it, not without expending much of our Arts in the process.

"With the magic streams dry, the creatures in this world that depend on this source began to perish. The griffins died or flew to the sea, to soak up what little magics remained free flowing in the waters. The dragons went mad and hoarded gold in order to soak up the magic from its mineral properties. Some of our kindred left us, searching for places in the world where magic might still be wild. We diminished… we were dying."

She licked her lips. "But you wights, you *humans,* felt no ill effects. You thrived and multiplied. The glimmer of magic remained in you, sometimes waking in a select few to become wizards, magic users. So, our thaumaturges decided that instead of beggaring our magical stores for what we could eke out honestly… we would simply take."

"People. You took *people.*" Arken gripped the bars of his cell, looking as if he'd like to wring her neck.

For the first time, saying these words out loud, Morwë felt their true horror. She wondered if he really would kill her, given the chance. He'd have the right.

Her head bobbed once. "Your kneph—breath, spirit, soul, whatever you like. We stole. And it fueled our Arts, kept us alive. But the sun became too hot; it burned us. We could not go out under its glare, and then we could not go out at all. We grew the taiga so that the trees blocked out all sunlight, created hidden paths beneath their branches that we walked for many generations. And then the flames came."

She closed her eyes against the hot light of memory, burning the protections between the Unseelie and the sky. "Some wights in our old land grew too strong. They banded together and set fire to the taiga."

"Too strong," Arken muttered sarcastically. "Right. They finally were able to fight back, more like."

Morwë's head dropped, acknowledging the hit. "Many died. My father led us south, to these mountains. Our thaumaturges found tunnels through the rock, and made others." She shook her head, throat parched. "That is all there is."

"Why the Caleahanach Mountains? Why *here*?" Arken pressed.

She hesitated. "My father traveled for a time in his youth, before he took the throne. I think this was one of the places he went." *Where he found my mother.*

Morwë's Arts moved restlessly through her veins, a warning. "The guard will wake up soon," she informed them. She pulled herself up, gripping the bars with shaky hands. "Will you help?"

"Yes," Micah spoke up quickly. "We will, Morwë."

"I'll come back—once Enzella is better." She hesitated. "I would work another healing, but...."

"Don't worry; it's fine," the boy assured her. He moved the arm slowly, showing the range of movement. "Tell Enzella I hope she gets well soon."

From the honesty in his eyes, Morwë knew he meant it. With exhaustion tugging at her shoulders, she reached out to briefly touch Micah's head. He colored, but didn't move.

She glanced at Arken and mumbled, "They are too good for this place."

Then she followed the witch lights from the cellblock down the stairs, winding her way through the tunnels to her chamber. Slipping past her magical defenses, she laid a hand on her sister's bandaged cheek.

Zel snuffled in her sleep and curled into the pillow.

Promise me, Morwë, her mother's memory rasped. *Take care of your sister.*

I will, Morwë thought, lying down beside her and letting her eyes finally close. *I promise, Mother.*

THIRTY-TWO

MORWË

Morwë avoided everyone as Enzella healed. She refused to let anyone into her rooms, summoning food from the kitchens when she needed it. It was supplied with only a little grousing, perhaps due to her adamant commands and icy demeanor.

Enzella wore Morwë's patience to a frazzle. Her sister pestered Morwë for all the stories she could claw from her memory, legends and history and any memories she had about their mother. After she had talked herself to death and Enzella was finally sleeping, Morwë would creep to the prison cells and deliver a status report and food. She had realized no guard had been tasked with feeding the prisoners—Micah was considered hers to feed or starve, and Arken was surely being deprived food to weaken his will. She would deliver a portion to Micah that the brothers could share, and then she would go back to her room and sleep until Enzella prodded her awake to entertain her again.

The next day, after Enzella had fallen asleep, Morwë glanced at the trunk in the corner of her room. The servants who had cleaned out her mother's chamber had wanted to go through the trunk, but Morwë had told them in the coldest voice she had ever mustered that the trunk was her inheritance, and she'd flay anyone who touched it. She hadn't opened it yet. Running her hand over the aged wood, Morwë lifted the lid, the hinges creaking like a last gasp. It felt macabre, to pick through her mother's possessions.

More macabre than seeing her die? she asked herself, *Besides, it might contain things we could use above ground.*

Shaking the shivers from her shoulders, Morwë sat and turned the key in the lock. She lifted the lid.

On top was the rock with the vein of silver running through it, the one Mother had asked her to put in the trunk. Morwë sent her Arts into her witch lights to brighten the room so she could inspect the rock.

Turning it over in her hands, Morwë wondered why it had been important to keep. She could see nothing special about it, though the silver vein might be genuine. Holding the stone gave her a feeling of... peace. A steadying influence. As if Morwë held her mother's hand still.

Foolishness. It was a hunk of rock, nothing more. Still, by the smooth edges, Igrainne had had it a long time. It had meant something.

And I never asked what, Morwë thought, setting it carefully aside.

She lifted out two very fine gowns she barely remembered seeing her mother wear, heavily embroidered with fine silks and trimmed with fur. She draped them over the back of a chair. Underneath them, a stuffed black bag softly clinked as she touched it. Pulling open the drawstrings, she dumped it into her lap. A tangle of silver strands and gold chains poured from the bag, as well as clumps of jewels. Untangling the mass, she found broaches, earrings, necklaces, diadems, rings....

"Where did she get these?" Morwë whispered, fingering a broach encrusted with rubies that looked very old. *Oh*, she realized. *Father must have given these things to her.*

She dropped the thing as if it had bitten her.

She dumped all the jewelry back into its bag and set it aside.

Though the jewelry might rightfully go to the next wife her father took, it wouldn't matter if they were gone before then. The jewels could be useful when they left. Though moonlight knew what wights used for payment.

Digging further into the trunk, she found gloves, handkerchiefs, and a few more items of clothing. Pulling those out, she uncovered a small threadbare quilt, carefully pieced together. Morwë lifted it out and stared at it, fingering the stitches between her thumb and forefinger.

Mother had made it during her pregnancy with Enzella, after being forced into bed rest by Father and the thaumaturges. She had needed something to keep from going mad. That was when Morwë had been pulled from youngling classes. She remembered cutting some of the fabric squares, sewing them into blocks for the quilt.

Morwë laid it across her lap, touching the different textures. She could remember a little toddling Enzella dragging this around with her as she learned to walk, which impeded the process. Her sister had never let go of that thing until the tutors pried it out of her hand and forced her to make her letters.

Ingridon had tried to ruin it several times, Morwë recalled. *Out of spite.*

She stood and carried it over to Enzella, who frowned in her sleep. "Here, Zel," she said, tucking the blanket around her sister. "It's yours, after all."

And Mother had kept it.

Morwë blew a strand of hair out of her eyes and with some effort, turned back to the trunk. There wasn't much left in it, just a few more plain dresses, a thick shawl, a small strand of wooden beads that looked as if the string could break at any moment, and—

Morwë gulped, her fingers ghosting over the object before she lifted it out.

The cloth body had no discernable features. It didn't even have legs; just a dress and arms and a head, but the rag doll sported tiny, neat stitches.

"But he tore it up," Morwë whispered, rubbing a finger over the blank face. Ingridon had torn it to shreds when she was a toddling, and she had cried and cried when she was forced to go to the youngling dorms without it—

And Mother had found it, and stitched it back together, and kept it safe.

"I never even named her," Morwë told the dark room. Surrounded by the mysterious fragments of her mother's life, she stared unseeing at the wall, trying to fathom the woman who had been stolen against her will, lived with a people she hated, bore children in darkness, but....

She pressed the doll to her chest and rocked it. "Hush a-bye, don't you cry, go to sleep ye little baby. When you wake, you shall have all the pretty little horses...."

THIRTY-THREE

ENZELLA

"How do you feel, Princess?" the thaumaturge asked Enzella, gauging her reaction with sharp eyes.

Enzella shivered. His two-toned eyes bored into her, and she didn't know which to look at. "Itchy," she mumbled, glancing at Morwë who stood just behind him, hovering like a hawk waiting to pounce on prey.

"Try to sit up," Toren urged.

Scooting away from his assistance, Enzella levered herself up in bed, panting at the searing pain that raced down her side. When she grimaced, the cuts on her face ached as well.

"Princess—"

"There." Enzella glared at him, trying to breathe past the burn. "See? I can do it."

"Zel," Morwë muttered.

"Such signs are encouraging and bode well for your recovery, my princess." Toren lifted the cup steaming at her bedside. The pungent smell of herbs and magic tickled her nose. "This will help you heal from the inside."

Enzella stared into the cup and then looked up at her sister. Morwë nodded once. She must've watched him brew the mixture.

Toren held the cup as she drank, but Enzella insisted on

steadying it herself. The taste was worse than the smell. After two swallows, she had to stop and gag.

"It would be better if she drank the whole cup," Toren told her sister.

"I'm right here," Enzella snapped. "Can I have some water? I'll drink some more in a minute."

Morwë poured her a cup of water and Enzella gulped the water, washing the awful taste from her mouth. Then she cast a baleful look at the cup in the thaumaturge's hand. "All right. Again."

She managed to get the whole potion down in three more installments, interspersed with stomach heaves and glasses of water. The concoction made her feel dizzy and heavy, like her tongue was made of lead and her blood from mortar. Her stomach wasn't settling.

Morwë plumped the pillows behind her so she could lean back but remain upright. "Do you feel all right?" She pressed the back of her hand to Zel's forehead.

"Strange," Enzella admitted in a small voice. "Stomach's not happy."

"Mm. That's the potion. Let me see him off, and I'll get you more water." Morwë moved to the doorway of her chambers with Toren.

Enzella lifted her head, pricking her ears to pick up the muted conversation.

"You didn't come here just to bring Enzella a potion, did you Toren." Morwë's gaze could have pinned lesser men to the wall.

"Regrettably, no, my princess." Toren bowed. "At the fourth bell, the Erlking is calling a special session of court, and requires your presence to deal with several matters of state."

"I cannot leave Enzella."

"My lady," Toren said deliberately, "Your presence has been requested specifically. The official summons will arrive before the bell. I thought to forewarn you."

Morwë pressed her lips together until they were white. "Then consider me forewarned." Enzella could hear the crackle of ice in her voice.

Toren wisely said nothing more, merely bowing low on his exit of her chamber.

Morwë shut the door and leaned against it, her shoulders slumping into shadow. She took a long slow breath and looked up. "Heard all that, did you?"

Enzella nodded, fuzzy but awake.

"It seems I must go to court, but I won't leave you alone when you feel sick. Let me find someone trustworthy to sit with you."

Enzella nodded again, her mind seizing on a detail. "Why did Toren tell you about court?"

Morwë lifted one shoulder in a shrug, pouring her another glass of water.

"Did Demyen send him?" Zel asked around a yawn.

Morwë froze, water sloshing out of the pitcher into the cup. "Why would you say that?"

"Toren's his son. He's next in line to be leader of the cabal," Enzella offered.

"Demyen's son," Morwë muttered, helping her sip the cool water. "Circles and circles. Do you think you can stay awake long enough for me to go and come back?"

Enzella nodded, her brows drawing together. "Who are you going to get?"

Morwë's lips twitched upward. "It's a surprise."

THIRTY-FOUR

MORWË

Morwë did not put the guards to sleep this time; she told them the truth. "I'm retrieving my sister's wight to attend to her."

The bigger one spoke up. "Any prisoners leaving their cells will need to be manacled, my lady." The words were thick and garbled. His jaw was the wrong shape for speech; it looked as though it unhinged like a snake's.

"Very well," Morwë said impatiently. "Bring me a set of manacles, then." She waved a hand. The two lower Unseelie guards stepped aside with only the slightest hesitation, and an icy stare got her two salutes and bows.

Sweeping down the hallway, Morwë retrieved the keys from the ring on the wall and approached Micah's cell, the bigger Unseelie guard following.

In the glow of his tiny witch light, Micah looked up at her in surprise. In the next cell over, Arken jumped to his feet. "What are you doing?" he demanded.

Morwë ignored him and unlocked the door of Micah's cell. "Step out."

Micah cast a scared look at his brother, but stepped out. The Unseelie guard fastened a pair of manacles around his wrists.

"Answer me!" Arken insisted, reaching through the bars. He only evaded the guard's swing because he could see in the dark, and the guard did not move fast.

"Address the princess again and I'll cut out your tongue," the guard sneered. The crooked grin on his face indicated that he would enjoy it very much.

Behind him, Morwë shot Arken a poisonous glare. In her best frost voice, she snapped, "This wight is required to attend to his mistress, my sister. He will be returned once he has performed his duties." *Stop calling attention to yourself, you dolt.*

She imagined even true fire could not compare to the burning of Arken's blue eyes as he watched her leave the cellblock with Micah in tow. Thankfully he kept his head and held his tongue. Morwë felt a guilty twinge that she couldn't take the time to assure him all would be well. But all would *not* be well if she didn't get Micah to Enzella and herself to the throne room before the fourth bell.

Hurrying through the tunnels, Morwë used her Arts to cloak them from view so that busybodies or curious glances would not slow them. "I've been called to court," she told Micah as she pulled him along the hallway. "I can't refuse, but I need someone to sit with Enzella and make sure she's all right. She was dosed with a healing potion, but you'll need to give her water and to make sure she doesn't throw up."

"All right," he whispered.

"You'll both be safe," she assured him. "I have protection spells around my room. I just can't—" Horrified, Morwë stopped speaking as her voice cracked. She couldn't show weakness! Not now. Not when she needed every bit of her armor about her to step into the court.

"I understand," Micah whispered.

They journeyed the rest of the way in silence before Morwë swept him into the family suite and into her room, bypassing the protections on the door.

Enzella was still sitting up in bed, though she was drooping terribly. When she saw Micah in the doorway, the fuddled expression on her face dropped away and she smiled as best as she could under the bandages. "Micah!"

"You approve?" Morwë moved to the tray of food on the side table and reheated it with her Arts.

"Yes." Enzella patted the bed. "You can sit here, Micah."

"Are you all right, Zel?" the boy asked, touching her hand. His wide eyes took in her bandaged face.

"Apart from the stabbing." Enzella's smile twisted, revealing the crack in her cheerful façade.

"You and Micah can share this food." Morwë had assured it was free of contaminants. "Make sure she gets at least a little food and water, Micah, and then she can sleep. If her stomach is settled enough, she can lie down. I'll be back as soon as I can."

"How many bells?" Enzella mumbled.

Morwë unlocked Micah's manacles. "Shouldn't be more than two. I can't think what Father could talk about that would last longer than that. But don't open the door, no matter what," she warned Micah. "The door is spelled to keep intruders out. The garderobe is through there," she pointed, "and if you're tired, you can sleep, too."

Micah nodded. "I'll take care of her."

Morwë inhaled, the relief those words offered making her almost lightheaded. She ran a brush through her hair, retrieved a fancy court dress with her father's sigil on it, and slithered into it behind the screen in the corner. When the summons finally arrived, Morwë secured a strand of black beads around her neck and left, Enzella having proclaimed her fit for battle.

THE THRONE ROOM was still bare black stone roughhewn from the mountain, but a witch light chandelier hung over her father's carved onyx throne, and another hung over the room at large. Sconces filled with witch lights lined the walls. Along both sides of the room, the higher Unseelie sat or stood, murmuring gossip in each other's pointed ears. No one knew why the Erlking had called this session of court, and everyone had a theory.

Morwë usually avoided any type of court function because she hated the scrutiny, but this night she hated it because she had to sit so close to Ingridon, knowing the subterfuges to which he'd stooped to get his own way. In the seat closest to the throne, he lounged and sharpened his dagger. The sound grated on her, but she kept her teeth clenched together. She wouldn't give him an opening. Not today.

Her implacable mask in place, Morwë sat in her seat on the lower dais until the herald announced, "The Erlking of the Unseelie, Yemelyan Onyxeyes!" Then she stood with everyone else as her father entered the room and sat on his dark throne under the baldachin, its black swaths of cloth and feathers throwing the Erlking into shadow. Today he wore the onyx crown of office along with his personal sigil. Its tall stone points glinted razor sharp in the darkness. With a hand wave, he seated his audience.

Morwë sat and placed her hands in her lap, making sure not to clasp them too hard.

"Today I pass judgment on two of my subjects that would ignore my edicts and try to escape the boundaries I have set on my realm." The Erlking's fingers flicked. "Bring them out."

Two prison guards each dragged a prisoner forward along the floor.

At the snap of her father's fingers, Toren stepped out of the crowd and placed his hands on the first imp's face. Arts flowed along his skin, seeking the imp.

The prisoner's body convulsed, his face opening in a silent scream.

Morwë curled her fingers into her palms as the distinctive white patches appeared upon the prisoner's skin. Toren had drained him of any excess kneph and whatever magical Arts he may have possessed.

The prisoner slumped in the guard's hold as Toren moved to perform the same ritual to the second imp. By the time he finished, the imps were gibbering and crying, their eyes blown wide with need. Kneph-sickness was not a pretty sight.

The Erlking stood up from his throne, and the prisoners threw themselves against their chains, fighting the guards.

"Let it be known that the names of these two will no longer be spoken in my realm," the Erlking said. "All who challenge my edicts and eschew the consequences will share their fate. As punishment for their disobedience, I say that they shall be skinned."

A violent hush fell over the court. The prisoners screamed, begging for a quicker death than that. Morwë bit her tongue to keep herself from reacting.

The guards moved to haul the prisoners away, but the Erlking lifted a hand. "No. Their punishment will be meted out here and now."

Ingridon sat up in his chair and laughed.

Please don't let me be sick, Morwë thought.

A susurrus passed through the crowd, shock changing to fascination and a murderous glee as the guards brought forth a long, sharp knife.

And then the screaming began in earnest.

Morwë kept her gaze on a point at the far end of the throne room as the guard began his work on the first prisoner. The crowd began to jeer and take sick delight in the pain being displayed for their benefit. "Skin his backside next!" Ingridon called, his teeth gleaming bright and sharp.

Movement at her elbow. Morwë shifted her gaze, skating hurriedly over the growing puddle of blood on the stone floor. Toren had appeared at her side below the dais. As she stared at him from the corner of her eye, he met her gaze levelly, the silver of his eye glinting knowingly.

And suddenly Morwë hated him, hated them all, that they thought they knew so well what she thought, what she wanted.

She hated the torture and the ruthlessness, and the misery that battered her until she thought she couldn't breathe. She hated that Toren and Ingridon and her father and the rest of these imps felt entitled to any part of her.

Deliberately freezing her features into the most distant distain, Morwë pulled her gaze from Toren's and set it upon the far archway again, blocking out the screams and the blood and the terrible rip of flesh peeling away from muscle. She sent her thoughts away, seeking the magical defenses around her room, which stood solid. She touched the two lives within, assuring herself of their safety and wellbeing, before seeking out the presence in the prison level that vibrated with worry and anger and fear. She breathed in an unsteady breath as she touched his essence.

Arken.

THIRTY-FIVE

ARKEN

Arken couldn't keep himself from pacing the cell like a caged animal. Micah had been taken away a while ago—he had heard the distant echo of a bell, the way these faefolk kept time in their interminable dark. How long until Micah came back?

If Micah ever did come back.

Arken warred with himself. He was still loath to trust Morwë and Enzella, but if he couldn't, then he was entirely alone in the dark, and that tore at him. He hated feeling like this, helpless and wretched.

He took a deep breath and clutched the bars of his cell with one good hand and one magically stricken hand, pressing his forehead against the frigid metal. Even now, Morwë's image floated behind his eyes—wild black hair, bright keen eyes—a mountain storm in the form of a girl. She left an afterimage on his sight the way lightning did. Just as powerful, just as dangerous.

And then without warning, Arken felt her—could sense her presence very close to him. He couldn't explain it, except that he knew in his bones it was indelibly, irrevocably Morwë—and she was frightened.

Arken, he heard, and he couldn't say whether it was with his ears or his mind. The strain in her tone made his hands flex on the bars.

Why would she be reaching for him?

"Morwë," he whispered, so that no guards would overhear him.

The sensation he felt trembled.

Who else did she have except Enzella, who was injured and ill? Everyone else around her was a threat—her brother, her own *father,* who had offered her to Arken like he had been passing a dish at supper.

She would never reach for me unless she was desperate.

"Morwë," Arken said again, throwing caution towards the wind. If what he felt really was her, and she was frightened, then something had happened. She was the only one who could bring Micah back safe—and Arken was stuck here, in this cell, helpless. All he could do was reach back. Arken tried to put all the steadiness and reassurance he could into his voice. It didn't make sense that he should comfort her—his enemy, for all intents and purposes. But he wanted to. By God, he wanted to.

He had the strongest sense that if he turned his head, she would be there, at his shoulder, looking at him with that bottomless gaze. But he saw nothing in the dark, not even with his fernseed-blessed eyes.

Arken closed his eyes and forced himself to breathe slowly. He did the only thing he could do, when the barest touch of sensation brushed his arm. He placed his hand there, imagining that he touched her hand. "Morwë," he said. "Morwë." As if she was his last hope and touchstone.

Because, in a way, she was.

THIRTY-SIX

MORWË

The torture stretched for an eternity.

"Make sure to get a big piece!" Ingridon jeered from beside Morwë. "We need something to hang in the gate caverns to discourage other imps from sneaking out."

The screams had stopped. Morwë wasn't sure if the imp had died or merely passed out from agony, but now that the struggles had ceased the guards were industriously peeling away the flesh. The crowd jeered with the terrible relief that it wasn't them under the knife.

Her nose twitched from the awful, cloying smell of blood… and vomit and urine. The other prisoner had pissed himself, thrown up, and fainted from fear, in that order.

Finally, the guards held up some horrifying facsimile of skin for the Erlking's approval. Morwë couldn't feel her fingers, they were so cold and bloodless.

The Erlking waved a hand. "Take the other away and finish it; we have other business to attend to."

The guards took away the bloody mess and the other prisoner, but once they were gone, the floor was still smeared with blood and bile.

What else could there be?

The Erlking stood and took in the crowd, spreading his hands. "Let it not be said that I do not hear the concerns of my subjects," he said. "You are worried about this new land, and our position of power within it. You worry about Unseelie strength. But I say we are stronger than ever, having shed all weakness. And we will gain more power still."

The Erlking turned toward his children. "I have chosen to unite two of our most powerful thaumaturges to usher in a new age of magic. Morwë, my First Daughter, will wed Toren Demyenson at the new moon."

Morwë's thoughts fractured.

He'll marry you off, her mother's ghost whispered as the crowd shouted around her. *He'll foist Enzella on someone.*

Morwë jumped when Ingridon hissed, "Stand up and smile, idiot. Greet your future husband."

Toren stood at the bottom of the dais, waiting, his eyes on her.

The expression that passed over her face was more a baring of teeth, but she doubted the crowd knew the difference. She placed her hand, icy, limp, in Toren's, and waited until the crowd's noise died down.

"Thank you, Father," she said, and the lie made the ice floe in her body crack. Up through the fissure came something boiling, but she kept a grip on her tongue. She could not lose control. Not here. Not now. "Please excuse me while I speak to my... betrothed."

Her father nodded indulgently.

"Is that amenable?" she asked Toren in a colorless tone.

He nodded and assisted her down the dais steps, tucking her hand in his until they were out of the throne room and down the corridor. Then she couldn't wait another minute and ripped her hand from his grasp. "Did you know?" she demanded. "Did you?"

He tilted his head to the side like she was some particularly puzzling bug. "Yes."

She summoned her Arts instinctively.

He lifted his arms and brought them down hard in a chopping motion. The power she had gathered shattered and dispersed back into her, leaving her gasping with the backlash.

"Look at it this way, Morwë," Toren said in a cold voice as she clutched her aching hands. "I will be a better choice for you than Hadrian. I have more power and more status. And your father won't be Erlking forever." He gave her a significant look. "Not with an Heir like your brother. He is too impatient by half, apt to lash out without forethought—and he has no magic to support him."

The feel of his magic registered along with his words. "You. It was *you*."

Toren tilted his head to the side inquiringly.

"I couldn't taste your magic in the potions, but I have it now," she whispered. "Your magic broke my wards. You hurt Enzella, and then you had the unmitigated gall to come crawling back to heal her?" Her voice rose with anger until she was nearly shrieking.

"But I gave you warning," he snapped. "I broke your wards when I could've slipped Ingridon past them without you knowing. Your sister is a liability, and you know it, Morwë." His tone changed, cajoling now. "But I can help you keep her safe. No one would stand against the two of us, powerful as we are. And our children more powerful still." He wound a lock of her hair around his fingers. "I won't mind the trying," he said hoarsely.

"If you think for one moment I will ever let you touch me, you are dreaming."

Toren's eyes glinted, one keen and knowing, the other an unfathomable pool of darkness. "It's a dream I've been having for a long, long time."

THIRTY-SEVEN

MICAH

The door creaked slowly inward, rousing Micah from his doze.

He flinched awake, instinctively putting himself between Enzella's sleeping form and the intruder. Then the brazier's light lit Morwë's face. She shut the door behind her and moved to stare at her sister, looking unbearably weary.

"Morwë?" Micah whispered.

She settled onto the bed, and then curled into a ball. "I'll take you back in a moment," she said. "Just give me a moment."

Micah sat up, ignoring Enzella as she snuffled in dreams, and watched Morwë hold her knees in a death grip, surrendering to full body shakes. She shivered for nearly a whole three minutes—he knew because he began to count his own breaths.

And then she locked her shoulders and sat up, composed again behind a mask. "Was everything all right?"

Micah nodded. "She ate and then slept. She's been sleeping for at least a whole bell. It's been quiet."

She closed her eyes in relief.

"What happened?"

"I'd best get you back. Your brother will be worrying."

Micah stepped away from the manacles she picked up. "Morwë. Tell me."

She stared at him, face blank. "I'd like to tell you and Arken at the same time."

He froze. "Is it bad?"

"We'll… need to leave sooner than planned."

Micah let her clasp the manacles on his arms and shroud them from view on their way back to the frigid cells. At the entrance, she sent the guards to sleep and addled their minds.

Stepping into the cell block, Micah gagged. It smelled like a butcher's shop, the copper scent of blood thick in the air.

Before Micah could pick him out, Arken saw them coming. His brother hugged him through the bars. "Are you all right?"

"Yes," Micah assured him. "What is that smell?"

"They skinned a prisoner up here," Morwë said. "The first skinning was in court."

Micah's stomach churned.

And then Arken said something curious: "Is that why you were frightened?"

Micah just barely saw Morwë flinch. "It's become clear that time is running out for Enzella and me, and we need to go sooner rather than later. Tomorrow."

THIRTY-EIGHT

MORWË

"Tomorrow? Can we pull that off?" Arken rubbed his weakened hand. It looked strange to see the wizened, arthritic fingers attached to the strong, corded forearm.

"The moon is waxing," Morwë said. "There will be enough light for you both to see. I can send the guards to sleep. Enzella…." she faltered. "Enzella will still be injured but she should be able to ride." Provided they went slowly. But she had no guarantee of that.

"Have you told her?" Micah asked.

Morwë unlocked his cell and motioned for him to step into it. "Are you mad? Of course not; she can't keep anything to herself. Let me see your arm."

He extended a hand, and she wrapped her fingers around his wrist. "As far as I can tell, the bone is healing. Does it feel all right?"

"It itches," he said as she shut the cell door. "Aches sometimes, when it gets too cold in here."

"Can't you heal him all the way?" Arken asked.

"I can't heal it any further," she said. "If we go tomorrow, I'll need the power."

"Arken, you know she's right," Micah said quietly. "She can't heal your hand for the same reason. It's only one more day."

"Once we're out, I can try to reverse the spell." Morwë hoped. She had never tried to undo one of her father's workings before. "I may need the power for other tasks, though."

"Like what?" Micah asked. "Healing Enzella?"

"No, I can't heal Enzella. I can't work Arts on my own blood. I need it for tasks like masking our trail. Keeping us invisible from what pursuers may come. Or luring them away from you and your brother." Morwë flexed her hands at the thought.

"I thought we were going to stick together," Micah objected.

They had discussed their plan of action, where to head initially, and how to throw off pursuers. They hadn't gone into contingency plans.

"They'll be looking for Enzella and me," Morwë pointed out. "If they close in and things go poorly, you could take Enzella with you, and I'd lead them away. Wights are beneath the notice of most Unseelie. Unless they have the kneph hunger." The most important thing was to keep Enzella safe.

"I don't think your father is the type of man to forget important details," Arken said. "I'm surprised he hasn't come to visit."

"There's unrest in the lower caverns," Morwë said. "Packing imps too tightly together will do that. He must keep his hand on those who would make trouble before he can indulge in other matters. He has a plan to deal with the restlessness, but... that's another reason we have to leave."

Arken's head came up. "What happened?"

"He's going to marry me off."

He snarled. "To who?"

"A powerful thaumaturge."

"Is he as much of a scumbag as your brother and that guard?"

"Who, Hadrian?" she said blankly. Oh, for the days when Hadrian was the worst of her worries. "Toren is just as bad. Maybe worse, moonlight take his eyes."

"Is there a difference between Unseelie and imps?" Micah tilted his head to the side. "Enzella talks that way, too."

"Is that really important right now, Micah?"

"I'm just asking," Micah protested.

Morwë turned the words over in her mind, trying to explain. "As we call you wight, human, you call us faefolk. There are—were—many kinds, in different colonies and clans. As you are Altesians, we are Unseelie. Imps and sprites are… lower class. Rabble, base Unseelie."

"Scum, you mean." Arken set his mouth in a hard line.

"If you like," she sighed. She looked over her shoulder at the guard. "I have to get back. He will wake soon."

"Tomorrow night," Arken repeated, reaching for her hand. "Your word on it?"

She met his blue gaze and nodded. "Moonlight take my eyes if I lie."

"Well, let's hope it doesn't," Arken muttered, surrendering her wrist. "I have a feeling you might need them aboveground."

CHAPTER

THIRTY-NINE

ENZELLA

When Enzella woke, a little groggy but no longer in pain, Morwë was bustling around the room, stuffing clothes and other items into a sack. "What are you doing?" Enzella asked, shaking her hair out of her face and picking at the bandages on her face. She wished she could peel them off, but Morwë insisted they were there to keep the cuts from getting infected.

"Packing, Zel. How do you feel?"

"Lots better."

"Can you come here?"

Enzella slipped out of the covers and padded over to her sister. "Nothing hurts." She twisted a little and winced. "Only if I bend funny."

"Good." Morwë put her hands on her shoulders and said, "I need you to get boots on, and think hard about if you want to take anything from your room. We're going to leave."

"Leave?" Enzella's eyes opened wide.

"Yes," Morwë said, tone brisk as she turned away. "We're getting Micah and Arken, and we're leaving. Put your boots on, like I said."

Enzella scrambled to obey, shoving her feet into her boots. "I don't want anything."

"Are you sure?" Morwë folded up some objects in a cloth and tucked them into the sack. "Think about it—"

"I don't want anything," Enzella repeated, eyes flashing. "I just want to go."

"Fine. Sit here and eat this." Her sister pointed to the bowl cooling on the desk. "Keep your strength up."

"Have we got food to take with us?" Enzella asked, picking up the spoon.

"Yes, I took several loaves of bread from the kitchens, and I've got flasks of water." Morwë pushed her hair distractedly away, and then straightened to braid it back.

"Where are we going?" Enzella asked around the food in her mouth.

"Wherever Arken leads us."

She broke into a huge smile, ignoring the pain as her scabs stretched. "We'll have an adventure!"

"We'll see," Morwë muttered. "Put these on as well." She tossed a bundle of cloth at her sister.

Unwrapping the bundle, Enzella found a black cloak with a deep hood, a scarf, and gloves that went halfway up her arms. "Why do I have to wear this?"

"The *sun*?" Morwë settled her own cloak around her shoulders.

"Do you think Father was telling the truth when he said it would burn?"

"I don't know, Zel. I don't want to take any chances."

"Do you think it will be enough protection?"

"What did I just say? I don't know. Put it on."

Grousing, Enzella put the ensemble on and went back to eating. Sometimes she hated bossy Morwë. "So when will we go?"

"Whenever it's quiet and folk are preparing for sleep, near the dawn bell."

After Enzella finished her food, they sat in silence for a long while. Morwë braided Enzella's hair back and tucked it under the cloak's hood before swaddling her face in the scarf, doing the same for herself. Then they sat and waited. Enzella swung her legs idly off the bed. She was sure Morwë was doing something magical to sense the colony's movement, to check and see when it was safe.

"Did you take anything?" Enzella finally asked.

Morwë looked up. "What?"

"Did you take anything of yours? To bring with you?"

"No. My books would be too heavy to take. We need to travel light." Morwë patted the bag in her lap. "Just essentials. And a few things of Mother's."

"Mother's?" Enzella repeated, sitting up straight.

"Your quilt, remember? I showed it to you?"

"Yes, but that's mine, not Mother's."

"Mother made it," Morwë pointed out.

"What else?"

"Her jewelry, in case we need to barter, or... or trade...." Morwë's voice trailed off, sounding unsure. "And some other odds and ends. I'll show you once we're away." She set her shoulders, voice growing hard. "They're settling. It's time to go."

Enzella took Morwë's gloved hand and held her breath as they crept out into the hallway. At every bend or fork in the passageway, Morwë would pause and look both ways before hurrying them along. If anyone came by, Morwë forced them into a crevasse to hide. The darkness was deep along here, and Morwë always stood in front of her, but each time Enzella stopped breathing until whoever it was passed by. Once they came upon bodies entwined in the hallway, but they were occupied enough not to notice.

They finally made it to the cellblock, and Enzella sighed in a huge gust as Morwë snapped her fingers and sent the guard into a deep sleep. "Hold the bag while I get the keys, Zella," Morwë instructed. Enzella hefted the sack and hurried as fast as her side would let her to Micah. The wound was beginning to ache.

"I missed you!" she exclaimed, pulling the scarf down from her mouth. "We're escaping! Isn't that fun?"

Morwë came up behind her and inhaled sharply. "Where's Arken?"

Enzella's heart skipped a beat. The other cell was empty.

FORTY

MORWË

"Morwë, they came and took him," Micah forced out, white faced, as Morwë turned the key in the lock and opened the door.

"Who?" Morwë could feel her pulse thumping in her ears.

Enzella grabbed Micah's hand and held it as he stepped out of the cell.

"Your brother, and that other man," Micah replied in a shaky voice.

"My father?" Morwë demanded, voice tight.

"No, the guard—your brother's friend. Please, Morwë, we can't leave without him."

Her mouth twisted. Ingridon and Hadrian... with Arken. They had decided that his time was up. "How long ago?" she asked, her hope slipping away.

"A few hours. I'm not sure," Micah gulped.

"How many bells rang?"

He hesitated. "Two? Maybe three? I can't...."

Morwë met his pleading eyes. Her traitorous mouth said, "He might already be dead."

"He isn't! I swear he isn't!" With his free hand, he clutched at her. "He's my brother."

"And you've met *mine*. Arken's chances aren't good."

"We've got to try," Micah begged. "Please. *Please,* Morwë."

Her gaze flicked between him and Enzella. Part of her wanted to toss them both onto a horse and be gone from here. She didn't know where Arken had been taken. And once she found him, she couldn't fight Ingridon with her Arts. He was her blood. And she had no skills in combat.

"Lady," Micah whispered, eyes shining with unshed tears and desperate certainty, "I don't know the mountains, and I can't see in the dark. We will not make it without him."

The doomed silence settled around them all like a shroud.

Morwë drew in a long, slow breath. "Enzella, you take Micah to the stables. Saddle the horses. Go to the gate cavern and wait for me there. If I don't arrive in one bell's time...." Morwë trailed off. She was the only one who could release the spells on the gate. If she wasn't there, they couldn't get out. She swallowed hard. "Never mind that. Go on."

Enzella nodded, eyes wide. She pulled on Micah's arm.

"Thank you," Micah whispered before Enzella tugged him away.

Morwë closed her eyes and didn't let herself consider what would happen if she didn't come back.

She waited until they had gone. Then she squared her shoulders and called up her Arts, the power crackling in her veins. She sent herself out through the colony, searching for Arken—his blue eyes, his unflinching hands, his steady anger. And then she felt him, the anger, the pain... the unrelenting grief of failure.

Morwë opened her eyes and stared at the sliver of moonlight trickling through the cell. What had Father said about it? *'Nothing kills the will as much as hope that never bears fruit'?*

She would prove him wrong. Prove them all wrong.

Hold on. I am coming.

FORTY-ONE

ARKEN

rken fought to breathe past the pain as he waited for the lash to come down again. "Oh, a whipping," he had said. "How original."

The pale devil had just bared his teeth in some facsimile of a smile while the other one chained him to a pole.

Now he was eating his words.

The whip whistled as it arced down again. Arken set his teeth in time to stifle his cry as the barbed end met flesh. Blood dripped down his back from the open welts. They'd been doing this for a while, and he was starting to see stars from the pain and the blood loss. His muscles trembled. *I feel like a horse that's just run a hundred miles,* he thought hazily, resting his head and as much weight as he could against the pole.

"Would you like to try again?" Ingridon sneered. "What were you doing in our caverns?"

Arken forced his mouth to move. "My answer… isn't going to change." He lifted his eyes to glare at Ingridon. "I stumbled on it."

The backhand sent Arken flying back as far as the chains would allow. At the movement, his body screamed with agony.

"I think your tongue will loosen soon enough." Ingridon coiled the whip back into loops, handing it to Hadrian. "Maybe sooner, if I had my carving knives. Or a set of thumbscrews." The men laughed.

Arken's back muscles spasmed as he tried to control the pain. He was going to die here. This torture wouldn't end any other way. But he'd be damned if he'd betray Micah. With any luck, his torture would be the distraction they'd need to get out of the mountain. He'd die—but Micah would live. He had to believe that.

"Hmm." Ingridon circled him, eyeing his clenched fists, the set of his jaw. "Interesting."

Arken looked up to meet his gaze, and wished he could muster up enough saliva to spit.

Like a snake striking, Ingridon reached out and pried his left hand open, twisting Arken's second finger viciously.

They all heard the bone crack. Arken gasped, stars exploding behind his eyes.

"The dog yelps," Hadrian chuckled.

"Keep after him," Ingridon told his friend. "I'll go get the thumbscrews. We'll get you to sing yet, dog." His footsteps retreated down the passageway.

The finger had broken in such a way that bending it made Arken want to faint again. He could not clench that hand without sending shooting pains through his finger. He sucked air through his mouth, panting, praying to faint. Then, at least, he might feel some relief.

"You are a miserable cur," Hadrian said conversationally, unsheathing his sword.

Arken barely saw him move before the weapon flashed towards him. He tried to dodge, but the chains would not allow him to move. The hilt slammed into the knuckles of his other hand, the one the Erlking had withered.

Arken shouted as the fragile bones gave way. His knees threatened to buckle as the yawning maw of pain raged through him.

"You know all the tricks: yelp, pant, whine… now all that's left is beg." Hadrian set his sword at the back of Arken's neck.

Arken bared his teeth. He'd bite his own lips bloody before that happened. He looked up, to spit what little moisture he had left in his mouth—and froze.

Hadrian gasped. An unseen force thrust his body across the room. His head hit stone with a solid thwack.

Arken twisted around as best he could. "Morwë!"

FORTY-TWO

MORWË

Her hands thrumming with energy, Morwë threw Hadrian with all the force she could muster into the wall. His head cracked against the stone, and he fell in a crumpled heap.

She dashed to Hadrian's body and dimly noted he still breathed as she searched him. The keys to the chains were in his pocket. Fumbling through them, she found the right key and ran to Arken.

"Morwë, you have to go! What are you doing here?" Arken forced out, sounding stronger than she knew he felt.

"What does it look like?" The key scraped against the shackles as her hands trembled violently.

He shook his head, blue eyes wide as he stared up at her. "You came back for me."

The key turned in the lock. "No choice. We couldn't leave without you."

Arken's throat bobbed. "You could have. But you came back for me."

Not interested in belaboring the point, she pulled the shackles off. "What's the matter with you? Blood loss?" His back was a mess of blood and whip marks.

"Somewhat," he mumbled. "Mostly the hands."

She hissed, seeing the broken fingers misaligned. "Can you stand?"

"There's nothing wrong with my legs," Arken insisted, straightening inch by painful inch as the skin on his back stretched. The blood dripped off him to land in coppery smears on the stone. "Point me in the direction of the surface and I'll crawl if I have to. Hand me my shirt and tunic?"

She snatched up the fabric and steadied him with hand on his elbow. "Here, I'll do it. Your hands are in no state to do anything. I can fix that, but not now." She eased the shirt and tunic over his head.

He hissed when the fabric met his back, but growled, "Just do it. We've got to get out of here. Saints above and below, Morwë. Why did you do it? You've got to open that gate. If they catch us—"

"They *won't*." She looked him dead in the eye. "Micah said we wouldn't make it without you to guide us down the mountain. And he's right. Zel and Micah need both of us." Pressing her lips together, she got his arms through the sleeves and draped her cloak around him as gently as she could. "Hold onto me."

Morwë supported him through the tunnels as they ran from prying eyes. She could feel Arken's heat through her cloak, and the slippery blood that dripped down his arms and back. How much time did they have? When would Ingridon return? She had seen him leave and acted, figuring she wouldn't get a better chance.

When they came upon an alcove that recessed a little deeper into the rock, she pulled Arken into it and used her belt knife to tear strips from his shirt. Arken winced and braced himself against the icy rock. Morwë bound the fingers of his right hand together to stabilize them, knowing there was little she could do at the moment for the smashed and brittle bones. Arken hissed through his teeth but didn't protest.

Tying off the knot, Morwë took another strip of cloth and reached for his left hand. "This will hurt," she told him, "but I need to put your finger back into place, and we don't have time for healing now."

"Do it," he said, gritting his teeth.

She set her own teeth and took hold of his fingers before giving the digits a swift yank to realign the bone.

As much as he tried to hold back, Arken yelled sharply, sweat rolling down his face as he gasped through the pain.

"Hold on," Morwë murmured, hands shaking as she started to tie the broken index finger against its neighbor for a brace.

They both froze at the sound of rapidly approaching footsteps.

Morwë looked up into Arken's haggard face, seeking out his wide eyes through sweat-plastered hair. She hauled him around by the arm so that his taller build and the long black cloak covered them both. He braced his arms on either side of her. She laid a finger to her lips as the footfalls and a chorus of laughter rounded a bend in the passage.

He stared down at her, eyes wide with fear and something else —fierce certainty. If they were discovered, he would fight.

Morwë knew her face must look the same. She was close enough to breathe his breath.

"Good one, mate," an imp cackled over what must have been a just-told joke. "Ohh, lover's tryst!" He whistled at their shape in the alcove.

"Give it to 'er good," the other said. The smell of wine wafted through the hallway with them.

"Make it last!" the first imp called back as they continued on their way. "Hallway tumblers are so overeager!" They both hooted in unison, continuing to utter unsavory comments on the nature of desperation as they walked on.

Neither Morwë nor Arken moved until the two Unseelie were safely around a corner and their voices had faded. Morwë squeezed her eyes shut as tremors overtook her body.

"Charming," Arken murmured, though his voice shook from relief. "Which way now?"

She nodded, eyes opening. "It's not far," she forced out. She moved to help him. "Are you all right?"

"I'll be all right when we're out of this mountain," Arken breathed. He leaned against her, and Morwë gripped him tightly, very aware of the warm blood still leaching from his body.

DIM WITCH LIGHTS lit the large entrance cavern as Morwë and Arken stumbled down the stairs.

"Arken!" Micah called, running to his brother's side to take some of his weight. "What happened to you? Are—"

"I'm all right, Micah," Arken rasped. "Time to go."

"I've got the horses!" Enzella said, still swaddled.

Micah took in his brother's state with a single look and paled. "We'll have to help him onto the horse." Micah ran for one of the horses and led it towards Arken.

"Step into my hands," Morwë said as Arken reached for the horse's mane with his mangled hands. "I'll toss you up."

Arken winced when his hands would not cooperate. "Don't worry about me, Morwë. Do whatever it is you have to do to get the gate open."

"Yes, Morwë. Open the gate."

They all whirled around.

Ingridon stood at the top of the steps.

"Morwë?" Enzella whispered, voice wavering.

Morwë's eyes darted from her brother to her sister, heart in her throat.

"Open the gate, Morwë," Arken ground out, his eyes trained on Ingridon. "He's only one man. We'll hold him off."

"Go ahead, you traitorous wench. Open it. Open the gate," her brother sneered, slowly descending the stairs. "I knew someone must have helped the wight escape, but you? *You?*" Ingridon shook his head. His hair flashed in the low light. "Set off the spells to open the gate, and every Unseelie thaumaturge will come running. You know how much power it takes to open the gates. And then where will you be? Weak. How will you fight them off then? What will you do... against Father?" He took another step, unsheathing his sword that gleamed a dull blue in the witch lights. "And you can't use your magic tricks on me, Morwë."

"Morwë, open the gate; we can outpace him," Arken urged. "Micah, you ride with Enzella." He gave his brother a shove. Micah ran to the other horse and boosted Enzella up before mounting.

"Where will you run?" Ingridon called, his lips curling back to show his teeth. "Where will you hide? I'll find you, Morwë. I'll follow you to the end of the mountains, to the end of the earth if I have to, you traitor to your species. Traitor to your own blood!"

Arken hauled himself onto remaining horse using his forearms and extreme force of will, as well as muttered cursing. "Climb on, Morwë; don't listen to the bastard!"

Morwë took a deep breath and locked her shoulders. "My blood is half human. I'm traitor to nobody." She closed her eyes and poured her power into the spell components that controlled the cavern's large rock gates. As the magic infused the spell, the gates thrummed with power and unlocked, slowly swinging inward. She felt her Arts' levels decrease with the amount of effort it took.

"Morwë, come on!" Arken urged, holding out his left hand as the horses danced nervously. The cold night air whipped at her skirts. She reached for his arm blindly, unable to tear her eyes from her brother.

Ingridon dragged the tip of his sword along the stone. "I'll consume your little wights as dinner, and then I'll make you watch—you think what I did to Zel was bad? You have no idea!" His face twisted into a ghoulish smile. "I'll carve her up piece by piece and make you watch, slow enough that you'll wish for her death! And then I'll kill you, just the way I told Father to kill our waste of a mother, you worthless lump of flesh!" He spat at her, nearly to the floor, nearly upon them.

Morwë could feel he was right—the spell alerted the Unseelie thaumaturges, and they were coming. The alarm had sounded. The fear that she had tried so desperately to keep at bay clawed its way up her spine and around her throat, tightening. In moments they would be overrun.

"If you run, I will find you, and I will kill you!" Ingridon yelled, holding out his sword. "I promise you, Morwë! I promise you that!"

Through the terror thrumming in her ears, she could just barely pick out Enzella's panicked voice. "Morwë?"

"Micah, ride out! We'll be right behind you!" Arken commanded.

One horse bolted for the open gate, her sister's cry flowing back to her. *"Morwë!"*

The memory crashed through her like a boulder. Enzella, confident, proud: *"Morwë's the best thaumaturge in the underground."*

Morwë's hand found Arken's forearm and grasped it. She opened her mouth and screamed.

Power erupted from her, and more power came to her call, following the spell lines that powered the gate, burrowing into the rock, up from the ground, into the mountain. Following the natural fissures, it poured into the stone as she screamed, igniting—something.

More, Morwë thought. *More!* She barely felt Arken haul her up across the horse's withers.

"You can't stop me!" Ingridon howled over the growing rumble from under the ground. Dust began to sift from the cavern roof.

Yes, I can, she thought, feeding all the power she had in her body, all the strength in her fingers to the stone. The mountain no longer felt hard and immutable—it flowed through her mind, molten, vibrant—alive.

Arken wheeled the horse around and made for the gate, but still she could not look away from her brother. Blood gushed from her nose as for a moment, Morwë *was* the mountain—tip to toe, living stone, to do with what she willed.

Then the cavern collapsed.

FORTY-THREE

ENZELLA

The darkness was lifting.

As the sky grew paler over the mountain's broken crest, Enzella watched wide-eyed as softly falling snow coated the land. The white powder dusted the branches of the firs and the poplars, landing lightly on her cloak and settling in between the fabric's folds to mix with stone dust. In front of her, snowflakes settled on Micah's head and ears, melting into his dirty hair. On the other horse, Arken held Morwë in front of him and pressed onward, finding a path down the mountain.

Morwë still hadn't woken up.

Enzella's stomach twisted. She gulped and stared at the sky as snowflakes spiraled down in a complicated dance. They had made a mad dash from the gate cavern and down the mountain as the stone collapsed. Enzella could still taste the grit on her tongue from the cloud of dust that had billowed out behind them as they ran headlong down the slopes. It must have filled in all the tunnels the thaumaturges had hollowed out. And now, after the rocks settled, the peak of the mountain—Micah had said it was called Ceridfel—was crooked.

And Morwë had done that. But it had been a *while* since then; why hadn't she woken up?

As Enzella tilted her head back, a snowflake landed on her eyelid, another on her nose. She squeaked.

"Are you all right?" Micah asked, trying to twist around to see her. "Is it your wound? Do you need to stop?"

Enzella licked the snowflake off her nose. "No." She stuck her tongue out to catch another flake and wash away the dust in her mouth.

When he caught a glimpse of her over his shoulder, Micah laughed.

Arken reined in his horse until he was even with Micah. "I think we can stop and rest a bit. If there are any pursuers, they're not close. We would have heard something by now. And dawn ought to be soon—I think we're safe for the moment." A muscle in his jaw flexed. "I've got to do something about my hands."

"Do you think we'll *have* pursuers?" Micah looked between his brother and Enzella. "The mountain did collapse."

"They have magicians; I wouldn't overestimate them," Arken muttered.

"Even thaumaturges die if you drop a mountain on them," Enzella pointed out, leaning out to catch a particularly big flake. She missed, and it melted against her cheek. She licked it off anyway.

Micah glanced around. "You want to stop here?"

"Up in that grove, maybe," Arken said, nodding towards it. "If you can dismount and take Morwë from me, that would help."

"I'm awake." The quiet voice rasped with exhaustion.

"Morwë!" Enzella exclaimed.

Her sister slowly straightened in Arken's arms. "What happened?"

"The mountain fell down," Arken said, assisting her. "Do you think you can slide down on your own, or should Micah catch you?"

"I can do it," Morwë muttered with grim determination, shifting slowly.

"Hang onto my arm if you need to."

Micah dismounted within the grove and reached up to help Enzella.

Enzella launched herself into his outstretched arms but paid for it when her side pulled. She gasped.

Micah eased her to the ground. "A little warning next time," he teased gently.

"Next time," she said as the pain eased. "Morwë, the mountain is crooked now! They're all dead! The horses almost fell maybe four times! It was amazing!"

FORTY-FOUR

MORWË

T he impact of Enzella's words hit Morwë just as she had finished easing herself down the horse's shoulder. Her knees buckled. Only a white-knuckled grip on the horse's mane kept her upright.

A second later, Arken reached down and pinned her against the horse with his arm. "Are you all right?"

Of course, he has no grip, Morwë thought, as her heart hammered in her chest. The sensation of being pressed against him was... different. "Yes." She locked her knees and pried her fingers open. "You can let go now."

Arken moved his arm, and Morwë turned to lean against her sister.

"Do you remember the ride, or did you faint right away?" Enzella demanded, wrapping her arms around Morwë's waist. "It was all in the dark, Morwë! I had to tell Micah where to go; he couldn't see! Arken could, of course."

"Take a few deep breaths and let me sit down, Zel," Morwë said, hoping her sister could not tell how her hands were shaking.

Dead. All. She had killed them all. How many Unseelie had come with them to the mountain, fifteen hundred? Three thousand?

Maybe I am my father's daughter, too.

She ran a hand over her face and felt her gloves catch on her lips and chin. She pulled off her glove and touched her face. Dried blood.

"You had a nosebleed; do you remember that?" Arken asked, slithering off the horse.

"Yes; I didn't faint until the cavern collapsed," Morwë said, scrubbing at the blood. She scooped up some snow and rubbed it over her face. "Are you all right, Zel? How is your side?"

Enzella sat down beside her. "Same as before. I'm hungry."

Her mouth watered at the thought of food, her stomach twisting in emptiness. "Get the bread out of my bag," Morwë told her, "and give some to Arken and Micah, too." She glanced to the east and saw the bright light flare over the horizon. Pulling her hood over her face, she tugged Enzella's over her head as well.

"Morwë," Enzella complained as she tried to pass the food around.

"We don't know what it will do," Morwë said, wincing as the world around her brightened. "Don't be foolish." She chewed a hunk of bread, but it did little to curb the ache in her stomach. She drank from the water skin to ease her parched throat and turned to Arken. "How are your hands?"

"Well, they've been better," he admitted with an ironic twist to his mouth, holding his share of bread awkwardly between his wrists.

"And your back?" she pressed.

"The bleeding's stopped. Don't worry about that now. If you can do something about this hand, I'd be grateful." He indicated the left hand that had only had one finger damaged.

"Eat first. Then I'll look at it." It was the least she could do to atone for her family's horrors. Morwë turned back to her own portion as the snow continued to fall.

She felt a strange pain in her chest, a deep ache that would not relent, and a weakness in her fingers. They wanted to tremble as she held the bread to her mouth. But Morwë steeled her muscles until she had eaten all the bread, and then leaned back against a tree trunk. Her spine fit between the grooves of the bark, and the tremors in her body passed as she let the tree trunk support her. But she felt just as hungry as before.

What is the matter with me? Her eyes tried to close against the increasing light and the utter exhaustion that clawed at her bones. She scooped up more snow and pressed it to her face, barely registering the cold. *Well, I did bring down a mountain.*

Morwë let her hands drop to her lap as the word whispered through the back of her mind. *Murderer.* The accusation bit deep, threatening to cast her into a deep well of oblivion.

I didn't mean to. I didn't know.

Killer, then. But they were still dead.

Ingridon would have killed me. *Killed us all, without a thought.* Morwë watched her sister continue what she thought was clearly a clever game of "catch the snowflakes on her tongue." Enzella giggled each time one missed her mouth. Watching Zel, Morwë felt the deep chasm within her close, just a bit, and she regained her poise.

Maybe I am not a full monster, then, if I can feel this weight.

As true sunlight flooded through the trees, she pulled her scarf over her nose and did the same for Enzella. "Aww, Morwë," Enzella complained, muffled by the scarf. "I want to keep catching snowflakes."

"Shh," Morwë murmured. "We'll probably move on after I do a working on Arken. Go help Micah with the horses." She turned to Arken. "Let me see your hand."

He held out his left hand. "Should I take the wrappings off?"

"How?" Morwë asked, some black humor leeching into her tone.

Arken shot her an exasperated look.

She managed to laugh a little. "No. I don't know how much I can do right now. The bandages will help support it." She took his hand and felt along the index finger. She had put it back, but now she searched for the break as well as any tears to the ligaments and muscle, or damage to nerves. She called up her Arts—and nearly reeled.

Stars sparked behind her eyes as she tried to transfer her power from herself to Arken. Where normally a deep pool of power resided, now only a mere trickle flowed. Morwë gritted her teeth until the roaring in her ears passed.

"Morwë? What's the matter?"

She looked up to meet Arken's worried eyes.

"Nothing," she ground out.

"My hand can wait, you know, if you need to rest…."

"Stop talking," Morwë snarled, and forced her Arts to knit his finger back together.

Though it felt as if she peeled away at her own skin to heal him, she did it. As she breathed through the pain and the weakness, she felt gratified to see him wince and gasp. "There," she sighed. "It will probably need another healing later. Bones take a while."

"Micah wasn't wrong," Arken said after a minute, blinking rapidly. "That was freezing." He flexed the fingers of his left hand. "But it doesn't hurt anymore."

"Good," she murmured, tugging her gloves back on.

His eyes flicked back to hers. "Thank you, Morwë."

She waved away his thanks and stood up. "Shouldn't we be getting on?"

FORTY-FIVE

MICAH

They reached the outskirts of Peridun by late morning. Micah swallowed and reined in his mount as he took in the sight. The gates hung broken and sagging from the entrance to the village, and the snow blew in through the opening, collecting in drifts around the walls. He hadn't been able to see any of it that terrible night.

"It's so quiet," Micah whispered. He had lived nearly his whole life in Peridun. He couldn't recall a time when there were no voices ringing out through the streets, animals baying, or the clatter of tools and dishes on the wind. Even in the middle of night in the dead of winter, you could faintly hear the rumble of voices or quiet strains of music from the one tavern at the center of the village.

It's a ghost town, he thought, swallowing past a lump in his throat.

"Come on," Arken said, swinging off his mount. He helped Morwë down with his good hand. "We need to search for any supplies that weren't stolen or shipped off with Father James."

"And a wagon," Micah said automatically as Enzella slithered off from behind him to land in a snowdrift. She was so swaddled in black, he couldn't even see her eyes, but Micah knew she was all right from the laugh she let out upon landing.

"Not a wagon," Arken said, glancing around him at the snow that hadn't let up for hours. "That won't do us much good. We'll have to find a sleigh." He strode off through the gates, Morwë and Enzella trailing behind him like black shadows.

The shorter shadow turned around and lifted a hand. "Come on, Micah!"

Swallowing past the dryness in his mouth, Micah swung off his horse and led it into the village.

The scenery looked normal—no dead bodies or scorch marks from fire. *Of course not*, Micah told himself, *they needed us alive.* He twitched, remembering the screams as black-clad figures pulled him out of bed and into a throng of people. Unseelie laughter echoing through the night air as the humans cried. Watching families separated and pulled apart, and the ones who resisted stupefied by magic.

He swallowed hard. If not for the open and broken doors, he could have believed the villagers would be back at any moment. But snow collected in the doorways leading to darkness. No hearth fires burned. No lamps glowed.

He closed his eyes against the agony of loss and guilt.

"Micah?"

Enzella looked at him, her eyes barely visible through the hood and scarf.

"What," he muttered, scratching his horse around the ears.

"Are you all right?"

I'm afraid I'll never be all right again. "Everyone who lived here is dead now. Almost everyone I've ever known." He glanced oddly at Enzella. "Everyone you've ever known is dead, too."

She shrugged. "I don't care that much."

He stared at her. "What?"

"Ingridon was horrible and tried to kill me. Jezra and Hadrian and Toren helped hurt me. Father killed Mother, and everyone else was glad she was gone." Enzella's face was stony.

It pained him to see her innocence whittled away. "You have a point."

The gelding nudged him, hoping for a treat. "Let's find you something to eat, hmm?" Micah whispered to him, starting for home. There might be a supply of Bess's oats left, or maybe a few wizened apples the horse would like. Micah rubbed his hand over the black bay's coat. *We ought to name them.*

Enzella hurried to keep up on short legs as Micah moved through the streets. He'd know the way home blindfolded.

When they reached home, Micah swung around the side and towards the run in shed where Bess had lived rather than look at the front of the cottage. He untacked the bay and rubbed him down. "What do you think we should call him?" he asked after a time, pouring out a measure of oats for the horse. Enzella had hovered nearby in silence for a long time, which was odd.

The ramshackle shadow took a hesitant step forward. "I don't know."

"I was thinking Spot, or Star, or maybe Onyx," Micah said, pointing to its blaze as the horse happily munched oats.

"Not Onyx," Enzella said immediately, her face twisting.

"All right. How about Star?"

"I like Star," she admitted. She took another step forward. "You didn't answer my question. *Are* you all right?"

He gazed off into the gray sky, sending snowflakes spiraling as he exhaled. "No, Zel. I'm not all right."

"I'm sorry."

In the light of day, he knew the truth. "It wasn't your fault." Micah touched her shoulder. "Come on, let's look for supplies." He led the way through the snowy ground, flakes crunching underfoot, to the front of their cottage. Then he stepped in the doorway.

There in the corner stood his mother's loom, ready for a new project now that the cloth she had woven had been turned into a new blanket for a baby. His niece.

"She's probably born by now," Micah said to the empty room.

"Who?" Enzella tilted her head to the side.

"My sister's baby. My mother went to help her… the baby's probably born now. I wonder if it's a boy or girl."

"You lived here?" Enzella asked, her eyes scanning the small front room with curious eyes.

"My whole life."

A door led back to his mother's room, and the narrow stairs to the loft above. The hearth was cold, and the cupboards stood empty, perhaps taken by Arken when he had had to supply Father James and the children. Micah didn't want to think about the alternative.

Micah pulled on the iron ring to open the cellar door. "Hand me that candle, Zel."

"What's down there?"

He struck the flint and the wick caught, a warm gold light spilling down into the darkness. "Food, I hope. You want to come?"

"No. I don't want to go underground again."

He raised an eyebrow in surprise. "All right. I'll see what's down here and hand it up to you, then."

As Enzella poked around upstairs, Micah climbed down the ladder into the cellar and held the candle aloft. In the cellar he could see sacks of grain, a few casks of salted fish, and a few crocks of unknown origin, probably pickled vegetables or preserves his mother put down earlier in the year. Some of it was missing, but it didn't look like a herd of caribou had come through to clean them out.

"Micah," Enzella called down, "here's Arken."

Micah looked up. "Was it you who went through the cellar?"

"Yes," Arken said, coming down the ladder. "We ran out of room in the wagon and couldn't take it all. But that works in our favor."

"Did you find a sleigh?"

"Yes, there was one in Elara Johansen's barn. We'll need both horses to pull it, though."

"Star's out back in Bess's shed," Micah said absently, starting to take crocks off shelves.

"Who?"

"We named my horse Star." Micah glanced at Arken. "Where's Morwë?"

"Sitting with the other horse outside. She's tired."

"Still?"

Arken shot him a look. "She *did* bring down a mountain. That would tire anybody."

"Right," Micah mumbled. "And your hand's no good. And Zel's still healing."

A shadow appeared above the door. Morwë said, "I can help. What do you need?"

FORTY-SIX

ARKEN

With only Micah totally hale, it took time to gather their supplies. Arken had only one hand that worked and a back that screamed at him. They had to make sure Enzella didn't overtax herself and reopen her healing wounds. Morwë could only make one or two trips at a time before stopping for a rest.

Arken didn't let on how much this worried him. He busied himself with carrying what he could and hitching the horses to the sleigh one-handed. The snow still had not stopped.

"Do you think we should go on?" Morwë asked him as Micah and Enzella ferried casks and sacks from the cellar to the sleigh. Enzella had a good time rolling the casks along the ground.

Arken slid a sack off his shoulder and onto the sleigh, ignoring the flames that licked up his back. Pain was for later. "The snowfall hasn't gotten thicker. With two horses, we ought to make good time. We could make Cairenoch in three days." He glanced around at the empty cottages as the wind whispered through the streets, and then up to Ceridfel's new shape. "To be honest, I'd rather camp along the road than stay here. We don't know that we're safe yet."

Morwë nodded. "It's unlikely that many could have survived… but it is possible."

As Enzella and Micah came laughing out of the house, Arken murmured, "Best keep that between us for now."

Allies now, Arken decided as they discussed their options, *fully allies*. In the mountain, he had still been wary of Morwë, and trust had not come easily. But she had come back for him.

He shivered as his back stung, feeling the lash lick his skin again, the bones break. He had tasted death… and then wild, unlooked-for hope had flared to life. Because of a princess who owed him nothing.

Arken swallowed as he watched her gaze at the street, just a figure in black except for her eyes, shadowed by her wide hood. The most astonishing woman he had ever met.

"That's it!" Micah called as he hauled his last cask into the sleigh and dusted his hands. "I don't think the horses could pull more than that."

"There's still some empty space in there," Arken said, narrowing his eyes.

"Well, we need somewhere to sit," Micah pointed out. "Plus… I was thinking… maybe we could bring Mother's loom to her."

Arken pursed his lips and turned the idea over in his mind, weighing the time it would take to dismantle and transport the loom. "It's a good thought," he said at last. "But once we get to Cairenoch and let everyone know what's happened, we can make firmer plans about the future. It's only a few days' journey back. We can get it for her then." *It would be enough*, Arken thought, *to bring you back to her, Micah.*

He swallowed. *I still can't believe we made it out alive.* It was all thanks to Morwë.

Micah looked away, the corners of his mouth turning down.

"Hey," Arken said, placing a hand on his brother's shoulder. "It was a good idea. Doesn't she have a hand loom somewhere? We could bring her that. And some of her thread and yarn, so she could start a new project."

"It's in her room! I'll get it." Micah dashed back into the cottage.

"Have we got everything else we'll need?" Arken asked, glancing back at Morwë and Enzella, who were organizing the contents of the sleigh.

"Food, blankets, oats," Enzella sang out. "Clothes. Some tools."

"Water?" Morwë said. "Though with the snow…."

"We can stop by the village well on our way out." He went over the list in his mind. "What tools do we have?"

Morwë checked the sleigh. "Two axes."

The axes could be used as weapons in a pinch, but only at close range. They'd have to get close to any threat, a dangerous idea, especially with the large mountain wolves.

Arken glanced at his hand in disgust. *Useless. If only I had thought to take a weapon, or ask Morwë to get me a sword. Can't shoot a bow with one hand.* He sighed in irritation. Maybe Micah remembered how to shoot. Arken had taught him, several years ago. He'd been able to hit the broad side of a barn in a pinch.

Better than nothing. Arken walked upstairs to the nearly empty loft and pulled his father's bow and quiver from behind the door. He hadn't wanted to use it after Darren had died, and at the time, Arken hadn't been able to draw it well. Now, six years later, he could—if he had two working hands.

Oh well. Arken balanced the bow and quiver in the crook of his arm and carried them down, taking care not to jar his fingers.

As Arken stepped out of the house, Micah finished stowing away their mother's hand loom and spools of thread.

"Micah, did you get the extra water skins?"

His brother groaned long-sufferingly and rolled his eyes. "Yes, *Father*."

Arken set the bow in the back of the sleigh. He wrapped his good arm around Micah's head and pulled him into a headlock. "None of your cheek, youngster," he laughed as Micah loudly protested. *I can't believe we made it out alive.* He let him go and ruffled his hair. "Last call!"

"Can't think of anything," Micah said, tying down the last of the contents.

"All right." Arken swung into the driver's seat. "Let's go."

ARKEN WAS PARTLY glad to only have two horses; he could drive a team of two with one hand, but more than that he wasn't sure he could handle. The sleigh bed was piled high with all the supplies the horses could pull. Micah and Enzella perched on the back of the sleigh and snatched at snow-covered branches that came too close. Enzella chattered like a starling, her head constantly swiveling to take in the world.

Morwë sat next to Arken on the seat. He could barely see her eyes through the swaths of cloth, but they flickered every time she glanced his way.

After about two hours of travel, Morwë said, "Give me your hand."

"Don't worry about me," Arken replied automatically. "Save your strength."

"I'm not going to do a working," Morwë countered. He could imagine the unspoken "you fool" at the end of her sentence. She continued, "I want to study what's wrong with it. I have to reverse a curse as well as heal bones."

He glanced at her. Swathed in her scarves, he could only see her eyes, but they met his levelly. Her brows drew down as if to ask, "what are you waiting for?"

"If you're sure." Arken scooted towards her and placed his right hand in her lap. He set his teeth against upcoming pain.

She stared down at his hand. After a moment, she carefully unwound the fabric strips. "I think it's only the bones in your fingers that are smashed," she mused in a dispassionate voice. "The others look intact."

Arken kept his eyes on the path ahead. The sight of his swollen, twisted flesh and bones made his stomach lurch, to say nothing of the latent pain that throbbed in the back of his mind.

Morwë's touch was feather-light and capable; the spikes of pain from moving broken fingers were not as terrible as they might have been. When his whole body twitched, she didn't move until he had his breath back. "I think I could align the bones, at the very least," she said. "Do you want me to try?"

A sour taste welled up in the back of his mouth, but there would be no profit in waiting. Arken pulled the horses to a halt.

"Why are we stopping?" Micah called from the back.

Arken said over his shoulder, "I didn't think we should be moving when Morwë puts my fingers back in place." He fixed his gaze on a far-off treetop and took a deep breath. "Do it, before I lose my nerve."

"Would you like to bite down on something?"

"No. Just do it." He made sure his tongue was well away from his teeth.

Morwë's grip around his hand tightened and pulled.

The world roared in Arken's ears. His vision went black as waves of fire flared from his fingers and rushed up his arm to his shoulder.

"Arken!" Morwë snapped in his ear, taking hold of his chin.

"I'm all right," he ground out, clinging grimly to the seat with his good hand to stay upright. His vision slowly returned, but his stomach lurched at the thought of more pain. "Do the next one."

"I did them all."

Incredulous, Arken turned to stare at her as she bandaged his fingers, using twigs she had stripped of needles for splints.

"Who needs magic, when you work that fast," he mumbled, his mouth twisting up in a shaky grin.

FORTY-SEVEN

MORWË

Morwë was grateful for her wrappings as Arken urged the horses on. No one could see her flinch.

"Who needs magic, when you work that fast."

If only he knew. Healing just one bone in Arken's hand hours ago had left her shaky and sweating, and even now setting the bones in his other hand made her want to slump. Only rigid discipline and pride kept her spine ramrod straight.

She had not told the complete truth. She *had* wanted to heal his hand—or at least part of it. But earlier, it had taken so much out of her she had nearly blacked out. She had to wait—gather her strength—and then….

What's the matter with me? Morwë wondered, gripping the sleigh's seat as they continued through the forested valley. *I've never felt so completely drained before.*

You've also never dropped an entire mountain before, her inner self pointed out. *You've never faced any consequences so great.*

Her Arts had always been her armor, her strength. No one could hurt her. Without them, she felt as though she was missing a limb. She felt… vulnerable.

You don't have to waste your strength on him, her traitorous inner voice cajoled. *Save your strength. You'll need it. Who knows what you'll have to face? What good will it be to heal his hand?*

But she had said she would try. And besides... she felt a terrible need to atone, somehow, for everything. For the mountain. For his torture. *For being what I am,* Morwë admitted to herself.

Her eyes flicked to Arken, driving the team one-handed through the snow. *Both of us handicapped, in different ways.* She felt the truth of it, now, that they never would have escaped without the both of them working together. She tried to imagine making this journey without him and clenched her jaw. *Zel and I need them.*

But what happens when we reach Cairenoch? They would have no more reason to be beholden to each other. All debts would, for the most part, be paid. *What happens to us then?*

She didn't have a good answer.

"You'll need to keep your hand elevated, to keep the swelling down," Morwë said, reluctant to break their silence but obligated to point out the obvious.

Arken held up his right arm and winced. Oh yes, she still had to do something about his back as well. "Would that I could," he said. Then he gave her a considering look. Scooting closer, he draped the arm lightly across her shoulders.

Morwë's whole body stiffened.

"Are you all right? I didn't mean...." He started to pull away.

"No," she said quickly, forcing herself to relax. "Keep it there. It will help the hand."

"You're sure?" Arken asked.

"Morwë doesn't like being touched," Enzella said from quite near them. Arken and Morwë both jumped. "Hadrian always tried to get her alone but she—"

If Arken's hand hadn't been injured, Morwë would have lunged at Zel. "*Enzella,*" she growled, turning as best she could to glare at her sister. "What. Have I. Told you."

Enzella shrank back against Micah, eyes narrowed. "Don't

give away knowledge, except when it's necessary, and it *was*. You *don't* like being touched."

Abruptly, the anger died. Enzella hadn't been revealing weakness. She had been protective of her. "It's all right, Zel," Morwë whispered. "No harm done."

Arken started to shift away from her, but Morwë reached up and grabbed his wrist. "Leave it."

"You're all right with it?"

She looked up into his concerned face and nodded.

Arken eased closer to her, and she let go of his wrist. "Not too heavy for you?" he checked.

"No." Morwë turned back around and fixed her gaze firmly on the horses' ears. She didn't want to think about the flash of understanding she caught in his eyes. His body was very warm against her side.

Arken let the tension between them stretch and relax like pulled taffy. Morwë's stiff shoulders loosened under the strange, warm weight of his arm. Once Enzella had been distracted by a story of Micah's, Arken shifted beside her. "So, what your father said, that first night—he meant it?"

"Very probably," she said, voice flat.

His voice dropped into a growl. "Did it happen often?"

Morwë frowned. "Threats? No, but I suspected he would try to marry me off soon. What good is a daughter, apart from that," she muttered sarcastically. If she hadn't been leg-shackled to Toren for a power union, she would have been killed at whatever point Ingridon rose to power. Unless she had tried to wrest the Unseelie from him. A tantalizing fantasy, that, but the thought made her bones ache with tiredness. She had none of that power, not now, and the prospect left a bitter taste in her mouth.

Arken frowned. "I meant… never mind."

Sudden clarity broke over Morwë. "You meant was I forced."

Arken was *angry,* and on her behalf. The surprise drove the truth from her. "No. None were strong enough." Toren, though— he had had more training, and very well might've bested her.

Another compelling reason to run. "But I couldn't have defied a command from the Erlking." But she *had* defied him in the end, hadn't she?

She shrugged, forgetting Arken's arm around her shoulders. She lifted a hand to steady it.

"I didn't mean to startle you," Arken confessed. "You'll tell me if I do, won't you?"

She looked him in the face, her hand still resting on the wrist about her shoulders. "You don't startle me. You...." *Surprise me,* her mind supplied. *Steady me.*

"You don't startle me," she said with finality.

He stared into her eyes a long time, and then he nodded. "All right."

As they rode on, Morwë concentrated her vision on the pair of horses ahead, and not on the slight press of Arken's knee against hers as the sleigh slid on.

The way he had looked at her, when she had entered the torture chamber to find him chained to that pole, it had been an expression unlike any she had ever beheld. Mostly shock, to be sure, but mixed with... awe. Wonder. And then they hid in the hallway, and he pressed her against the wall—not to threaten, not to take, but to protect.

He held me in his arms all the way down the mountain. In some ways, he held her now, his warm arm and side against hers, but he did not hold her against her will. He did not imprison. He felt like... like....

The breeze blew down the path and caught the snow, making it dance in the air. It rustled through her cloak and tangled in her scarf, whispering against her ears.

It said: *refuge.*

A word that had little meaning before today.

FORTY-EIGHT

MORWË

"We'll have to soak the shirt," Morwë declared after she and Micah had looked at Arken's back.

"You could just leave—"

"*No*, we could not just leave it; do you want your back to be a mess of festering sores?" Micah snapped.

Arken winced. "That doesn't sound ideal."

Morwë and Micah shared a look of exasperation. "Sit," Morwë said, pointing to the ground in front of the fire.

They had made camp at nightfall and cooked a simple repast over the fire that Arken and Micah had built. Now they would have to deal with Arken's other wounds. After the whole day, the blood had soaked into his shirt and dried, sealing it to the wounds.

"I brought my apothecary stores from Peridun," Micah said as he set water to heat over the fire. "Let me look through them. I'm sure there will be something to help. I was an apothecary apprentice," he told Morwë. He walked to the sleigh and began sorting through bundles as Arken eased himself to the ground and rested his forearms on his knees.

Enzella's head lifted from where she sat on the other side of the fire, but her gaze returned to the flames in front of her. She pulled a branch out of the fire and watched the makeshift torch flicker and flare as the deep red seeds of flame gusted in the faint wind.

Morwë said, "Put the stick back, Enzella. Fire is dangerous."

"I used to be scared of fire," Enzella said, "but look Morwë, it's beautiful! It dances through the air in bursts of gold and orange and red, but underneath a blue glow hides in the logs."

"Beautiful things are often dangerous," Arken said. "But as long as you approach them with a healthy respect and use a little wisdom, they won't hurt you." He looked up at Morwë.

She glanced away, pulling off her gloves. She dipped a clean cloth in the warm water and laid it atop Arken's shirt. "Does it hurt?"

"Stings a little. The warmth is nice."

She repeated the process, and once the shirt was soaked, she gently peeled the bottom of the shirt away from his back. Arken growled like an injured wolf. "All right, that hurt."

"If you had let us tend to it earlier, it wouldn't hurt as much," Morwë pointed out.

Arken lifted his head off his knees and smiled wryly. "It had already dried by then. Same problem, except now we're further down the road. Keep going. It can't hurt more than the whipping did, and I survived that."

Grimly, Morwë peeled the shirt away section by section, as new trickles of blood flowed.

Micah arrived to help ease it over Arken's head. "Should've just cut it off."

"And waste a perfectly good shirt?" Arken protested through clenched teeth.

Morwë flinched as his abused back came into full view, striped and crisscrossed with flay marks. "We'll clean it and then put aris-wort on it," Micah said. "It keeps infection at bay and numbs slightly, so it will help with the pain." He held up the bunch of leaves. "I'll make a poultice."

Enzella appeared at his shoulder. "Can I help?"

"Yes. Ariswort might be good for your cuts as well," Micah said.

"Then I'll clean his cuts," Morwë said, wringing out the cloth. She carefully sponged away the dried blood and made sure the wounds were clean as Arken growled intermittently.

His back was tanned to a deep bronze, as if he was often stripped to the waist in hotter months. It felt strangely intimate to touch his bare skin with her ungloved hands, and stranger still to catch glimpses of the hair that dusted his chest and curled under his arms. When she neared his neck, Arken shivered.

Morwë froze. "Did that hurt?"

"No."

"Are you cold?"

"No," he said though his teeth. "Keep going."

Morwë glanced about them. That had to be a lie. The snow had stopped a few hours before, but it still lay heavy on the ground. They had had to scrape the ground free and pile branches on the ground to act as pallets beneath their blankets. The picketed horses and sleigh were also positioned to block what wind might spring up. But it was still cold. *We just have to finish quickly and get him into clean clothing.*

As she cleaned the last of the cuts, Micah and Enzella came back with a bowl of murky green paste. Micah said, "Arken, this will sting, but then the hurt should fade."

"My favorite," Arken muttered. "Go ahead."

Morwë helped Micah slather the sticky paste onto the wounds. Arken hissed. It made her fingers tingle, so she could imagine how it felt on his back. Once it was all on, Micah dabbed the remaining mixture onto Enzella's cheek as Morwë carefully bandaged Arken's wounds with strips of clean linen.

"Be sure not to make any sudden movements to reopen the wounds," Morwë said.

"I'll have to learn not to breathe, then," he chuckled.

Morwë swallowed the knot of guilt in her throat. "Is it that bad?"

Arken shook his head. "No. It feels much better than before, truly. Thank you."

Morwë ducked her head. "I didn't do anything." How could she, depleted of her Arts so?

Her fingers twitched on the bandages. Saliva built in the back of her mouth, and she felt her stomach rumble. It was as if she was still hungry, even though they had just eaten not an hour ago. She swallowed, but that only made it worse.

"You've done everything." Arken carefully reached around with his good hand and clasped her ungloved one.

She stared at their entwined fingers—his so large and tanned, hers bone white, except for the stained black tips. She gently disentangled their fingers, avoiding his eyes, and gathered up his bloodstained shirt. "What should I do with this? I hardly think you could call it 'perfectly good'."

"Keep it," Arken said. "You never know what we might need. If you soak it, most of the bloodstains will come out."

As Morwë bundled it up, something inside her whispered, *The blood. Lick it.*

She stared at the bloodstains, unseeing as her stomach cramped. She shot a glance at Arken. No reaction.

Blood. Fresh. Lick it. Taste it. So hot. So Alive, the voice urged.

Micah handed Arken a fresh shirt and tunic, and helped his brother ease the shirt over his head.

Morwë could not look away from his whip marks. If she pressed her lips to his shoulders, the blood would flow between her lips—on her teeth—

"Morwë? Do you want me to take that?" Micah held out his hands for the bundle.

She wordlessly handed it to Micah. Then she slipped into her bedroll laid out beside Enzella, who was already snoring by the fire. She pulled the blankets over her head to hide her shaking.

Moonlight, what is happening to me?

CHAPTER

FORTY-NINE

ENZELLA

Enzella woke slowly in the morning, wind tickling her nose just as dawn peeped its first rays over the mountain almost directly east of the valley, the one Micah called White Mountain. She sat up and looked at the fire, now a pile of glowing red embers that Arken was coaxing to life.

He flashed her a crooked smile. "Breakfast will be ready soon."

Enzella's stomach growled at the thought of food. She stood up and shook off her blankets, going to hunt for a convenient bush to do her business behind. Morwë and Micah were still unmoving blanket lumps.

When Enzella returned, the others were waking, and the sun had emerged from behind the mountain. It shone down onto the white snow, making the whole world glitter and shine brighter than any gem or witch light she had ever seen. It lay in perfect swaths across the branches and the ground, except for their camp-site and where their horses were picketed. They nosed the snow away to get at some of the grass underneath.

Enzella's eyes watered from the brightness, but she blinked the tears away, swiping at her face with her gloved hands. She turned her hands over, then squinted up at the sun through her thick hood.

Father had said she would burn. Morwë too. But… why?

Surreptitiously, she slipped one hand out of her glove and inched her fingertips out of her long sleeves until they touched the light. She turned her hand over, staring at the light on her skin. It… didn't feel like burning.

Something exultant and wild welled up inside her. Enzella pulled the scarf away from her mouth as her heart beat out a rapid tempo. Then she pulled her hood back from her face.

"*Enzella!*" The water skin in Morwë's hands hit the ground, its contents splattering.

"It's all right!" Enzella squinted at the blue sky and the morning glare. The light against her face felt warm, a gentle caress. She lifted her bare hand to feel that warmth. She pulled the scarf from her neck and let it drop to the ground.

Morwë ran to her and pulled her into an embrace. "Don't you know what could have happened?" she shouted. "How could you be so stupid, Zel?"

Enzella frowned at the quaver in her sister's voice. "But it doesn't hurt," Enzella protested, pushing against her sister. She wanted to feel the warmth again. "It doesn't. Father lied! Look!" She smiled and spun around, kicking up snow around her feet in a shower of white. "See, Morwë?"

Micah shook his head at her, but he was smiling. "You took one hell of a chance, Zel."

"It's warm! It's light!" Enzella beamed, even though the cuts on her face smarted in pain at the motion. "Try it, Morwë!" She wriggled in eager anticipation.

Her sister stared at her, the sunlight shining all around, before she slowly peeled away one of her gloves.

Morwë inched her pale hand into the sun's glow—and yelped. They all heard the sizzle of burnt flesh.

Enzella's stomach plummeted into her toes.

Morwë jerked her hand back into her sleeve.

"Are you all right?" Arken wanted to know as Morwë drew her glove over the angry, blistering burn.

Micah said, "Here, put snow on it, that will help. We have a little poultice left—"

"Leave it alone," Morwë hissed.

"But…" Enzella whispered, staring from her own hands to her sister, who had drawn into herself, glaring at the ground. "Morwë…."

"*Leave* it, Zel." Morwë turned away and stalked back to the campsite where breakfast bubbled in a pot. Arken followed her, still badgering her. Micah shot Zel a sympathetic look, but he too walked back to the fire.

Enzella's shoulders slumped as she gazed around, bereft of the world's previous wonder. "…I didn't mean it…." she whispered as guilt gnawed her insides.

What had happened?

CHAPTER

FIFTY

MORWË

"Enzella didn't mean anything by it," Arken said, trying to keep up as Morwë stalked away into the snow.

"I know she didn't." That was the problem, and Morwë's aching hand was the result. "She doesn't *think.*"

"She wanted you to share in her joy."

"Would that I could," Morwë whispered. Hope *was* dangerous. She had felt it fill her whole being when she saw Enzella lit with sunlight and unharmed. And then to have it snatched away at the awful sting and sizzle on her fingers—she felt like someone had carved away an essential part of her, even though the hope had only been there for a moment.

"Why would the sun burn you and spare her?"

Morwë stopped walking and said dully, "Maybe she's more human than I am." *Mother, you were righter than you knew. Enzella was the one thing that you did right. I'm the one that's all wrong.*

"That's not true," Arken snapped.

Morwë whirled on him. "How do *you* know?"

"If you were less human, you would've left us to die. You didn't. And anyway, I've heard a lot of faefolk tales, and burning in sunlight has never come up in them."

"Because all the stories you've heard are so true."

"They usually have a grain of truth, here and there. And you'd think if it was a widespread affliction, there would've been a reference to it." He gestured to the hand curled up against her chest. "What else could it be?"

Morwë stared down at her gloved fingers, flexed them. "Enzella doesn't have any magic."

Arken snorted. "Neither does your brother, and I suspect he'd burst into flames on the spot in sunlight."

The scarf around her mouth hid her fleeting smile. "I'll have to think about it," Morwë said reluctantly.

Arken urged, "Come back to camp. You need something for your fingers."

"No, I don't—"

He held out his hand. "Come on. You got your chance last night; it's my turn to slather goo on you. Fair's fair." His easy smile transformed his face, and Morwë's breath caught.

"I suppose I must, if only to keep things *fair*," she grumbled.

"If you're very good, maybe I'll let you check my bandages before we head out," Arken laughed.

Morwë was very glad for the scarf covering her face.

FIFTY-ONE

MICAH

"It wasn't your fault, you know," Micah told Enzella in a low voice as they walked behind the sleigh together. Morwë sat up front with Arken again, but her posture was more hunched than the day before, more wary of the light that might intrude through her hood.

Enzella didn't reply, just trudged along beside him through the sleigh's tracks. Her scarf was wrapped around her head to keep it warm, but her hood was back and her hair shone in the light, only a few shades darker than the snow. In contrast, the slashes on her cheeks shone red since she had peeled the bandage off. It sent a chill down Micah's spine that her own brother had cut her like that.

"Really," he said again. "You couldn't have known."

"But why did the light burn her?" Enzella said in a tiny voice. "I'm fine."

Micah shrugged. "I don't know, Zel."

Enzella just sniffed and pressed a hand against her side.

"You want to stop walking for a bit? It's been nearly an hour."

She shook her head.

Micah sighed. This girl was more stubborn than anyone he'd ever met. She didn't want to admit that her stab wound pained her. Micah tightened his cloak around himself and glanced up at the sky. The sun shone almost directly overhead, and his stomach growled uncomfortably.

"Well, I'm hungry, so I'm going to get a few of the honey oatcakes," Micah decided, jogging ahead to swing himself into the back of the sleigh. He rummaged in the food rucksack and pulled out some of the cakes. "Do you want one?"

Enzella didn't say anything, but as he busied himself with the food, he heard her swing into the sleigh beside him. He handed her an oatcake, and she bit into it, wincing a little as the movement pulled the scabs on her face. After a while, she leaned into him, inch by inch. Micah didn't move, and eventually her head was on his shoulder.

"I just… wanted her to feel this," Enzella mumbled around the food in her mouth.

"Feel what?"

She gestured to the wood crystalized with snow. "This. The wonder."

Micah blinked and took a closer look at the world to see what Zel, who had never experienced the light of day before, saw.

The snow lay thick along the ground and in the trees, the weight making the branches bow towards the ground. Sunlight seeped down through the evergreens and made the snow sparkle like diamonds. The whole world, except for the jingle of the horses' harnesses, had gone soft and muffled. Micah exhaled slowly as he chewed his oatcake, and his breath formed a white cloud that spiraled into the air and disappeared.

Along the path behind them, Micah saw a flicker of movement. He tapped Enzella and pointed. "Look."

She followed the direction of his finger and gasped, a piece of oatcake falling out of her mouth. "What is it?"

"It's a forest cat." The brindled cat blinked yellow eyes at them and whisked its massive tail as the sleigh pulled them further and further away.

"What's that?"

Right, Micah reminded himself. "Forest cats are big feral cats that have long, thick fur and very strong legs and big paws. We saw them here and there at home—they'd eat the mice, rats, and possums that would come after the grain."

"It's so fluffy," Enzella said, steam exhaling sharply from her mouth as she sighed. "Do you think there are forest cats in Cairenoch?"

"I'm sure there are, here and there. They're all over Altesia, but you see them more in the small villages. They come in all different colors and shades. We think they're lucky."

Enzella wiped the partly chewed bite of oatcake off her lap. "Why?"

"They can walk back and forth between home and hearth and the wild places of the land, I think. They belong to both and neither. To ask them to choose would be wrong. So when you see them in the forests or in your barnyard, you think it's lucky." Micah rubbed his arm to rid it of the ache that had set in. "It has something to do with us being a part of the land, part of the mountains. No one in their right mind would try to tame the Caleahanachs. But if you live with them, you can go in and out of their wild places safely. And so they keep the homesteads safe...."

But had they, if Peridun was ransacked?

Micah squinted at the receding mountain to the west. Ceridfel *had* crushed the Unseelie, but that was mostly Morwë's doing.... He shook his head. Parsing the meaning behind myth and lore was his mother's domain; he had just inherited her love of story-telling. Even if it did seem as though myths had caught up with them.

Micah glanced at Enzella. "Do you want to hear a story about forest cats?"

Her eyes widened. "What kind of story?"

"You'll see," he chuckled, settling into the rhythm of a tale he learned at his mother's knee. "It is said, when the first wayfarers crept into the kingdom of Altesia-as-would-be, following Taliesin, the first explorer into the mountains, that the cats called to them.

Their song wound out of the deep valley forests between the mountains in a sonorous descant, and the travelers felt it settle, resonant, into their bones. They thought the mountains themselves were singing to them. 'Your place is here,' the mountains said. 'We know to whom we belong.'

"So they settled and farmed, and cut down the trees, and time passed. And then one night, a farmer woke to find paw prints all around his farm. Well, he and his wife were sore afraid, because they had never seen such tracks before; they had no idea what animal they belonged to. They worried for their horses, cows, and young child, just a baby. Every morning they would find the tracks around their farm."

"But why didn't they know it was a forest cat?" Enzella insisted.

"Because they had never seen one before," Micah explained. "They didn't know what kind of a beast it was, if it was some new kind of wolf, come to kill, or what it meant that the tracks circled and circled but never came too close. So one night, the farmer stayed up all night, staring into the dark from his barn, and he saw the dark shapes on the prowl, pacing, watching...."

Enzella sucked in a deep breath, her eyes as wide as dinner plates.

Micah hid his smile. "The farmer raised his crossbow to shoot at the dark shapes when suddenly, out of the dark woods, came a deep, dark snarl. Eyes glowed from the woods."

"A forest cat?"

From the front of the sleigh, Morwë cleared her throat. "Stop interrupting Micah and let him tell the story."

Enzella frowned but apologized.

Micah's ears burned. "As the farmer stepped out of his barn, lifting his lantern high, a massive timber wolf stepped from the woods, drool dripping from its maw. His heart quaked, and his crossbow shook in his hand. But three dark shapes flew for the wolf, diving for its throat, clawing at its eyes. The forest cats drove the wolf away from the farm. The next day the farmer told all his neighbors about the wolf, and they hunted it down and killed it. And forest cats became highly revered in Altesia."

The rest of Enzella's oat cake sat in her hand, entirely forgotten. "So the cats were protecting the farm the whole time?"

"Yep."

"Why do they do it? Protect?"

"That's what good neighbors do."

Enzella frowned in deep thought. "Because they love you?"

Micah squinted up at the mountain peaks. "Yes. I guess they do."

FIFTY-TWO

ENZELLA

"Morwë, when we get to Cairenoch, what will we do?"

"I don't know, Zel."

Morwë's voice was muffled from the scarf, but Enzella suspected she had sighed.

When they had stopped for a rest to let Arken stretch, Morwë switched places with Micah and walked along behind the sleigh. After walking with her for a while, Enzella swung up to sit in the back and ask all the question that were bubbling up inside of her.

"Will we stay there?" Enzella pressed.

"If it's safe. Or we might want to go elsewhere. Karneesia is a big place, it seems." Morwë gestured to the land around them.

"Well, will we get a house, like Micah's?"

"Possibly. We'll need a place to live, food, work, perhaps, if our money runs out. First we'll have to sell a few things."

"What things? Can I see?"

Morwë hesitated, then clambered back into the sleigh. She went through the boxes and bags until she found the sack they had taken with them from the mountain. Reaching inside, she pulled out a much smaller soft velvet bag and opened it. "These were Mother's."

Enzella gasped at the tangle of riches inside.

The stones caught the sunlight and reflect it through their tiny facets, shining brighter than they ever did in the glow of the witch lights. Together they sorted through the tangle. An emerald ring, the stone as big as a baby's eye. A sapphire choker. A diadem made of geodes. Ropes of silver and gold. One long strand of perfectly round, luminous beads.

"Pearls," Morwë said, fingering the strand. "They come from the sea."

Garnet broaches, diamond earrings, gold bangle bracelets. Rubies and amethysts, dark as blood, crusted into crowns. And on one small bracelet, small stones made of obsidian, the special kind that thaumaturges enchanted into witch lights.

"I don't remember her wearing any of this," Enzella said with a frown. "Except maybe the witch light bracelet. She used it to see."

"Much of it Father probably gave her. That's probably why she didn't."

"And so we can sell some of it and buy a place to live?"

"Hopefully." Morwë sifted through the jewelry thoughtfully. "If anyone has enough coin to buy them from us."

Enzella looked over her shoulder towards the front of the sleigh. "What if we lived with Arken and Micah?"

"No, Zel," Morwë said firmly.

"Why not?"

"We're not their family. They wouldn't want us living with them. They might...."

"What?"

"They might not want to see us again."

"What? Why?" Micah was her friend! Why wouldn't she see him again?

Her sister struggled for words. "Bad things happened to them, Zel. They might not want to be reminded of it." She glanced toward the boys at the front of the sleigh.

"Bad things happened to *me*, too. I got stabbed."

"Are you feeling poorly?" Morwë asked, alarmed. "Let me see—"

"I'm *fine*; it just itches." Enzella kicked her legs as they dangled off the sleigh. "Are we family?"

Morwë gave a muffled snort. "Last time I checked."

"Do we have more?"

Morwë's voice gentled. "We don't know if Father and Ingridon—"

"No, not *them*. Other family. Wasn't Mother from here?"

Morwë stared at her. "How did you know that?"

"I showed Mother Micah's necklace. She named the mountains for me. Ask Micah!"

"I believe you, Zel." Morwë swallowed. "I don't know anything about Mother's people." She stirred the tangle of gems in her skirts. "I wish I did."

Enzella pulled her legs up and wrapped her arms around them. "Morwë, do you think Mother loved us?"

FIFTY-THREE

MORWË

Morwë gave the only answer she had. "I think she cared for us as much as she was able."

"That's a cagey answer," Enzella said grumpily.

"It's an honest one," Morwë retorted.

"Don't you think she did?"

"I think... she could have," Morwë admitted. "But I don't know, and that's the truth. She was stolen, Zel. She was stolen and married to a monster. We don't know how or why. She had us. She was never allowed to escape. She lived underground for twenty-six years. Her life was sucked away in precise increments. She was all alone and yet surrounded, all at once. I think that she gave what she could." Morwë wrapped her arms around herself as hunger gnawed in her gut. It seemed like she was always hungry, these days, could never be satisfied with simple food.

Her mother had been trapped. She had been married against her will. She had been hurt in every way a person could be hurt. And Morwë had watched it ever since she had been pulled from youngling classes at ten annuals to help tend to her mother and Enzella.

She had always felt different, but that difference had grown since that day.

She had resisted all the strictures, all the pressures on her, because she had seen, *in her mother,* what could happen.

It wasn't foolishness, or oddity. It was a subconscious decision to protect herself.

I didn't hate you, Mother. Not at all.

"I suppose it doesn't matter," Enzella said with finality. "I loved her." She peered up. "Morwë, do you love *me?*"

Morwë stared into her sister's large eyes, owlish in their proportions, her skinny fingers that Morwë had counted when she was just born. She had been there when Enzella drew breath. Morwë murmured, "I don't know, what does it feel like?"

Enzella tilted her head to the side. "Like something in your chest is trying to get out?"

Oh, thank you, Enzella, for describing every day of her existence. "Like a wild animal?" Under her scarf, the corner of her mouth turned up.

"Sometimes," her sister said seriously. "It hurts, too, but sometimes it's like—like all the snow is melting in the sun."

Morwë shook her head ruefully. "I wouldn't know about that."

Enzella studied her. "Well, I think you do. You wouldn't have escaped with me if you didn't."

"I made a promise to Mother."

"You wouldn't have made the promise if you didn't."

"I might've lied."

"Then you wouldn't have kept it. So I think you do. And I love you back." Enzella sat up and wrapped her arms around Morwë in a hug. "And if we don't find Mother's people, that's all right. We can be a family, just the two of us."

Morwë swallowed around the lump in her throat. "That we can, Zel. Just the two of us."

Enzella pulled back and began playing with the jewelry again. "Why did Mother need *three* crowns? Father only had the one."

Morwë took a deep breath and disentangled a necklace and the bracelet from the diadems. "These were gifts from Father for our births." She tapped the ruby crown. "This was Ingridon. The amethyst was mine." She lifted the clear geode diadem. "This one was for your birth."

Enzella took the diadem in her hands and turned it over, looking at it. "What were they for?"

"Our presentations to the people," Morwë said. She could remember her mother holding a tiny bundle, wearing the shimmering geode crown in front of a sea of imps. She did not smile. She never had.

The rest of the event was a blur in Morwë's memory, because Ingridon had pushed her down a flight of stairs, and her new gown had ripped.

Enzella set the crown on her head. Too big for her, it slid down and balanced precariously on her nose and ears. She laughed. "Aren't you going to put yours on?" Enzella asked, using one hand to keep the diadem on.

Morwë touched her own lightly with one finger. The purple stones had seemed nearly black underground. Now the color shone clearly from their depths. She set the crown on her hooded head. "Ta da."

Enzella dissolved into a fit of giggles. "At least yours fits better than mine!" She took her crown off and put it back in the bag.

Morwë did the same, bundling everything away except for the long rope of creamy pearls. "These I know Mother inherited as part of her position. Pearls come from the sea. You find them in shells. They must be very old. I never heard of any Unseelie reaching the sea."

"From before the Sundering?"

"Yes."

"There must be a lot of history to them, then," Enzella said. "I wonder how many necks they've been around?"

Morwë fingered the strand. "I wonder how many of them were slit."

FIFTY-FOUR

ARKEN

That night, as they ate around the campfire, Arken rolled his shoulders irritably. The whip marks itched something fierce, and Morwë warned that they would probably scar. She said she needed to focus on his hands first, which Arken agreed with, but he knew something else was going on.

As a logger, Arken knew utter exhaustion when he saw it. Morwë never seemed to grow stronger from rest or the time that passed. Ever since the mountain fell two days ago, even the smallest tasks threatened to push her beyond her strength. She hid it well, but he hadn't perched beside her for two days on the sleigh for nothing.

He glanced through the tongues of fire to Morwë as she listened to Enzella recount some animal that she and Micah had seen that day, maybe a snow rabbit or a fox. Arken could only see part of her face in the twilight; her scarf and the hood covered the rest. She nodded in the right spots, but the slope of her head and the dark circles under her one visible eye spoke volumes.

Is she sleeping? Arken wondered. He knew she was eating, for all the good it did.

Unbidden, the bubble and hiss of burning flesh came back to

him, along with the smell. Arken glanced down and swallowed hard. He forced himself to finish the food on his plate.

He couldn't help but overhear bits of the girls' conversation in the sleigh earlier. *I understand not wanting to be a burden, but what are she and Zel going to do now? She burns in daylight. What kind of future lies ahead for them?*

He rubbed the back of his neck and considered her posture again. *When the whole world posed a threat to me, I didn't sleep well either.* Those days in the dark had been the longest of his life.

They finished supper as a mostly silent affair, punctuated by questions from Enzella and the occasional stamp from the horses tethered by the sleigh as they cleaned their dishes and packed their stores back again. Arken was sure they were all as relieved as he was when Morwë cut Enzella off before she started another story.

"And then a hawk—"

"No." Morwë unrolled Enzella's blankets. "No more talking. Time to sleep."

"Awww." Enzella slumped. "But I'm not tired."

Morwë pulled back her hood and shook her hair out. "You have to go to sleep. You have to get used to sleeping during the dark."

"Who says night is the right time?" Enzella complained as she climbed into her blankets.

"They do." Morwë motioned to Arken and Micah. "And all the rest of the wights, I'm sure. We have to get used to it."

"Why—"

"Hsst." Morwë laid a finger against her lips. "No more talking. Shut your eyes. Sleep."

With a little more grumbling, Enzella pulled a blanket over her head and made a big show of wriggling around to show she was most emphatically *not asleep.* But ten minutes later, she started to snore.

"You, too," Morwë said, feeding another branch gingerly to

the fire, careful to stay out of range of the flames. "You've got a long day tomorrow."

Arken raised an eyebrow. "Me, or Micah?"

"Both," Morwë said shortly. "I'll take first watch tonight."

Hiding a yawn, Micah obediently rolled himself into his blankets.

Arken glanced at her over the fire. "I'm not tired." He stretched his legs out and leaned back on his good hand.

Morwë huffed. "A likely story." Drawing her knees up to her chest, she tipped her head back to look at the stars.

Arken watched the firelight play over her face. "Have you ever seen stars before?"

She shot him a saturnine look. "You mean last night?"

Arken snorted. "You know what I meant."

Morwë's gaze returned to the night sky. "I *have* been outside before," she told him. "In the taiga, our community was only partially underground in barrows and warrens, and aboveground, the trees had been magically grown so that they blocked out all light. It always smelled like tree rot," she whispered. "The war bands would leave to hunt, but I never could. Not until we left."

She shifted to mimic him, leaning back on her hands. "But yes, I saw the stars. Once."

Arken stared up at the constellations of the cat and the centaur that galloped over the Caleahanachs and didn't say anything.

"They told us not to look," Morwë continued after a long moment, gaze flicking to the dancing flames. "We spent the whole journey under magical domes that blocked out all light, night and day. To protect us from burning. Father commanded us not to leave the domes for our own safety."

Arken tilted his head to the side. "But you looked anyway."

"I looked," Morwë confirmed.

The flames lit her pale face in a gold light, illuminating her sharp features and her eyes, now downcast. "Why?" Arken whispered.

Her voice was dry. "Mother asked me to help her out of the

caravan one night when no one was looking. She wanted to see the sky for the first time since she was taken. And when she looked, I looked, too."

"And what did you think?"

"I think… they're very far away."

"That they are," he nodded. "But very bright and beautiful. Did she tell you about the northern lights?"

Something flickered in Morwë's face, an expression he couldn't describe. "…I heard her mention them, towards the end when she was very sick. What are they?"

"Some winter nights, when the skies are very clear, lights appear in the sky and dance." Arken smiled. "There are different legends surrounding why they show up, and why they change colors. Some think they're harbingers of doom or famine, but I've never thought so. They're too lovely to be something so terrible." He looked at Morwë. "Others say they're the last vestiges of magic from the land, dancing in the sky before disappearing. The ghost of magic, if you will. That's what my mother always says."

"What do they look like?" Morwë tilted her head back to look at the stars. "Like stars, or the moon?"

"They look like…." he tried to pick the right words. "They look like tongues of green or purple fire that reach all the way up to the sky, sometimes… other times they look like a river of colors in the sky, flowing along the air."

"Where do they go?"

"To the Lloren sea, maybe. Or towards the far north."

"I've never seen the sea."

He laughed. "Neither have I. But it's supposed to stretch as far as the horizon, and then further on. Our priest, Father James, is from Cadruissau, on the coast. He left there when he was young, but he described it to me. They have schools there, to study anything a body has a mind to, and he said that their learning told them the world was mostly water, with land just floating along on it."

"You're sure he wasn't taking advantage of the country boy?" Her mouth curved into a slow smile.

"Maybe," Arken shrugged, smiling in response. "How could you know for sure, unless you got on a boat and sailed to the ends of the earth?"

Except for the crackle of flame, the land grew silent, the dark forest blending into the black velvet sky above them. After a long time, Morwë sighed, her expression what he might call wistful. "I would like to see those lights."

He fed another branch to the fire. "Maybe you will, this winter."

"Only if they don't burn me." Her mouth twisted and grew hard.

Arken looked up. "They won't, Morwë."

"You don't know that." Her head drooped and shoulders slumped.

"Maybe not," he said quietly. "But I know that you need sleep. Get some rest."

"I said I'd take first watch."

Arken shot her a look. "Morwë."

She avoided his gaze. "I don't need to sleep."

"Saints above and below, Morwë." He rolled his eyes. "Everyone needs to sleep."

She glared at him. "If someone comes upon us in the night, I need to be awake to sense them."

"Do you still think we have pursuers? It's been two days." Arken glanced around the dark forest. "If someone was on our tail, do you think they would wait so long to make their presence known?"

"It is still possible, but… more unlikely. I would have expected a threat by now," she whispered.

He got up and walked around to her side of the fire. "Go to sleep," he said, sitting down beside her.

"Are you trying to boss me like I do Enzella?" She arched an eyebrow but didn't move away.

"Well, it's a tactic I've seen work."

She huffed. "If I go to sleep, will you wake me up to take second watch?"

"Depends on if you actually sleep." He grinned at her disgruntled expression.

"I doubt it," she muttered as she crawled into her blankets, shooting him an irritated look.

Arken laughed softly. "Shh," he said. "Close your eyes, and I'll tell you about a time I saw the northern lights." It had been the last winter with his father still alive. They had gone up to hunt elk around the valley rim and had stayed up late talking around the fire, just like this night. And then colors had lit the night, arcing above them in a dizzying array. "It was the most beautiful thing I had ever seen," he admitted.

But Morwë didn't hear him. She lay beside him, breathing softly, fast asleep.

"The most beautiful thing I had ever seen," he whispered.

FIFTY-FIVE

INGRIDON

Ingridon lay in the dark for what seemed like eons, screaming when he had the breath and fainting when the pain swelled or his air grew too thin. Rocks crushed his legs, pressed in on his shoulders. The rocks piled all around him allowed air to pass through only the smallest of cracks.

He had nothing that would help him. His sword was buried and unreachable outside the tiny pocket of space that had formed when the roof caved in. He scrabbled at the stone until his nails broke and his fingers bloodied. With every breath he managed to take, he silently cursed Morwë and her Arts, a gift he had never coveted until now.

I'll kill her, Ingridon vowed. *I'll do it in this life, or my curse will continue beyond the grave. She will rue the day she traitored her people, her blood.* His lips peeled back in a cracked and dirty snarl. *She will not get to say she destroyed the Unseelie people.*

Ingridon's throat grew parched and his tongue dry as dust. More and more often he could not draw the breath to scream. He stared at nothing in the utter darkness and wondered if he'd even know it when he died, or if death would only be much of the same, trapped forever under tons of earth and stone.

Sometimes the tight space would seem to grow even tighter

and press in on him to an unbearable degree. He would grow so panicked he would lose consciousness. But he always woke up to the pain, the darkness, and the silence.

Sometimes Ingridon imagined that he could see a witch light shining through the cracks in the stone, and then he'd make as much noise as his damaged throat could stand, clawing at the cracks until his hands could take no more and the light faded.

A mirage, Ingridon always thought afterward, *a hallucination. I am dying now.*

But he did not.

He had no idea how long he had been trapped under the mountain when there came a great groan from above him, stone against stone.

Another hallucination, he thought, only twitching in response.

But the rumble continued, and dirt began to shift and move around him. Ingridon moved as much as he was able and yelled, a broken, dry rasp of sound.

I'm here, he mouthed. *Here!*

With a great rending, the stone peeled away from above him, and the glow of witch lights shone down into his tiny prison. Ingridon lifted his head and stared up into the face of the Erlking.

"…Fffaa…." he moaned, choking on the sound.

"My son," his father said, reaching down to him and grasping his shoulder. "Drink this." He held out a leather skin bag and guided it to Ingridon's lips.

Ingridon gulped from the skin, nearly choking as the freezing cold liquid passed his lips. He swallowed as much of the water as he could before his father pulled it away.

"Hold still," Yemelyan commanded, his black eyes deep pits in his face. "I must free your legs."

"Crushed," Ingridon rasped.

"We will deal with that once they are free," Yemelyan said. The Erlking held out his hand and the power spread from his palm to the rocks. They twitched and groaned like living things. Then with a great crack, they broke, falling away from Ingridon's lower legs.

Ingridon screamed. Darkness threatened to take his vision again.

Yemelyan grasped Ingridon's mangled legs in impassive assessment. "Broken, but not unmendable," he pronounced.

"How?" Ingridon gasped. *Your Arts don't work on your own blood.*

Yemelyan straightened and walked away for a moment. "I would have returned for you earlier," Yemelyan explained, his voice carrying back to Ingridon, "but had I found you without a way to heal you, it would have served no purpose."

He returned to Ingridon's field of vision, towing a stumbling figure. By the light of a cracked witch light, Ingridon peered into the darkness. His eyes widened at the sight of a bruised but familiar face. "Hadrian."

"Ingridon—" Hadrian rasped, but Yemelyan placed his hands on either side of Hadrian's head, cutting off his words. Yemelyan stared into Hadrian's eyes as magic swelled around his hands. Hadrian's skin began to glow.

"Once you consume him, the healing serum I placed in his body will begin to work on your legs. Then we can build up your strength." Yemelyan pushed Hadrian down beside Ingridon in the hole. "You need to be in your prime to confront your sister. It was she who collapsed the mountain, was it not?"

"Yes," Ingridon hissed.

The Erlking's face twisted into rage for a blink, then smoothed back into its immovable mask. "I will deal with her in due time. Morwë has upended my so carefully laid plans for her and this place. I had to consume Toren and the rest of the thaumaturges to gain enough power to come to you." He sighed. "Now I'll need another stud."

"Ingridon. Please," Hadrian begged. Beneath the glow of enchantment, Ingridon could see the cuts and scrapes in his skin. "I am your friend—"

"And loyal, I am sure. And loyalty demands sacrifice," the Erlking said, his voice iron-hard. "You owe your allegiance to the Erlking and Heir, and you swore your life to us. And now your life is required."

Breath rattling in his chest, Ingridon stared at the man who had been at his side since they were both in youngling school, who had fought with him numerous times over the years, who always supported him, always had his back. He pulled back his lips in some facsimile of a smile. "My friend," he whispered, reaching toward Hadrian.

Without warning, he wrapped his bloodied fingers around Hadrian's neck. Ingridon used what was left of his strength to shove him to the ground and pry open his mouth. He inhaled as Hadrian struggled, greedily leeching the kneph from his body.

As the life force flowed into him, Ingridon felt feeling return to his lower legs—intensely painful feeling, but the healing had started. He held Hadrian down until he had drained him dry, leaving only a shriveled husk behind.

Ingridon wiped his mouth with the back of his hand, and it came away streaked with blood. Ingridon growled as Yemelyan pulled him to his feet, still not fully healed.

"I've left a few imps alive in the mountain," Yemelyan said, once Ingridon had found his footing. "Come, my son. We must restore your strength."

"And then Morwë?" Ingridon said, baring his teeth.

"Yes. And then her."

Be ready, Morwë, Ingridon thought, following Yemelyan as he swept into the darkness. *We are coming.*

FIFTY-SIX

ARKEN

"What are you thinking about so hard?" Arken asked the next day, glancing at Morwë as they took a rest and ate around noonday. He and Morwë had stayed with the sleigh while Micah and Enzella watered the horses at a nearby stream. Snow was gently falling again, and they were both turning into white-crusted lumps as they stretched their legs.

Morwë blinked and straightened, some of the snow trickling down the back of her cloak. She broke her long silence. "Magical theory."

"Oh." Arken raised an eyebrow and looked away, biting into part of a sausage. "Well… can't help you there."

Morwë rubbed her scarf-covered nose with a gloved hand. "I've never *had* to think about it before. Unseelie Arts are instinctual, and taught as such. Your training concerns your will, how to shape a formless magic and force it to obey. Not… finesse." She looked at his bandaged hand, her eyes glinting.

"So you're trying to go about magic in a different way?" Arken checked.

"I've never experienced a power deficit," Morwë said shortly. "I'm trying to find the best way to channel power."

"A hand's a hand," Arken shrugged. "I don't know there's any other way to go about healing it."

"Yes, but…." Morwë clicked her tongue, annoyed.

Arken tried to hide his smile. "Go ahead and tell me; we've already established I don't know anything about magic."

"I thought that first I'd have to heal the bones, muscles, ligaments, and then remove the curse."

"The wasting effect."

"Yes. But… if the damage to your hand is a result of brittle bones and weakened muscles, then we could consider it *all* part of the curse. We convince the magic that because of the curse, they are one and the same thing."

He looked at her, his eyes widening. "You mean, remove the curse and maybe the whole hand is healed?"

She nodded. "Yes, if the magic sees it that way."

"You talk like the magic has a choice in the matter."

"It's wild," she said. "If undirected, it could do a great many unintended, harmful things."

He remembered the fear on her face when he had tried to interrupt Micah's healing. *Ah. Bad.* "Well, lifting it together would make a certain sense," Arken mused. "What are the risks?"

"I don't know," she confessed. "I suppose a revitalized hand that is still injured could make the injuries worse."

"How much worse could it get?" Arken shrugged, finishing off his sausage.

"If the damage was bad enough, and I had no reserves to heal it, infection would set in. We'd need to take the hand at that point." Morwë's brows drew together. "It's amazing it hasn't gotten infected yet."

They both gave Arken's hand a long look, and he tried to repress the awful lurch in his stomach. He'd seen festering injuries; working with wood, axes, adzes, saws, and the like tended to result in the loss of fingers or deep cuts when apprentices weren't careful. He'd seen a boy swing with an axe, miss the log, and hit his own leg. The cut had been deep, and quickly turned puss-filled and sickly, sending angry dark veins from the wound up the boy's leg. They had to take the leg, in the end. They were almost too late, the doctor from Cairenoch had said. A day or two more, and the infection would have spread to the rest of the body, killing him.

"'We'?" Arken repeated, smiling weakly. "I don't think I'd be much help at that point."

"Neither would I," Morwë said darkly.

Arken passed his good hand over his face. "You know that Micah was the apothecary's apprentice. I know he's at least seen an amputation." He pursed his lips as he thought of his brother having to perform that task.

Morwë said, her voice dry as parchment, "Well, if the worst comes, you'll at least have that."

Arken made a face and stared ahead of them as the constant pain from his smashed hand pushed its way through his mind. They still had another day to travel before they would reach Cairenoch's outskirts. If something disastrous was going to happen, he'd rather it happen where they had a doctor… but he didn't want to put his mother through that sort of worry, not after all this.

"I think this hand is pretty much useless right now. And that won't change over time. I'm willing to gamble on removing the curse if you are." He took a deep breath, trying to ignore the twist deep in his stomach. "If this had happened before I met you—not the curse, obviously, but the smashing—I probably would have lost the hand anyway." He looked up and met Morwë's eyes, sharp and wary under her hood. "I'm willing to let you try, if you think there's a chance."

"Arken—"

"It *is* my hand," he reminded her.

She turned away from him and watched the snow blow in from the east. "All right," she said at last. "Give me your hand."

His eyebrows shot up. "Now?"

"Did you want to wait for something?" Morwë snapped.

"No. But if you were worried about power, we can wait until you're ready—"

"I have enough power," she insisted, sitting down in the snow beside the sleigh. She pulled her cloak close to her body, shielding her lap as she shucked off her gloves in its shadow. "Put your hand in my lap."

Arken hesitated and then closed the gap between them, sitting next to her and placing his mangled hand in the shelter of her cloak. She unwrapped his hand without jarring it, and placed his hand between both of hers. "I need you to think about your hand before the curse, hale and whole. Fix it firmly in your mind."

"Picture that removing the curse will give me back an undamaged hand, you mean."

"Exactly. This will not be pleasant," Morwë warned him. "Once I start, I'm not sure I can stop until the curse is fully removed."

"I didn't expect it to be," Arken said, gritting his teeth. He clenched his good hand around the shaft that ran from the runners to the bed of the sleigh and took a deep breath in through his nose, picturing his hand as she had said. Then he nodded.

Deep cold flooded his arm, and an intense pressure followed, not unlike trying to pry a cork out of a wine bottle. Arken tried not to move as the pull continued, as if the cork was very stubborn and hardened, and while it needed to come out, it also needed to come out in one piece. The sensation built, traveling over him like a lightning strike that kept burning, racing through his veins from tip to toe. Arken held onto the sleigh until the knuckles of his good hand turned white and his broken finger throbbed. He breathed in short gasps. The pressure, the cold, and the lightning seared together. It felt like his skin wanted to peel away from the rest of the flesh and bone in one fell swoop.

Just as he thought he'd go mad with the agony, the pressure released with an audible pop.

Arken blinked his vision clear. Had Morwë pulled his whole

hand free from his wrist? Or maybe that had been the sound of his jaw finally relaxing.

Arken stared at his hand in Morwë's lap as the hurt faded. Still attached. He flexed it—no pain, no fractures, no arthritic bones or parchment-thin skin. It was healed! He inhaled sharply, the relief overwhelming—just as Morwë collapsed.

"Morwë!" Arken caught her before she slumped sideways onto the snow-covered ground. Her head lolled forward. He pulled her into his lap, frantically unwinding the scarf around her mouth while shielding her from the sun. "Morwë, can you hear me?" He held a hand against her face, reached for the pulse point under her jaw. The beat under his fingertips was slow and faint, with just the barest breath passing her lips. "God's wounds, Morwë," he cursed, scooping up a handful of snow to press against her bone-white face.

"Arken? What happened?" Micah led the horse they had dubbed Zephyr out of the woods, blinking in concern at the tableau in front of him. Enzella struggled through the snow behind him, leading Star.

"Morwë fainted; how do I wake her up, Micah?" Arken demanded, still supporting her head. Micah thrust the horse's reins into Enzella's free hand and rushed up to him. "Chafing her wrists will help. That gets the blood moving."

"The sun. Mind her skin," Arken snapped.

Micah pulled off his cloak and laid it over the unconscious woman before reaching for her hands.

"What happened?" Enzella waded through drifts with both horses trailing behind her. "What's wrong?"

"She fainted," Arken said again, swallowing hard. "Morwë, wake up."

CHAPTER

FIFTY-SEVEN

MORWË

"Morwë, wake up."

Who was calling her? Her head felt so heavy. Her whole body ached, but especially her hands. Why did her hands ache?

"Nmmm," Morwë mumbled, clenching her eyes shut and trying to pull her hands out of someone's grasp. Who had her hands? "L'go."

"Morwë?" said a voice by her ear. "Can you hear me?"

She groaned and turned into whatever she was leaning against. Her head and neck felt like stone, stone that throbbed angrily. "Y's. L'go." She tugged weakly at whatever held her hands.

"Can you open your eyes for me?" the voice insisted, prodding her.

Someone demanded, "Morwë! Morwë, open your eyes. Right now."

That was Zel's voice. Zel was calling her. Morwë managed to peel back one eyelid to take in part of a chest and beyond that, a brilliant blue eye trained on her.

"She opened her eyes!" Enzella's voice crowed.

Morwë groaned again and squeezed her eyes shut. The noise

made her head pound like she had stuck her head inside the Lych Bell.

"Shh, Zel. Give her a few minutes. You're all right, Morwë. Take your time." Someone slid fabric over her hands. Her gloves. Why hadn't she been wearing her gloves?

"Stop. Talking," Morwë forced out, burying her face in the warm fabric and inhaling the scent of pine and warm skin. As words murmured softly around her, memories slowly filtered back. The journey on the sleigh. Arken's smashed hand. Their conversation about magic. Then… the awful, gut-wrenching sensation of uprooting the very core of herself, plundering nearly every fragment of magic in her body to tear her father's curse from Arken's hand—and then the blackness taking over when she had finally wrested it free.

She groaned again. Her mouth felt bone dry—her whole body did. "Water?"

"Can you sit up?"

Morwë opened her eyes and pushed away from—from Arken's chest, which she had apparently been leaning against this whole time. "Hnng." The world spun in front of her eyes.

"Breathe. Take your time. Here." Arken held a water skin to her lips. "Don't choke."

A fine thing to tell me, she grumbled to herself. *Like I'd be able to help it.* But she was careful as he tilted the bag up towards her mouth. She swallowed water until she had drained it dry.

"You took a damned risk, you know that?" Arken told her in a low voice under the sound of chatter and the jingle of harnesses.

Morwë slowly turned to look at him. Sticks had been stuck haphazardly into the ground and a cloak spread over them, a makeshift canopy. Her face was exposed, she realized, touching her cheek absently. "Did it work?"

"That's not the point."

She sniffed. "Well?"

Arken glared at her and held up his hand, revitalized and

whole. "Yes. Are you happy? For a second I thought you were dead, Morwë. Why did you do it?"

"I said I would, didn't I?" Her stomach rumbled, her mouth flooding with saliva. "I'm hungry."

"Have some more water." He held out another bag, but she reached to take it.

"I can hold it."

By the look on Arken's face, he doubted this, but he kept his mouth shut and handed her the water skin, for which she felt oddly thankful. Neither did he comment on the tremors in her hands as she held it up and drank deeply from it, swallow after swallow. Finally her arms shook enough that she had to lower them, but she could have drunk until this bag was dry, too.

"What would you like? Bread? Oatcake? Jerky?"

She licked her lips at the thought of salt. "Jerky."

Arken unbent his legs and rummaged in the sleigh, emerging with several strips of jerky that he cut up with his belt knife and handed to her, one chunk at a time. She chewed and swallowed each one, holding her hand out for the next until he was empty-handed.

"Do you feel well enough to stand up?"

Morwë pulled her hood over her head and wound the scarf back in place as her stomach gurgled, full of food. But she still wanted… she needed…. She licked her lips again under the scarf, her tongue flicking against the wool.

Arken dismantled the makeshift canopy and called Micah to reclaim his cloak. Then he held out his hand to Morwë. She gripped his hand, felt the new strength in his limb that she had given back to him as he pulled her to her feet. She swayed and Arken steadied her, his hands on her arms until she found her balance again.

"Not feeling faint?" he checked.

She shook her head, rubbing her hand against her chest. The weakness was still there, but she wasn't seeing spots. But the ache

—that was growing stronger. A deep, gnawing pain in her gut that churned with need. A craving. She craved….

Her fingernails dug into the itchy, dry skin beneath her gown.

"Morwë, I…." Arken looked down and then met her eyes. "Thank you. I'm in your debt."

"We're even," she said automatically, staring into his blue eyes. "I said I would help you in return for your help escaping."

"No, we're not. You didn't have to bring yourself to the brink for me—you *shouldn't* have—but I'm grateful." He clasped her hands. "Thank you. I owe you."

The words echoed in her brain, even as Morwë finally found a name for the sensation that was eating through her bones, clawing its way up her throat, the one that insisted it needed, craved, *feed me—*

Moonlight, she realized. *I need kneph.*

Morwë stared into Arken's face and felt her stomach drop.

No.

FIFTY-EIGHT

MICAH

Micah tapped his brother on the shoulder. "What's that?" He stood up in the back of the sleigh and shaded his eyes as he peered ahead.

Arken cursed under his breath. "We've got a tree down," Arken called, pulling the sleigh to a stop.

The tree that lay across the path was old, its gnarled branches heavy with snow and a lot of dead wood. The roots splayed out of a deep hole beside the road to Cairenoch. Micah had never seen a tree that large fall like this before.

"Micah, get the axes out of the sleigh," Arken said, handing the horses' reins to Morwë and jumping down. "We're going to need to shift some of this tree."

"Couldn't we go around?" Enzella asked, tilting her head to the side as she clambered over the sleigh's contents to reach her sister.

"We could try," Arken said, glancing up at her, "but I'd rather not."

"Why?"

"Zel," Morwë muttered.

"Not enough room for the sleigh between the trees, for one

reason. For another, on unknown ground, with the snow covering up any dangers, the horses might flounder."

"That tree must weigh a ton." Micah handed the axes down to Arken.

Enzella offered, "Morwë can move it."

"Zel, Morwë just fixed Arken's hands," Micah said quickly. "She needs to rest a bit. Besides, no reason to waste magic on something Arken and I can do."

"Yes, I've got to put the new hand to work." Arken flexed his healed hand. "But we won't be going anywhere fast. Enzella, if you and Morwë can set up camp, we'll try to get the tree moved so that we can get an early start in the morning. Let's go, Micah."

Micah hopped down from the sleigh and took the axe.

"The trunk is mostly off the path," Arken said, pointing out the sections off the tree that weren't covered in snow. "I figure if we can work on the branches and get them out of the way, we'll be able to get around the rest of the tree."

"Smart." Micah tested the edge of his axe.

"Just make sure you don't chop your foot off," Arken said in a low voice. "No one will be able to fix you."

Micah followed him to the tree. "Morwë's that bad off?"

"She fainted, didn't she? And she's been shaking all afternoon."

Micah stared at his brother. "Really?"

"Yes, I sit right next to her." Arken shot him a look. "Let's get to work."

They began chopping into the branches, most of which was dead wood, and quickly shed their cloaks as the sweat poured off them. They severed the first large branch, and Micah paused to wipe the sweat from his eyes. He squinted along the road. "Arken!"

His brother turned at the urgency in his voice and followed Micah's pointing finger.

"Riders," Micah said unnecessarily. Along the road to

Cairenoch rode upwards of fifteen horsemen, coming towards them fast.

Arken cursed under his breath. "Soldiers."

Micah stared hard at the group of riders. "How can you tell?"

"Two of them are wearing helms." Arken stepped back from the tree trunk but kept a firm grip on his axe. "And they ride in formation. It looks like two squads."

"From Cairenoch?"

The sound of Morwë's voice behind them made both Micah and Arken jump. "More likely from Cruever," Arken said, recovering first. "Father James said he would go to the capitol and ask the Crown for help."

"And what do you think they will do when they reach us?" Morwë said in a low voice.

"We're not going to let anything happen to you," Arken said firmly, his eyes on the soldiers.

Morwë hissed wordlessly.

Arken ignored her. "Zel, run get my bow and quiver from the sleigh."

Enzella, who Micah hadn't even realized was there, dashed back towards the sleigh.

"What *do* you think they'll do?" Micah took up his axe as well, though much good it would do him.

"Discount us, hopefully." Arken narrowed his eyes. "Soldiers don't think much of anyone who doesn't bear arms. With any luck they'll ask us questions and pass by." Zel ran up, panting, with his bow and arrows. Arken set the quiver beside him and strung the bow, leaning on it to wait as the horsemen bore down upon them.

The horses kicked up clouds of white powder as the riders came with as much speed as they could safely manage. As they grew closer, Micah could make out the royal seal on their armor and the swords they carried.

The soldiers reined in and stopped on the other side of the tree, the horses throwing up their heads and stamping, steaming from the ride.

"Who are you, and where do you come from?" an officer called in a commanding voice.

He had a captain's insignia on his helm, which rode low over deep-set dark eyes that squinted hard at the tableau in front of him. His mouth turned down, perhaps burdened by the thick black moustache that sat atop it. Behind him, a dark-skinned woman with a sergeant's badge inspected them with intrigued eyes.

Arken said in a hard voice, "What of it?"

Micah resisted the urge to kick his brother hard in the shin, and by Morwë's shifting weight, she felt the same way. Enzella threaded her fingers with Micah's, and he gave her hand a comforting squeeze.

"I am Captain Alastair Konstantin. I was dispatched by the Crown to investigate a priest's claims that a calamity has overrun Peridun and left no survivors." The captain scanned them with hard eyes, lingering over the two black-clad figures with more interest than Micah liked.

Arken raised a skeptical brow. "Two squads of soldiers. Wonderful. I can see the Crown was highly concerned."

Micah could nearly feel Morwë's teeth grind together, but before she could say anything, a soldier behind the captain shifted in his saddle and turned a gimlet eye onto Arken. His face was scarred and leonine. "None of your cheek, boy," he ground out, "or I'll teach you the meaning of respect—"

"That will do, Corporal." The captain frowned at the scene before him. "I have been detailed to investigate these disappearances and possible threat—"

"No threat," Arken said flatly. "Not anymore."

An eyebrow rose high on his forehead. "So you have come from Peridun. The priest did say a young man had ventured back to search for a brother." His gaze passed over the small party and rightly identified Arken as the young man and Micah as the brother. The captain's mouth flattened. "Now explain what you meant about no threat. The priest was positive there was a need for haste, and Cairenoch certainly thinks something of ill omen has taken place. They report that one of the mountain peaks shifted in an earthquake."

Enzella's voice carried clearly from her place at Micah's side. "Morwë brought the mountain down."

FIFTY-NINE

ARKEN

Arken watched the shock ripple through the soldiers on horseback and tensed.

Morwë clamped her hand onto Enzella's shoulder, and as close as he was, Arken could hear her frustrated growl. "Zel...."

Captain Konstantin leaned forward in his saddle. "And what do you mean by that?" he asked, deep suspicion in his tone.

Arken stepped between them and told the captain, "Look, we can tell you all of what happened, but it's a long tale, and we're not going anywhere as long as this tree stays here. I'm sure you'd like to hear it straight through and not piecemeal."

"We'll take your statements now, then." The captain dismounted, and the squad followed suit. "Corporal," he said, speaking to the man who had growled, "Take your squad and put them to work moving this tree. Sergeant Horne, with me." The captain strode off without waiting in the direction of their camp, his female sergeant following.

"Is this good or bad?" Micah mumbled.

"We'll see," Arken said, eyeing the soldiers.

Acidly, Morwë asked, "Arken, do you think you can manage to keep your needling to yourself?"

He shot her a quick grin. "For you, I'll do my best."

"And Zel?" Morwë continued. "Stop. Talking."

Enzella wilted under her sister's glare and nodded. Morwë stalked towards their camp, her spine ramrod straight. After a quick glance at their siblings—Enzella had leaned against Micah and he was comforting her—Arken hurried after Morwë. "You don't have to be so harsh."

"I'll be harsh if that's the difference between getting out of this alive or not."

"I said I wouldn't let anything happen to you."

"If they decide to kill us, then there's nothing you can do about it, is there?" Morwë hissed.

Arken gripped her hand, pulling her to a stop. "Morwë. You saved my life. I would step in front of an arrow for you." He hadn't planned to say it, but it was the utter truth of what he felt. She deserved it.

Under her scarves and wrappings, he saw her dark eyes widen from shock, enough that he could see a clear ring of white around her irises. Before he could reassure her that he didn't think it would be necessary, the captain cleared his throat, pulling Arken's attention away.

The sergeant picketed their horses with Star and Zephyr while the captain leaned against the sleigh and eyed their group. Once the sergeant had dealt with the horses, she flanked them from the other side.

"I'd like to hear this tale," Konstantin said at last, having finally eyeballed everyone to his satisfaction. "From the beginning to its termination." He gestured at them to begin.

"Would you mind if we got the fire going?" Arken gestured to wood that Morwë and Enzella must've gathered but hadn't had a chance to light before their guests had arrived.

"Sergeant Horne?" the captain asked. "If you would."

The woman stepped forward smoothly and with her index finger drew a few symbols in the snow. With a pop, a small flame flared up among the wood.

Enzella gasped.

Micah hurried to feed the fire tinder and blow on it, coaxing the flame to grow and catch more of the wood. "You're a wizard?"

The captain scoffed. "Of course she's not; just how much of a country boy are you?"

Arken glared at him over his brother's head. "The kind that doesn't see many wizards."

"I'm not a wizard," Sergeant Horne said quietly. "Wizards gain their education and degrees from universities. I only knew a few spells and incantations, most of which are battle defenses. There are a few useful tricks in there, though, like this one."

Morwë nudged her sister and pointed one gloved finger towards Micah. Enzella followed it obediently, sitting beside him as she pulled her hood away from her face to savor the fire's heat.

The sergeant gasped at the sight of Enzella's sharp and fey aspect.

Enzella froze, her eyes huge.

Arken shifted so that he was between her and the sergeant.

But the captain did not react at all. After a moment of absolute stillness from everyone, he reached into a pocket, pulled out a cigar, and lit it from the fire. With an exhale of smoke, he looked Arken dead in the face and said, "Faefolk."

It would be a poor idea to lie to this man.

Morwë's hand closed onto Arken's arm, as if she expected him to do something stupid—or to warn him. Likely she had come to the same conclusion.

Arken simply said, "Yes."

Captain Konstantin stared off towards the Lady's Mirror and puffed on his cigar, the end glowing cherry-red as he inhaled. In a quiet voice, he said, "Thought so. You, too?" He nodded to Morwë.

She lifted her chin and nodded, presenting a haughty visage. But Arken could feel the hand on his arm trembling.

"Mind taking off your hood, miss?"

"She can't," Arken said sharply. "Sunlight burns her."

"But not the little 'un?" The captain raised an eyebrow.

"No. We don't know why."

The captain mulled this over for a time, puffing on his cigar. "Two human boys and two faefolk girls walk out of the forest. Sounds like something out of a tale. Well, lad, let's have it."

"What do you want to know?"

"Tell us the story of what happened at Peridun," Captain Konstantin grunted. "Start at the beginning."

Arken shifted. "The beginning starts with Micah."

Micah's eyes went wide as everyone looked at him. He coughed and cleared his throat. "Me?"

"Yes," Sergeant Horne said, sounding firm. She had recovered from her shock. "Start at the beginning." She pulled out a small book from her pocket and licked her pencil stub.

Micah cleared his throat again and began to recount what had happened during the night that the Unseelie attacked and what had happened to him later. He spoke of meeting Enzella and Morwë, stumbling over it a bit as he kept glancing to Arken. But they hadn't ever discussed what to say when they reached Cairenoch.

We'll just have to hope they believe us, since the captain is a sharp one for lies.

"And that's when Arken came," Micah said, handing over the narrative with what sounded like relief. The captain shifted his gaze, and Arken continued the narrative. He recounted all that had happened until their mad escape where the mountain crumbled around them. "That was the day the snows started. And since then we've just been making our way here," he finished.

Captain Konstantin uncrossed his arms and pulled the cigar out of his mouth, knocking some of the ash from the tip. "Go back to the mountain."

Arken frowned. "What about it?"

"How did you escape?"

"I just *told* you—"

The captain shook his head, hard enough to make his mustache shake. "Not you." He nodded towards the girls. "Them."

"I brought the mountain down."

Morwë's words rang over-loud in the silence. The crackle from the fire did nothing to muffle them.

Sergeant Horne blinked in shock, but the captain made a low noise in his throat, almost a growl, his brow nearly obscuring his eyes.

Well, Morwë knew that this would be the result of walking into a nest of wights. They would never understand—never even comprehend.

"My magic fractured the stone. It all fell inward, into the honeycomb of tunnels my people had made in the mountain. You don't have to worry anymore. They're dead."

"You know this for a fact, do you?" The captain's eyes searched out Morwë's.

Morwë's lips tightened. "Not for sure. But we were not followed. If there were survivors, someone would have come after us."

"Why is that?" the sergeant pressed.

Captain Konstantin grunted, but Morwë answered anyway. "For vengeance. We would not have been allowed to live for such a crime, much less escape."

Konstantin ground out, "Sounds like you faefolk are a pretty murderous bunch."

Arken took a step forward, eyes flashing. Morwë grabbed his arm and hung on.

"Unseelie," she corrected. "It is a characteristic of the Unseelie, not all faefolk. And since there are only two of us left, you needn't worry."

Morwë tugged on Arken's arm when he refused to give ground. "You are not allowed to injure the hands I worked so hard on," she warned him in a low voice.

Arken's blue eyes narrowed for a moment but quickly began to dance. "I'll do my best to keep them safe," he whispered back.

Captain Konstantin's words rang out. "How do I know what you have told me is the truth?" He raised one vast brow. The cigar in the corner of his mouth glowed like a brand.

Morwë met his eyes with a gimlet stare. "I suppose you don't. But moonlight take my eyes if I lie."

The sergeant put aside her pencil and notebook to step forward. "Do you consent to a test, to prove your words?" she asked smoothly.

Arken frowned. "What sort of test?"

"A truth spell," Sergeant Horne said, the corner of her mouth turning up.

"You said you knew tricks. I don't like the sound of *trick*," Arken began scathingly.

"I consent," Morwë broke in, before she could change her mind. She clenched her hands in her lap. If it would safeguard Enzella, she would submit to whatever wight Arts she had to.

"Morwë—" Enzella whispered from the fireside.

"It's all right, Zel." She held up a stalling hand. "I'll be fine."

"It will not hurt," Sergeant Horne promised, stepping forward. She unbelted the large pouch at her waist. "If everyone could please step back, except you, miss." She nodded to Morwë.

Arken did not move until Captain Konstantin caught his eye and nodded. Arken reluctantly pulled away.

Sergeant Horne brushed the snow away from the ground in front of her to reveal bare ground. Then she pulled dried herbs from her bag and a small vial of some substance. She uncorked it and poured a tiny amount of the liquid onto her fingers. She drew a series of glyphs over the ground and then sprinkled the herbs over the symbols.

Morwë found herself watching in fascination. She had never seen a wight do magic before; it seemed to be entirely different than the way she used her Arts. Her Arts welled up from within her, but Sergeant Horne pulled power from the earth, using her symbols and supplies as a conduit to make sure the power did what she wanted to do.

When all was written to the sergeant's satisfaction, she struck a spark with a flint striker and lit the herbs.

The fire blazed up from the glyphs in a sharp, hot flare, and then settled into a small, steady flame, only burning the herbs where she had drawn the symbols.

"I am Mirat Horne, a sergeant of the Crown," the sergeant said. The flames stayed steady over the glyphs. "Say your name," she instructed Morwë.

Morwë licked her lips. "I am Morwë, First Daughter of the Unseelie Erlking." The flames flickered.

"Your whole name, please."

"Daughter of Igrainne," Morwë added. The flames steadied.

"This is a truth spell. All lies will be revealed, all falsehoods uncovered," Sergeant Horne intoned. "Say something untrue."

Morwë hesitated, feeling her cheeks heat, but no one could see under her scarf. She murmured, "There is nothing human about me."

Instantly the fire shuddered and turned a deep, violent red for several seconds before returning to its normal cheerful demeanor.

"You see that it does reveal lies you may say."

Morwë's throat tightened. She nodded.

Sergeant Horne squared her shoulders. "Please repeat the key portions of your testimony under the spell cloak."

Withholding a sigh, Morwë did as she was bid, repeating the important parts of her story. "The Unseelie are dead. We are the only two left. We mean no one harm," she finished.

The sergeant looked over her shoulder to Captain Konstantin for confirmation.

He scowled. "Will you cause any harm to any human in Cairenoch or the surrounding area?"

Morwë opened her mouth—and hesitated, the clawing hunger still alive and desperate within her. "I—I swear I intend no human in Cairenoch or the surrounding area harm."

The fire flickered but remained the same color.

Captain Konstantin's eyes narrowed as the sergeant finished the spell and blew out the flames.

He had caught her wording.

"Right," Konstantin said, "I'm satisfied that, to the best of your abilities, your accounts are true and correct." He shot a side eye towards Morwë. "However, I know that Sergeant Horne's spell is dependent on how *you* perceive reality, not objective facts. As such—"

Arken, seething beside her, broke in, "If you're trying to make this some sort of inquisition—"

"It is *not*." The captain's flat voice struck with all the force of a hammer and anvil. He gave Arken a long, slow look before glancing back to Morwë. Then he undid his chinstrap and removed his helm.

Morwë sucked in a harsh breath.

Free of the helm, the captain's close-cropped black hair was mussed. It had been cut short enough for her to see that the tops of his ears did not round to a natural human shape—they flattened to a point. More subtle than hers and Enzella's, but distinct.

"Faeblood," Morwë murmured.

"Some generations back," the captain said in a low voice. "No magic in me, though—just the ears. So you'll know," he continued, "This is not based on faefolk hysteria. This is an investigation over *danger*." His eyes shot to Arken.

Morwë realized Arken had frozen, had barely even breathed since Konstantin had removed his helm.

And it wasn't over the ears.

"Ask," said Konstantin abruptly.

"You… you didn't shear your head for us," Arken said hoarsely. "Not for Peridun." He glanced around the camp, and Morwë tried to see what he saw. "No braids. No queues. What's happened?"

"The princess is missing," Captain Konstantin said shortly. "She disappeared five days ago, and her lady's maid is dead. No one can find a trace of her. We don't know if it was an animal attack, raiders, or if another country kidnapped the heir to use against us. We could be at war. That's why it's imperative to deal with *this* threat, ensure the two events are not related, and make certain we will not be attacked from this quarter. We won't survive a two-front war."

"It couldn't be related," Morwë said. "Five days? I know for certain it couldn't be. No Unseelie were allowed outside the cavern since the sack on Peridun."

"Even so. It's a danger too close for comfort." Konstantin's hands clenched and released. He met Morwë's eyes as the last licks of the sunset sank below the western mountain, Fulla's Sorrow, far in the distance. "I believe you when you say you have no *intent* to do harm," he continued, emphasis resting on the word. He nodded at Arken. "And I believe this boy's story. You can't twist ones like him—they're honest as the day is long. So we will part ways in the morning. I will take my squads towards Peridun in the morning to ascertain if the threat is well and truly dead. Nothing less will satisfy the Crown. However, Sergeant Horne and Corporal Vastic will return with you and yours to Cairenoch."

Arken snapped, "So we need guards now? You just said you believed us."

"Use your head, boy," Konstantin barked. "Trust is not easily given, and mine takes a long time to earn. Horne and Vastic will monitor you in Cairenoch, but they're not throwing you in the lockup. They're going with you to keep you safe."

"*Safe?*"

"Arken," murmured Morwë, a thread of steel entering her voice.

"You don't know the state of Cairenoch," Konstantin said darkly. "It was in a whirlwind when we left, and the town council and that priest were having a hell of a time keeping the peace. We're not ceding to faefolk hysteria, but they just might be. However, servants of the Crown in attendance should give them pause. Horne and Vastic will keep you safe."

He turned his gimlet eye onto Morwë. "I assume you will not try to leave the area before we return." *Or else*, the sentence implied.

"No," she said flatly.

"Good." He nodded. "Coordinate with Sergeant Horne on logistics, and let her handle any problems in Cairenoch. That's what she's trained for. Isn't that right, Sergeant."

Sergeant Horne saluted, having cleaned up the truth spell. "Yes, sir. Good hunting."

Captain Konstantin cast a black look at Ceridfel's crooked peak. "Let's hope there's nothing left to hunt."

THE HUNGER WAS SO MUCH STRONGER NOW that there were more wights.

The soldiers had built more campfires and were in the process of preparing the evening meal. Morwë had told Enzella to stay by their fire; she didn't want some wight getting nervous and hurting Zel—Zel could make anyone edgy, but luckily she was happy to feed twigs to the fire and watch the flames as Micah told her stories. If only Morwë could say the same.

Morwë curled her arms around herself and tried to control the shakes.

There, her Arts whispered. *So close and alive, full of life—they wouldn't miss one sip, just one—*

Morwë gnashed her teeth.

The price is too high, she vowed. *And I gave my word.* She dug her fingers into the earth, trying to anchor herself. Trying not to scratch the dry patches on her skin, flaking and turning gray.

"Are you all right?" Arken settled beside her.

Her fingers tingled. The hunger that threatened to choke her subsided enough for her to speak. "Fine."

"You don't look it," he said softly.

"How would you know?" she snapped. Dusk was only just falling; she wouldn't feel safe unwrapping her hood for half an hour more.

"I can feel you shaking," he said, staring at the fire. "Everything's going to be all right. We'll go to Cairenoch in the morning and the soldiers will go on their way." His voice was low and quiet, like he wanted to soothe a frightened animal.

Better he think me frightened than hungry. "And then?"

What would they do, she and Zel? Where would they go? This vast human world stretched out before them—and Morwë knew nothing of it. How would she keep her promise to her mother then?

"Then we meet my mother," he said, and she heard the note of longing in his voice. "And then we'll see, I suppose. We'll have to find a place to stay. My sister's home isn't very big. We'll weather the winter here, and then come spring…." He swallowed. "We're both displaced, you know."

Morwë knew. Her hands clenched, dirt digging into her gloves. But his displacement was her fault.

"It's all right to be afraid," Arken continued. "We're all scared." He took her hand.

Morwë stared at their entwined fingers. He treated her like an equal—she the Erlking's first daughter, and he a… a human peasant. Villager. It should offend her. Repulse her.

No one had ever held her hand before. He was not afraid of her. *I'd step in front of an arrow for you,* he'd said. He'd meant it.

"My mother's name is Luned," he continued, rubbing his thumb over her palm. "She's a weaver, and she makes beautiful scarves, cloaks, belts—and she knits, too. I wouldn't be surprised if you and Enzella end up with something she made after the first week or two. It's how she shows she cares."

Morwë let out a skeptical breath. "How do you know she'll care for us?"

"Because I do."

She gave him a sideways glance. "You didn't like me at first."

"I didn't trust you," he corrected. "But I cared."

"Why?"

"Perhaps because no one else seemed to. But I can guarantee Mother will be happy to have you with us for as long as you want."

To Morwë, it seemed a sweet but utterly implausible dream that an unseen woman would willingly take in two faeborn girls. Inconceivable. But she said nothing, preferring to remain in this dreamlike place where Arken told her he cared. Reality was cruel and hard and she would return to it in a moment, but she'd have this small, foolish dream, just for a while.

As they sat and watched the flames, he still held her hand.

Morwë made herself pull away first, rousing her bones to move away from the light and warmth to her bedroll as hunger gnawed at her ribs in the dark.

SIXTY-ONE

INGRIDON

"Deserted," Ingridon said, taking in the settlement by starlight. No people moved; not even animals wandered through the empty streets.

"You said you left the young alive, did you not?" Yemelyan's black eyes consumed the sight before him.

"Yes, and the elderly." Ingridon opened his mouth, like he could taste remnants of phantom terror in the air. The thaumaturges had subdued all who resisted, but hadn't silenced the wails and the cries. "They must have fled like rats to the next settlement."

Yemelyan exhaled slowly, his breath spiraling into the frigid air in a pale trickle. "Cairenoch."

Ingridon cocked his head. "What, Father?"

"The town to the east. Cairenoch." Yemelyan turned slowly around, surveying the ruined gates. "That is where your sisters have gone."

"How do you know?"

The expression on his face turned distant and remote. "I've been there before."

Ingridon flexed his hands, gripped his sword hilt. "Their blood will color the snow for what they've done."

"No."

"But Father—"

Yemelyan turned his black gaze on his son. "Do not question me, Ingridon."

Ingridon choked.

Yemelyan turned away. "There was a greater purpose for moving our kind into these mountains, plans that still remain intact, even though your sister has acted rashly."

"Rashly?" Ingridon burst out. "Destroying everything we've built, betraying our family, was *rash*?"

"You fool," Yemelyan said in a low voice. "It was never about lands or ruling or territory. It was about *power*. For all her impetuousness, your sister still has her part to play. You will not indulge your bloodlust until her role has been fulfilled."

Ingridon narrowed his eyes. "What are these plans, Father? Why haven't I heard of them? Why—"

Yemelyan's words rang out like a thunderclap. "Am I not still the Erlking of the Unseelie? Do not question me, Ingridon. I will not tell you again. As of yet you are still useful to me and to my plans, but they can be modified." His black-stained lips twisted. "Everything can be modified."

Against his will, a frisson of fear snaked through Ingridon. Ingridon lowered his eyes and bent his neck. "Yes, Father." Inside, he wanted to rage, to roar at his father that *he was the* Heir *and would not be spoken to this way!*

But, he realized, eyes on the snow, *Heirs are only useful if the ruler dies.* And his father had no plans for death any time soon.

Yemelyan's robes flowed over the snow with a quiet hiss. "Yes," he said, almost to himself, "they have fled to Cairenoch. And so history repeats. But they have allies with them. Those two humans. Let us even the field of play." He held up his hand. A dark glow emanated from his palm and coalesced in a ball of shivering darkness. The ball lifted from his palm, spun a moment in the air, and then flew off into the forest, disappearing from sight.

He flexed his hand, opening and closing the black-stained fingers, frowning.

"What was that for?"

A howl rose above the trees, and more joined it in song. Through the trees, pairs of glowing green eyes approached, more and more responding to the call of his father's magic.

"Calling allies of our own. Come, my son." Yemelyan waved a hand. "We must find your sisters and remind them of their duty to family." Then he proceeded onward, followed by the conclave of eyes.

Yemelyan had been using magic at a rapid rate—for healing, tracking, creating domes to shield them from light. He would need to replenish his reserves soon.

Hadrian's face flashed into Ingridon's mind, before he shoved it ruthlessly away. Hadrian had done his duty. Given his life in service of the Erlking.

Yemelyen expected that. From everyone.

Ingridon swallowed.

SIXTY-TWO

ENZELLA

Enzella hung off the side of the sleigh as far as she could, peering intently into the new strangers' faces. "I'm Enzella," she said brightly. "And you're Vastic, and you're Mirat Horne."

The snow had finally stopped. Their little company had set out in the early morning hours towards Cairenoch, the downed tree moved and out of the way. The rest of the soldiers rode for Peridun, their armor shining in the winter sunshine.

Sergeant Horne smiled at her, but the corporal huffed. "We know our own names."

Enzella cocked her head. "You sound grumpy."

"That's 'cause I am." He scowled at her.

She stared at the long scar that bisected his high, broad cheekbone. "How'd you get your scar?"

"Cut myself shaving, didn't I," he growled.

"I hope you got better at it."

Vastic's eyes narrowed.

Enzella froze, wobbling precariously over the snow. Such flippancy would have earned her snide words or a cuff to the head from Ingridon, at the very least.

Sergeant Horne had a coughing fit into her elbow. Micah

seized the back of Enzella's gown and tried to pull her back into the sleigh, his ears bright red in embarrassment.

"Cheeky young miss, ain't ya?" Vastic ground out, but his mouth twitched. Enzella saw it curve before he turned to peer into the tree line.

She beamed before elbowing Micah. "Stop tugging on my arm."

Wheezing, Micah let go reluctantly. "Don't blame me if you fall on your head."

She wasn't afraid of the fall. Not now. Enzella tried to follow Vastic's eye line into the forest. "What are you looking for? Forest cats? Micah and I saw one a few days ago."

"Nothing so lovely." Vastic shifted in his saddle, sharp eyes alert and wary. "Not everything is sunshine and roses in the Caleahanachs, girl. Life is hard, the winters are long, and the mountains are full of beasts."

"But the forest cats help you, don't they? Micah said they protect farms and bring good luck and things." She sat back on her heels.

Vastic grumbled, "Wild animals do what they want. They hold no loyalty to anybody."

Enzella deflated. "Oh. But then, what about all the stories? Where did they come from?"

"You like stories, girl?"

Enzella hesitated. "Yes?"

"Here's a story for you." Vastic's horse sidestepped closer, bridle jingling as the horse huffed a breath of white fog from its nostrils. "Has he told you about the timber wolves?"

Enzella shook her head.

"These mountains are full of 'em. But timber wolves ain't regular wolves. They ain't right. Some folk say timber wolves are men who give in to a beastly nature."

Mirat Horne made a noise in the back of her throat. "Is this going to be fit for her ears?"

Vastic shot her an impatient look. "Reality's fit for everyone."

"I've heard worse. Beastly nature," Enzella prompted, waiting.

"Right. Men who kill others, men who beat on their wives and children, they slowly give in to the beast. One day he just walks into the woods and never comes out because a wolf has burst from his skin, making him the same outside as he is inside. A monster."

"But humans don't have those sorts of Arts," Enzella said practically. "How could that happen?"

Vastic rolled his eyes. "It's a story. Magic happens in stories without explaining how. But others have a different explanation. Folk say that in days past, some faefolk had the ability to change forms, to be a man one minute and a beast the next. And when the magic all left Karneesia, these faefolk got stuck, or they went mad, forgetting their two-legged form. But they know there's something they've lost. So they hunt humans, become man-eaters. They're driven by hate. That's why when you see those yellow eyes in the dark, you run. They're uncanny—a man staring out from a beast's body, looking to kill."

Enzella's brow wrinkled. "I thought you said this was a story."

Vastic raised an eyebrow. "I did."

"But some faefolk *did* change to beasts," Enzella said. "Not the Unseelie. But some of them. It was written down in our histories. Morwë told me. So… maybe it's true."

Micah turned the color of clotted cream. "If all stories have a grain of truth…."

"It's just a story," Vastic ground out. "Story, old wives' tales, hearsay, faeble. Don't mean a thing."

Enzella propped her elbows on the sleigh's side and rested her chin in her hands. "It wasn't a story at all. Stories have a beginning, middle, and end. I know that much."

"How about if I tell you a story?" Micah shot a quelling glance at Vastic.

She pouted. "But I want Vastic to."

"Zel, I don't think—"

"I've got a story," Vastic said. "I traveled in a mercenary band as a young man before coming home to join the guard. We went as far south as Darikar, and I heard this story in a bazaar. Don't worry," he said, smirking at Micah. "It's appropriate."

Enzella crossed her arms. "And it's a *real* story?"

"Yes. It's called The Thief of Darikar." Vastic cleared his throat. "So in the far away city of Darikar, right on the edge of the Sarkan desert, there was a thief named Hassan. And he could steal anything. Get into anywhere. No bolted door, no locked trunk was safe. He stole coins and diamonds and jewels, ladies' veils and fans, men's maps and chains of office, swords and daggers of soldiers. Anything he felt like."

Enzella leaned forward. "What did he do with all of it?"

"Well, some of it he kept, but sometimes he gave the money to destitute mothers or families who had been thrown out of their homes. He gave presents to strangers on the street. And sometimes he gave back what he stole, because what he really liked was stealing to prove he could. So no one ever knew what would happen to their valuables, if they'd be here today or gone tomorrow. So one day the caliph—"

"What's that?"

Vastic sucked his teeth. "Like a ruler, a lord. The caliph has gotten complaints about Hassan the thief, see, but no one is more annoyed than his daughter. The caliph's daughter is just tired of it, because she had wanted to wear a necklace of her mother's to some fancy party, and it isn't in her jewelry box. So that's the last straw. And she wants to get the better of him, so she issues a challenge to Hassan the thief—she says there is a treasure absolutely impossible to steal, no way in the world, and if he will just stop being a—" Vastic coughed, looking at Enzella, "a nuisance, she will tell him what it is."

"Of course Hassan is curious. He's stolen some amazing things. And he's also offended, because he knows he's the greatest thief who ever lived. So he comes to the caliph's daughter and asks what the treasure is, saying he'll devote all his energies to this and not steal another thing until he accomplishes his task.

And the daughter—she's a princess I guess—the princess says, 'finally!' And she declares, 'the treasure is my heart, more closely guarded than the most prized rubies, and you will never be able to steal it, unsatisfied man.'"

"More closely guarded than rubies," Enzella repeated, entranced.

Micah snorted.

Vastic nodded at him. "Right. So Hassan is fascinated; he's never stolen a heart before. So he brings the princess fragrant and rare flowers from Cadruissau, and composes poems and songs to her beauty, and gifts her puppies and kittens to dote on. But it doesn't work. He doesn't have her heart. He competes in duels for her honor. He climbs mountains, goes on epic adventures in her name and still does not have her heart.

"This is very discouraging for Hassan, who up to this point was a very good thief. He gets depressed, and the princess notices, so she makes time to sit and talk with him since he isn't running around trying to give her the jewel of Achad Lloren or anything. And finally Hassan tells her that she was right; he doesn't know how to steal her heart and he's not a good thief after all. He's very sad at this point."

Enzella propped her chin up in her hands. "Poor Hassan."

Vastic snorted. "And the princess says, 'well, Hassan, that's because you were wrong. Love is not something you can steal. But I was wrong, too. A heart can't be taken away and locked up; that's not good for it. Hearts can only be given.' And she gives Hassan, the unsatisfied thief who never knew what he wanted, her heart. And that's the story of the Thief of Darikar."

"All right," Micah conceded. "That story was pretty good."

"What was her name?" Enzella asked.

"Hm?" Vastic raised an eyebrow.

"The princess! The caliph's daughter. What was her name?"

The corner of his mouth turned up. "Yasmin."

"Hassan and Yasmin," Enzella repeated, picturing them in her head. "I like that."

CHAPTER

SIXTY-THREE

MICAH

The stories only tided Enzella over for so long before she was back to peppering Micah with questions. "Where are we going?"

"To Cairenoch; you know that," Micah reminded her patiently.

"No, I mean, where does your sister live?"

"She and Leofric, her husband, live a little ways out of town," Micah said. "He's a merchant's son that's taken up farming."

"Poorly," Arken muttered from the front of the sleigh.

"You don't like Leofric?" Micah asked, surprised.

His brother raised an eyebrow. "You do?"

"I don't know him well," Micah confessed. Selma had met Leofric when she had gone to Cairenoch several years ago to help some distant cousins with their brood of children and their farm, and the two had married after a short courtship. Micah had only been eleven at the time, and hadn't spent much time with his brother-in-law beyond a few scant visits.

"He's an ass," Arken said flatly. "I don't know what Selma sees in him."

"An ass?" Enzella's brows drew together. "Like Ingridon?"

"No!" Micah hastened to assure her. "No, Leofric…."

Arken made a face. "He's just southern stock."

"What's that mean?" Enzella asked.

"His people are merchants from the hill countries, Trellester and the like. They only moved to Altesia a generation or so ago. He still doesn't understand the way we do things. And then Selma went and lost her head and said she had to have him, but he didn't want to move to Peridun." Arken glowered at nothing.

"He didn't *want* to?" Micah's brows shot up. "I thought the reason was there was more opportunities in Cairenoch...."

Arken shrugged. "Maybe that was another reason."

"Why would he move to Peridun?" Enzella asked curiously. "I thought he lived here."

Arken glanced at her. "In Altesia, the family lines travel through the firstborn girl. Sons leave home and live with their wives' family and help them with the farm or business."

Vastic nodded, bringing his horse closer. "Leave and cleave."

"What's that?" Enzella said.

"It's from scripture—'a man should leave his father and mother and be united to his wife'," Micah told her.

Arken continued. "It doesn't matter as much where younger sons and daughters end up—some go to the cities to find work, or join the church, or go into the guard, but Selma's my mother's only girl—she should have inherited the house and land we had in Peridun."

Enzella peered at Vastic. "Is that why you joined the guard?"

He nodded once. "Younger son, no prospects." He fingered the scar and bristles on his chin. "Did well for myself, I think."

"Mother should've talked sense into her, but Selma's always wanted bigger towns with more people." Arken shrugged. "And she's always been set on her own way. So, she said she was going to move to Cairenoch and marry Leofric, and nothing we said could sway them. When Micah and I marry, we'll leave home, and Mother will be alone, or she'll have to move in with one of our families, and that's seen as shameful. Leofric should have come out to join Selma and Mother, but he shirked his responsibilities." Arken glanced back at Enzella. "That's all in the past now, though. There's no real harm in him. All talk and bluster; don't worry."

Enzella looked up at Micah. "But if they were all home with you, wouldn't they be—erm, have been kidnapped, too?"

The thought hit Micah like a rock. "You're right," he croaked.

"I'm glad they weren't."

"Me too," he said, feeling a rush of goodwill for Leofric. If he hadn't been a stubborn lowlander, Arken and his mother wouldn't have been away when Selma's pains started. Arken would've been taken too. And then… who knows? "God works in mysterious ways, I guess," he whispered.

Enzella leaned against him as they approached a fork in the road. Micah put an arm around her shoulders and swallowed hard. Very mysterious ways

Sergeant Horne pulled her horse close to Arken and said, "Best to go around Cairenoch to your brother-in-law's farm."

"You think there'll be trouble?" he asked.

"I think it's best to avoid any complications it might cause. There's no reason you need to go into town, is there?"

"Well, I'd like to see Father James at some point, tell him I got back, but it can wait for a day or two." Arken clucked to the horses and they took the left fork, away from the Lady's Mirror Lake and around the town.

Enzella waved goodbye to the glimpse of the lake through the trees. "Why is it called the Lady's Mirror?"

"Didn't I tell you?" Micah asked, surprised.

"No."

"It's very flat and reflective," he said. "On clear days, depending on what side of the lake you're on, you can see all the mountains in the water. The Caleahanachs are female, you know."

Enzella sat up straight. "The mountains are *girls*? Morwë, did you hear?"

"I did," Morwë said.

Micah laughed. "All the peaks—Fulla's Sorrow, Queen's Crest,

Ceridfel, even Watchtower. It's Altesian lore that the land is female, and she's married to the river."

"What's the river's name?"

Micah smiled at her. "Glais."

"What's that mean?"

"'River.'"

"Micah, stop teasing," she complained.

"He's not," Sergeant Horne offered, making Enzella jump a little. "The land is a lady, and she can't be changed or moved, but she loves her man, who's changeable and mysterious and just a little dangerous. He goes by other names when he leaves the mountains, but his waters never fail, his springs never run dry. They say no one's ever found the river's origins."

"Are you from the mountains, too?" Enzella asked with simple curiosity.

"Altesian through and through," Sergeant Horne said with a small smile. "I'm from Cruever, the capitol. A long time ago, my mother's people came from Cadruissau or maybe Udresh—warm sands and the sea. But one of my ancestors had restless feet and came up to the mountains, so here I am."

"And you like it?" Enzella said. "Vastic told me about the wolves, and Micah told me about the forest cats and Clever Reeny."

"Clever Reeny was one of my favorite stories as a child," Sergeant Horne confessed. Her smile grew. "I love the Calea-hanachs. In the spring, the mountainsides fairly burst with color, flowers of all shapes and hues in bloom. And in the fall, all the leaves turn brilliant yellows and reds, as if a fire swept over the land. But I've never seen a forest cat."

Enzella sat up very straight. "I have!" She proceeded to tell Sergeant Horne all about their spotting earlier on the trip, in exquisite detail.

The sergeant was very appreciative. "You don't see them much around the bigger towns and cities," she said. "That sounds very exciting."

"It was," Enzella said, her mouth stretching wide in a smile, highlighting her wide-set eyes and sharp cheekbones, right to the ears with their flared points. The cuts on her cheek had healed well with the ariswort.

A shred of doubt crept into Micah. He bit his lip. Would his mother see the little girl who had sat by him in his cell, who had shared his pain and sorrow and gave him hers as well? Or would she see something else?

He didn't have long to wait. Little more than half an hour passed before Arken pulled the sleigh to a stop in the midst of a modest farmyard.

The door opened, and Micah saw the flash of a blue shawl. Instinctively, he jumped from the sleigh and crossed the farmyard, floundering in snow drifts until he found his footing and recovered. His eyes were locked ahead of him.

His mother's red-rimmed eyes widened. "Micah!"

He fell into her arms, sobbing, and she held him up. All of it poured out of Micah in his cries—the horror of death, the terror underground, his black despair that he would never see her again.

And yet here she was.

"You're all right," she said in a choked voice. "You're—*here*."

The waver in her voice, when she was usually so strong, struck a chord in him. Abruptly, Micah pulled back to see her face, the brown and graying hair that had hung past her waist shorn off around her chin. She had grieved. She had thought him dead.

"Yes, Mama. I'm all right," he said, desperate to reassure her of his wellbeing. "You see?" He clutched her tightly. "Arken and I are both all right."

SIXTY-FOUR

ARKEN

Arken lifted Enzella down from the sleigh and reached for Morwë.

"I can manage," Morwë said tightly.

"I know," Arken said. He held his hand out anyway, and she finally gave in and used his hand to steady herself as she stepped down.

"Arken! What were you *thinking*?"

He turned to see his mother striding through the snowdrifts towards him, agony on her face.

Arken stepped forward. "Mama, I can explain—"

"How?" she demanded, clutching her skirts in her fists. "How, when you were barely thinking at all! When Father James told me what happened—told me you had gone back—I died a thousand times!" Her voice broke as she clutched the front of Arken's tunic.

"Mama, I had to get Micah." Arken put his hands on her shoulders and squeezed. "I'm sorry. I couldn't leave him." His vision blurred.

Luned sobbed. "Foolish boy, don't you know I could have lost you both?"

"I'm sorry," Arken said again. "I couldn't see any other way."

She threw her arms around him, weeping. He hugged her back, closing his eyes as the tears streaked down his cheeks.

"You're home! You're alive!"

Arken lifted his head to see Selma and Leofric standing at the door of the house, their eyes wide and astonished—and then confusion and fear growing as they took in the guards, strangers, and Enzella, with her hood thrown back.

"Faefolk!" Leofric spat, his beard bristling. "You've brought faefolk to our door?!" He squared his shoulders and moved towards them aggressively. Arken let go of his mother and interposed himself between Leofric and the girls.

Sergeant Horne swung her horse into Leofric's path. "These women are under my protection, not to be harmed. Any move against them will constitute an attack on the Crownsguard."

Corporal Vastic, who up to this point hadn't cared a jot about the hysterics of the situation, seemed cheered at the thought of a fight. He leered at Leofric and spat.

Leofric tried to glare around Sergeant Horne's horse. "I'll not have it! You betray your people, your family—"

"Quiet!" Luned's voice rang through the farmyard like a whip crack. She glared Leofric down with steely blue eyes. "Leofric Vitrear, I'm ashamed of you. Forgetting the rules of hospitality. Insulting guests before we've even heard their tale. Enough."

In a last ditch effort, he said, "This is my house, and—"

She drew herself up straight, pinning him with her gaze. "Are you claiming to be head of this family, Leofric?"

I was right, Arken thought. *Ass through and through.*

The battle of wills stretched between them, battling for dominance—and finally Leofric looked away. Arken's mother turned to the guards, Morwë, and Enzella. "I am Luned Sawyer. Come in, and welcome. We would like to hear your tale."

CHAPTER

SIXTY-FIVE

MORWË

"You expect us to just—just believe this?" Leofric said. "The word of *faefolk*?" It sounded like he spoke of the lowest form of life. By the look on his face, Morwë thought, it wasn't too far off the mark.

Enzella flinched and leaned into Morwë. Morwë wrapped an arm around her and glared at the man, stubbornly refusing to shrink away.

Micah and Arken had retold the whole story again for their family, and Sergeant Horne finished with the orders from her captain. But their brother-in-law remained stubbornly skeptical.

"No," Arken said in a hard voice. "I expect you to believe *mine*."

"These are the ones who slaughtered a whole village! Who's to say these won't just murder us in our beds, too?" He made an angry gesture towards Morwë. "This one hasn't even uncovered itself—"

Arken was on his feet and reaching across the table before anyone could blink.

His mother exclaimed. The guards put their hands on the weapons. Enzella gasped.

Morwë lunged for Arken's arm to hold him back.

"You watch your mouth," Arken growled. "She's not an 'it,' and you'll remember it, or—"

Morwë yanked on his arm, pulling him back into his seat. "It's an easy enough request," Morwë said, ice in her voice.

Arken turned to look at her. "Morwë, you don't have to satisfy his vulgar curiosity."

"I can certainly take off my scarf if it makes Master Vitrear more *comfortable*." Morwë very much doubted that it would. "You only need to close the shutters and light the lamps."

"Will that satisfy you, Master Vitrear?" Sergeant Horne said gravely. "You should know that my captain believed their tale, and he has the full confidence of the Crown."

Leofric still glared but did not protest as Vastic got up and shut the farmhouse shutters. Luned set a lamp on the table. Beside Morwë, Enzella wriggled happily in its glow, enchanted once again by the firelight. Arken's jaw ticked.

Morwë pulled back her hood and unwound the scarf. Her dark tangle of hair fell around her shoulders as she bared her face.

Luned went very still and pale, staring at Morwë fixedly.

Why was Luned looking at her so? Morwë had seen enough wights by now to assure herself that she and Enzella were not markedly different. Their features were thinner, sharper, and their pointed ears signaled their heritage, but they did not have qualities exaggerated by magic like some faefolk.

"I am neither ghost nor specter," Morwë told the room flatly. "Think me monstrous if you like. But I am flesh and bone, just like you."

"You may be bloody solid, but you're not staying in my house, and that's my final word on it," Leofric growled, banging his hand on the table.

"I never asked you to house us," Morwë said with bitter dignity. "Zel and I will go."

"If they go, I'm going with them," Arken declared, staring his brother-in-law down.

"Arken!" Selma exclaimed from the doorway to another room where she was holding her baby. "Leofric, you can't let him."

Grumbling, Leofric got up from the table, his chair scraping along the floor to speak to his wife in a low voice.

"You don't need to come," Morwë told Arken through her teeth. "I'm sure the sergeant will follow wherever Zel and I go."

The sergeant gave a quiet nod.

"I do," Arken insisted. "I want to go with you, Morwë. Besides you don't have anywhere to go."

Luned pursed her lips, watching the two of them closely.

"Surely there are lodging houses in Cairenoch for travelers," Morwë said practically. "We will go there."

"How? You don't have any money," Arken said.

Morwë took a deep, obstinate breath and reached for the bag they had brought with them, overturning it in her lap. She sorted through the items to find the velvet bag. Enzella caught the odd rock and doll before they fell to the floor. "Thank you, Zel," Morwë murmured.

Morwë opened the velvet pouch that clanked and held it under Arken's nose. "This is how," she said in a low voice. His eyes grew very big at the sight of the jewels inside.

Enzella reached for the quilt still in Morwë's lap. "This is mine, see?" she told Micah. "Mother made it for me." She spread it over the table and smoothed it out.

Micah, who looked as upset as everyone else, nodded. "Very pretty."

"She made it when I was a baby. Morwë helped." Enzella set the rock and the doll on the quilt and inspected them, turning them over in her hands.

Luned's eyes focused on the items in Zel's hand and widened.

Arken said under his breath to Morwë, "You'll attract too much notice. You can't pay for lodging with a diamond earring or jeweled bracelet. If thieves don't come after you, some small-minded fool will say you stole it and call out the watch. We can find somewhere else."

"There is no need for you to come," Morwë insisted. In fact, he *shouldn't* come. She had no idea what to do about the kneph-hunger, and it was dangerous for him to be around her. Too dangerous.

"Of course not, but I can't just let you go off alone—"

"We *won't* be alone, the guards—"

"—Are *guards*. No offense," Arken murmured over his shoulder to Sergeant Horne.

"None taken," she said easily.

Luned's eyes flicked back and forth from the quilt to the rock to Morwë's face. "You will not be staying at the inn, nor camping somewhere along the road." she said, her voice breaking through the chatter.

"They will not stay here, I said!" Leofric insisted. "This is my house—"

"No, they won't stay here. They will go—we will *all* go—to the Obelyn farm."

All the humans frowned.

Morwë exchanged a puzzled look with Enzella, then stared at Luned blankly. "Where?"

"You can't go *there*," Leofric finally said, scandalized.

"Why not?"

"It's been abandoned for years! It's probably haunted! And anyway, by law, it's not claimable. The whole area was turned back to the land."

Luned did not look away from Morwë's face. "The Obelyns left the house and land to their daughter and any of her heirs."

"Everyone knows it was a slap in the face to the families who owned the bordering properties; their daughter died years earlier."

"Not died," Luned said, eyes luminous as she watched Morwë. "Disappeared." She glanced down at the objects on the table and picked up the funny rock with the silver vein running through it. "I've seen this stone before."

The world all around Morwë went quiet.

Luned held the stone out to Morwë. "What was your mother's name?"

Morwë's hand shook as Luned set the stone in her palm. "Igrainne," Morwë whispered.

"I knew it." Luned's eyes filled with tears. "I *knew* it. You have every right to go to the Obelyn farm. Igrainne Obelyn, my best friend, disappeared twenty-six years ago. And now here you are, with your mother's face. You've come home."

SIXTY-SIX

MORWË

The farm, Luned said, was called Wardwood. It had belonged to the Obelyn family for many generations, passed down through the oldest daughter, as things were done in Altesia. When Igrainne had disappeared many years ago, her parents had grieved deeply, but never thought her dead. Instead of ceding the land to a neighbor or much distant relative, they had sealed the property in trust for their long-lost daughter. This and many more things Luned told them on their ride to the farm, but much of it didn't register with Morwë.

Leofric and Selma had not wanted Luned to leave, but she had insisted. "How can I leave my best friend's daughters alone? I must go; she would want this."

Morwë could still feel Luned's arms around her in a fierce, impassioned hug. "You have her look," Luned had whispered in her ear. "I knew, the moment I saw your face. I knew."

Ahead of them, Wardwood loomed. The woods had encroached into the fields in the years since the Obelyns' deaths and Wardwood's subsequent abandonment. Overgrown and fallow, the fields sprouted gorse and brambles dotted with snow. At the end of the disused road stood a large wood and stone house with ruined shutters hanging askew from the windows.

Nature had encroached there too, but the structure itself looked solid and sound.

Arken pulled the sleigh to a stop and helped them out.

"We have to introduce you to the house," said Luned, straightening her skirts.

"Is the house alive?" Enzella gasped, her eyes wide.

"No, but it's traditional." Luned took Enzella's hand in her left and reached for Morwë with her right.

Morwë let Luned lead them through the gate and up to the threshold of the spider-webbed and snow-crusted house.

"Wardwood," Luned said, her voice ringing through the silence of the farm. "Here are Morwë and Enzella, daughters of Igrainne, Obelyns by blood and right. The land is no longer desolate. Your bereavement is over. They have come home."

As her words died away, Morwë felt—something. A shift, as if something dormant and inward-focused had—not precisely turned to look at her—but acknowledged her presence.

Morwë breathed in the scent of snow and dust, the musk of wild animals who had passed by and left a mark, and beneath it the smell of rich earth, and stone, and clear water. Then Luned reached down and lifted a loose flagstone to reveal a small metal key.

"I was here when they closed the house, after Bera and Kor's death," Luned explained, straightening. "They paid and pensioned the servants, sold the outermost lands that were tenant farms, and then locked the house up tight. But they always believed that someone would return." She inserted the key into the lock and, with the groan of disused hinges, pushed open the door.

The group stepped into Wardwood.

Inside the house, it smelled musty and stale, full of dust. Luned led them along a dark wood-paneled passageway and into a much larger space. The others fumbled for flint to light torches, but Morwë could see clearly. At the far end of the hall stood a huge empty fireplace with an intricately carved mantle, taller than

Zel and wider than Morwë could reach across. Stout wooden tables and chairs stood in the center of the room, silent sentinels, while finer furniture had been bundled to the side and covered with cloths. It made the room appear to contain lurking ghosts.

The torches finally caught, and color bloomed along with light. Morwë could see the places where tapestries had once hung in between the tall, shuttered windows. Wardwood had glass windows, unlike Arken's home in Peridun or Leofric's precious farmhouse.

Morwë turned in a careful circle, eyes lifting to the vaulted ceiling above as the reality sunk in. Her mother was not some nameless wight of no consequence after all. She had lived in this fine house, walked these flagstones, touched these walls.

Igrainne Obelyn. Her mother.

After a survey of the state of the house, Luned took charge with easy authority and decided that for now they'd better camp in the main hall, the easiest part of the house to clean and keep warm on short notice, thanks to the fireplace. The nearby pantry and buttery, once cleaned out, would also give them a place to unload their supplies from the sleigh.

Luned sent the menfolk out to see to the horses and inspect the state of the stables, and Enzella tagged along behind them, her eyes agog and mouth hanging open. Sergeant Horne generously offered to unload the sleigh; probably, Morwë suspected, to get out of cleaning duty.

"What a good thing I brought along brooms and dust cloths," Luned said, tying back her shorn hair into a kerchief and tying another cloth around her nose. "Use this broom to get rid of some of these cobwebs—but don't kill the cobs if you can help it; they've done a fine job of keeping down the rest of the bugs." Luned used her own broom to sweep. "Once we get rid of some of the dirt, we'll scrub down this floor to make it really clean."

Morwë set to her task, brushing the fine silver threads from the rafters and corners. A few dried herbs still hung from the rafters in the pantry, petrified and brittle. "Should I take these down?" she asked humbly, feeling ignorant of both manual labor and wight customs.

Luned looked up. "Oh, yes. But save them—we could use them for kindling, if they're dry enough."

Sergeant Horne entered, rolling a barrel. "Where do you want this, Mistress Sawyer?"

Luned straightened and surveyed the area. "Just pile it in whatever corner looks the cleanest—I haven't swept the pantry yet."

Sergeant Horne nodded and righted the barrel on its end. She had to dodge Arken on her way out the door again.

"The stables look sound enough for now," Arken said, rolling up the sleeves of his shirt. "I think part of the roof might need to be replaced, but we've got the horses in the box stalls and they're happy with their grain. Micah and Enzella are rubbing them down. Vastic's gone to do a survey of the grounds. I came to see if you want me to start a fire—it will be dark in a few hours."

"My, yes, and then we'll need to eat something." Luned nodded, moving across the floor with her broom. "Morwë has some ancient herbs you can use for tinder."

Arken flashed Morwë a grin when he took the fragile stems she offered. "My thanks for the use of Wardwood's bounty, mistress."

Morwë drew herself up—but then saw the spark of mischief in his eye. "It was little enough," she said airily, waving a hand to get him out of the way of her broom. She needed to get the cobweb in the corner, and she'd need to stand on the barrel to do it.

Arken bowed out of her way and stacked tinder and kindling on the empty iron firedogs. With a strike of flint, he got a spark and set to coaxing the wood into flame.

Clambering up onto the barrel, Morwë straightened and

brushed her broom along the walls and windows, careful to allow the scurrying spiders to escape. She swept up the threads, intricate as a woven cloth, as well as the dead carcasses of bugs snared in the webs. She was glad of the scarf still around her nose and mouth as the webs fell and Luned swept them up.

Morwë bent over and leaned the broom against the wall, crouching to ease off the barrel. But she misjudged and nearly toppled over—and suddenly Arken was there, gripping her waist and gloved hand to keep her upright. Morwë steadied herself. "Thank you."

"Always," he said. "Help you down?"

She nodded. He set his hands around her waist. She gripped his shoulders, and he lifted her to the floor. She felt so warm in the circle of his arms.

Over Arken's shoulder, Morwë saw Luned give them a considering look.

Then the hunger struck, roaring up in her like an inferno from a spark on deadwood. Morwë wanted to set her lips to his skin, dig her teeth in and consume, *consume*—

Morwë jerked away from Arken and grabbed the broom, her hands clutching the wood so hard it creaked.

No, she insisted, even as her insides cramped and her arms shook. *I will not. Not him.*

Enzella burst through the door, panting. "The house is so big!" Her eyes danced with delight. "And it's ours?" She fairly leapt into Morwë's arms.

Locking the hunger away, trapping it as firmly as she knew how, Morwë caught her sister and spun her around, holding her tightly. "Yes," she whispered, though she could hardly fathom it.

Enzella wriggled free and bounded over to Luned. "Can we see the rest of the house? Can we? I've seen the grounds. Vastic's a grouch but he let me come. We found a badger den but I couldn't look in," she said regretfully.

Luned laughed and straightened. "I think this is as good a

time as any for a break." She winced and put a hand to the small of her back.

Arken took the broom from his mother's hand and kissed her cheek. "Go on. I'll help the sergeant unload." He kindled a torch in the fire that now flickered merrily and handed it to her.

Luned smiled at her son and led the way up the narrow stair in the corner of the hall. Enzella pulled Morwë along behind. Arken snagged the other broom out of Morwë's hands as she passed and winked.

"This is the servant's stairway," Luned said as they climbed the narrow stair. "You saw the main stair when we entered through the front. This stair comes out by the master bed chamber."

Morwë stored that information, sorting through it in her mind. "Were they wealthy, the Obelyns?"

Luned paused in the hallway as Enzella and Morwë emerged from the stairwell. "Don't know I'd call it wealthy, per se. Well off. They had servants—a cook and two maids and a stable boy, but no one else. They weren't titled; the Obelyns worked their own land as well as renting portions of it to tenants, though they rented more and more as they got on in years. There are much richer farms to the south and west of Cairenoch. But their ancestors were some of the first to arrive in the area and claimed the land as the law allowed. The Obelyns have always held kinship with the land."

Luned lifted the torch she held, and the flame illuminated some of the darkness, though Morwë and Enzella could see past it. "There are four or five solars on this floor, and after that visitors were put in pallets in the hall." She walked along the dust-ridden floor until she reached the middle door along the right wall. "This was Igrainne's solar." She turned the knob, and with great protestations, the door swung inward.

Morwë stepped inside the room, cloth-covered tables and chairs lurking like ghosts in the corners. A four-poster bed stood against the far wall, hung with draperies. At the foot was a large oak chest. Enzella tried the lid, but it was locked.

Luned crossed to a window and tugged at shutters; Enzella helped her, and they finally unlatched them and pulled them open to let the winter sunlight spill into the room. Some creature had nibbled the carpet in years past, but the sunlight revealed the pattern and weave. Enzella started pulling off drop cloths, sending clouds of dust into the air with abandon.

My mother lived here, Morwë thought, and caught sight of her face in a mirror, mottled but clearly her swathed in black. Her mother's eyes stared back from the looking glass.

"What is so special about this rock?" Morwë plucked it from her pocket and turned it over in her hand. "I don't understand. How did it let you know me?"

Luned reached for the chunk of stone, and Morwë let it go with reluctance. When it was in her hand, she felt better. Not hungry and restless.

"Your mother was very beautiful, did you know that?"

Morwë nodded. The traces had lingered even as illness ravaged her.

"And she was the heir to Wardwood—the only one. She had suitors coming out of her ears," Luned laughed, "from landowners to butcher's boys."

Enzella plopped into an uncovered chair and propped her hands beneath her chin, for once not interrupting.

Luned turned the rock over in her hands. "I was there when one of beaus presented her with this—a chunk of silver ore from the Eskdahl mine on Queen's Crest, just newly opened. He had gone there to work, and came back with proof that he could save up for a marriage settlement, and he wasn't afraid of the work. A nice lad," Luned said softly.

"What happened?" Enzella whispered.

Luned wiped a tear at the corner of her eye. "Igrainne disappeared. She was walking home from Cairenoch around Midwinter, the longest, darkest night of the year, with no moon to light it.

Cairenoch always has a festival that night, with cakes, cider ale, music, that sort of thing. Dancing, too," she added. "Igrainne loved to dance. She left town but never reached Wardwood. People suspected she ran off with a swain, or got taken by the timber wolves or some other haint… but I never thought so." Luned sniffed. "She was the heir, and her parents had no one else. There had been a younger brother, but he died. She wouldn't have left the land. Not if she had a choice."

"I always assumed Father stole her," said Morwë. "She hated him enough."

Luned covered her face. "Oh, Igrainne…."

"You couldn't have done anything," Morwë said, throat tight. "No one stood against the Erlking and what he wanted."

But I did.

Her eyes widened at the realization.

"What happened to the lad?" Enzella reached out with one finger and gently touched the silver vein in the stone.

"Went back to the capitol heartbroken. I never saw him again. Poor boy."

"Poor boy," Enzella echoed.

"Did she love him?" The words did not come easily to Morwë's tongue. "Is that why she kept it? Held onto it?"

Luned shrugged. "I couldn't say. She never told me if she did. It could be she wanted to keep hold of a piece of the mountains— a piece of home." She wiped her eyes one last time and then clapped her hands together, motioning them to follow. "Come along. Let's find something for you to wear."

Wardwood had chests of belongings and clothes, plate and silver and linens, all packed away in storage. Luned opened chest after chest to Enzella's curious eyes, answering her questions as Morwë stood silently by. Enzella was soon distracted by a stick and hoop of wood, which Luned explained was a game, and she ran off to the great hall to try it.

Luned chuckled. "I'll set aside some clothes for her. Now." She eyed Morwë's shape with a keen eye. "Here. Try this gown and surcoat; I think they'll fit you fine. And this one, too—oh, and this. I found you a fresh shift, too. I'll see if there are more smocks and hose in this next trunk." She piled several changes of clothes into Morwë's arms. "You're much the same size as Igrainne."

"These were my mother's clothes?"

"Yes. I think everything else wouldn't fit at all. I'm going to have to search for anything remotely Enzella's size, as it is."

Morwë trailed back to her mother's bedchamber in something of a fog. She laid the garments over a chair and unlaced the fine black velvet gown, somewhat worse for wear after travel. She let it drop to the floor and stepped out of it, then pulled off the soiled shift. She avoided looking for any patches of skin that looked gray and dead. She put on the new shift and let its folds settle over her. Then she shook out a deep blue gown and drew it over her head, lacing it closed.

Morwë fingered the fabric's thick folds. The garments didn't smell of must or age, to her great surprise—merely a sweet floral scent, as if they had been packed away only a short time ago.

Morwë turned to the mirror and plaited her hair, staring at her reflection. She touched the mirror where a cat with large eyes stared out at her from the carved frame. Had her mother seen the same image reflected back at her, twenty-six years ago? Except for her ears. She traced the points, finding the subtle differences in her appearance that made her Morwë.

"Mother, I'm home," she whispered.

She brought the matching sleeveless surcoat over to the mirror and smoothed it into place as Luned opened the door, carrying a pile of clothes. "I can't find anything Enzella's size, but some of these will be fairly simple to cut down," she said, tossing them over another chair. "My, that looks well on you!"

Morwë touched the deep dips in her surcoat that fell to her hips. "Is it supposed to be cut so low?"

Luned laughed. "The length means you're a landowner, a lady, not a working woman like me." She moved her apron to show Morwë her surcoat's sides were only cut to her waist. "But don't think you won't be working. It will take all of us to get this house clean. Here's an apron." Morwë took it and tied it on, her lips turning up in a small smile.

WHEN LUNED HAD TAKEN a break from cleaning to begin supper preparations, Morwë had put on her scarf and cloak and gone walking. Everyone else had been able to see the grounds, and she wanted to see them before the last of the light went. She went out through the pantry, past the overgrown vegetable gardens crusted with frost and down the hill towards the fields.

The land unrolled before her like a parchment, one she knew would take time to decipher, dotted with fields and woods, inhabited by the unfamiliar mysteries of Altesia. But it was hers.

The thought was strange.

She heard someone follow behind her. She stopped by a massive oak with bare branches lit by the last flare of the sun and waited.

Arken walked up and stopped beside her, saying nothing.

It made her awkward in the twilight, reluctant to pull her scarves away from her face, even though the sun finally dipped below the mountains and she was safe.

"It's a lot to take in," Arken said at last, staring at the overgrown garden.

"Yes," said Morwë.

"But I'm glad," he said, casting a glance at her from under his still-ragged hair. "I didn't want you to feel like you didn't belong anywhere. Hated the idea, actually," he murmured.

Morwë had no idea how to respond to that.

"Mother brought me here once, when I was very young. We were visiting relatives in Cairenoch. I think I was being a handful, so she left Selma with the relatives and took me on a very, very long walk. We ended up here. It wasn't quite so wild then, but the woods were making their mark on the place. We didn't go beyond the gate." Arken stopped again, and turned to her. "It hurt her, to see the place so lonesome."

"Did she tell you what had happened?"

"No. Only that her best friend used to live here, and she missed her." The corners of his mouth turned down. "She's torn up that she couldn't do more."

Morwë shook her head. "She couldn't have known. And my father was too powerful. No one could have gotten my mother out of his stronghold."

"No?" Arken raised an eyebrow. "I got you out."

She drew herself up. "I rescued *you*."

"You helped a little," he said, mouth curving up in a smirk.

Morwë fairly tore the scarf away from her face so she could level the full force of her glare on him. "If you think," Morwë said, ice in her voice, "that after all of—"

"Morwë," Arken laughed, putting his hands on her shoulders, "Morwë. I was *joking*. I would never—" His voice wavered a moment, then steadied. "I know without a shadow of a doubt that we never would have made it out alive without you. I owe you my life and both my hands."

She swallowed, her anger derailed and her composure shaken. And she realized, from the thrum under her breastbone and the way her body warmed in a way that it never had before, that this was not the kneph-hunger. It was—something else. A sort of desperation, a longing that had no name. She didn't know what he could see in her face, if he would recognize it.

She couldn't even decide if she knew what it was.

"Well, you helped," she said, voice hoarse.

Arken laughed, filling the air with the joyful tune of his voice. "You look lovely, by the way."

She smoothed her hands over the fabric of her new dress. "My mother's."

He winked. "Well, you didn't get your beauty from your father."

Her eyes widened in surprise. The warmth in her flared to a burning.

Then his blue eyes drifted to her mouth.

A nameless dread welled up in her, stirred by hunger and black memory. Her body locked and her heart pounded hard enough to beat out of her chest. *He will—and then what—what—*

But Arken didn't kiss her. Instead, he pressed his forehead against hers and closed his eyes. Their noses brushed.

Morwë could see every single one of his eyelashes, dark against his cheeks. She could breathe his breath, just like in the dark passage under the mountain, when she had pulled him into an alcove to hide. She shook with the hunger for his life force, the fear of his nearness, the way no man had been to her, and—and—

Morwë caught her lips between her teeth hard enough to draw blood.

Arken opened his eyes, pulled back. He opened his mouth to speak.

She rasped, "You shouldn't have done that."

He blinked, confused, but she pressed on. She must warn him. Before he did something foolish. Before she gave in to the rioting emotions that threatened to tear her apart. "You shouldn't. Because I—I—I don't want to hurt you." She turned away, horrified at the break in her voice.

He caught her gloved hand, held it fast. "Morwë. What's wrong? Won't you tell me?"

Morwë pulled, but Arken didn't let her go.

The need clawed through her, growing ravenous for his blood, his life, his breath, anything she could get. It took her voice and deepened it to a growl. "I'm so *hungry*."

CHAPTER

SIXTY-SEVEN

ARKEN

Arken couldn't help but flinch.

Morwë's eyes had darkened to black, bottomless pools, her voice rough and rasping as she spoke. And it had startled him.

And she saw it. Raw agony crossed her face, and she jerked her hand away, leaving her glove in his grasp. "Morwë!" Arken called after her, starting to follow. "Morwë—"

But she was running flat out towards Wardwood, towards what had quickly become a sanctuary, a safe haven.

Away from him.

Arken braced his hands on his knees, breathing as if someone had punched him in the gut. He never imagined something so small—a *flinch*, mountain's bones!—could hurt her, and him, so much.

But it had.

Morwë carried herself with guarded reserve and with strength. She was prickly and snappish, with a wildness that drew him in ways he couldn't explain. *But it was protection,* Arken realized, straightening like an old man with arthritic joints. *No one could hurt her if she didn't let them.*

Yet he had.

Against all odds, unbeknownst to both of them… she had let him in.

And he had caused her pain.

Arken leaned back against an old oak, shrouded in shadow, and pressed his hand against the tree. The cold wind passed over him like a sigh.

The two of them were connected. She had called to him in a vision, pulled him out of that prison, rescued him from torture. He had carried her down the mountain and supported her when she was weak. She had healed his hands. They had formed a fragile trust. His mother's best friend had been Morwë's mother.

And Wardwood knew her. Arken couldn't put words to *how* he knew, but seeing Morwë in the center of the hall earlier today had made him sure, down to his bones. It allowed the shock and disbelief that clung to him to fall away.

He loved her.

His head and heart finally coalesced and put to words what he had felt instinctually for a few days now. But strangely enough, she had felt more attainable as an Unseelie princess than as the heir to Wardwood.

And now he had wounded her when she was vulnerable.

Vulnerable because….

Arken stopped. Why had she been so hurt? So afraid?

He had wanted to kiss her here, behind the house. He almost had. But that hadn't caused her fear.

"I don't want to hurt you," she had said.

Oh, Morwë.

He walked back to Wardwood and entered the kitchen in the midst of the supper preparations. His eyes automatically found her, sitting beside her sister, but her face was trained stubbornly on the fire in the grate, and she did not look at him.

Arken kept his eye on her as they ate. He picked at his food, but she ate even less.

But Morwë had said she was hungry.

Arken frowned. Hungry for what?

SIXTY-EIGHT

ENZELLA

Zephyr nibbled at Enzella's fingers as she fed him a carrot after supper, and she giggled. She stroked his dark muzzle as he crunched, whiskers brushing her hands. He blinked liquid eyes at her, following her movements as she turned to Star and gave him a carrot as well. The stable door creaked, and Enzella looked over her shoulder.

Arken stepped into the stable, the lantern he held casting a warm glow over the surroundings. "Dark in here, isn't it?"

"Not to me!" Enzella held out one of the carrots Luned had given her. "Do you want to feed the horses too?"

He smiled, but it didn't reach his eyes. "Sure." He took a carrot and fed it to Star, scratching the horse behind the ears. "Enzella," Arken said quietly, "have you noticed anything... off about Morwë?"

She frowned. "Why?"

"Humor me."

Enzella looked away and shrugged. "She's tired."

"Because she's overtaxed herself?"

"What's that?"

"Over extended. She did too much."

"Yes."

Arken licked his lips. "Has that ever happened before?"

She shook her head. "No, but she always had kneph before."

"What's that?"

Enzella hesitated. "Promise you won't get mad."

Arken frowned. "Why would I get mad?"

"Micah got mad." She hunched her shoulders, eyeing him warily. "Promise."

Arken stared at her a moment, and then nodded. "All right. I promise." He sat down on a rickety stool, waiting.

Enzella turned to Star and petted his neck, finding it easier to look at the horse than Arken. "Kneph is what makes Unseelie magic work."

"Food, or fuel?"

She nodded.

"And Morwë needs it?"

Enzella raised one shoulder. "I guess, but she doesn't like to drink it. I think it must be a bad thing," she said in a small voice.

"Why?"

She shot him another look.

Arken held up his hands. "I promised, remember?"

"Kneph is what we—they—stole wights for. It's life force." Enzella held herself still, waiting.

He didn't cry, like Micah had, or lash out at her, like Ingridon would've. He just flexed his hands on his knees, over and over again. "That's right," he finally said. "I'd forgotten."

"She didn't drink, or at least not much," Enzella hurried to assure him. "She doesn't like it."

"Will you tell me why?"

"She doesn't like the way it makes her feel."

"So it's like a drug?"

Enzella hesitated. "I don't know what that is."

He thought about it. "It makes you feel excitable. It changes your perception of the world. You feel like you can do anything."

"I guess. All the imps were crazy for it. I was too young. You don't get to drink until you leave youngling school."

"So it's *not* food," Arken said to himself. "It is more like a drug, because you don't need it, but Morwë's gotten used to it."

Enzella shrugged again, but he wasn't looking at her.

"What will happen if Morwë doesn't get kneph?"

"I don't know," Enzella whispered, but that wasn't true. The imps her father drained of power went mad, slavering and screaming, trying to reach or bite anyone that came too close. When they started to bleed from their eyes and noses, the war band finally put them to death.

Arken's eyes narrowed. "That bad, huh?" He sighed. "Come on. Let's get inside, it's too cold out here."

Enzella took his outstretched hand and swallowed, ashamed she hadn't even thought of what might happen to Morwë. "But she's only tired. Not completely drained. If she just rests, she'll get better... right?"

"I don't know, Zel," Arken said, squeezing her hand. "I hope so."

But there wasn't much hope in his words.

SIXTY-NINE

MORWË

That night in Wardwood, on a pallet in the great hall beside Enzella, Morwë dreamed of her mother.

Morwë knew who it was, even though she could only see the figure's back as she stared at the massive fire in Wardwood's hall.

"I had forgotten the size," Igrainne whispered in the velvet night. "How could I have forgotten?"

Morwë walked to the figure still staring dreamily at the fireplace.

Igrainne reached a hand out to touch the carved mantle. Morwë could see the fire through her arm. "It grew so small in my memory. But that is Yemelyan's way—he makes everything around him small. Including me."

Igrainne's shade turned and looked Morwë in the face—and Morwë saw a girl no older than her, with a laughing mouth and canny eyes under a fountain of hair, black as her own. They even wore the same dress.

"So you've come home, Morwë. That is good. Wardwood is all I can give you, and you need so much more."

"Mother," Morwë said, as the hunger crawled through her, the craving turning her bones to wax. *This is a dream,* she told herself as she looked at her mother's young face, and because she knew it to be true, Morwë said what she could never have said aloud, below ground or above it. "Mother, I'm frightened."

Her mother said nothing.

"How can I keep Zel safe from me? Luned—Luned is here. She would care for Zel, and I—"

"I did not raise you to cower and fall at the first sign of hardship," Igrainne said.

Hot anger coursed through Morwë, cutting through some of the tethers that bound her. "You did not raise me at all!"

Igrainne acknowledged the hit, pain flickering. "Then I did not raise you to be a coward."

"You don't understand."

Igrainne opened her hands to Morwë, held out the hunk of stone that she had carried all those years with the Unseelie. "You are my daughter, the heir to Wardwood, and tethered to the fells and the valleys of this land," Igrainne whispered. "You are also steeped in the magic of your father's people. You are the only one who can stop him."

"What are you saying?" Morwë whispered.

"He stole everything from me. Hope, faith, even the memory of love. But I won't let him take you."

Morwë's throat tightened against the burn of tears. "Did you ever love me?" she asked the ghost.

Igrainne tilted her head to the side. "If you had asked me in my last days, I would have said no. But I believe I loved you as best I could. I love you now, all that I could not give, trapped as I was."

She met Morwë's gaze again, the formerly laughing eyes glassy and blank. "See him for what he is, Morwë. You're the key to his desires—the only thing he wants."

Far away, something howled.

"Beware, Morwë," Igrainne said, lifting the stone, a reminder, a talisman. "Beware—"

Morwë sat up, drenched in sweat and shaking. Someone was screaming.

They had all spread their bedrolls in the hall, better to heat the one area that was clean. Enzella curled into a ball, her hands clamped to her ears, but everyone else was sitting up—all except Mirat Horne, who screamed and thrashed in the grip of dreams.

"Horne!" Vastic knelt at her side and shook her. "Wake up!"

Her screams only grew louder.

Luned clutched a quilt around her shoulders and touched the sergeant's forehead, beaded with sweat. "She's burning up."

The kneph-hunger raged in Morwë like a hungry fire, but when Arken looked at her, confused and entreating, she slid towards Horne and reached for the tiny pool left of her Arts.

The magic came to her call, painful though it was, and she felt Horne's pain—agony—from two different directions.

An unfamiliar magic lay over Horne like a miasma, joining her to something far away. Traveling down that bond flew a magic Morwë knew far too well—the insatiable hunger of Unseelie Arts. The pain Horne felt was a sympathetic response from the unfamiliar magical bond—but if the Art's hunger followed the tether back to her, then the pain would be real, and Mirat's kneph stolen.

Without more conscious thought, Morwë brought her hands up to force the Arts back—and recoiled.

She could not touch the magic's source.

Changing tacks, she reached for the miasma, felt the thread of the bond that led away from Horne—and snapped it.

Horne's screams stopped. She collapsed in a dead faint.

Morwë fell backwards from the magical backlash. Sturdy arms caught her and held her steady so she could catch her breath.

Hunger, the urge whispered, *Need. Sate us. Just one taste... you will need it,* her Arts insisted. *You are too weak, and you must keep your promise....*

Morwë levered herself out of Arken's hold and buried her face in her hands, shoulders shaking.

"What happened?" Vastic growled, no hint of sleep left in his voice. He loomed over the sergeant's still body, the muscles in his bare chest flexing and looking for a target. "What did you do?"

Horne opened her eyes, gasping like a fish.

"Just breathe," Luned soothed. "Take your time. You are safe."

"Are we?" Horne rasped, sitting up from her bedroll, her hand reaching for something—knife or sword. "The captain—he was in pain. Dying. I felt the life leave him, bit by bit." She clutched the cross around her neck with her free hand. "They were all screaming. He could hear them. It was…."

Morwë said, "You had a link to him. A magical connection."

"Yes," Horne said. She reached out with a hand, her fingers opening and closing, searching. "It wasn't much, but… I can't feel him anymore," she whispered.

"That is my doing." Morwë lifted her head. "I broke the link. They were trying to use it to reach you."

Horne licked her lips. "Is… is he…."

"Yes, I fear he is dead."

Micah spoke up for the first time. "How do you know?"

"The magic," Morwë said. "The magic that pulled the life from Captain Konstantin, that tried to reach for Horne. I could not touch it." Morwë met Enzella's eyes.

Her sister pulled her blankets up to her chin. Her eyes took up her whole face.

Arken's hand on Morwë's shoulder tightened. "That means—"

"Yes," Morwë said, blank with despair. "Someone with my blood. My father is alive."

SEVENTY

MORWË

ool, Morwë thought, clutching her shawl around her. *For believing Yemelyan would just lie down and die under the weight of a mountain. Fool.*

The dream replayed in her mind, her mother's ghost whispering "Beware" over and over again. Unconsciously, she dug one-handed through their bag of belongings until she found the stone with the silver vein.

"What does this mean for us?" Horne asked hoarsely. "What is our enemy?"

"He's a nasty piece of work," Arken growled.

Morwë clenched the stone hard enough to make her skin sting, as the edges bit into her flesh. "He's coming for me."

All faces turned to her.

"I'm the one who brought the mountain down. You all have to go—leave Wardwood, go as far away as you can—"

"You think he'll just ignore the two humans that got away?" Arken snorted and crossed his arms. "He didn't strike me as the type to discount loose ends or to leave anyone unscathed."

"Then we'll all go," Morwë said desperately, "but we've got to run."

"What about protection?" Horne said. "I know some spells. Can you…."

Morwë shook her head, spoke the damning words. "I don't have enough magic to light a candle."

"But I thought—" Micah broke off. "You mean, it didn't come back?"

"You need kneph," Arken whispered.

She could not look at him.

"Where will we run?" Luned said practically. "To Cairenoch, full of people? Cruever? To the woods, in winter?" She shook her head. "If you run from the wolves, you will never be able to stop. They'll either catch you, or you'll fall down and die."

"So what do we do, Mother?" Micah gripped the back of a chair, his knuckles turning white. "You don't know—you didn't see what the Unseelie were capable of. Do we just wait?"

Morwë reached for Enzella, held her tight. "Please forgive me."

"For what?" Enzella mumbled.

"All I wanted was to keep you safe," she said, tracing the silver scars on Enzella's cheek, "but all I've done is condemned us to a slow death."

Enzella pulled back, her brows pulling down low over her eyes. "How," she demanded, "are all of Father's killings and pain and evil your fault?"

"Zel, I have nothing," Morwë said. "I can't stop him."

"If he only wants to kill us, no," Enzella said.

Morwë blinked and rested her chin on her sister's head. She stared blindly at the dancing firelight.

Beware, Igrainne's shade had said. *You're the key to his desires. The only thing he wants. See him for what he is.*

Morwë thought of her father. The Erlking of the Unseelie, who ruled with an iron fist and a calculating, scheming mind. Who had been born the second son, and had left the colony to travel and explore other lands. Who had stolen a wight woman for his wife.

Why Igrainne?

She had had a laughing face. Morwë supposed that might have been enough for some men. But for Yemelyan?

Igrainne Obelyn. The heir to Wardwood, with a connection to the land.

A land that had a history—if only in stories—of magic.

Morwë sat up straight, not hearing the conversation that swirled around her.

Yemelyan's rule had been a force of fear and power, held through his Arts as the strongest of the Unseelie. He had had three healthy children when others struggled for one. Ingridon was his firstborn and heir.

But Ingridon had no Arts.

The Erlking's title didn't flow from one to another with peace. Yemelyan himself was proof of that—he had unseated his father and older brother.

A strong Unseelie ruler took power ruthlessly, with both hands.

She was the second born. The one with the skill for magic.

But a girl, she reminded herself.

Would that have stood in her way if she had decided she wanted power? If she had decided that Enzella was an acceptable loss?

No, she admitted. *I'm the Erlking's Daughter.*

The answers stood just beyond her grasp. She just didn't know the question.

"He wants something," Morwë said, breaking through the conversation. "I don't know what, but he wants something. Something from me."

Arken touched her shoulder. "And what will he do then?"

She shook her head slowly. "I don't know."

CHAPTER

SEVENTY-ONE

ARKEN

Arken conferred with Horne and Vastic about the night's revelations as soon as dawn crept over the horizon. They fed the horses and walked the perimeter of Wardwood's grounds, discussing options.

They didn't know how fast the Erlking would be traveling or the numbers they'd face. They did suspect he would come at them during full dark when he was strongest, even though Enzella reminded them he had the ability to create darkness to cloak him. He liked to use fear as a weapon, and night was a better time for such tactics than day.

Horne used what little magic she had available to her to ward the inner boundaries of Wardwood, but according to her, it would not keep anyone from wandering onto the grounds. It would only warn the occupants when and where it happened. Scant protection, but better than nothing.

They discovered the wards worked sooner than they had expected. Around midmorning, Arken felt a tingle shoot down his spine—as if someone had just walked over his grave.

Horne shot up from her seat. "Three people. Main road," she exclaimed. "And horses."

"But it's light out," Luned said, picking up the dust cloth she had dropped. "It can't be faefolk."

"Sun shield, remember?" Enzella said. "That's how we traveled to the mountains."

Arken snatched up his bow. "Wait here until we know who it is." He set an arrow to the string as he and the soldiers pounded outdoors and took positions behind trees and rock fence lines, waiting for the intruders.

In several minutes, through the break in the trees came three riders, two wearing helms and quilted leather tunics—and one in a habit.

Arken relaxed his bow. "It's all right," he called to Vastic. "That's Father James! He was the priest in Peridun."

"That's as may be," the soldier said, but his hand stayed on the grip of his sword. Arken recalled what their captain had charged them with—protecting Morwë and Enzella from any threats, whatever they were. *The town council and that priest were having a hell of a time keeping the peace,* Konstantin had said. *"We're not ceding to faefolk hysteria, but they just might be."*

Arken's hand tightened again on his bow.

When they were in hailing range, Arken lifted a hand. "Father James!"

"Arken!" The priest dismounted so fast he nearly tumbled off his horse. He ran and caught Arken in an embrace, clutching him tightly. "God be praised!"

Arken hugged him back and was surprised to find tears blurring his vision as the old priest's shorn gray hair pressed against his cheek.

"I had meant to send you a message," Arken said, voice thick. "But we've been a little busy."

"Of course." The priest stepped back to look into his face. "I prayed for your return. We all did."

"It was a near thing," he said roughly.

"Miracles always are." Father James smiled. "But I had faith in you."

Arken's eyes flickered to the two men behind the priest. They had the look of volunteer soldiers unused to bearing arms, and Arken didn't miss the derisive curl of Vastic's lip as he and Horne approached to flank the men.

The priest introduced them. "This is Kell and Einur. They accompanied me." He hesitated. "I'm afraid the tales we heard from your brother-in-law were... varied, to say the least."

"Leofric needs to keep his damn mouth shut," Arken growled. "Sorry, Father."

"Is it true you're sheltering faefolk?" one man with small, beady eyes said, his tone belligerent.

"Charged with the protection of two ladies, under orders of Captain Konstantin of the Crownsguard," Horne said in a clear voice.

"An' I got full discretion in how I discharge my duty," Vastic growled.

The militiamen reared back while Father James nodded. "That's what I suspected."

Arken opened his mouth to defend Morwë and Enzella, but stopped. Actions spoke louder than any words he could say. "Would you like to come in and meet our miracles, Father?"

The priest's eyebrows shot up, but he merely said, "It would be my great pleasure."

SEVENTY-TWO

MICAH

"Father!" Micah sprang up from his seat in the kitchen to throw his arms around the priest, who looked shockingly different without his long gray locs. But his craggy brown face smiled at Micah just the same.

"Alive! Thank God!" Father James clasped Micah on his shoulders. "The others?"

The smile slid off Micah's face. He shook his head. "No. Just me."

Father James's eyes softened as he touched Micah's forehead. "Ah," he breathed, "But even one life saved is more than we hoped for. What an incredible blessing."

Micah swallowed down the lump in his throat.

One of the militiamen cursed and crossed himself upon seeing an unveiled Enzella and Morwë.

Vastic started forward with a growl, but Father James snapped, "Kell! Apologize."

"Sorry, Father," the man muttered.

"Not to me," Father James said in a low voice. "To these ladies."

"But they're faefolk, Father," the man said, casting an uneasy glance at their pale visages and pointed ears.

"And?" Father James asked. "No matter how different, they are stamped with the indelible touch of the Creator, just as we are."

"They've got an evil, unnatural look," the one insisted.

"I could name several humans that could fit that description without pausing to draw a breath," Father James said flatly. "It is what is in a man's heart, not on his skin, that determines his character." His eyes narrowed on the man.

Micah thought, *Case in point.*

He continued, "I am a priest. It is my job to affirm that hearts can always change, thanks be to God, no matter the penitent. Now, Kell...."

Vastic stepped up behind the priest, smiling evilly.

Kell muttered his apology and stepped back, but his eyes were wary.

Luned came up beside them and said, "Father, we are glad to have you here. May I introduce you to the true owners of Wardwood?"

"I would be delighted," Father James said.

"This is Morwë and Enzella, daughters of Igrainne Obelyn. They helped Micah and Arken to escape," Luned said quietly.

Father James's face took on a curious expression that slowly dawned into understanding. "I never knew the Obelyn family. It was before my posting, but I know the story. Igrainne's daughters. What a marvel! The Lord truly works in mysterious ways."

Enzella came forward curiously, but Morwë remained where she was by the large table, her face impassive.

"Were you the one who put the stuff in Arken's eyes so he could see in the dark?" Enzella asked, looking up into the old priest's face. "What kind of magic was it?"

"If there was magic in the fernseed's virtue, it did not come from me," Father James said with a smile.

"Well, I think you should do it for everyone," Enzella said seriously. "Especially Micah, because it was hard for him to see in the dark, and we'll need it."

Micah flushed and ducked his head.

"What's this?" Father James asked.

"We're not out of the woods yet, Father," Arken said heavily.

So, after bringing out more chairs for the strangers, they sat down and told him all, including the night's events and their suspicion that the Erlking was alive, and bound for Wardwood.

Father James rubbed his temples. "These are dark times indeed." He told Horne, "I will pray for your squad and companions."

"Thank you, Father," she murmured. Vastic only gave a short nod.

"Won't you all consider coming to Cairenoch?" Father James asked. "The town has walls, men with which to defend—"

"No," Morwë said flatly.

All eyes turned to her.

"The Erlking is coming for me," Morwë said. "I'm not going to put others in danger. Besides, walls and weapons can do little against his magic. I am the only person who can stand against him. You'd better tell your town to prepare, priest. If I fail, you will all be in worse danger."

"Do you know why he has fixed on you?"

"I thwarted his plans," she said shortly. "Everything he has done thus far has been for a purpose, formed long ago. He stole my mother, made sure his children would be both Unseelie and human. He wants to use me for something. I just don't know what." She stared at her hands in her lap.

"You were gifted with a unique power and heritage he wanted to exploit," the priest said, with keen awareness.

"Yes."

"If you have gifts he wants to use for his own wicked purposes, then it stands to reason you also have the ability to use them to counter his wishes," he said reasonably. "Power or magic is not a good or evil—it just is. The wielder determines how a tool is used. Maybe you were given your gifts for just this reason."

Morwë said wryly, "This wielder cannot use their tool without harming others."

"Ah," Father James breathed, his face falling. "And you will still stand against him?"

She looked up. "What else can I do?"

"Many things." The priest smiled. "Run, or hide, or give in—but you have chosen to fight, and to protect those you do not even know. A noble, selfless choice, and I honor and thank you for it. Let me do what little I can to bless those of you here."

Enzella leaned forward. "And the fernseed, too."

He laughed. "Aye, and that."

SEVENTY-THREE

ENZELLA

Enzella stared up at the ceiling from where she lay beside Morwë, listening to the sleepers breathe. She had tossed and turned all night without sleeping. Once or twice Morwë had woken and mumbled at her, thinking that Enzella wasn't used to their new sleep schedule.

That wasn't it. The thoughts of Father kept her awake.

Enzella shuddered, remembering the punishments of the Unseelie court—the skinnings and impalings on pikes and the slow cracking of ribs under piles of stones. And now Morwë was their only defense against him, along with the daubs of fernseed oil Father James had put in their eyes.

But what if the stories were true? What if the mountains *did* recognize those who were friend and foe? Surely—oh, surely that counted for something in their favor. Enzella pressed a hand to the stone floor, wanting to feel what Morwë had said she had felt —a recognition from the house. Or the ghostly touch of her mother. But there was nothing.

I wish I could feel Wardwood. I wish I knew if the mountains knew me.

Enzella sat up, not able to stay under the covers a second longer. It was near dawn now. She'd be safe enough. She slid her slippers onto her feet and grabbed her cloak. She would go see Star and Zephyr. Maybe then her legs would stop shaking.

As dawn peeped over the horizon, she eased herself out Wardwood's door and stepped into the light snowfall, following the overgrown flagstone path to the stable. While part of it sagged to the side, the portion where Star and Zephyr had stalls was solid, and Micah and Corporal Vastic had rigged tarps to keep out the wind. She reached in and petted the soft, dark noses that snorted in the air, creating clouds of steam.

The world was quiet, snow settling onto her shoulders and the tree branches and Wardwood's roof with barely a whisper. "Can I tell you a secret?" Enzella whispered to Zephyr, who was nuzzling her for the possibility of a carrot or some sugar. "Yes?"

Zephyr was still convinced she must have something edible about her, and sniffed her hands. Enzella opened them to show they were empty and patted his neck. "I feel silly, but I wish—"

A dark shadow fell over her, shutting out all light. Zephyr snorted, blind as well.

Hard gloved hands clamped down on Enzella, covering her mouth so she could not scream. Her captor spun her around and pushed her back into the stable wall.

"No, go on, Zel," he hissed. "Tell us. What is the big secret?"

Ingridon!

She struggled, icy with terror, fighting like a wildcat to scream, to escape the blackness of the dome around her. Safety was Wardwood's walls, Morwë's arms. If she could just *get away*—

"None of that," Ingridon growled. "Father wants to speak to you, imp. You've been a naughty girl, haven't you?" He struck her face, and Enzella knew nothing more.

CHAPTER

SEVENTY-FOUR

ARKEN

When no one saw Enzella upon waking in the morning, they didn't immediately panic. She was young and curious; she was probably exploring the house after what Morwë had said was a restless night. But when she didn't arrive promptly to help with breakfast, they walked through Wardwood, calling for her in old storage rooms, the wine cellar, and disused parlors. No response.

"I'll check the stables," Arken offered. It was the next logical place to look.

That's where he found the message.

"Morwë," Arken said, coming to the kitchen door.

She must have seen something in his face. She stilled, the knife in her hand trembling. He moved and grabbed her hand before she cut herself instead of the sausage she was slicing for breakfast.

"What is it?" she whispered.

"I think you need to come and see," he said quietly. Vastic and Horne both stood and followed as Morwë threw her hood over her head.

In the stable, the horses snorted in the back of their stalls, their eyes wide and wild. In the walkway, blood pooled from the dead rabbit left butchered on the ground. The blood was tacky and drying; it had been there for a while.

Horne cursed when she saw the scene. "He got past my wards somehow. I didn't even feel it!" Vastic growled in wordless agreement.

Morwë stood and took in the message scrawled in blood on the stable wall, expression flat.

"What does it say?" Arken prompted her.

Morwë blinked. "What?"

"I can't read that," Arken said patiently. "What does it say?" He could read simple printing; he had gone to the village school for a few years until he had joined his father on the mountains, felling trees. But this script was elaborate and flowing, defying his ability to parse.

"Midnight," Morwë said dully. "The copse of standing elms. Come out and play."

Arken blinked. "That's not—"

"Not something Father would say, no." Morwë flattened her lips. "It's more Ingridon's line."

Arken couldn't stop the twitch he gave, remembering the feel of the lash. "All right," he muttered, and turned to Horne and Vastic. "One powerful magic user, one swordsman."

Horne nodded decisively, cracking her knuckles. "At least now we've got a time and place instead of the unknown. Do you know where this copse is?"

"No, but I bet Mother does."

"I'll ask," Vastic said, starting off. "We can scout it ahead of time. Maybe Horne will be able to lay some traps."

"We'll be able to plan better now that we know what we're facing," Horne said to Morwë. "We can come up with a strategy—"

"Don't you understand?" Morwë snapped, her eyes flashing as she whirled on them all. "This was a message for me. They've got *Enzella*. I can't do anything to them magically. If anyone tries anything, they'll kill her." She nudged the rabbit corpse with her foot. "This? It's an example. A warning of things to come." Her shoulders slumped. "They might kill her anyway."

Arken pulled her into his arms and held her. "We're going to get her back," he said firmly.

"How can you be so sure?" she said, twisting out of his hold.

He swallowed, tried not to let that hurt. "I have faith. And your sister is not as helpless as she seems. Enzella's got a good head on her shoulders. However bloodthirsty your brother is, I don't think your father would kill her. It wouldn't serve his interests."

"And you know him so well?" she snapped.

"Yes," Arken said. "*Ingridon* is the hothead. Your father is the tactician. He knows the value of the pieces he holds."

Morwë pressed a hand to her forehead. "I don't know how to do this."

"Do what?" he whispered, feeling his heart pound uncontrollably.

"Any of this," she hissed. "I don't know how to defy my father. How to save Enzella, save all of you. I can't—" She pressed her lips together, looked away.

"We'll stumble through somehow." Arken touched her hair, her cheek. "That's the important thing. That we try to do the right thing, even if we're not sure how."

She glared at him. "When you went after Micah, did you have a plan?"

"Yes. To find him, and bring him home. Wasn't much bothered with the how."

Her eyes widened in horror. "What?"

Arken smiled. "It worked, didn't it?"

"What would you have done, if I hadn't helped you?" she said slowly.

"Thought of something else. Plans fail, anyway. We'll do as much as we can to prepare, and then it's out of our hands."

"And that's *comforting*?"

"To me it is."

She pushed away from him. "Not to me. I can't gamble Enzella's life on a chance. There's only one thing left to do."

A hot spike of alarm pierced him. "Morwë—"

But she was out of his reach, running from him. Again.

SEVENTY-FIVE

ENZELLA

Enzella woke up face down in cold snow and darkness. Her face felt hot and puffy.

Ingridon must have hit me again, she thought, head fuzzy. *Morwë will bring me a tisane or poultice to feel better.*

Then she remembered.

"She's awake, Father." A booted foot met her side, none too gently. "Get up, imp."

Putting all her previously abandoned Unseelie safeguards back in place, Enzella slowly sat up and drew her legs under herself, in case she had the chance to run.

Stone walls hemmed her in on three sides. A curtain of darkness made up the fourth, shrouding everything inside the cave from the light. But they were Unseelie. Their eyes did not need any light besides the stone in the center of the cave, enchanted into a witch light.

At one time, Enzella had been comforted by darkness as a hiding place.

Now the dome contained the two beings she feared most in the world.

"Enzella." Yemelyan's voice sounded unchanged from its usual lilt, no hint of emotion in it.

She swallowed, eyes on the snow beneath her, blown in through the mouth of the cave.

Snow crunched and hissed as Yemelyan moved towards her, his robes sweeping across the ground. "Look at me."

She clenched her fists and didn't move.

Ingridon grabbed her hair and pulled her head back, shaking her. "You've been away too long, little sister," he hissed. "When you hear a command, you obey."

Enzella squeezed her eyes tight. He'd have to pry her eyelids open.

"Ingridon," Yemelyan said. "Go and check the perimeter while I speak with your sister."

"Father—"

"That was a command." Yemelyan's words had a bit more force behind them.

Ingridon dropped Enzella. She fell back in the snow. Enzella opened one eye to see him wrap his cloak around his mouth and nose before stepping outside the shield of darkness. She didn't know if it was relief or fear that held her still.

"Sit up, child."

Slowly, Enzella did as she was bid. It was one thing to bait Ingridon. It was another to defy Father. But she still didn't look at him.

Yemelyan sighed lightly. Then cold fingers reached under her chin and tilted her head up. He touched the raised scars on her cheek.

Enzella shook, her knuckles whiter than the snow.

"Ingridon often acts without input from his brain," Yemelyan said. "It was the wrong approach. I see that now." He *tsked*, a sound of faint annoyance. "It only galvanized your sister away from home, instead of inspiring her to greater heights." His fingers left her face.

Enzella chanced a look at him through her eyelashes. But Yemelyan's dark eyes were not on her; instead, he stared off into the middle distance, lips pursed as he thought.

"You never came to see me."

He came back to himself and looked down at her.

Enzella could not quite believe herself, but once she opened her mouth, she could not hold the words back. "Not once, when Ingridon stabbed me." She pressed her hand to her side, where the flesh was still red and tender. "Why not?"

"Why would I need to?" Yemelyan said, vaguely curious. "You would recover, and your sister was tending to you."

Enzella's throat tightened, and she shook her head. "You didn't care. You wouldn't even care if I had died." Her eyes burned. She didn't want to cry, but she couldn't help it. She had seen what family looked like—in Arken and Micah, and Luned, and even in Leofric, as rude as he was—family meant caring. Love. All families, except hers.

"Mother would've cared," Enzella whispered vengefully.

"You are very like your mother. You have her spirit. But did *you* care," he said, "when you thought I was dead?"

Enzella froze. Her heart skipped a beat.

Yemeylan smiled. "You see? We are Unseelie, Enzella. We cannot change our nature."

"I'm *not* Unseelie!" she said vehemently. "I'm half human. I'm an Obelyn! I belong at Wardwood, with Morwë."

"Wardwood?"

She stuttered to a stop.

Behind Yemelyan, several eyes snapped open. They glowed in the gloom.

"So you've discovered your heritage," Yemelyan said. "Very good."

Enzella tried to keep an eye on both threats. "Why 'good'?"

"I hoped you would—after I had to adjust my plans to Morwë's meddling."

Yemelyan reached out, as if to touch her face again, but she swatted his hand away. "Stop touching me!" Enzella cried. "I hate it, and I hate you!" The truth finally spilled free.

"Yes," Yemelyan laughed quietly. "Very much your mother's spirit."

"You're a coward," Enzella spat. "Hiding in your little bubble of darkness. But guess what, I'm not afraid of the light. I don't burn. And I'm not afraid of *you*."

"Ah," he breathed. "Excellent. You don't seem to understand, Enzella. I *wanted* you to be half human. I wanted you to inherit gifts from both sides of your family. Unfortunately, your sister is the only one of the three of you that seems to be a perfect cross. But perhaps you will serve some purpose after all, too."

"I won't," she said stoutly. "You can't make me."

"We shall see," he said, "I have a few new tools at my disposal now."

Out of the depths of the cave padded one of the glowing pairs of eyes. It was a wolf—huge and muscled, its shoulder the height of a grown man's waist, with wicked teeth and claws it flexed against the stone.

Enzella's breath hitched. Was this a timberwolf? Her stomach lurched in a mix of horror and pity. No intelligence she could see lingered in the wild eyes.

Yemelyan laid a hand on its back like it was a pet. "You don't want anything to happen to Morwë, do you? After all, she can't heal herself."

Enzella stared at him. "What do you want with Morwë?"

"I want her to help me," her father said, smiling. "And you will ensure that she does."

"Or what?" she demanded.

"That remains to be seen," he murmured.

"You'll hurt me," Enzella said flatly. "Or kill me. Something."

Yemelyan just tilted his head, eyeing her like she was an odd insect he had encountered.

"You think Morwë will do whatever you want, obey your plans because you have me, and you can pit us against each other. But she'll never be what you want," Enzella said mulishly. "No ruthless ice queen. This proves it. She loves me, so my sister will sacrifice to protect me. You've never loved anything, so you murdered our mother and killed your people. For what?"

She spat on the stone floor. "I'm not afraid of you anymore. There are more important things than safety, and I've seen them." Home. Love. Family. All worth far more than the pittance he offered. "All you can do is kill me, and I've already seen that."

Enzella crossed her arms and turned to face the wall, ignoring his chuckle. He wouldn't win. Morwë would find a way to stop him.

She tried not to listen to the creeping doubt that insisted, *"But what if she can't?"*

SEVENTY-SIX

MORWË

None of them, not the soldiers, not Arken, not even Enzella, knew what Morwë's father was capable of. Whatever he wanted from her, he could take. He had proven it—he had taken Enzella. Morwë had no resources left, and none would stand a chance against him anyway. He was her blood. She had utterly failed to protect them. What could she do to enact a rescue?

Morwë sat, silent, in the planning session for a time, but she couldn't stomach it anymore. All their words buzzed around her like flies, stinging her with their naiveté. As snow continued to fall outside, Morwë left. She disappeared into Wardwood, padding along the stone corridors without a torch. She didn't need one, after all.

She passed all the rooms Luned had taken them to before—back when this might've been a place of safety. A place to belong.

No chance of that now. Yemelyan had ruined even that faint hope.

But one door Morwë hadn't peered behind. She turned the knob of the intricately carved door at the end of the hallway and stepped into silence.

Colored lights shone across the bare dusty floor in a blaze of green-blue-purple, and her eyes could not make out the shape. Then Morwë lifted her eyes. Above the small altar in the center of the room, a large window was set with colored glass. Small geometric pieces of glass formed a picture of a silver mountain range over a deep blue lake. Above the lake, in a dark sky, hung gemstones of green, blue, and purple.

Morwë could not pin them down. At once they appeared as tongues of fire, then streams of water, then tails of the wind flowing over the mountains. Their lights sparkled down over the short wooden bench behind her, bathing it in their otherworldly glow.

She had never seen a display of color and art like this, not even from enchanted witch lights.

Lights, she thought. *Northern lights.* Rivers of magic, dancing in the sky.

Arken found her there after a while. His lantern illuminated the room as he stepped inside. "Mother was worried about you," he said quietly.

"I'm not the one who was kidnapped," Morwë snapped, keeping her eyes stubbornly on the glass.

"That wasn't what she was worried about," Arken said. He set the lantern down carefully on the altar, the warm flame lighting the carved cross that stood there. He examined the craftsmanship studiously, wiping away the dust and cobwebs until the wood began to shine, some of the beauty uncovered. He waited.

"You're all going to die," Morwë said finally. "My father—" She swallowed. "Your blood is on my hands."

"What's done is done," Arken said, a surprising heat in his voice. "Micah and I would have died under Ceridfel without you. And Enzella, too." He shook his head. "You did the right thing. The blood is on your father's hands, and there's enough there he won't even notice it. We can only think what to do now."

"What *can* I do?" Morwë sank down onto a small bench against the wall. "There's nothing left but to give in to what he wants. I haven't got the power to oppose him. And he's got

Enzella. We've got no room to maneuver. I'll go alone tonight and turn myself over to him, and maybe that way you will live—"

"No," Arken objected, reaching for her, "we are not going to let you sacrifice yourself for us. Absolutely not."

"If not for you, then for *Enzella.*"

"She wouldn't want you to, either."

"I am her older sister. I have no choice. If I give in, he'll keep her alive to keep me compliant. If not...." She could barely think of that possibility.

"We're not going to let him win. Not like this."

She thumped her fist onto the bench. Stubborn, thickheaded fool! "There isn't any other way, Arken!"

"We've got to try *something*, Morwë! Otherwise he's going to have free rein to do to Cairenoch what his minions did to Peridun —and who says he'll stop at Cairenoch? That's a good enough reason to stand up to him. We're the country's only hope, even if they don't know it. No one else in Altesia has magic on his scale to oppose him."

"Don't you understand?" Morwë demanded, her voice raising to a wail. "I can't do anything against him; Enzella ensures that. And even so, I *haven't got the magic!*"

"I've been thinking about that." Arken looked at the stained glass above him, and then at the cross in his hand. "For power, you need kneph. And that's life-force, right?"

She nodded tiredly.

"What if I gave you some of mine?"

She lifted her eyes to his, the blood draining from her face. "No."

"Morwë—"

"No!" She stood to put more space between them. "I won't do it, Arken. I won't steal from you. It's—"

The truth, what she had always known, hearing the screams of prisoners, witnessing the fading of her mother's life before her eyes, fell from her lips. "It's *wrong*. I won't be like him." It seemed there was a limit to her martyrdom after all.

Arken followed close on her heels. "Morwë. It's not theft if I give it freely."

"You don't know what you're saying," she said with a voice of ice.

"You're not listening to me," Arken said harshly. "I would give *everything* to keep my family safe. But you only need a bit. Isn't that right?"

"If you want to keep your family safe, take them away from here," she said as she looked up at him. "Run as far as you can and pray he won't come looking for you. Leave me."

"*Morwë*," Arken said, cradling her face. "Better ask me to leave my own heart behind." Then he bent his head and kissed her.

She tried to push him away, but he held her tight, wrapping his arms around her as his lips caressed hers, not to plunder, but to give. A rush of emotion swooped through her, weakening her knees, parting her lips to let him in. She gasped into his mouth at the feeling of his body against hers.

Then her Arts screamed *Yessss*! and reached into him to pull on his kneph, unspooling him into her.

Morwë fought in earnest then, against her Arts, her instinct, and his arms as the sense of *Arken* washed through her in a wave. Deeply personal, indelibly himself, he surrounded her, fragments of thought and memory floating by. Her Arts drank it all in, craving, more, more, *more*—

Morwë broke free and hurtled across the room, pressed against the wall, breathing hard. Everything in her told her to run before she gave in to the craving, the monster… but the sight of Arken on one knee, breathing heavily with a gray face, froze her to the spot.

She had hurt him.

Moonlight, what have I done, Morwë despaired, remembering her words to Captain Konstantin.

"Are you all right?" she whispered. "Arken?"

"Yes," he rasped, lifting his head. His dazed blue eyes met hers. "That was… different."

She wanted to rail at him, call them both every sort of fool. "Why did you do it? I *warned* you—"

"It was my choice," Arken said. "Look at me, Morwë. I chose. I don't regret it. It was for you."

"*Why?*" She nearly choked on the word.

He gave her an odd look. "I know what I gave you. Can't you see?"

She opened her mouth—and stopped. His essence still hummed through her, surrounding her in every way as if he still held her safe in his arms. The bits and pieces he spoke of floated through her mind. His first sight of her in the gate cavern, seeing her as a caged bird poised to take flight. Her eyes outside his cell. Her biting tongue. His mistrust that burned away to conviction when she came for him. The vulnerability she tried so hard to hide. The way she gave all she had to heal his hands. His utter certainty that....

"How?" Morwë demanded. "How can you *love* me, knowing what I am? What I've done?"

"Because you're you. Even before I knew you had any connection to this place, to me. Even if you don't—don't feel the same, I wouldn't choose any other way." His voice changed to rueful. "I will, however, need a hand off this floor."

She forced her bones to move and bend. She had done this. She had to fix it. She lifted him, and he leaned on her without hesitation.

"Do you think it will be enough?" Arken asked.

She touched his face, resolute. "It will have to be. Because I swear on my life, I'll never take from you again."

"I won't hold you to that," Arken said gently. "Whatever you need, I want to give. I'll give it all to you if it means you won't give up hope."

Mother never said that love was so dangerous, Morwë thought, taking his arm to help him from the chapel.

SEVENTY-SEVEN

MORWË

The moon hung like a silver sickle in the black night sky, thin and waning into something wicked and desperately sharp.

They all came with Morwë, even Micah, though Arken had tried to dissuade him—"Enzella's my friend," he insisted—and Luned, though Morwë had pleaded with her to stay behind. "I'm the only one who knows where the elms are," she had said practically. "I'm not going to let you wander around in the dark."

And, of course, the soldiers were coming regardless. Their duty, they said, to defend the realm against all threats. They were armed with swords, and Arken had his bow. Micah and Luned had a knife and axe each.

Morwë carried nothing except the Arts that hummed in her veins and the silver-veined rock in her pocket. It made her feel close to her mother. She wanted that tonight.

They walked deep into the overgrown woods until they reached a stand of trees, beyond which was a black nothingness—deeper still than the night all around them. None of their torchlights penetrated it. It was Yemelyan's spell.

Morwë took a step forward and the impossible darkness dissipated. Yemelyan stood in the middle of the stand of trees. At his right hand, Ingridon gripped Enzella's arm.

Luned sucked in a harsh breath behind Morwë, seeing for the first time her best friend's nemesis and nightmare.

The dark cast around her father's mouth was darker still, and his eyes shone so stark against his white skin they almost bled shadow. It was disconcerting, to say the least.

Enzella tried to run towards them.

Ingridon sneered and hauled her back. "None of that," he snapped, and shook her, hard.

Vastic pulled his sword from his sheath and took a step forward.

A chorus of howls erupted from outside the grove of elms. Through the trees, they could all see the glow of eyes.

Arken touched Morwë's wrist. "Timber wolves."

Yemelyan gave Arken a long, considering look that Morwë did not like at all.

"Well, Father," Morwë said, her voice gone cold beyond recognition, "Here I am. Do you want to kill me? You don't need wolves for that."

"The wolves will keep your compatriots busy while we discuss other matters. I don't plan to kill you, Morwë. You've accomplished much. I'm very proud."

Proud?

"I used the wrong approach with you," Yemelyan continued, the corners of his lips turning down. "I assumed that you would react to pressure in the same way I had. I did not take temperament into account—and perhaps gender," he murmured.

"What?" Morwë said, decidedly off balance. The world seemed too still, frozen.

She glanced around and found Arken, his family, the guards— all motionless. For one horrible moment, she thought them dead, but then she saw vapor pass their lips into the cold night. Ingridon and Enzella were the same way, still and unresponsive.

"What is this? What did you do?" she demanded. It was like nothing she had ever witnessed before.

"Pausing the moment to avoid any pesky interruption," her father sighed.

She met his gaze and clenched her hands. "Release them."

"Not until you know all," Yemelyan said, with equal steel.

"All of what?"

"Your purpose in all this." Yemelyan lifted a hand and motioned to the land around them. "Did you think I chose your mother on a whim, some flight of fancy?"

"Igrainne," Morwë corrected. "Her name was Igrainne, and you stole her."

He tilted his head to the side. "I did. The Unseelie would have disappeared in a few more generations from sterility. No one could find a solution. But I could see a way where my close-minded father and brother could not. And I left, and I came to a land that still remembered the shape and weight of its vanished magic. And that memory, that virtue, dwelt in your mother. Igrainne."

He blinked, and Morwë reminded herself to breathe.

Opening his eyes, Yemelyan continued, "I speculated that children between us would receive not only the Unseelie Arts, but also that recognition of wild land-magic."

Wardwood, Morwë thought. *It* knew *me.*

"So I made her mine and killed to pave a way for myself and my descendants to rewrite the course of Unseelie history." Yemelyan frowned and glanced at Ingridon and Enzella, still frozen in struggle. "But of all my children, only you inherited the perfect mix of wight and faefolk."

"Are you trying to tell me," Morwë said, as the wind blew snowflakes through the trees, "that—"

"You are fated to rule," her father said, his regard piercing her.

"I am second born—"

"Then you change your birthright, as I did," Yemelyan said harshly, his black eyes glittering.

"Is this why you chose to freeze our audience, so Ingridon wouldn't hear you endorse a second-born girl as queen?" she snapped.

"The one with the power makes the rules, and the usurper with more power changes them. You know that," Yemelyan chided.

"It's the Unseelie way," she said bitterly. "Am I supposed to believe you're not angry, that you won't kill me as soon as you can, all for the sake of a plan that's worthless now? Everyone is dead. There's no one left for you to rule."

Her father waved away her protests. "What are a few thousand imps? They were always expendable. But there's rabble here, wights in plenty. Oxen ready for a yoke. With the magic of the land at our disposal, it would take less than a thought to make them bend the knee."

They were always expendable.

Yemelyan eyed Arken's hand that still lay frozen on her wrist. "I'll admit to some irritation that you foiled my plans for you and Toren; I had planned to give you the most powerful thaumaturge to ensure the line remained strong. But if you want the wight, I shall let you keep him. We need fresh bloodlines. I won't keep up terrible breeding practices. You can keep all the wights if you like." He cast a glance over the group.

"People who have known freedom don't like being kept." Morwë forced the words through numb lips.

He snorted. "What do we care for that? We can rule this valley, these mountains. I thought so all those years ago, and I knew it was possible when I set fire to the taiga and led us back. In fact, your mountain stunt confirmed it. You don't possess the power to collapse an entire mountain. Not even I could have done that."

The memory of flame, scorching heat, and ash filled her mind. "*You* set the fire?" Morwë whispered. "But...."

"I said that the wights' magic users had tried to burn us out," Yemelyan shrugged, as if the lie was of no importance. "It was a necessary fiction. I had to return to these mountains to test my theory. And it was correct. With your blood, we can tap into the magic buried in the land, use it, mold it to our will. You can *rule*, Morwë."

A vision appeared of her crowned in darkness, dressed in the finest velvets and silks, a scepter lit by witch lights in her hand. She could command all before her to bend the knee—any wight who looked at her askance, even her own magic-less brother. She could even spill his blood into the snow if she desired. At her side stood Enzella, stark and unsmiling, and Arken at Morwë's feet, looking up at her with a mixture of adoration and fear as he clutched the hem of her dress. Everything she could want. Power. Adulation. Fear. The ability to bring her enemies under her heel as she commanded the mountains to do her will, exploited the people for their life force….

But that's never been what I wanted, the tiny voice inside her whispered. And Yemelyan—whether from blindness or plain inability—had never understood that.

Nothing matters to him, Morwë thought. Not his people—he set fire to the taiga, killed a good number of Unseelie to force their migration south to the Caleahanachs. He didn't care for the rest of his people that had perished under the mountain or for his family —he had killed his wife. He was willing to let her depose Ingridon, who had always been the favored son, just for her ability to give Yemelyan power.

Once that power, visions of crowns, a scepter, fire and blood would have tempted her. Because she had been trapped and desperate for any semblance of safety.

But Morwë knew the taste of something else now—a flavor that was cleaner and richer than fear that made the figures in her vision bend the knee.

But that yearning—that *hope*—was as faint and flickering as a candle flame, almost as transient as the torches that struggled in the winter night. She had nothing to feed it, not enough promise of survival, not enough power to bring it to fruition.

Power.

Not enough power, Morwë thought, feeling far away. *Yes. He put into words what I've known in my gut since the moment it happened. I couldn't have brought the mountain down alone—not under my own power. I would've died or failed. The mountain came to my call and saw my intent. It lent its strength to mine and collapsed itself down onto the colony—all because* it knew me.

The land knows to whom it belongs.

"And Enzella?" Morwë heard herself ask.

"I will ensure her safety."

Why bother turning over a new leaf now, Father?

Morwë stared at her sister, frozen in their brother's cruel hold. She had promised Mother to look out for Zel. She had escaped to keep her safe. She had been willing to tear down their dark world for her.

Would Morwë tear down another?

No, that wasn't the right question. The question was, would Enzella want her to tear down this new world, in which Zel had found such joy, for her sake?

Morwë closed her eyes and shook her head. "No."

The conviction reached down her bones to the earth, dug through the topsoil and down into the bedrock of the mountains. That grounding was enough to bring them back into sync with time. Beside her, Arken sucked in a breath and shivered, hands twitching towards his quiver.

Morwë looked her father in the eye. "You're asking me to be a tool that you can use to lay waste to these people, these mountains," she said, calling up what power she had regained from Arken's kiss to readiness. She wrapped her fingers around the chunk of stone in her pocket. "And I am too much my mother's daughter to let that happen."

Yemelyan's eyes narrowed, and he opened his mouth to respond.

Then Enzella, whose gaze had been fixed on Morwë the whole time, bit down on Ingridon's hand and bolted from his hold.

Ingridon bounded after her with a snarl.

Morwë nearly let a bolt of her Arts fly, blood or no, but Ingridon leapt back, barely evading an arrow that passed within a hair's breadth of his nose.

Arken set another arrow to the string as Enzella made it across the stretch of snow between the two groups and dove for Morwë. "You just try again, scumbag," Arken said. "We'll see if I can put out *your* eye."

Ingridon drew his sword. "Yes," he hissed. "We will."

Morwë clutched Enzella to her. "Are you all right?"

Her sister nodded and buried her face in Morwë's shoulder. "I am now."

"Foolish, obstinate girl," Yemelyan said, in a low, clipped voice. "You had your chance." Power swelled around him, and Morwë stiffened. "Now watch everyone you care for be cut down, and know that at the end, you will give me what I want in spite of it all."

The power released, and a chorus of spine-tingling howls erupted from the wood.

Then the first timber wolves sprang.

SEVENTY-EIGHT

ARKEN

Arken put an arrow through the first glowing eye that sprang for their company, taking a brief second to marvel over the draw of the bow. At fourteen, he hadn't been able to pull it. But now, his arms drew his father's bow like he had been born to it. Then he put out another eye.

Vastic launched himself at Ingridon with a growl.

The fiend laughed as their swords clashed. Their blows fell too quickly to follow, and they were too close for Arken to get off a good shot.

Morwë stepped forward and threw up her hands. The air between her and her father shimmered and billowed, like the heat above a fire. Black veins appeared on Morwë's hands and on her face.

Arken made a mental note to not let anything get in the way of very dangerous magic. He shot another wolf in the throat.

Micah pushed Enzella into the center of their circle before swinging his axe at a snarling wolf that harried Luned. But their mother didn't need protection; she handed off her dagger to Enzella and hacked with her axe whenever a wolf got too close.

Protecting their backs, Horne traced signs on her blade and

murmured under her breath before she swung at sharp teeth aimed for her throat. Green fire burned along the length of her blade. The wolf shrieked.

Then Arken was too busy defending his flank of the circle to bother with the others, besides a hurried prayer for their safety.

The beasts were big and tough, with a strange light in their eyes, a madness that was decidedly un-wolflike. Arken shot arrow after arrow at snarling mouths that would turn and regroup before assaulting them again.

When a wolf got under Luned's guard, Enzella leaped forward and stabbed at its glowing eyes. "Help us!" she called to the silent woods. "Help us! We are your people! Come and help us!"

Arken didn't know if she was praying or what, but he added his own silent entreaty to her cry as his bowstring twanged over and over.

There seemed to be no end to the wolves, and besides defending their circle, he also killed two beasts that had flown at Morwë. Arken could not forget that at some point, he would run out of arrows.

Enzella shrieked, and Arken swung around.

Ingridon pull his blade out of Vastic's chest.

The soldier fell to the ground. Arken heard his death rattle.

Ingridon stepped over the body and started towards them, sword dripping blood, eyes promising death.

Arken moved to get a better line of sight, raised his bow, and fired.

His aim was poor. Instead of sprouting from his chest, the arrow caught Ingridon in the shoulder, and he fell back with an awful curse.

As Arken set another arrow to the string, Yemelyan snarled. Taking a moment from his fierce magical struggle with Morwë, the Erlking made a gesture at Arken.

The air shifted, something shooting too fast to see, too quick to dodge. Arken set his teeth. How did you brace for magic?

In between one breath and the next, Morwë appeared in front of him. What had been meant for Arken struck her squarely in the chest.

SEVENTY-NINE

MORWË

The magical blow was strong enough to make Morwë's ears ring, so much so that she could barely hear Arken's frantic voice.

"I'm all right," she gasped, and reinforced her shield that protected their tight circle of fighters. It was the truth. Besides the force of the blow, the spell had not affected her. Father couldn't harm his own blood through magic. And judging by the hair-raising curses he spewed, the spell's backlash caused him no small discomfort.

Morwë only had time to give Arken one nod before Yemelyan renewed his barrage against her shields, but that had been enough for Luned and Micah to close the gap in the circle as Horne, armed with the only other suitable martial weapon, ran forward to engage Ingridon. He had pulled the arrow out of his shoulder and was bleeding freely. But wounded animals were the most dangerous.

Stepping away to allow Arken the range of his bow once more to keep the yawning, frothing maws at bay, Morwë deflected two more magical blows aimed at their circle before Yemelyan brought his hands together in an arcane gesture. His power coalesced and descended on her with the force of sledgehammers, relentlessly hammering her defenses.

Morwë heard Enzella crying out, but couldn't make out words over the force of the barrage.

The blows drove her to her knees, blood gushing from her nose as her Arts wavered under the onslaught. Morwë pressed one hand flat to the earth, clenching her mother's rock in the other so hard that it bled.

Yemelyan's magic bombarded her shields, reaching for those behind her. She could not even lift her head. Under the assault, she felt her shields buckle.

"Mother," Morwë cried.

Her blood dripped to the ground from her nose and her hand. Morwë gasped for air. The power in her veins slowed to a trickle as she gave all she had to defend the tiny circle behind her. A few more hits, and her shield would break. They would be at her father's mercy—and he had none to give. She could see the truth of it in his eyes. They would all die, and she would be left alone. Morwë reached desperately for anything, anything at all—

Someone else's hand closed tightly onto her hand braced against the earth. The hand forced her fingers into the dirt, digging them into the frozen soil.

Morwë tried to blink her vision clear.

The hand over hers was silver and ethereal—Morwë could see straight through it.

Beneath her, she felt the presence of Wardwood wake, and below that, something far greater—a vast sea of magic beneath the earth, locked away and dormant.

But she could *feel* it.

Morwë clenched her hand in the soil and beckoned to the magic, showing it the way through the rock and loam. It came to her call, filling her to the brim. Strengthened by the rush of power, she reinforced her shields into a solid wall and took a deep breath.

Morwë lifted her head at Yemelyan's passionate curse.

He glared at—at *Igrainne*, crouched beside Morwë, gripping

her hand. Igrainne's semi-solid form stared at her husband through Morwë's shield.

"You're dead," Yemelyan hissed in a strangled voice.

"Yes," Igrainne's shade said solemnly. "You killed me. But you never touched my soul."

Rage crossed his face. Morwë had never witnessed an emotion that strong on the Erlking before.

Morwë's shields rippled under his new onslaught. She had to add to and reinforce her shields repeatedly. Where had Yemelyan gotten all this power? He had killed the squad of Crownsguard for their kneph, but this felt *overwhelming*. Even with the magic borrowed from the land, she was barely staying ahead.

Her mind whispered, *Well,* he *survived the mountain's collapse, and Ingridon, too. Who's to say there weren't more?*

Yemelyan called his own people expendable. Perhaps not all the deaths under the mountain could be laid at her door.

Morwë flinched as her shields flickered again. The colors of magic danced before her eyes, bright and vibrant. She dared not turn her head to see how Arken or the others were doing against the wolves and Ingridon's sword.

This couldn't continue. She was entirely on the defensive, her father attacking without care to manage his resources.

She had power at her fingertips, waiting, if she could just think what to do, how to use it. But that was the trouble—even with borrowed power, she could do nothing directly.

Yemelyan threw another spell, and the colors in her shield ripped again to absorb the blow. They shimmered and flowed… almost like the auroras in the stained-glass chapel window.

Panting, Morwë lifted her head and clenched the tendril of an idea tight. She didn't know if it would work. And if it did, she would burn, just as surely as Ingridon and Yemelyan would.

Her shoulders shivered and shook from the pounding her shield was taking.

Morwë stared at Igrainne's ghost.

"I did not raise you to be a coward," Igrainne said, in a voice like dry leaves.

At least I know that Enzella will be safe.

Morwë closed her eyes and dug her fingers into the earth, reaching for the aquifer of power in the land.

What had Arken said northern lights could be? Harbingers of doom. The ghost of magic. She pictured the stained glass, a whirl of color with all the power of the sun, hidden from sight.

By my mother's blood. By my inheritance.

Morwë touched the power, and called.

Power filled her senses, coming up from the ground as if she had unblocked a dam. Snow blew around them with all the force of a gale as the power brought forth the wind.

And then—there was light.

CHAPTER

EIGHTY

ARKEN

L ight swelled around them, descending from the sky and coming up from the ground, rushing among them like tongues of fire and bathing them with color—blues, greens, purples, and reds. The night glowed with light.

The sight took Arken's breath away.

The cold, fierce wind moved like a living thing, swirling around them in a brilliant haze, nearly bowling him over with its force. When it passed him, it left Arken feeling scoured clean, all impurities burned away. Maybe that was the snow it blew along with it.

He had never been able to *see* the wind before.

The wolves that harried them became disorganized in their assault. Then, out of the forest, came the sound of growls and howls, a fierce battle cry.

Arken lifted his bow, but what stepped from the woods were not wolves. Forest cats with huge green-glowing eyes charged forward. They battled the wolves, driving them from the circle of fighters with bloody claws and fangs. The wolves fled into the night, yipping as they went.

"They came like I asked," Enzella cried. Then she burst into tears, dropping her bloody dagger in the snow.

The forest cats took up a circle around the grove of trees, waiting, watching. Bearing witness. Only their tails twitched.

No one can hide from light. It eats away at darkness, destroys it utterly. Even the black shield that Yemelyan tried to erect dissolved under the waves of green and purple light, consumed.

When the supernatural light touched them, the two Unseelie men screamed. They tried to run, to cover themselves, but there was nowhere to go to escape the flames of light. The men's flesh began to melt and burn, even through their clothes.

Arken flinched and covered Enzella's eyes. She had her hands pressed to her ears.

Then Arken heard a noise that made his hair stand on end.

Morwë knelt on the ground, surrounded by the flow of the lights as they danced and eddied. She screamed. Her skin writhed as oily, noxious smoke poured from her hands and her mouth. But the auroras burned that away, too.

"Morwë!" Arken tried to run to her, but Luned caught his arm.

"You mustn't interfere," his mother said urgently and held him fast even though he tugged. Micah had to catch Enzella to prevent her from running forward, too. "She knew what she was doing."

Arken's heart caught in his throat. He saw what was happening to Ingridon and Yemelyan. The lights would not rest until every bit of corruption had been purged. The lights consumed them, leaving only dead and empty shells on the snow.

Morwë must have known what would happen.

And she chose to do it anyway.

The lights formed a whirlpool around Morwë, a mix of all the colors in a dizzying array, spinning faster and faster as the black smoke unspooled from her, burning away. Morwë's voice grew thin, as if the lights were burning that away, too.

But when the last wisp of black smoke had dissipated, the northern lights faded and blew away with the wind, leaving them in darkness with only the barest guttering torches for light.

Morwë fell sideways into the snow, and Arken threw himself forward to catch her.

EIGHTY-ONE

MORWË

It was so much worse than Morwë had expected. Thousands of fiery darts piercing her skin, peeling it away, paring her down to her marrow, never ceasing as the world was consumed in fire. Her scream went on for eons as the fire traveled down her throat, setting her insides ablaze. Everything was laid bare. Every part of her was separating, burning away.

When the tot in youngling class called her a half-breed, she ignored the girl, then smiled when the tot woke up screaming with a smooth, shiny head and all her beautiful locks on her pillow.

She and Jezra jeered at an imp who could not learn a spell, hexing him until he spat with a mixture of rage, pain, and blood.

If she could have, Morwë would have covered her face, but the memories kept coming.

"I hate you," her younger self told her mother after a long day of caring for her needs and chafing at the indignity of it all. She dashed a basin of water to the ground, shattering it into thousands of shards that sliced into her arms and legs and feet.

I didn't mean it, Morwë tried to say, but the fire kept illuminating all the dark, terrible parts of her she thought she had hidden and buried.

"When I take the throne, I'm going to kill you," *Ingridon told her twelve-year-old self.*

Hadrian pressed his cold lips on her, his hands grasping her tight enough to bruise. She slapped him away and felt the horrible urge to make him feel like a used, inanimate object in turn. She threw him into nasty brambles and stinging nettles and listened to his howls with pleasure.

There was nowhere she could go from the light. Nowhere she could hide.

Her father inspected her coldly, viewing her as if she were a vexing disturbance rather than a daughter. "You have become far too outspoken."

"I would let you have… even her," *her father told Arken as her heart dropped into her stomach.*

Her Arts burned through her, splattering Hadrian and Jezra with piebald burns, and she smiled.

The stone around her crumbled and sent the mountain down, falling, crushing. Murderer.

Igrainne stared at her, lank gray hair blending in with her decaying flesh and flat stone eyes. Her rotting lips moved. "You did nothing. He killed me and you did nothing."

If she could have found the moisture, she would have wept. *It is all true*, Morwë told to the light. *I am what they say.*

The light found the deep well that held her Arts. Her limbs stiffened, bracing against the relentless fire. *Not that, not that*, her Arts chanted, twisting way. Trying to hide. *Not that.*

The winds spun around her, whistling in her ears, saying *Yes.*

What will I be without it? Morwë asked.

Hands cupped her face.

"You will be who you have always been," Igrainne said, young again, with eyes alight. "What you were always meant to be. You will be Morwë, the Erlking's daughter, the Obelyn heir. If you choose."

"Morwë, breathe!" someone commanded. "I need you to breathe."

What will I be? Morwë wondered.

"I said I'd give you whatever you needed," the voice said grimly. "And I will. I swear it."

Morwë breathed in, and then the pain was gone. Only light remained.

And then there was nothing at all.

EIGHTY-TWO

MORWË

The voice chattering on like a sparrow woke Morwë from her sleep.

Morwë blinked, the pillow under her head unfamiliar, but soft and comforting all the same. Breathing in, her lungs remembered the fire, but nothing hurt, except maybe some soreness from her hands.

"Morwë? Morwë, are you awake?"

She blinked again, doing her best to keep her eyes open. Slowly, her vision settled and focused on Enzella leaning over her. She licked her lips. Her mouth tasted brackish. "Zel?"

"I'm here." Enzella snuggled against her on the bed, for it was a bed, in a room with a window on the far wall. The shutters were open, and daylight streamed in.

"Where are we?" Morwë lifted a bandaged hand and carefully stroked her sister's hair.

"Wardwood," Enzella said. "You've been asleep for three days."

Morwë's hand stilled. Three days. She took a deep breath. "Are they—"

Enzella nodded and burrowed closer. "Dead. But guess what, when the wolves tried to run away, forest cats came and fought them. Then they stood guard until it was over. They left after that, but Arken's found paw prints around Wardwood every night."

Arken. There was something she was supposed to remember about Arken. "Tell me what happened, Zel."

Zel wriggled happily, glad to be able to use her best skill. "The lights came, and they were so beautiful, they almost looked alive, and they spun around you and a bunch of black smoke poured out of you, and then you fell over. Arken grabbed onto you, but you were as white as snow and weren't breathing, so he—"

"Kissed me," Morwë said, touching her lips. She could still feel him there, in the back of her mind.

"Yes, and then you started breathing again, and so we all went back to Wardwood. In the morning Luned cleaned out Mother's room for you and we put you in here, and Micah and Arken buried Vastic." Enzella's face fell. "He died; do you remember that?"

"Yes, I remember."

"I cried," Enzella said, looking away.

Morwë stroked her hair. "That's all right. That's… that's human."

Enzella nodded into her shoulder, the cloth muffling her sniff. She took up her narrative again. "Sergeant Horne rode for Cruever to tell them what happened to the captain and his squads and that you took care of Father and Ingridon. Luned and I have been cleaning," Enzella added, perking up a bit. "She taught me to bake bread, too. Though it burned a bit on the bottom. More than a bit." She made a face.

"That's good," Morwë whispered, touching Zel's nose. "You'll have to make it again so I can have some."

Enzella beamed. "I will. I'll make more today. Morwë?"

"Yes?"

"I'm glad you didn't die. It was really horrible when you were screaming."

"I'm glad too." She touched Zel's cheek. "I love you, you know."

Her sister's smile blazed. "I love you too. Bunches and bunches." She threw her arms around Morwë.

That's when Morwë realized—they had won. They were both alive, and that tiny sliver of hope—it had made it possible. Her throat tightened.

Mother. Thank you.

The door to the room opened and Luned poked her head in. "Enzella... oh!" Her face broke into a broad smile. "Morwë!" She came in and carefully smoothed Morwë's hair away from her face. "I'm so glad," Luned said, her voice cracking.

Morwë felt her eyes prick with sudden tears as she smiled. "I hope I haven't been too bothersome a patient."

"Not at all," Luned said firmly. "Are you hungry? Thirsty?"

"I think...." Morwë pursed her lips as her body, on its way to waking up, informed her of its demands.

"Ah. Enzella, why don't you go tell the boys that Morwë is awake while I help your sister."

Enzella danced away, glad to spread her tidings through the house.

Luned helped Morwë out of bed and into the garderobe. As they left it, someone knocked at the door. Luned called for them to enter as Morwë sat on the side of the bed to rest her weak legs.

Arken opened the door carrying a tray. "Thought you'd be hungry."

"Thank you," Morwë said, in a voice she didn't recognize.

Luned looked between them and softly excused herself.

Arken pulled over a small end table and set the tray down. "It's soup. Mother made it, not Enzella." He flashed her a small smile. "Did she tell you about her bread?"

Morwë nodded. "I'm afraid she's going to make more. I wanted to try it."

"Practice makes perfect, as they say." He handed her the bowl and spool, and she cradled it carefully, sipping at the broth. "Mmm." Her stomach rumbled, intent on food. She didn't feel the other hunger anymore. She took another spoonful.

Arken grinned. "Potato soup. Good for what ails you."

The heavy door creaked open, and a large brindled forest cat pushed its way into the room. It stared at her with startling green eyes, its ears and tail upright.

"We've had some visitors the past few days. This little guy has been the only one of the bunch that wanted to come inside," Arken said, eyebrows lifting.

Morwë clenched the spoon. "He's not little."

The forest cat gave her an approving look and jumped onto the bed, rubbing against her arm. Hesitantly, she touched his long soft fur, and the cat settled down beside her. He stretched, yawned to display many a sharp fang, and began to knead her leg industriously. He made a sound like grinding rocks.

"He's purring." Arken scratched the cat behind the oversized ears. "It's like he was waiting for you, and just tolerating the rest of us."

"Did they really chase off the wolves? Not just one of Zel's fancies?"

"Yes, they trounced them well."

Morwë copied his scratching motion. "Well, thank you very much, good sir."

The cat's tail twitched in acknowledgement.

As Morwë finished off the soup, the silence stretched between them. She said, a little desperately, "So Zel said that Sergeant Horne left for Cruever?"

"Yes; she needed to report her captain's death and the rest of the squad, but she said she would heavily emphasize you saved all our lives, and probably all of Cairenoch as well." Arken took the bowl and put it to the side. Under his fringe of hair, he shot her a look full of mischief. "You may get a title and more holdings out of all this."

Morwë choked. "What will I do with that?" She was leery of telling the rest of Altesia what she was and what she had done, but she supposed it was out of her hands. "What will you do? Now, I mean. Will you go home to Peridun?"

Arken shook his head, looking at the strip of sunlight on the floor. "No. There are too many ghosts in Peridun, and we won't find many willing to move to an empty village in a hurry. I wouldn't want to be alone." He shrugged. "Selma's here. And Mother won't want to leave you and Enzella here all on your own."

"Good."

Arken lifted his head.

She hurried to say, "I—I'd miss your mother if your family left."

"Just Mother?"

Morwë opened her mouth, but no sound came out. She cleared her throat. "Not just her."

Arken shook his head and smiled. "You'll need someone who knows the land, if you want to make a go at revitalizing Wardwood and the fields. We're not farmers, but I think I could learn, if you're not opposed to the idea."

"No," Morwë said, burying her fingers in the forest cat's fur as he continued to rumble beside her. "No, I'm not opposed."

"It would be a change to try planting instead of cutting down trees," he mused.

"Yes," she said faintly. Planting. Roots in the earth. Stretching out leaves toward…. She bit her lip.

"What is it?"

"I won't be much help," she said in a low voice. "You can't plant if you burn in the sun. I don't think I could wear scarves and a cloak throughout the summer."

He gave her a strange look. "After all that, you really think you'll burn?" He glanced back at the light streaming into the room from the window.

Morwë's lips parted, but the words got stuck in her throat.

Arken stood and held out his hand, and, moonlight help her, she took it.

Morwë leaned on him as she had on Luned. Her legs felt as wobbly as a foal's, but she made it to the edge of the sunbeam. It lay gleaming gold, spilling from the window in a stream across the floor, and the darkness fled, just as it had three nights ago.

Do I really think it will?

She squeezed his hand for luck. Then, heart pounding, Morwë let go and stepped into light.

Warmth played over her face in a smooth caress. Pleasant. Gentle. Tender.

Morwë opened her eyes, wincing a little. In the brilliant morning light, snow covered the fields in a glittering white haze. The trees that framed the house spread empty branches, but she could picture them green with leaves, blowing gently in the wind and framed against the vast expanse of the mountains and sky.

"It's so bright," Morwë whispered, pressing a hand to her mouth. Her eyes were watering. "It almost hurts…."

"No one can look directly at the sun," Arken said, moving to her side. "It's too bright for anyone's eyes."

Morwë blinked away the tears. "Everything looks different now." She looked up at him, his blue eyes shining, and for the first time, she reached for him first.

Arken wrapped his arms around her. She fisted her hand in his tunic and pressed her lips to his without fear as they basked in the light. He cradled her tenderly, kissing her back. A promise of things to come. A future full of light.

After a time, Morwë broke the kiss and wound her arms around him, leaned her head against his chest to stare out the window over Wardwood.

"Tell me what you know about planting, Arken. I want to learn, too."

If you enjoyed this book and want MORE sweet happily ever after moments for Morwë and Arken, you can sign up for my newsletter on my website (www.ClaireTrellaHill.com) to receive the **EXTENDED EPILOGUE** as well as two other short stories about the characters!

Thank you so much for reading *The Erlking's Daughters*!! Please consider leaving an honest review at your favorite retailer or review site.

Again—thank you.

ACKNOWLEDGMENTS

I started this story my freshman year of college. I finished the first draft the year after I graduated—the second book I ever completed, and the first fantasy. I've revised, edited, or reread this story just about every year since. My eyes turn towards other stories now, but I wanted to share this story because it's what nineteen year old me wanted to tell, and what she wanted to hear. Morwë and her cold, prickly self will always have my whole heart.

So the book is really for me. But I hope you like it, too.

Thanks to my in person WriteCreate group who read the first drafts one section at a time every month, even when most people didn't write fantasy.

Thanks to Priscilla for reading it when it still had holes, I'm pretty sure, and saying it sounded as good as a published novel (patently false, but it was encouraging!).

Thanks to Alexandra for your cheering and unabashed fangirl flailing, and for the map and fan art you sent me. Thanks to both you and Katherine for helping to name a character all those years ago. RIP Alastair Constantin.

Thanks to the Things with Feathers for their publishing advice and beta feedback, specifically M.L. Farb and Brielle Porter and Beverly Twomey, who assured me it was NOT too dark and helped straighten out the POVs to be stronger.

Thanks to my real people job folks for giving me job security and making it possible for me to live and write on the side. Don't ask how many of these ideas I've had at work and needed to write down ASAP.

If I have missed anyone in the ten (oh boy) years since this story's start, thank you!! We will chalk it up to the time.

As always, thanks to Mom and Dad, who aren't fantasy people either, but remained encouraging and supportive when that was all I wanted to write.

And, as ever. Soli Deo Gloria.

ALSO BY CLAIRE TRELLA HILL

<u>Gothic Vampire Romance</u>

Black and Deep Desires

Parfit Gentil Knyght: an Addie and Etienne Vignette (Newsletter Exclusive)

<u>The Karneesia Chronicles</u>

The Erlking's Daughters

Mistress of Wardwood and Other Stories (Newsletter Exclusive)

<u>Tales from Karneesia</u>

Coming Soon: When a Dragon Comes Courting

Coming Soon: Come by Water

ABOUT THE AUTHOR

Claire Trella Hill will read anything, but fantasy romance and gothic fiction are her favorites. Born and raised in Houston, Texas, she still lives there because she is impervious to 100 degree weather. She also has a bad habit of making her characters in the Sims and continuing their stories. When Claire isn't writing, she can be found with her nose glued to her library app, assisting with the last tricky pieces of a puzzle, swilling Dr. Pepper, collecting vintage romance covers, or cuddling with her cat.

You can connect with her on social media or sign up for her newsletter on her website ClaireTrellaHill.com.